The H...

KT-426-849

30130502376227

The House of Dolls

David Hewson

W F HOWES LTD

This large print edition published in 2014 by
W F Howes Ltd
Unit 4, Rearsby Business Park, Gaddesby Lane,
Rearsby, Leicester LE7 4YH

1 3 5 7 9 10 8 6 4 2

First published in the United Kingdom in 2014
by Macmillan

A CIP catalogue record for this book is available
from the British Library

ISBN 978 1 47126 647 8

Typeset by Palimpsest Book Production Limited,
Falkirk, Stirlingshire
Printed and bound by
www.printondemand-worldwide.com of Peterborough, England

This book is made entirely of chain-of-custody materials

For Eddie

PART I

MONDAY 17 APRIL

CHAPTER 1

'Vos?'

Laura Bakker walked through every room of the Rijksmuseum looking for him. 'Pieter Vos?'

A slight man of medium height, hunched in a pale-green winter coat that had seen better days. Seated on a bench in front of the biggest doll's house she'd ever seen, Vos seemed both young and old at the same time. His posture, his long brown hair, his creased and worn clothing spoke of middle age. Yet his face was unlined, interested, alert. That of a favourite teacher or a caring, patient priest. And his blue eyes, fixed entirely on the doll's house opposite, had the bright, hard glint of a piece of pottery on the mantelpiece back home in Dokkum. Unwavering. Intelligent.

She'd read the file before De Groot dispatched her from the police station a short bike ride away in Marnixstraat. Pieter Vos, thirty-nine. Resigned from his position as Brigadier in that same station two years before after the failure of the investigation into the disappearance of his daughter Anneliese. Now living a downbeat bohemian existence on a

3

houseboat in the Jordaan, struggling to survive on the paltry remains of his premature pension.

Bakker pulled out the folder she'd brought. Papers, photos scattered everywhere. She swore. Heads turned. Then she scooped up the strewn documents and pictures from the floor and crammed them back into place.

He was staring at her by then. A look she knew. It said . . . *that was clumsy.*

'Vos?' she asked, glancing at the ID photo to make sure this was the right man. In the force Vos was even more boyish in appearance. Events had aged him.

De Groot was his boss. A personal friend too from what she could gather. Heartbroken by Vos's resignation and the loss of a famed Amsterdam police officer to . . . what?

Trying to repair his ramshackle houseboat on the Prinsengracht no more than a five-minute walk from the desk he once occupied. The early newspaper cuttings lauded Vos as a scourge of the city's underworld, a languid, modest detective who'd torn the city's gangs to shreds with a shrug and a smile. Not that there was much to read. He'd shunned the limelight when he was in post. Fled from it when his own daughter went missing, shattered, or so the papers said, that his own diligence as a police officer may have brought about her abduction. A fruitless search followed and then Vos was out of the force. Anneliese was one more name in the missing persons files. A case in the archives, gathering digital dust.

He had a lead coming out of his pocket, earphones on. She leaned down, gently pulled them out, was surprised to hear the loud jazz-rock of 'Willie the Pimp' coming out of them.

'Pieter Vos?' she said again and found herself reaching out to touch his arm, not quite knowing why. The long, uncombed hair and shabby clothes . . . there was something fragile about the man. It was hard to associate this quiet, absorbed figure with the Brigadier who put so many in jail. 'You haven't got time to listen to Zappa. Commissaris de Groot wants to see you in your office. Pick up your stuff. We're off.'

'What do you know about Zappa?' he asked in a kindly, amused voice.

'My dad liked him. Used to play that stuff all night long if he could get away with it. Get moving. We're off.'

'Why does Frank send me children?' he asked then put the earphones on again.

She sat down next to him on the bench, folded her arms, thought for a moment then reached into his pocket and yanked out the lead for phones.

The look on his face was a mixture of surprise and outrage.

'That's quite a thing,' Bakker said, pointing at the display case in front of them.

The doll's house of Petronella Oortman was complex and a good head taller than Pieter Vos.

An Amsterdam canal mansion in miniature. Three floors, each with three rooms and an adjoining staircase corridor. A kitchen, a parlour, a nursery, furniture and paintings, crockery and delicate, miniature draperies. He couldn't stop staring at it and she knew why.

'My name's Laura Bakker. Twenty-four years old and no child, thank you.'

When his bright blue eyes fell on her she had nothing else to say.

'Missing the green fields of Friesland, Laura?'

It was the accent that did it. Amsterdammers looked down on everything outside the capital. She came from the provinces. People there were simple, stupid even.

'There's more to Friesland than green fields,' she said.

'What does your father do when he's not listening to Zappa?'

'Farmer.'

She was tall. Lanky even. Her fine red hair was pulled back behind her head, a practical decision for work. Laura Bakker didn't give much thought to how she looked. Her long face was pale and, she felt, unremarkable. Not much different from when she was seventeen.

'Do you miss him?' he asked.

'Yes but he's dead,' she said. 'Mum too. Not that this matters. Just get your stuff, will you?'

He didn't move.

She took out another folder from her bag, almost

6

spilled the contents of that on the floor. He looked at her, one dark eyebrow raised, then went back to gazing at the doll's house.

'That cost Petronella twenty, thirty thousand guilders. As much as her mansion on Warmoesstraat I guess. Which is probably a coffee shop now, selling bad marijuana to drunken Brits.'

'You look like you were expecting me, Vos. How's that?'

'Magic. Didn't you read the files?'

'They don't say anything about magic. Plenty else . . .'

'Oortman was a wealthy widow. Her money came from the silk trade. Which kind of lived alongside slavery and spice. So maybe . . .' He stroked his chin, trying to find the right word. 'Maybe things aren't that different.'

'Warmoesstraat? Is that where you buy your dope?'

'I said it was bad.'

'It's all bad, Vos.'

'You're young, Laura. What do you know?'

'I know the daughter of the vice-mayor's gone missing. Katja Prins. Not the first time apparently. But—'

'Frank called me. He said he was sending their new aspirant. A simple country girl who thought she might catch drunk drivers in Dokkum. And when that didn't happen felt she could make a difference in Amsterdam. He gave me your name.'

The blood rushed to her cheeks. Her fingers automatically clutched the simple, silver crucifix around her neck, over the plain black jumper.

'By simple I'm sure he meant . . . unspoilt,' Vos added in his quiet and diffident voice. 'Nothing untoward. He said you crashed a squad car . . .'

She wasn't going there.

'Your daughter was snatched by a man obsessed with dolls. There's something like that with the Prins girl . . .'

She placed the photo on his lap. An antique porcelain child's doll in a white pinafore dress and a police evidence label next to it. There was a hank of blonde hair in its right hand. The pinafore had a large bloodstain covering most of the front.

Her long index finger jabbed at the gigantic model opposite.

'Looks just like that one over there, in the Oortman house, doesn't it? Just like the one he sent you? Except for the blood and the hair.'

Vos sighed.

'The hair was in its left hand with me. The bloodstain was smaller.'

'Katja was staying at a tenement in De Wallen . . .'

'The daughter of the man who runs the city council living in the red-light district? Doesn't that tell you something?'

'She hasn't been seen for a week. We're testing to see if the blood and the hair are hers. The doll was left outside her father's house last night. In a miniature cardboard coffin. Just like he did with you in Marnixstraat . . .'

No surprise. Just a sad, resigned smile. It seemed his natural expression.

'Did Frank tell you Wim Prins's wife was my partner for seventeen years? Anneliese's mother?'

The heat fled her cheeks.

'No.'

'Amsterdam's a small place. Not as small as Dokkum . . .'

Vos went back to looking at the little rooms, the furniture, the doll marooned in a tiny nursery four centuries before.

'Katja's a crazy little junkie,' he said, almost to himself. 'Her own mother was too. She killed herself. The girl hates her stepmother. What's new there?'

'Vos . . .'

'She's tried to extort money out of her father before. He always refuses to press a case. It seems she has a cruel imagination . . .'

'And if you're wrong? If this is the same man who took your daughter?'

A shrug.

'Then I expect you to do a better job than I did. You must excuse me.' He rose from the bench seat, stretched his arms, took out a set of keys. 'I have to go . . .'

'Do you think you'll see him here, then? Is it as easy as that? He'll walk in and you'll know.'

Her words seemed to disappoint him.

'No,' Vos replied. 'But I want him to see me. Good day, Aspirant Bakker. I wish you well in your career.'

Then he plugged the earphones back into the phone, put them in his ears, and left.

CHAPTER 2

Jimmy Menzo sat in a cold basement by the grey-brown bulk of the Oude Kerk. The faint drone of a pipe organ made its weedy way through the high slatted window. Outside, in the shadow of the squat church, the first morning whores writhed behind the glass of their cabins, waving their come-on gestures to the tourists wandering wide-eyed down the street.

Some stopped. Some walked on into the coffee shops. Doped or screwed, he got into their wallets either way. The city was a money machine. His. Not going to change.

Menzo had fled the slums of Surinamese when he was nineteen, abandoning the squalor of South America for the Netherlands, a harsh new world he entered with nothing more than a handful of guilders in his pocket, two powerful scarred fists and a head full of envy and ambition.

Two decades on he lived in a mansion near the waterfront, not far from the red-light district with his coffee shops and brothels, his cabins for rent to the freelance hookers and, most profitable of all, his hands around the drug supply chains threading through the area the locals called De Wallen.

From Centraal station in the north to Spui, from Nieuwmarkt to Damrak, the heart of Amsterdam belonged to the man who'd left the hovels of Paramaribo with nothing but some ragged clothes and a few hundred US dollars ripped off a failed coke shipment.

He'd earned this prize. Fought for it. And good fortune had put his one last rival, Theo Jansen, in jail.

That was two years before. Twenty-four months had passed in which Menzo battled night and day to seize every last fragment of Jansen's empire, changing loyalties through money, through persuasion, through hard fists or the barrel of a gun when needed.

It was war of a kind and, like most modern conflicts, this one would never end.

Now a couple of kids fidgeted across the table from him. About the age Menzo was when he first turned up in Holland touting a fake passport and a forged work permit. Ugly like him, brutal, looking for opportunity. From Surinamese, once a little piece of Holland on the edge of South America. Short, stocky wannabe thugs not long arrived in town, one dressed in a shiny blue tracksuit, the other in red.

Four weapons on the battered wooden table. Two machine pistols, a couple of semi-automatic Walther P5s, the same kind the police used. Which was no coincidence, not that he said.

The two hunched, scared figures opposite couldn't stop looking at them.

'We'd planned on staying longer.' The blue one. The bravest.

Menzo threw a briefcase on the table, opened it. They went quiet, stared at the spread of green money.

'Fifty thousand US dollars. A couple of Antilles passports. Two tickets to Cape Town. Business class.'

'Business class,' red kid repeated, reaching for the case.

A bronchial, smoker's laugh. Menzo was about the same size, pug-like and thuggish, strong, not one to shirk a fight. Pockmarked surly face. Narrow eyes. Swarthy skin.

He passed over a sheet of paper with Miriam's tidy, female handwriting on it. A Prinsengracht address.

'Miriam can fill you in. Afterwards you go here. It's a shop. There you get the money. And the tickets.'

They looked at the paper like dumb school kids given impenetrable homework.

'When can we come back?' blue kid asked.

'You don't. You take the money and do what I did. Make your own way. I've friends over there. They can get you started.'

The two kids looked at each another.

'What kind of shop?' the red one asked.

Menzo liked their idiot questions, rifled through the pockets of his jacket. Black silk suit, sharp, tapered, tight. Made for him by a tailor in Bangkok where he went for business and a little pleasure.

Two business cards, the same pretty picture on the front. A miniature Amsterdam canal mansion in wood. Tiny pink chairs with tinier figures on them.

Poppenhuis aan de Prinsengracht.

The Doll's House on the Prinsengracht. He gave the kids a card each.

'Dolls?' red kid asked.

'Don't worry,' Menzo told him. 'They're not there any more. Someone got rid of all the pretty things a while back.'

'I got a sister here,' the blue one said. 'She just came out. Working in one of your restaurants. She needs me. If I leave—'

'I'll look after your sister. Make her manager. Give her a bar. Or something.'

A big, friendly smile.

'Ask anyone. You do what Jimmy Menzo asks and no one ever touches you. I look after my own. Even when they're someplace else.'

'We've got a choice?' blue kid asked quickly and Menzo thought maybe he'd underestimated this Surinamese brat, new off the plane, two hits to his name, police chasing him up and down the mainland and the Caribbean.

'Sure you've got a choice.'

He lit a cigarette, listened to the asthmatic tones of the distant church organ. It was spring outside. Still cold with squally rain between brief spells of sun.

He took away the briefcase, put it on the floor. Their eyes were on the weapons.

Menzo got up from his seat, smiled at them. Launched himself at the table, seized the nearest machine pistol in his right fist. Waved the barrel in red kid's face, then the blue. Laughing all the while.

'Miriam?' he yelled.

The door opened. Taller than Menzo, physique of a basketball player. Just touching thirty. Long face, one quarter Chinese she said and he believed it. A Trinidad girl, she barely spoke Dutch. Just English.

'What?' she asked.

Brown fur coat. What kind he didn't know or care. She got all the money she wanted. Gave plenty in return.

'These boys aren't up to it,' Menzo said. 'Drive'em to the station. Put'em on a train somewhere. They're pissing me off.'

The Surinamese brats shuffled on their seats, dumb young eyes on each other.

The woman walked up, threw some filthy English insults in their direction, glared at them with her big white staring eyes.

'Fifty thousand dollars? How much you punks make back in Paramaribo?'

Silence.

She leaned over them. There was a presence to her, both enticing and threatening. Menzo loved the way she could scare a man and make him want her at the same time.

15

The kids were shivering. More than they did for him.

'How . . . much . . .?' Miriam wanted to know.

'Money's no good if you don't get to stay alive,' blue kid mumbled.

Her long fingers wound into his lank, greasy hair, shook his head. Hard. Menzo watched, chuckled.

'You get to stay alive, boy!' she yelled at them. 'More alive than we ever was when we showed up here. You get to live somewhere warm and cheap and sunny. Where no one knows who you are. How hard can it be?'

Their eyes were on the floor. Menzo put the long black weapon back on the table next to the others.

'Not hard at all,' he said then opened the case again, plucked a wad of the dollar bills, waved them in their faces.

'What are we supposed to do?' red kid asked.

Battle won.

'Whatever Miriam tells you. Flight goes to London at six o'clock. You're in Cape Town for breakfast. Looking at a new life.'

He patted the black gun.

'You hear that? A new life. A little gratitude wouldn't go amiss.'

Menzo waited. Miriam Smith waited, standing back on her heels, folding her arms through the brown fur coat.

'Thanks,' said red kid obediently.

'Yeah,' said the blue one and stared at the cold stone floor.

CHAPTER 3

As usual Sam had stayed with the woman Vos had befriended in the security office. He retrieved the little dog, said thanks, then led him outside. The rain was holding off. He placed the white and tan fox terrier in the front basket of his rusting black pushbike, adjusted the plastic windscreen at the front, pulled two elastic bands out of his jacket pocket and snapped them round the bottom of his wide, unfashionable, creased and shabby jeans to keep them out of the chain.

Zappa had given way to Van Halen. He pulled out the phones and stuffed them into his pockets. One look at his jeans, the decrepit black bike, the dog in the front. Then he set off into the morning traffic for the ten-minute ride to the houseboat on the Prinsengracht.

Cyclists and trams. Cars and motorbikes. Baffled tourists wandering among them all, not knowing which way to look.

He'd asked Frank de Groot straight out: was there any news of Anneliese? The smallest piece of evidence to link her with the Prins girl apart from a doll? The silence that followed said everything.

17

Just eighteen months old, the dog circled the basket three times then settled, got bored and, as the bike picked up speed past Leidseplein, rose to his haunches, put his long nose and beard into the wind, turning from side to side with delight, mouth open, white teeth in an apparent grin.

The first spot of rain and he'd be back behind the windscreen. But spring was beginning to peek out from behind the grey shroud of winter. The lime trees showered the streets with their feathery seeds like tall statues scattering pale-green confetti for a wedding to come. The dog would enjoy his second lazy summer on the water, basking amidst the ragged vegetable and flower pots on the deck, enjoying the attentions of camera-happy tourists. More anonymously, Vos would too. And before the year was out the boat would be finished finally. He could try to think about what might come next.

A furious ringing of bells from behind, an exchange of cross words in English. Then, as he entered the long straight cycle path that ran alongside the canal, Laura Bakker pedalled briskly to his side muttering curses about tourists.

She was riding a rusty olive-green granny bike with high handlebars, sitting stiff-backed, a strand of red hair escaping to blow behind her in the spring breeze. The grey trouser suit looked as if it belonged in the 1970s. So, in a way, did Laura Bakker.

One hand, he saw, worked her phone. Talking while she rode, not looking where she was going.

Or, worse, texting. As he watched the thing nearly fell from her grasp. She only stopped it with the sudden, informed response of someone who recognized how truly clumsy she was.

'Vos! Vos!' Bakker cried when she'd got firm hold of the phone again. 'Listen to me! Stop, will you? Commissaris de Groot wants to see you to discuss this in person.'

A pleasure boat slowed on the canal. A pack of people in the front started taking pictures of them. Sam, paws on the front basket, little head into the breeze, shook his fur like a model posing for the camera.

'Why on earth did De Groot send you? Of all people?' Vos asked, keeping his eyes on the path ahead.

'What's wrong with me?' She looked offended. 'Just because I'm from Dokkum . . . it doesn't mean I'm a moron.' A glance towards Marnixstraat. 'Whatever anyone thinks.'

'I didn't say that,' Vos muttered then wove through a crowd of visitors wandering across the cycle track and quickly rode on.

'Your dog's very cute,' Bakker noted as she caught up again. A smile then. For a moment she looked like a naive student fresh out of college trying to persuade the world at large to take notice and treat her seriously.

'You don't know him,' Vos said.

'I always wanted a pet.'

He stiffened with outrage.

'A pet? Sam's not a pet.'

Laura Bakker seemed worried she might have offended him.

'What is he then?'

The gentle rise of a bridge approached. Vos pedalled harder, left her behind again, took his hands off the handlebar, throwing up both arms in despair.

The tourists tracking them on the canal launch loved this even more. An argument among locals. A lover's tiff even.

She was back by his side quickly, more of her red hair free now, flying back beyond her shoulders.

'This is childish,' Laura Bakker declared.

'Being pursued along the canal by a wet-behind-the-ears junior. That's childish,' he complained, and realized how petulant he sounded. 'Arrest me and have done with it.'

'I can't arrest people. I'm not allowed. Commissaris de Groot doesn't believe Katja's trying to extort money from anyone. He thinks this is to do with your daughter's case . . .'

Enough. He put out a hand to steady the dog then brought the bike to a sudden halt. The little animal yapped gleefully as if this were all a game.

'I told you. Frank called me this morning,' he repeated as Laura Bakker stopped by his side. 'No one demanded a ransom for my daughter. No one gave me the chance to save her. If—'

'Did you have much money?'

'I'd have found it. If he'd asked. But he didn't. For that or anything else. Anneliese was there one day. Then . . .'

Three years the coming July. It might have been yesterday. Or another lifetime altogether. Tragedy occurred outside normal time, everyday conventions. It possessed a bewildering ability to fade and grow brighter simultaneously. There was no such thing as closure. That was claptrap for the counselling services. Only a pain so insistent it eventually became familiar, like toothache or the ghostly ache of a missing limb.

'I'm fed up arguing,' she said briskly. 'Commissaris de Groot says he needs your help. You and him are supposed to be friends. It's not like it's the only thing he's got on his mind.'

Vos growled, a habit he'd picked up from the dog, then started pedalling again. She kept up, legs pumping at a steady, leisurely pace, big boots occasionally slamming against the frame. A gawky, awkward young woman. The kind of clumping, bumbling ingénue from the provinces that Marnixstraat's hardened city officers would pounce on and devour in an instant.

'Of course it's not,' he said, making an effort to sound reasonable. 'This is Amsterdam. How could it be?'

The houseboat was almost invisible from the road, an ugly black hulk marooned in the Prinsengracht beneath the line of the pavement. The cheapest on the market when he and Liesbeth sold the apartment, split the money, went their separate ways. It needed so much work and he couldn't afford even half of it on the pittance of a cut-down, early retirement police pension.

'There's a crook called Theo Jansen in the appeal court today,' she added. 'According to what I hear they think he'll go free.'

Another sudden stop. This time he forgot to reach for the dog. Sam barked testily as he was flung against the front of the wicker basket.

'Sorry, boy,' Vos murmured and reached out to stroke his wiry fur. 'What?'

'This Jansen chap's in front of the judge this afternoon. Likelihood is he's on his toes straight after . . .'

They'd almost cycled past the place. The court lay along the Prinsengracht too, close to Leidseplein. Most of Pieter Vos's working life, the police station, the courthouse, the cafes and brown bars of the Jordaan where he retreated to talk and think, lay within walking distance of his ramshackle houseboat.

'If the idiots let Theo out the first thing he'll do is start a war,' he said. 'Frank knows that as well as anyone. I hope he's prepared. What in God's name are they thinking?'

'They don't have much choice. You didn't stay to finish the job, did you?' She had a harsh and judgemental tone to her flat northern voice when she wanted. One that seemed old for her years. 'That's what they reckon in Marnixstraat. You quit and someone else screwed up in your place.'

A council boss's daughter either kidnapped or demanding a ransom for herself. The city's former gang lord about to get out of jail, looking for revenge against the Surinamese crook who'd seized his territory, the coffee shops, the brothels, the drug routes, while Jansen was in prison.

Pieter Vos could understand why his old friend was worried.

'You've got a lot to say for yourself, Aspirant Bakker. Not much in the way of tact.'

She leaned closer. Pointed a long finger in his face. Chewed nails, he noticed. No polish. No make-up on her face.

'I didn't join the police to learn tact. De Groot told me to bring you in.' She had green eyes, very round, a little on the large side, now gleaming with a mixture of determination and outrage. 'That's what I'm going to do. If I have to follow you around all day.'

He stifled a smile and pushed the bike gently forward again.

'At the risk of repeating myself, I'm no longer a police officer.'

The boat looked dreadful in the strong spring sun. Peeling black paint. A shrivelled and desolate garden around the deck. The railings rusty. The wood rotten in places. In front of the bows, by the next mooring, a small dinghy sat half-flooded in the dank canal water, just as it did the day, almost two years before, when Vos moved in.

This casual neglect, a lack of care and worry,

helped him feel easy in this quiet and leisurely part of the city. The Drie Vaten bar by the bridge to Elandsgracht. The little shops and restaurants. The people more than anything. The Jordaan was home. He couldn't imagine being anywhere else.

A portly figure strode out from the foot of the street, near the statues of Johnny Jordaan and his band. In his shabby jeans Vos never thought of himself as old. Nor did most of those he met as far as he could work out. They seemed to treat him like an odd adolescent, trapped in amber in his houseboat, listening to old rock, visiting the nearby coffee shop for a smoke from time to time, lingering over beers in the Drie Vaten.

Seeing Frank de Groot gave him pause for thought. At forty-nine the boss of Marnixstraat was just ten years his senior. But he looked like a man well into middle age now, lined face, neatly clipped dark hair and tidy moustache, both too black to be real. His wan, watery eyes appeared tired and worried. A gulf had emerged between them. Vos had gone nowhere, gone backwards maybe, since he locked himself in the houseboat on the Prinsengracht. De Groot had stayed in post and that had marked him.

'Pieter! Pieter!' De Groot rushed up and forced a small package into Vos's hands. 'I thought I might catch you here.'

'Here's where I live, Frank. Where else would I be?'

24

'Hanging round the Rijksmuseum,' De Groot replied with a glint in his eye. 'In the Drie Vaten eyeing up that pretty woman behind the bar. Not fixing your damned boat that's for sure. This dinghy . . .'

De Groot moaned about the half-sunken boat every time they met.

With a sudden clatter Laura Bakker turned up, shot out her long legs, slammed her heavy boots on the ground.

'I was on my way to Marnixstraat,' Vos said. 'Aspirant Bakker briefed me.' The green eyes were on him, surprised. 'She did a good job. All the same I can't help you.'

'Cheese!' De Groot patted the little package. 'I got it from that shop you like. Kaashuis. They said it's straight from the farm. It's Limburger . . .'

The dog was wrinkling its nose at the package.

'You're trying to bribe me with cheese? This is pathetic.'

De Groot nodded.

'True. Please. Can't we talk? Fifteen years we worked together. It's not a lot to ask.'

The commissaris wore a fixed smile.

'You're looking . . . bohemian, Pieter. More so than ever I'd say.'

Vos climbed off the bike, lifted Sam out of the basket, found the lead in his pocket and a spare bag from the supermarket.

He extended the loop of the leash to Bakker and held out the bag.

'You wanted a pet. Time to discover what it's like. Clean up after him. He can't do it for himself and there's a fine if you leave it.'

'I didn't join the police force to walk dogs,' she complained.

'Indulge us,' De Groot growled.

His voice could turn from amicable to threatening in an instant. She snatched the bag and the lead then bent down and cooed at Sam.

'Don't let him beg for food,' Vos ordered. 'And keep him away from other dogs. He doesn't know he's little.'

The two men watched Bakker chain her bike to the canal railings then wander down the canal, behind the happy, wagging tail of the proudly strutting terrier.

'That was a dirty trick,' Vos said.

'What?' De Groot asked, all innocence.

'Sending me the office dunce and hoping I'd take pity on her.' Vos stared at the wax paper package in his hands. 'I hate Limburger.'

'I'm not a cheese man, am I? She's not a dunce, Pieter. Didn't choose to be born in Dokkum. Kid just doesn't fit.' He thought for a moment then added, 'Also I think she may believe in God.' De Groot shook his head. 'What the hell she's doing here . . . I'm sorry. I thought she'd mess that up too. Why do you think I turned up?'

Vos lifted his bike onto the boat deck.

'Do I have to beg?' De Groot asked. Then he pointed to the half-sunken dinghy next to Vos's home, the empty hull covered by a grubby tarpaulin. 'I've told you a million times. You should do something about that. It's against the law.'

Vos put his hands to his head and sighed.

'It's . . . not . . . my . . . boat. Remember?'

De Groot hopped from one foot to the other, apologetic, but only mildly.

'Stuck next to your place like that. Looks like yours.'

'Inside,' Vos ordered then walked down the gangplank and threw open the tiny wooden door to his home.

CHAPTER 4

'De Groot wants us to go to Marnixstraat,' Liesbeth Prins said. 'Wim? Are you even listening?'

His office was one of the most palatial in the city hall on Waterlooplein. Long windows, a view. A feeble spring sun hung over the city beyond the window: the canal, the mansions and corporate headquarters, then the sprawling, chaotic community of De Wallen. There were more than eighty thousand people in the tightly enclosed fiefdom of central Amsterdam. Six months before, his Progressive group had seized a surprise number of seats in the elections then forged a fragile alliance with the tiny anti-EU Independence Party. And in the hard bargaining for seats that followed, Prins had won just what he wanted: the role of vice-mayor, with a specific brief.

He was forty-eight, a tall, imposing, unsmiling man. Liesbeth had known him since she was a teenager, though most of her life was spent with Pieter Vos. Now he'd risen from rich city lawyer to full-time politician on the city council, and a part of her had come to wonder: was that why he needed her? To complete the picture?

'I can't waste more time on her games,' Prins said flicking through one of the many reports on his desk. 'De Groot should have better things to do. God knows—'

'You think she can be that heartless?'

He took hold of her hands, made her sit down. Looked into her eyes. A big man. A sad man in some ways. There was never the familiarity, the humour, the playful closeness she'd shared with Vos.

'I know her better than you. She's been like this ever since Bea died.'

'Katja's sick.' Her voice faltered. She felt cold. Ill maybe. The black dress she'd picked that morning hung loose on her skinny frame. 'Christ, Wim. I know you never liked the fact she wasn't so bright. Not the star pupil. Some genius to take over your firm one day. But she's still your daughter . . .'

Prins placed the report on the desk. She saw the name on the cover in bold black letters: *De Nachtwacht*.

The Night Watch. The title taken from the city's most famous painting, Rembrandt's massive master work in the Rijksmuseum. A group of armed militia men about to patrol Amsterdam, to keep the city safe. Prins gave the same name to the key element in his election campaign the previous autumn. A promise to clean up De Wallen once and for all. No half-hearted measures any more. No compromises. From the start he'd pledged to make life unbearable for the dealers, the coffee shops, the brothels, the pimps and hookers who'd been there for decades.

No one expected him to win. But with the endless round of recession and austerity the popular mood had become febrile and unpredictable. People were looking for a change, any change. Then the Independence Party began to pick up votes on the back of suspicion about Brussels and the EU. They sensed an opportunity and joined the clamour. De Nachtwacht turned from a minor politician's pipe dream into a hazy commitment that put him second-in-command in the council, with the one man above him, the Labour party mayor, happy to stand back from De Nachtwacht entirely and watch from a distance the developing furore about its implementation.

'This,' Prins said, tapping his finger on the report, 'is more important than Katja now. I can't help her any more. I've tried. But maybe someone else's child—'

'The police want to talk to us.'

'You should have spoken to me before you called Marnixstraat.'

She shook her head. Ran three bony fingers through her scant, short fair hair.

'Someone leaves a cardboard coffin outside the door. There's a doll in it. Some hair. A bloodstain . . .'

'One more of her games . . .'

'A doll! A hank of hair. Blood.'

Prins closed his eyes for a second.

'There's nothing she won't do if she needs money for dope.' He eyed the desk and the reports there. 'They're like that.'

'Katja's not heartless. She wouldn't . . . taunt me with this.'

'You always see the best in people.' His arms came away. 'Especially when it's not there. Stay out of it.'

'How can I?'

He wasn't paying attention. Wim Prins was smiling, the way he did for the public these days.

Margriet Willemsen, the pushy young woman who led the Independence Party, had opened the door. Behind her stood Alex Hendriks, head of the council's general office. A diminutive, quiet man who seemed to live inside the sprawling council offices next to the Opera House on this open square near the heart of Amsterdam.

'We've a meeting about De Nachtwacht,' Prins said, for her benefit and theirs. 'Call me later . . .'

'You can make time if you want,' she insisted. 'For Katja's sake . . .'

Still smiling he put his arm round her, whispered, 'Tell De Groot I don't want this in the papers. I don't want to see her in court either when they pick her out of the gutter. We don't need that and neither does he.'

Then, brightly, 'Margriet. Alex.'

31

'Is everything OK?' the woman asked. 'We didn't mean to interrupt . . .'

'You didn't. Sit down, please.' The smile again. 'Liesbeth is just leaving.'

CHAPTER 5

The holding cells of the Prinsengracht courthouse. Basement rooms. No windows. No light. Stale, cold air.

Theo Jansen sat at a plain grey table waiting for his daughter Rosie and freedom. Fifty-nine years old, a giant of a man with the thick white beard of a fallen Santa Claus. When he was nineteen he'd started work as a bouncer for one of the Spui brothels patronized by rich foreigners, corrupt locals and the odd passing Hollywood star. The Seventies were a time of change. Drug liberalization, the consequent dope tourism and the spread of the red-light trade made the mundane profits of brothel-keeping seem tame.

Jansen was a quick apprentice, strong, fit, in the right place. He rose quickly through the gang ranks on the back of his fast fists, even temper, sharp intelligence and steadfast loyalty. Then his boss was cut down in the street during one of the periodic vendettas that gripped the Amsterdam underworld. There was no obvious successor so Theo Jansen, son of a lowly paid line worker from the Heineken brewery, stepped up for the title.

Three further executions, a flurry of generous bribes to politicians local and national, some strong-arm persuasion on the street and the old network was his. Until Pieter Vos came along.

Jansen didn't hate cops. They had a job to do. Some could be bought. Some could be scared off. Others turned away by subtle coercion brought elsewhere. Vos, a man as relentless as he seemed invisible at times, understood no such pressure. Quietly, doggedly he worked away, chipping at the edges of the city's criminal empires without fear, pulling in the small fry, offering them the choice between jail or turning informer.

Most chose jail, which was a wise decision. But not all.

The two men had met from time to time. Jansen liked Vos. He was an unconventional, modest man with a downbeat honesty and a fearless, perhaps foolish persistence. The city would always have police officers. Just as it would always be controlled to some extent by criminals. Might as well be one whose honesty could never be questioned.

Then the quiet detective's world was torn apart and so, in a way Jansen still failed to understand, was his. Three years before the cop fell victim to a personal tragedy that saw him leave the police, a damaged, broken man. Not long after, tempted by Klaas Mulder, Vos's successor, a small-time crook called Jaap Zeeger, a minnow Jansen barely knew, stood up in court and talked.

'Liar,' Theo Jansen spat out loud, just thinking

about those weeks he spent in the dock, listening to fabrication upon fabrication. Zeeger, led on by Klaas Mulder, had put him there and still Jansen didn't understand why.

'Liar,' he said again more quietly and then the door opened. Rosie, by her side Michiel Lindeman, the lawyer Jansen had used for a decade or more.

He smiled at his daughter. Thirty-two years old, her mother long gone from his life, vanished from Holland as far as anyone knew. Rosie would never abandon him. She'd stood by her old man throughout, had done since she was a teenager. Did her best to keep what remained of his empire running through a combination of strength and persuasion she'd learned from him over the years. She'd inherited his heavy physique and his outlook. A big, smiling, loud woman who never minced her words. Unlike Michiel Lindeman, a lean, humourless, middle-aged Amsterdam defence brief who'd come to make his name, and his fortune, representing crooks a few others didn't dare touch.

'Will I get out today, Michiel?' Jansen asked watching them sit down.

'All that money we've spent,' Rosie said, glancing at the lawyer. 'If Dad's not home for supper I'll be asking why.'

Lindeman took the hard cell chair so delicately it looked as if he feared the seat might break his thin and spindly frame. An act. This hard, unforgiving man was indestructible. Plenty had tried.

'Well?' Jansen asked again when he got no answer.

'It's up to the court. Not me.'

Lindeman always sounded bored. Odd given the money he was getting for every minute of his time.

'We've got the statement from Jaap Zeeger,' Rosie said. 'Signed affidavit. Klaas Mulder got all that crap out of him by force. Threats. Beatings.'

'If Vos had still been there none of this shit would have happened,' Jansen muttered.

Lindeman laughed.

'Vos would have got you straight. Be grateful he went crazy before he got the chance.'

Theo Jansen nodded. Before he set up on his own Michiel Lindeman was senior partner in one of the biggest city law firms. Alongside none other than Wim Prins, the new vice-mayor of the city council. The man who got into office by promising to clean up Amsterdam. That made Lindeman more valuable than ever.

'Get me out of here,' Jansen said. 'Book me a meeting with your old friend Prins. We can sort things out. Reach an accommodation. He knows we're never going away. Tell him he can trust a Dutchman. We'll both run that Surinamese bastard out of town. Then things can be peaceful again.'

Lindeman shook his head and sighed.

'You're a criminal, Theo. Wim Prins can't click his fingers and get you out. Even if he could . . .'

He went quiet.

'What?'

Lindeman stared at Rosie Jansen and said, 'Tell him.'

She seemed uncomfortable for some reason.

'Things are different, Dad. What was ours . . . maybe isn't any more. I did my best. I'm not you. Half the men we had are with Menzo now. Those that aren't are dead or gone.'

'Not all of them. I get to talk to people inside. I'm not alone in there.'

'Those people in jail are lying sons of bitches,' she hissed. 'Menzo's putting words in their ugly mouths.'

Jansen could feel himself getting mad.

'What's lost I'll take back. I've done it before.'

The lawyer looked round the room, pointed at the shadowy corners.

'See, Theo. There you go. Talk first, think later. What if this place is wired?'

Jansen shifted on his chair, felt his big shoulders move the way they did when a fight was coming.

'If they tapped into a private conversation between a man and his lawyer they'd never get to use it. I don't pay you to be insulted.'

Besides, there was no mike in the room. This was Amsterdam. The courthouse. They did things properly. Carefully. Legally. The Dutch way.

'You pay me to get you out of here,' the lawyer replied. 'To keep you out. If they think for one minute there's going to be a war that won't happen.'

'I'm not guilty!' Jansen slammed his heavy fist

on the table. Then more quietly, 'Not for that shit Mulder pinned on me.'

Rosie Jansen reached over and took gentle hold of his clenched fingers.

'We know that. They do too. I want you home. I want you to stay there. You had your time—'

'My time?'

They'd talked this through before. Reached a deal. He could see it now.

'You've got enough legitimate businesses to keep you comfortable for the rest of your life,' Lindeman said in a dry, tired tone. 'Rich and safe. Zeeger's affidavit doesn't make you innocent. The best we can hope for is release on bail on the basis of an unsafe conviction. You need to give them something that will get us an appeal. I want to be able to say in private you're out of De Wallen. Menzo's taken most of the firms you ran there anyway—'

'Stolen!' Jansen bellowed. 'Thieved behind my back while I was rotting in jail on some trumped-up—'

'It doesn't matter,' his daughter cut in. 'It's happened. You can't turn back the clock. No one can.'

'I'm your father, Rosie. Don't you know me?'

Her warm hand tightened on his. Her dark eyes shone at him, pleading.

'You can't. If you try they'll put you back in prison. Me too maybe. It's not just Wim Prins on our backs now. The government's coming down on us. Times are changing. They won't let things pass the way they did.'

'Throw them some money. That usually works.'

Lindeman shook his head.

'A lot's happened in two years. Change of party since you went inside. Change of mood. Not just in the council. Everything we grew up with's falling to pieces. You're a dinosaur, Theo. Time to get out of the way before the comet hits.'

Jansen blinked.

'You think I'll just roll over and let Jimmy Menzo have it all?'

Lindeman shrugged.

'If you want to go home and live with your daughter. Enjoy your money. Forget about how things were before. They're gone for good.'

Rosie smiled at him, looking the way she did when she was five, ten years old. His daughter could always wind him round her little finger and she knew it.

'That's what you came to tell me? That I'm an old man and I'm out of it?'

'Pretty much,' Lindeman agreed. 'I'm a lawyer. Not a miracle worker.'

They waited for him to say something.

'I'll think about it.'

Rosie wasn't smiling any more.

'I said I'll think about it,' Jansen repeated.

'We've got a pre-hearing meeting fixed this morning, Dad. They want an answer before it comes in front of the judge.'

'The court needs to know now,' Lindeman added. 'A commitment. A—'

'A piece of paper?' Jansen snapped. 'You want me to sign that? I, Theo Jansen, relinquish all my rights—'

'We don't have any rights.' Her voice was stern and rising. 'We don't have anything. We're screwed. Let's try and get out of this with a little dignity.'

There were tears welling in her solemn dark eyes and he always hated that.

'I want you home,' she said again in a voice so soft and gentle it belied her looks. 'I want us to enjoy things together. That place you bought in Spain. We never went there. Not once. All the things we never had time for . . .'

Jansen leaned back in his chair, looked at the ceiling, the bleak, windowless walls. In his mind he could see the city outside. April. Soon the new herring would be here. He could grab a beer in a brown bar, walk to a canalside stall, dangle a sliver of raw fish over his mouth, down it like a Pelican the way he did when Rosie was a kid and he wanted to make her laugh. You weren't supposed to do that in Amsterdam. It was common. But so was he. And she always giggled when he did it. That was enough.

Freedom wasn't something intangible. It had a taste. You could touch it, smell it. A fifteen-year sentence, ten inside if he was lucky, wasn't punishment. It was an execution of a kind, cruel and deliberate.

'You need to say it now,' Rosie insisted. 'Michiel has to tell them. If he doesn't there won't be a hearing. You go back to jail. And I go home alone. Dad, if you won't do it for yourself, just do it for me, will you?'

CHAPTER 6

The houseboat was thirty years old, fixed moorings with electricity, phone line, water and mains drainage. A stationary, rotting wooden hull on the canal the locals shortened from the Prinsengracht to Prinsen, close to the Berenstraat bridge.

'I'd hate to live in a pit like this,' De Groot said as he ducked his head and went into the cabin. Roses, chrysanthemums, a few vegetables were visible beyond the glass in their pots and raised beds. None of them prospering.

'How's Maria?' Vos asked, recalling the man's quiet, shy wife.

'Fine. She wonders why you don't come round any more.'

He said something about being busy. De Groot eyed the chaotic interior of the houseboat, the boxes of tools on the floor, rock posters covering the peeling paint on the timber walls, raised a single heavy eyebrow. Then followed Vos to the old pine dining table and sat with him.

'Busy doing what? Never mind. I want you back.

You can be a brigadier again. The pay's a bit better. Not much—'

'What's happened?'

Skimpy details. The night before, a miniature cardboard coffin was left outside Wim Prins's courtyard home in one of the smarter *hofjes* a kilometre north near Willemstraat. An antique porcelain doll. A hank of hair. A bloodstain.

'How did they want the money?' Vos asked, interested in spite of himself.

De Groot pulled a photo out of his coat pocket.

'They didn't exactly. There was a note in the doll's hand. Computer. No prints.'

One line, big bold letters.

Love's expensive, Wim. Get ready for the bill.

'What else? Did they call?'

De Groot shook his head.

'That's it.'

'Wim Prins doesn't love his daughter. She's a junkie. An embarrassment. If they wanted money they'd kidnap the kid of someone who cared.'

'I know you hate him. What he did with Liesbeth—'

'It's not that. Katja's just a younger version of her mother and God knows she caused him enough trouble.' It was a terrible thing to say. To think even. But true. 'Bea Prins killed herself, didn't she? She was an embarrassment and so's the daughter. Prins is a man with ideas. A mission. Clean up Amsterdam today. The country tomorrow.

43

A dead wife and a lost child would add some credibility.'

De Groot put the photo away.

'That's unfair. Inaccurate too. From what I hear De Nachtwacht isn't doing too well. It's easy to be a prude when you've got no power. Harder in practice. His coalition's shaky. His own party's having misgivings. My guess is the whole thing's dead before summer's out.'

'I don't give a damn about politics. Why isn't he in the police station now? Screaming at you to do something?'

'Who says he isn't?'

Vos laughed.

'Wim Prins wouldn't want me back. You're not here for him.'

No answer to that which said something.

'You can't ignore the similarities.'

Vos shook his head.

'What similarities?'

'The doll! Prins got a doll!'

'Did he get a picture of the Oortman house?'

De Groot threw up his hands in despair.

'For God's sake, are you still going on about that? It was just a drawing the bastard sent as a joke or something. Why do you waste all that time staring at something in a museum? This is real. The Prins girl's missing. No glass cases. Flesh and blood.'

Vos started hanging round the Rijksmuseum out of habit when he crashed out of the job. It was routine. Something to fill the day. De Groot was right. It was just a drawing that came with the doll, Anneliese's blood, a hank of her hair. One more odd fragmented link among so many. For some reason – the temporary breakdown in all probability – he couldn't get the picture of that place, with its tiny rooms, the fragile creatures trapped inside them, out of his head.

He had been over his daughter's case a million times. In the brief period he worked on it as a police officer. Later, in the quiet of the houseboat in the Jordaan until something – sleep, booze or a smoke – killed the never-ending circle of possibilities and riddles. There was a photo of her by the long window on the street side of the boat, next to a poster for a couple of concerts he'd been to at the Melkweg.

He walked over and picked up the picture.

Anneliese on her own eating an ice cream in the park. A little had melted on her bright blue dress. She was pretty, childlike. Almost a doll herself. But her eyes seemed blank now. Her smile a little forced. That was what time did to you. These thoughts had never occurred to him when the shot was taken on a warm June day not long before she vanished.

Vos put the photo back on the shelf. It seemed to embarrass De Groot.

'We don't know what happened. We never—'

'He sent you the same doll!'

A flash of memory: sitting at his desk in

Marnixstraat after an endless week of sixteen-hour days. Fielding frantic calls from Liesbeth asking where Anneliese might be. Just turned sixteen. Never late home from school, not without warning.

One of the aspirants of the time, a shy young kid called Oscar, came up with a cardboard box, a coffin shape sketched on the top with black felt tip. The lid bore a printed line drawing of what looked like the Oortman house, nothing else. Vos could picture himself opening it. Inside a doll. Hair. Bloodstain. Tucked inside the pinafore dress was a photo of his daughter, terrified against a plain background, duct tape round her mouth.

'I didn't know what was happening then,' Vos said. 'I'd no idea if it was a madman. A crook like Theo Jansen sending me a warning . . .'

'Jansen didn't murder kids,' De Groot said with a shake of his head.

'I never found a body, Frank. I didn't find anything.'

De Groot closed his eyes, murmured, 'True. Sorry.'

It was a feeble hope, an empty dream. For three months they'd turned the city upside down, raided Menzo's premises, Jansen's, harried sex traffickers, anyone Vos could think of. Anneliese had disappeared without trace. Vos felt some inner biological sense ought to tell him whether she was dead or not. But that wasn't there either. She was just . . . gone.

'Menzo would do it,' Vos suggested, with little conviction.

'Jimmy Menzo wasn't big enough to be in our sights back then,' De Groot replied. 'It must have been some . . . lunatic. Not your fault you couldn't catch him. No one could.'

Vos folded his arms and kept quiet.

'OK,' De Groot admitted. 'I don't know that either. We were just out of our depth. All of us.'

That bleak time would never leave him. Liesbeth getting crazier by the day. Accusing him of bringing this on by chasing the city's gangs. Spitting out secrets he never wanted to hear.

Vos had asked her to marry him so many times. She always said: *Why? Weren't they happy already?*

When Anneliese vanished he got the answer. Liesbeth was never his, not really. Worse, he was never hers and that still hurt.

No one got close to what happened. The two of them went down different roads, each to their own breed of madness. She rushed into marriage with Wim Prins. Vos entered a dull, penurious solitude in a run-down boat in the Jordaan, punctuated by trips to the Rijksmuseum to stare at Petronella Oortman's doll's house hour after pointless hour, the odd deafening concert in the Melkweg, evenings spent mostly alone in the Drie Vaten.

And bleak nights stoned senseless in the houseboat, sucking in the dense, dark smoke of the harshest weed he could find. Trying to obliterate something he couldn't put a name to.

'Katja hates Liesbeth for marrying her father,' he said, trying to convince himself. 'Taking the

47

place of her dead mother. From what I remember she's a heroin user. This is one more trick to get more money out of him.'

'Drugs,' De Groot said dryly, looking round the place. 'Terrible things. What if it's not?'

Vos frowned.

'Then it doesn't matter, does it? I'm off the payroll, remember? This is none of my business.'

'Make it your business. Come into the station and we'll talk about it. It's just some paperwork to go through. You could be back in place by tomorrow. Let's face it.' His eyes ran round the shabby boat. 'You could use the money. You're pissing your life away here.'

Vos fingered the packet of Limburger. It stank.

'I was thinking of opening a cheese shop.'

Frank de Groot roared with laughter.

'You? A cheese shop? As if the Jordaan needs another one. Please—'

'Frank.' Vos's hand went out to De Groot's arm. 'It nearly broke me. I didn't know who I was for a while. If I hadn't found some escape. This place . . .'

A sudden look of anger on De Groot's face.

'Do you think I never noticed? That I'd ask for any of this lightly? We weren't just colleagues. We were—'

'If Liesbeth called you from the office of the vice-mayor of the city council you'd do whatever she wanted. No choice.'

Frank de Groot swore. Then grinned.

'Sharp as ever. And there was me thinking you might have smoked yourself stupid in this hole.'

Nothing.

'It's no secret, Pieter. People have seen you in that coffee shop down the street.'

'Amsterdam resident. Card carrier. Nothing illegal. But if you want the truth . . .' Vos hated the lassitude, the idleness dope brought on. 'It didn't help.'

'I don't want you using that shit if you're back with us. I want . . .' He leaned forward, tapped Vos's skull through the long brown hair. 'All that's in there.'

'No.'

'I'm begging.'

'One hour in Marnixstraat,' Vos conceded. 'That girl of yours. Bakker . . .'

'What about her?' De Groot asked.

'She seems tense. Why?'

'Weren't you tense in your first job?'

Vos shook his head.

'No. Why would I be?'

'She's spent half the night reading up on Anneliese's case in the station. Reading up on you. She's a bit in awe I guess.' He groaned. 'Worried too. Her probation period's nearly up. The service assessment's coming.' A shrug of his heavy shoulders. 'She isn't going to make it.'

Vos waited.

'Amsterdam's no place for her,' De Groot added. 'A farmer's kid from Friesland who turns up here with a suitcase of bad clothes and an attitude.'

49

Something was missing.

'Why did she come then?'

De Groot groaned, a low, tired sound.

'Horrible story. Last Christmas. On the way back from church. Mother and father dead in a car crash. She might have been with them but she was doing unpaid work experience at the Dokkum police station.' De Groot shrugged. 'Drunk driver. She was in the car that went out on the call. Saw them.'

'Christ . . .' Vos whispered.

'After that she told Dokkum she wanted to join the force. Here, not there. I think the kid wants to tend the flock. Never a good idea.'

Vos groaned and put a hand to his forehead.

Heavy boots on the stairs that led down from the deck. He knew what he'd see. Laura Bakker there, Sam panting on the end of his lead. She'd stamped on the planks deliberately. He was sure of that. Had managed to slink onto the boat quietly without their noticing. Vos had no idea how long she'd been there, how much she'd heard.

'I'm not a girl,' she repeated in that flat sullen northern voice.

'True,' Vos said. 'We'll take Sam to the Drie Vaten. The bar on the corner. The woman there can look after him. And . . .'

He got up, found a bag of washing.

'. . . I can leave this with her.'

'The bar does your washing?' Bakker asked.

'It's just a temporary arrangement,' Vos said. Got

up, smiled, saw that this broke the ice a little. Shooed out De Groot with his hands, then her. 'Don't worry. I'm coming. I'll take a look at your doll.'

CHAPTER 7

Miriam Smith walked the two kids out of De Wallen into the quieter, more affluent streets of the Canal Rings, past imposing mansions, mostly apartments these days or hotels for the wealthier visitors. It was an ordinary Amsterdam spring morning. Chilly, the sky gently changing from weak sun to weak rain. Locals on bikes, heads down, pedalling hard for their destinations. Tourists wandering, on foot, on rented cycles, getting in the way.

The smell of bread and pastries from the bakeries. Beer from the bars serving early, thirsty customers. From time to time the harsh organic tang of dope on the air.

She made them carry the weapons in a black holdall, walking on and on, past Herengracht, past Keizersgracht and Prinsengracht, into the busy square of Leidseplein where the morning visitors were already out to play with their Heinekens and smokes.

'We could've took a tram,' red kid moaned.

She kicked the big bag he was carrying.

'Bright idea, sonny. The cops come and check

52

this stuff from time to time. Do you two have names?'

They didn't answer and looking at them she knew why. They were strangers before Menzo brought them together that morning. An odd streak of machismo meant that neither wanted to be the first to ask.

Down a narrow street there were Indonesian restaurants and sushi bars, cocktail joints and tiny coffee shops dressed with the Rastafarian flag and pictures of cannabis leaves.

They walked into the third one along. A tall West Indian behind the counter, Afro cut, woollen hat. Didn't say a word. Just turned down the reggae. Led them out to the Prinsengracht, one of the city's three great waterways encircling De Wallen, the last, an enclosing belt for Amsterdam that ran through everything the city had to offer, rich and poor, squalid and magnificent.

Opposite stood tall terrace houses, winches on gable rooftops ready to haul in furniture. Pigeons flapped stupidly across the tiles. There were houseboats and tourist vessels. A few smaller craft too.

The man walked them down some steps to a battered dinghy, took off the blue tarpaulin to reveal two bench seats, waved at them to climb in. Checked the outboard motor, showed them how to start it. Listened to the steady rattle of the little engine after he'd pulled the cord then shut it down.

He took out an old Nokia and a tourist map with points marked along the canal.

'When I call the first time you go here and wait. The boat's small, the water's low. No one will see you. When I call the second time you move.' He gave them the phone and the map. 'Here.' Two pairs of cheap fake-leather gloves. 'Wear these. Throw the weapons in the canal. Make your way to the place Jimmy told you about. Miriam's going to wait for you there.'

Blue kid pulled out the card with the picture of the doll's house.

'That's the one, bright boy,' Miriam Smith said. She grinned. 'You'll like Africa. It's where we're from.'

Red kid grunted something.

'Him.' She tapped the West Indian on the chest. 'Me. You too.'

They didn't like that. Surinamese toughs. From South America, not the Caribbean.

'You don't know shit about history,' the man grunted. 'Do you?'

'I know I'm hungry,' red kid said.

'Wait there,' Miriam Smith told him.

A couple of minutes later she was back with two cones of fries dripping in mayonnaise, a couple of cans of Coke and a pair of cheap collapsible umbrellas.

'Here,' she said and handed them over. 'I wouldn't want you to get wet. Take a look at this too.'

She gave them a photograph of a beefy, middle-aged man with a white beard.

'Who's this? Father Christmas?' red kid asked.

Miriam Smith laughed at that.

'Yeah. But you've got a present for him.'

CHAPTER 8

Wim Prins came up with the idea for De Nachtwacht a year before when he was thinking of running for the council, hunting for headline-grabbing ideas. He'd never expected to win a majority let alone seize the presidency. But the mood had changed. Austerity and a popular resentment for the old parties had given muscle to minority groups previously confined to shouting on the fringes.

He was Mr Clean. A new broom sweeping the city. His own history – a wife lost to drugs, a daughter who'd wound up with the same affliction – helped his position more than hindered it.

Here was someone who knew the cost of Amsterdam's liberal legacy. Pushing an anti-crime, anti-drugs ticket, he found himself in the headlines immediately. The mix had touched a nerve. And now he was in power, kept there by a deal with Margriet Willemsen's Independence Party.

No, with her. Thirty-two years old, ready smile, short, black hair in a business-like Sassoon bob, alert cobalt-blue eyes, bright, attentive face, not beautiful but hard not to look at. She was made for office. To begin with Prins couldn't understand why she'd never joined one of the major parties. That would have put her in Parliament already. Then they worked together to seal the coalition and he'd come to understand. Beneath the bland, politician's exterior burned a steely, individual sense of ambition.

Not that De Nachtwacht was without its obstacles. Alex Hendriks, head of the council's general office, was one of them.

He and Margriet Willemsen had spent an hour at the conference table in Prins's office going through the initial phase of the plan.

'We've got objections from the retailers, the restaurant association, some of the local community groups. A few of your own councillors are having second thoughts,' Hendriks said.

He was a short, furtive, anxious man, forever playing with his laptop or iPad or any one of the three phones he carried and checked constantly.

'The less money people waste on dope and whores the more they've got to spend somewhere else,' Margriet Willemsen said with a smile.

Hendriks shook his head.

'Not everyone's here for the culture. They're after—'

'Those are people we can do without,' Prins interrupted.

'I'm not so sure of that,' Hendriks continued. 'The trade associations are worried they're going to get hit on footfall by maybe twenty, thirty per cent. That's big money. People not buying food, drink. Clothes. Souvenirs. They're nagging their councillors. *Your* councillors.'

'Think of all the ones who'll come instead,' Prins said. 'Better people. Richer people.'

Hendriks stood his ground.

'They won't go down De Wallen. Why? To see a bunch of closed coffee shops? Some empty cabin windows? This is the centre of the city we're talking about. You could be killing it—'

'If you won't do it we'll find someone who can,' Margriet Willemsen broke in. 'We won the election—'

'You don't have a mandate to piss off everyone,' Hendriks snapped. 'Do that and they'll hang you. If Theo Jansen or that evil bastard Menzo don't get there first.'

The smile never left her face.

'What are you saying? That we need to look out for the crooks now?'

Hendriks didn't take his eyes off Wim Prins.

'You're threatening their empires. What do you think? They're not going to sit back and wait.'

'They won't have much choice,' Prins said. 'I talked to Marnixstraat this morning. Jansen's due to be released this afternoon. He and Menzo are going to be at each other's throats. We're the last thing on their minds. They can fight it out between each other and we'll clean up the corpses when it's done. There's never been a better time to throw out the rubbish . . .'

'And what about your daughter?' Hendriks asked.

The civil servant's pale face had colour for once.

'You're not the only one who talks to Marnixstraat,' Hendriks added. 'They're worried as hell about what you're asking for. They said—'

'My daughter's my concern. Not yours. Margriet was right. If you feel you can't pursue the agreed policy of the council you should resign. We can talk severance if you like.'

He was a coward at heart, Prins thought. Now was the time to test it.

'I'm paid to offer you advice, whether you want to hear it or not.'

'Thank you,' Prins replied. 'We've listened. Now will you kindly do what we've asked?'

The first phase was almost ready. Within a month the city would start to turn to the civilian staff who usually dealt with traffic and minor street crime. They would be empowered to enter coffee shops and arrest on sight. Pick up pimps, hookers and dealers, call the police and hand them over.

Hendriks kept tapping the table with his pen. But he hadn't started to make notes yet and that meant something.

'These are unarmed men and women we pay to hand out parking tickets. You're asking them to harass criminals in the street.'

'That's their job now,' Prins insisted.

'And when one of them gets beaten up? Or killed?'

'Then we crack down harder,' Willemsen replied.

'Is there really anything else to talk about?' Prins asked, glancing at his watch.

Margriet Willemsen shook her head.

Alex Hendriks picked up his three phones, tucked his iPad beneath his arm and left.

CHAPTER 9

Marnixstraat didn't look any different. Office after open office. Then, finally, homicide with its lines of desks, reports and photos on the wall, detectives, men mostly, working computers and phones.

Faces that were familiar. Koeman with his droopy brown moustache, eyeing Laura Bakker as she walked, the way he did every female officer, looker or not. Thin, miserable Rijnder, trying to work up a smile. Van der Berg, the genial office drinker, raising an imaginary glass when he spotted Vos approaching.

A brisk, brave man, little appreciated.

'Welcome back, boss,' he shouted as Vos got near. 'It's your round.'

Vos smiled, lifted a pretend beer, said nothing.

Then Klaas Mulder, hands on hips, leaning on the door of a meeting room.

The carefully sculpted fine blonde hair was thinning. Rugged face lined, the cheekbones more prominent, the grey eyes more weary. When Vos was a brigadier Mulder shared the same rank. Always saw himself as competition. Not a man to pool resources or information. Then, after Vos's departure, he was promoted to hoofdinspecteur, De Groot's deputy, picked up the skimpy case against Theo Jansen and built it into something that could jail Amsterdam's leading gang lord on obscure and perhaps dubious money-laundering charges.

Vos was still half-crazy at the time. But one day, when he was feeling serious, he skipped the coffee shop and the bar and went to the library to read through all the newspaper reports. Any prosecution that put Jansen in jail was probably deemed a good thing by the city hierarchy. It still didn't feel right to him. And now the evidence was unravelling. No wonder the man's smile looked counterfeit.

'Pieter. Good to see you back where you belong.' Mulder reached out and felt Vos's scruffy black jacket. 'You're wearing your old work clothes too.'

Before he joined the police Mulder had almost become a professional footballer. Trialled for Ajax. Just a dodgy knee stopped him, or so he told everyone. That didn't prevent him working out most days in a gym nearby. A tough, solitary, uncompromising man. He'd been lucky not to face a disciplinary hearing over some of his antics with suspects.

'Just passing,' Vos said and walked past him into the room.

Two sights there to take his breath away. A large porcelain doll on the table, twice the size of the one he'd received almost three years before. And Liesbeth Prins, pale, thinner than ever, standing in the corner, hand to her mouth, staring at him.

'Hi,' he said. 'Where's Wim?'

'Busy.' Her voice sounded fragile too. 'He'll come if we need him.'

'This is about his daughter,' Laura Bakker cut in. 'He should be here now. What . . .?'

Vos smiled at her, put a finger to his lips, waited until she was quiet.

He went over to a desk, took a pair of disposable gloves from the drawer, pulled them on.

The doll was still inside a cardboard box shaped like a coffin. Left outside Prins's home in one of the Jordaan's more beautiful *hofjes*, a quiet sanctuary of houses set around a private garden near Noordermarkt. The security cameras had caught a hooded figure flitting into the entrance around seven in the evening. Nothing of use on the box. Nothing on the doll either except the hank of hair, the bloodstained pinafore dress and that curious note: *Love's expensive, Wim. Get ready for the bill.*

The box was plain and ordinary. No line drawing of the Oortman house.

'Where's the hair?' Vos asked.

'Forensic have got it,' Mulder said. 'They came back thirty minutes ago and confirmed it's from the Prins girl. As is the blood.' The tall detective stared at De Groot. 'Am I working on this or not?'

'We don't even know if there's a case yet,' the commissaris replied. 'Give it time.'

The note was in a plastic evidence envelope. Vos looked at it and frowned.

'What?' Mulder asked.

'I already said.' He looked at Liesbeth. 'Prins doesn't love his daughter. Does he?'

She came a step closer. He could smell her perfume. The same as it always was.

'That's not true,' she said. 'Katja's been a nightmare for the last few years. Wim's done his best. Paid for medical help. Paid to keep her out of trouble. It didn't—'

'Does he love her?' he repeated.

'In his own way,' she replied, staring at him with the same sad, brown eyes. 'You won't understand. If there's something here that needs to be done . . .'

Nothing more.

'They sell dolls like that in all the tourist shops in De Wallen,' Mulder said. 'Could have come from anywhere. The kid's probably jerking him around.'

Vos nodded, looked at the figure in the box. It wasn't much like the one he'd received. He put both gloved hands underneath the back and lifted it. Heavier than he expected.

'Torch,' Vos said and held out a hand.

Bakker was there straight away, pulling a long police Maglite out of the pockets of her grey trousers and placing it in his hands.

Vos lifted the dress and shone the beam through the translucent plastic of the torso. A dim black shape was just visible.

De Groot swore and glowered at Mulder.

'Haven't forensic been over this thing?' he asked.

'I got the DNA. You told me you were bringing in Vos and Prins! I was waiting . . .'

'Good idea,' Vos said and took the torch away.

Carefully, piece by piece, he removed all the doll's clothing. On the neck, by a mark saying 'Made in China', there was what looked like a small speaker and a hole next to it that could have been for a microphone. The thing could talk. And play back a customized recorded message.

Vos gently pumped the doll's stomach.

Something crackled. There was an uncertain, electronic racket. After that came the shrieking.

The doll.

Liesbeth Prins.

Both of them.

Vos got his ear closer to the plastic head and tried to listen.

'Daddy! Daddy! Christ . . .'

A young girl's voice in agony and pain. A scream. A bellow of anguish.

A repeating refrain.

'Help me! Help me! Help . . .'

Liesbeth was on him, beating at his arm, shrieking, 'Turn it off for God's sake.'

The thing was on a loop. It was back at the beginning already.

Laura Bakker had her hands to her mouth, her face paler than ever. De Groot looked lost and helpless. Even Klaas Mulder didn't have a thing to say.

65

'It's Katja?' Vos asked.

'It's Katja,' she said. 'Christ, Pieter. Turn it off—'

'I don't know how.'

He looked round the room, opened his arms. 'Anyone?'

The doll kept squawking.

Mulder walked over, touched something by the ear. The screaming stopped.

Vos looked at him.

'There was a switch,' Mulder said dryly. 'You saw it too. Don't pretend . . .'

'No,' Vos said with a slow nod. 'I didn't see it. I'm out of practice. Slow. Stupid. I don't know why I'm here.' He looked at Liesbeth Prins. 'You need to ask your husband to come into the station. It doesn't matter if this is Katja's doing or someone else's. He should be here.'

He tore off the disposable gloves.

'What next?' Bakker asked.

'I need to pick up my dog from the Drie Vaten. I've got a houseboat to fix. There's a band at the Melkweg tonight I was thinking of seeing and . . .'

A hand on his arm. Liesbeth's sad eyes turned on him.

'The doll's bigger than the one I got,' Vos said, exasperated. 'This one has a message. Mine didn't. Anyone who read about the case in the papers could have done this.'

A sudden flash of anger on her face.

'And left it on my doorstep? It's the same man . . .'

'You don't know that. You can't rush to—'

66

'A young girl's missing. Jesus. Can't you hear her? Can't you see her? Anneliese—'

'Anneliese's gone. I tried. So did all the police officers in Amsterdam. We couldn't bring her back. I apologize. I did what I could. I failed.'

There was a harsh tone to his voice and he regretted it immediately.

The woman he'd lived with for most of his adult life, loved, never expected to leave him, put her bony fingers into her bag, pulled out a photo. Then another. Vos looked at them. Their daughter at her last birthday party. Bright eyes, long blonde hair, smile on her face. A future in front of her.

The second, he knew, was Katja Prins, not that he'd ever met the girl except through a picture in the odd gossip piece in the city papers.

Dead eyes, blank face. But the hair was much the same and the smile . . . was maybe the one Anneliese would have worn had she known. Fated, resigned, half-amused that life should amount to this and nothing more.

'Walk away from Katja and you walk away from our daughter.'

They were all watching.

'If I couldn't save Anneliese,' Vos said and heard his own voice rising angrily, 'what makes you think I can do it for someone else?'

Frank de Groot intervened, thrust an ID card into Vos's hand. An old picture. The same rank. And a piece of paper.

'Let me be the judge of that,' he said. 'I'll get

Prins in here even if I have to drag him every inch of the way. This is Katja's last known address. Some dump near Warmoesstraat. Tell me who you'd like assigned to work alongside you. We're busy here but take your pick.'

Laura Bakker stood stiff and nervous in her misshapen grey suit, sad green eyes staring at the floor.

'I'll take Aspirant Bakker,' Vos said.

De Groot blinked. Mulder was laughing.

'This is serious, Pieter,' the commissaris said in a gruff, annoyed tone.

'Yes,' Vos said. 'It is.'

Then put a hand to Bakker's arm and led her from the room.

CHAPTER 10

When Hendriks was gone, taking his papers and gadgets with him, Margriet Willemsen got up and walked to the window.

'What's this about your daughter?' she asked as Prins came to join her.

'Nothing.'

'Don't give me that, Wim.'

So he told her. She looked worried.

'What if Hendriks is right? If Menzo or Jansen or one of the other hoods is coming for us?'

'Jansen goes free this afternoon. Those two will be at each other's throats in a second. It gives us more ammunition to do what we want . . .'

'What's she like? Katja?'

'She was fine until two, three years ago. Just another teenager.' He shrugged. 'Difficult. Not so bright. Never said where she was going. What she was doing. Then . . . It was her mother all over again. God knows I've tried. Just a while back there was this place . . .'

The Yellow House. He'd paid through the nose for that, thought for a time it might be working.

Then she was back to the squalid tenement off Warmoesstraat, living like a tramp.

Willemsen picked up some papers Hendriks had left behind.

'I don't want this to get in the way. We're on shaky ground already.'

'What?'

'Hendriks is right. People are getting cold feet. We might have to trim things a little . . .'

'No,' Prins insisted. 'I won't allow it.'

She smiled.

'We're tearing up the twentieth century. Putting something new in its place. You can't expect everyone to leap on board from day one. Why should they?'

'Because we're right.'

'Right doesn't mean you get to win . . .'

Prins closed his eyes. Headache coming on.

'I want you to think about your daughter,' she said. 'That story's going to break one way or another. When it does I don't want to see you like this. You've got to look hurt. Concerned.'

'I am hurt. I am concerned.'

'Show it then. Katja going off the rails is proof we're on the right track. When she turns up we can use that.'

Margriet Willemsen came close, touched his chest very lightly for the briefest of moments.

'They'll find her. When they do get her out of Amsterdam. Put her in rehab in America or somewhere. No distractions. For her. For us.'

He didn't say anything.

70

'Do you understand me?'

His phone was ringing. He looked at the number: *Liesbeth*.

'Past caring,' he muttered and took the call.

CHAPTER 11

Vos insisted they go to Warmoesstraat by bike. He wasn't a cop yet, whatever Frank de Groot said. The ID card was in his jacket for convenience, nothing else. She seemed keen to avoid cars too. The previous week she'd been driving a station patrol car when it got into an argument with a tram.

'The tram won,' Bakker said wide-eyed, as if this was a surprise. 'Commissaris De Groot wasn't happy.'

'You don't have trams in Dokkum?' Vos asked.

'Dokkum's the most northerly town in the Netherlands. Did you know that?'

They found the dead-end turning down towards the canal.

'Trams, Laura. I was asking about the trams.'

'No trams.' A shrug, the briefest of giggles as she put her long fingers to her lips. 'Otherwise I wouldn't have bashed that one here. He just came at me! I told De Groot. Wasn't my fault.'

Vos climbed off his old bike. The little basket on the front seemed empty without the dog. He wondered how far he could push Sofia Albers,

72

the woman who ran the Drie Vaten. The odd beer and coffee seemed scant reward for dog care and laundry.

'Why did you pick me?' she asked. 'You could have had one of the proper detectives?'

'You seemed interested,' Vos said. He smiled. 'And I'm not a proper detective either.'

The joke didn't humour her.

'I'm an aspirant, Vos. They're going to fire me next week.'

'In that case let's make the best of things.'

She seemed to like a straight answer. Bakker looked up at the street sign and said, 'This is where it came from, isn't it?'

'What?'

'Your doll's house. Petronella Oortman lived in Warmoesstraat.'

She did, Vos thought. Not that anyone knew where. He'd tried to find out.

'Is it important?' Bakker asked.

A drawing of an ancient doll's house. A famous one. Stuck on a miniature coffin. After that nothing. Just a black and endless well of doubt and grief. Once, in a screaming match in the night, Liesbeth had yelled at him, 'You want her dead, don't you? You want to see her corpse?'

Not at all. He wanted to watch her walk down their street in the Jordaan the way she used to, happy, free, smiling, occasionally mischievous. To vanish like that, after such dreadful, terrifying messages, was worse than a bereavement somehow.

It left them both with a wound that refused to heal. A question that came with no possible answer.

'I think it must be,' Vos said, coming back to the present. 'I just don't . . .'

Understand. It seemed the wrong word. Some things were beyond comprehension, and perhaps Anneliese's disappearance was one of them.

Bakker wheeled her bike round the corner into the narrow lane running down to the water, checking the numbers on the terraces. The buildings became more run-down. She found a battered red door. Posters in the cracked and dirty windows. Bands, movies and dope. The sound of music from inside.

Recent rock. Which sounded like a pale copy of the originals he preferred.

'The doll he sent you,' she said chaining her bike on the railings. 'Where did it come from?'

'You mean you didn't look in the files?'

She folded her long arms.

'I haven't read everything.'

This wasn't going away. Not with Laura Bakker asking.

'We never found out,' he said. 'It was expensive. Looked antique but it wasn't. They're made in Germany. No one sells them in Amsterdam. Not like that cheap thing you've got in Marnixstraat now. Someone spent real money on this. Maybe . . .'

She waited then, when he said nothing, asked, 'Maybe?'

'Maybe he had it already. He was a collector.

Crinoline dress. Not much different from the kind of thing Petronella might have put in her doll's house.'

'It had her hair?'

'Yes.'

'And her blood?'

'Yes,' he said, feeling cold and miserable, wishing he was back on the boat with the dog and some beer. Maybe a smoke if things got bad.

'So you think she was dead already?' Bakker asked. 'He was torturing you? Not your daughter?'

When the case was alive he'd rarely had conversations like this, even with Frank de Groot. They were too close and personal.

'I don't know,' he admitted. 'He wasn't a lunatic like De Groot says. That's too . . .'

Words. Sometimes they wouldn't come.

'Simple?' Bakker asked.

'Quite.'

'I'm sorry,' she said and stood there, sad-faced but pretty in an innocent, adolescent way.

People joined the police for different reasons. He wanted to be a part of something that helped. That made the world better. Laura Bakker . . . he wondered. Frank de Groot was a clever, incisive man, as good a judge of character as anyone Vos had known. That remark about how she was trying to herd the flock . . .

The police didn't change things. He'd learned that early on. At best they offered comfort. Reined in the worst elements of a society so fractured it was incapable of healing itself. It was wise not to hold out too much hope, to set your sights too high. The cost of failure could be shattering.

'I'm sorry I said those stupid things,' Vos told her. 'About drunk drivers. I don't talk to people much these days. It's hard.'

For the first time she looked actively cross at something he'd said.

'You weren't to know,' she replied, then pushed past him, tried the doorbell. Heard nothing, banged on the woodwork with her fist.

CHAPTER 12

The girl who answered the door had short and greasy fair hair, a face so pale it seemed like parchment, a skinny, haggard frame. Long Indian cotton dress and a threadbare jumper which she clutched constantly, holding herself by the elbows where a grubby sweatshirt showed through.

Four floors high the terraced house stank of dope and sweat and drains. A communal kitchen, no sign of food. In the front room two drowsy men passing round a bubble pipe.

She was called Til and came from Limburg in the south. The source of De Groot's cheese. Bakker asked for her ID. Mathilde Stamm. Nineteen. The age Anneliese would have been now. Same as the Prins girl too.

They tried to talk to her about Katja. Gave up and went to the men smoking in the front room. Got nowhere. Back to the girl, pinned her in a corner, waited until she gave in.

Didn't take long once she understood Vos wasn't leaving without answers. Katja had lived in the squat for a year off and on. Til didn't know where she went when she wasn't there. No boyfriends around. Girlfriends either.

'No friends at all then?' Bakker asked before Vos could say another word.

The girl hugged herself more tightly.

'What is this?'

'She's missing. We think she could be in trouble.'

Til Stamm laughed.

'Just 'cos you can't find her doesn't mean she's missing. Katja gets up to stuff. Gets away with it too. Her old man's loaded. He runs Amsterdam, doesn't he?'

'He thinks so,' Vos said, looking around the house. It seemed as transient as Centraal station. A place people came and went. Not much more.

'Her dad can fix things,' the girl added. 'He sent her off to rehab.' She reached into the grubby jumper, pulled out a pack of cigarettes, lit one with shaking fingers. 'As if Katja cared.'

'Where?' Vos asked.

'The Yellow House. Behind the Flower Market. I don't have that kind of money.' She laughed again and it made her cough. 'Or needs.'

Laura Bakker looked her up and down and said, 'You mean Katja was even worse than you?'

Vos sighed. The kid flew off the handle, started throwing a flurry of curses, at Bakker, at him. The cigarette fell from her trembling fingers.

Taken aback by the sudden violent outburst Bakker retreated. The men with the bubble pipe didn't move. No one did except Pieter Vos who retrieved the cigarette from the dirty floor, held it out in front of Til Stamm, waited for her to calm down, then placed it back in her fingers.

'Do you like her?' he asked when she quietened down.

'Katja's OK. Not snooty. I think maybe . . .' She twirled a finger at her ear. 'Her head's not quite straight. But she never pushed her old man at us. We just saw him when she needed something.'

'Like what?' Vos asked.

'Like money. Or a get-out-of-jail card.'

'Why would she need that, Til?'

His voice was calm, his manner friendly.

Her eyes were on Laura Bakker. Only a few years separated these two but they might have come from different worlds.

'The usual,' the girl replied. 'I haven't seen her for a week or so. I told you. Sometimes she goes off on her own somewhere.'

She walked to the front door and flung the cigarette out into the chill day. Pulled a hand-rolled smoke from her jumper pocket, thin and half-gone. Her fingers trembled so much she couldn't light it. Vos took the matches and did that for her.

'This is important,' he said. 'She must have someone. A friend she liked more than anyone else. Was that you?'

The juvenile shrug.

'What about men?'

'I don't tell tales.'

Laura Bakker started squawking at that. Then went quiet when Vos looked at her.

'All we want to do is find her,' he said. 'Make sure she's safe. And then we're gone. Then . . .' He pointed at the joint. 'You can go back to doing whatever you want.'

'What kind of trouble?' she asked.

'The getting kidnapped kind,' Laura Bakker said.

Til Stamm looked at both of them, frowned, then meandered towards the worn wooden steps in the hall. They followed, up and up. The girl walked at the pace of an old woman. The sour, sweaty smell of unaired rooms got worse.

Four flights. At the top Til Stamm stopped, out of breath. Gasping, sucking on the joint.

'Are we here for the view?' Bakker asked, glancing out of the window. Nothing there but more dreary ancient terraces on the other side.

'She's shit at her job,' the girl said, staring at him. 'I'm surprised you put up with it.'

Vos smiled.

'She's learning. Country kid, from Friesland. I'm an Amsterdammer. Indulgent by nature.'

The door was already ajar. A room with a single bed. The sheets half on the mattress, half on the bare plank floor. Smell of dirty clothes and resin.

'A while back she brought this guy here. He was old. Weird.'

Vos walked in, looked around.

'What was his name?'

'Jaap. Never heard him called anything else.'

She walked to a chest of drawers, one leg of which was broken, a brick supporting the corner.

'Never paid his rent. Never paid for anything. Food. Smoke. You name it.' She clutched at her waist again. 'Who'd kidnap Katja?'

'We don't know,' Vos said. 'That's why we're looking. This Jaap . . .'

'He never said much.'

'She was with him?' Bakker asked.

'I don't do bedtime stories either.'

Vos raised an eyebrow.

Til Stamm folded her arms.

'I . . . don't . . . know. I think they were just friends. Katja brings people here sometimes. If she thinks they need a place to stay. She's a nice kid. A bit simple.'

He walked to the drawers, went through the papers there. Some were official. Reports from a probation officer. Court orders. A letter from a lawyer. He picked up the last and read it.

'Katja said we ought to put up with him,' the girl added. 'Jaap had been in trouble or something. It was all going to come good. One day we'd get paid . . .'

Her arm circled the squalid bedroom.

'Get all the money we're owed for this.'

'When did he leave?'

'About a week ago.'

'Around the last time you saw Katja?'

She frowned.

'I guess. I wasn't keeping tabs. Why would I?'

'What does Jaap do?' Vos asked.

'Do? He went out in the morning and came back at night. I didn't ask.'

That was it. Vos waved the paper he'd picked up, told her he was taking it, then the three walked downstairs.

The air outside was a little fresher. Laura Bakker looked uncomfortable. Vos didn't speak.

'So,' she said. 'The girl talks to you but not to me. What did I do wrong?'

'Nothing I wouldn't have done at your age.'

'I need to know.'

Vos looked at the paper again, thinking.

'She's nineteen. Dropped out of school. Out of home. Out of what we think of as life. How many job interviews do you think she's had?'

Bakker put her hands on her hips. An expression of exasperation he was coming to recognize.

'How many do you think I got?'

'Enough. You're bright. Educated. You wanted to be a police officer. In a quiet little country town called Dokkum.'

'You don't know me!'

He nodded.

'True. But I know Til Stamm. You behaved the way she expected. Life's easier sometimes if you do the opposite. When they think you're going to play hardball be charming. If they think you're the nice guy . . .'

'Always the nice guy. That's you. How was the dope they were smoking? Good?'

'Frank talking out of turn?'

'It's in the files, Vos,' she said, a little shame-faced. 'On your record when they gave you sickness retirement. I thought . . .'

She didn't finish the sentence.

'Thought what?'

'I thought you'd look older. And more wasted.'

He laughed at that and said, 'You shouldn't believe everything you read in the files.'

'Does this go down on mine?'

Before he could answer her phone rang. She took the call. Change of voice. Deferential not defensive.

'Any news from Frank?' he asked when she was done.

Bakker said, 'You've got to stop doing this to me.'

'It's the way you talk.' Vos unlocked his bike. 'From aggressive to . . .' He was about to say defensive but that wouldn't have been right. 'You've got to learn to listen to people, Laura. Especially when what they say doesn't seem to matter.'

'That kid in there was lying.'

'She was,' he agreed. 'So what?'

The round green eyes widened.

'So what? She was lying.'

'Til Stamm was doing what comes naturally with people like us. Does it matter?'

A quiet curse beneath her breath.

'Wim Prins finally got around to going to Marnixstraat,' she said. 'De Groot wants us back there to talk to them. Prins is busy apparently. A meeting to go to. He can't stay long.'

Vos held out his hand for the phone. She passed it over. He returned the call. Asked De Groot some questions. Gave no reasons for them. Then passed the phone back and pointed to her bike.

'Time to go, Aspirant Bakker.'

'To Marnixstraat?'

'To court. According to Frank they're going to let Theo Jansen out sometime over the next hour. He's promised to be a good boy. Let's hope we get there in time.'

She didn't move.

'Commissaris de Groot specifically told me to get you back to Marnixstraat. If I don't . . .'

'Frank can talk to Wim Prins. I don't want to miss Theo. It's been a while.'

'Will you please tell me what's going on?'

He showed her the piece of paper he'd taken from the bedroom.

'Katja's friend is Jaap Zeeger. A pointless little druggie and petty crook who was, for a while, the primary suspect in my daughter's disappearance. Turned out to be wrong. At least I thought so.'

She read the document. A summons to the court for that afternoon.

'Zeeger was on Theo Jansen's payroll,' Vos said. 'Maybe a few other people's too. Klaas Mulder got him to turn informer and put his boss in jail.' Vos climbed on the bike. 'Now he's retracted everything. He's going to help Jansen go free.'

The letter said Zeeger would be in court for the hearing.

'Why's he changed his mind?'

'Let's ask him. After we find out what he knows about Katja Prins. Since you're so good at multi-tasking you can phone Frank and tell him where we're going.'

Vos set off down the narrow alley back towards Warmoesstraat.

She followed, getting more shrill along the way.

'Vos! Vos! Why don't you call . . .?'

Her voice rang off the dingy brickwork. Spots of rain. Shouted pleas from behind. Something about him being infuriating.

Which was wrong, Vos felt. More . . . pre-occupied.

He turned, smiled, waved, then rejoined the busy street where, three and a half centuries before, Petronella Oortman had lived with her little wooden mansion and her family of dolls.

Vos bent down, pulled the elastic bands out of his pocket, bent down to put them on his jeans.

She was there straight away, hand on his shoulder.

'No, Vos. I've seen that once and I don't want to see it again. Here. I brought you a present. They're spares.'

A pair of shiny black bicycle clips. Brand new. He looked at her loose grey trousers. She had the same.

'Thanks,' he said.

CHAPTER 13

Two o'clock in Marnixstraat. Koeman sat silent in a chair, rubbing his droopy brown moustache, reading the *Telegraaf* sports pages.

Liesbeth Prins was in a huddle with her husband, eyeing the sharply dressed woman talking to Klaas Mulder outside the interview room.

'It's Katja's voice. In the doll,' she said. 'Her blood. Her hair.'

De Groot had played them the tape when Prins finally arrived. Fifteen seconds of agonized screeching. One word at the end, over and over again.

Vader. Vader.

'She never called me father,' Prins said.

'It's her . . .'

'I know it's her. She never called me father. Think about this. Please . . .'

He took her hands. Tried to peer into her eyes.

'I know this is my fault. I couldn't stop it happening with her mother. I should have done something . . .'

Liesbeth was starting to get angry.

'Katja couldn't do this herself. She's not up to it.'

'One of her druggie friends then.'

'Someone's taken her, Wim! The same man who took Anneliese. I know what this is like. I don't want to go through it again. I don't want it for you. We have to do something . . .'

'Such as?' he asked and the question silenced her.

He was glancing at the corridor. Margriet Willemsen was talking earnestly to Mulder.

'I don't like that woman,' she whispered.

'Mulder's our link man for De Nachtwacht. We've got a meeting.'

'Is Katja getting in the way of your schedule or something?'

'For God's sake!' He hardly ever raised his voice. 'I'll do whatever they ask. Just don't expect to—'

'What?'

'Believe it. The crap I've put up with from that kid. You don't know the half of it.'

She realized how much her anger hurt him. Struggled for something to say.

'I watched her mother lose it,' he said in a low, aggrieved voice. 'Day by day. Then Katja went the same way and there wasn't a damned thing I could do to stop her. Don't lecture me, Liesbeth. I don't deserve that. Why do you think I came up with De Nachtwacht in the first place? I want these scum and their poison off our streets for good.'

'This isn't about politics.'

'I never realized you and Katja were so close,' he said with a bitter look in his face.

'What are we going to do?'

'You can stay here if you like. If someone gets in touch . . .'

'I asked for Pieter. He's better than any of . . .'

He looked at her, open-mouthed, astonished.

'You think your crazy old boyfriend can fix this? He did that before, didn't he?'

It was so quick she never even thought about it. Liesbeth Prins slapped her husband hard on the face. One swift blow, open-handed.

She'd never struck him before. Thought about it though.

He had his hand to his cheek. Face going red, through fury, through the slap, she wasn't sure which.

The door opened. Klaas Mulder came in. The Willemsen woman stayed outside, staring at the blank walls.

'Is there anything else you want to ask?' Mulder asked, looking at both of them.

Prins straightened his tie.

'Is Pieter Vos back with the police?'

No expression on Mulder's stony face.

'He's helping out today. The commissaris thought it was a good idea. If there's a link—'

'They get cunning when they need something,' Prins broke in. 'Addicts have no morals. No feelings. They'll do anything. Doesn't matter how much it hurts. Their friends. Their family. Themselves . . .'

'We've got an open mind,' Mulder said as

Koeman noisily rustled the sports pages then folded the paper and placed it on his lap. 'As soon as we know something I'll be in touch.'

'You or Vos?' Prins asked.

'He's just helping out,' said Koeman from the chair. 'Don't you hear too well?'

Prins, in his smart politician's grey suit, bristled.

'I don't want any crap from you people over what we're doing. We won the election. We've got the right—'

'Like your wife said. This is about your missing daughter,' Koeman interrupted. 'Not you playing sheriff in the Wild West.' He got up. Stretched. Stared at Prins. 'Katja.'

'I'll remember you,' Prins said and walked out.

Mulder was staring at Liesbeth Prins. Amused.

'What am I supposed to do?' she asked.

'Go home. Wait. Keep your eyes open,' Mulder replied. 'If you see something odd let us know.'

She didn't look happy with that.

'Your daughter's case was all over the papers,' Mulder added. 'Anyone could copy it. There's nothing in what we've seen that hasn't been out there already. It could just be a bad practical joke.'

'Nice to see you're trying,' she said.

The two cops watched her leave.

'I never liked her when she was with Pieter,' Koeman observed. 'That bitch was playing him for a fool all along. Can't believe she's dragged him back into it again.'

'I told you. Vos is just helping out,' Mulder insisted. 'One day only.'

'Yeah,' Koeman agreed with a smile. 'I'm sure you're right.'

CHAPTER 14

Red kid. Blue kid. Bored in the boat, feet kicking the bag with the guns.

Empty cardboard cones smeared in mayonnaise and chip fat in the bows.

The phone was in blue kid's hand. It rang. He listened, checked the map again.

Black voice. Jamaican accent. The big man from the coffee shop doing just what he'd promised. Telling them where to go.

'Yeah,' blue kid said and put the ancient Nokia back into the pocket of his shiny tracksuit.

The canal reminded him of the broad, lazy river that ran through Paramaribo. The Surinam. It gave the country its name. Slow and grey too. Opaque. A place to hide things. He'd done that. Wondered if red kid had and whether he ought to ask his name. Not that he talked much. Or seemed to want to.

In a few hours they'd both be on a plane to somewhere new. He hadn't had time to do a lot in Amsterdam. One hooker, some smokes. Then Jimmy Menzo called.

His uncle had a boat on the Suriname river. When

he was young and the family was still intact they used it to go out of the city for picnics in the country. Good times. All gone. There was no future for his kind back home. They had to go abroad, to Venezuela, the Caribbean, across continents for that.

A tourist cruiser went past. People standing up to take pictures. Japanese mostly, cameras round their necks. These people weren't like him. They had money and real jobs. Enough to take them to Amsterdam then get out again. He didn't resent that. It was how things were. They couldn't help being born in Tokyo or Los Angeles or London. Any more than he had a choice about growing up four to a room in a Paramaribo slum.

'Are we going?' red kid asked then yawned as if this was just another boring day.

It seemed colder. The wind had got up. Rain was spitting from the dull, heavy sky. The trees that lined the canal kept shedding their light-green seeds. When the breeze caught they whirled around the little dinghy in a sudden storm.

His uncle let him steer the outboard when he got older. Those were good days.

Blue kid walked to the back, yanked on the cord, got the engine going, worked the little boat into the slow traffic of the Prinsengracht. Another throw of the die and he might have been one of the traders running up and down these waters, delivering things, moving them. Never having to worry about people like Jimmy Menzo. Never having to touch a gun.

But that wouldn't happen. In a day he'd be in Cape Town, at the foot of Africa, red kid by his side. He really had to ask his name. Not now though.

Four, five faster tourist boats cruised by, all of them taking pictures, which bothered him, not that he could do much except try to bring his hood up round his face. Then he checked the map and realized they'd almost passed the spot the West Indian had marked. He flung round the outboard, cut the engine to idle, steered towards a rusty metal ladder leading up to the pavement above.

The black guy was right. No one would see the boat. They'd wait there until a call came. From someone inside Miriam said after she'd brought them the cones of greasy fries.

He didn't like that much. It was important to see things for yourself.

Menzo probably had other people around. They'd be watching too. They'd see the two of them climb the rickety steps, look round the broad cobbled road outside the courthouse.

So what? If they did what Menzo wanted they were fine. If they didn't . . .

He wasn't going to think about that. He loved his sister. Wished she hadn't come all the way to Amsterdam on a wisp of hope and a forlorn prayer.

'Stay here,' he said. 'I'll be back in a minute.'

Then he jumped from the dinghy to the platform at the bottom of the ladder, tied up the boat the way his uncle showed him. Went up the ladder.

More trees shedding green leaves on the damp,

slow day. Police cars. People, lawyers and clients he guessed, smoking outside a severe stone building.

As he watched, an unusual-looking man with long hair and a young and striking face cycled to the main doors and started talking to the security officer there. He wore old clothes, almost ragged. Behind him, pedalling hard to keep up, was a tall red-haired woman, pretty but anxious, just as oddly dressed.

Another check of the cheap digital watch on his wrist, one of the few things that had come with him from Paramaribo. Almost three o'clock.

He walked along the waterfront, found the ladder again, went back down to the dinghy.

'I'm hungry,' red kid moaned.

'You'll have to wait,' he said. 'We got work to do.'

CHAPTER 15

The last time Vos met Theo Jansen was two weeks before Anneliese disappeared. The encounter was friendly enough. One hour in the gang boss's compact, unostentatious house near Waterlooplein, his daughter in attendance. No lawyer. Jansen thought he didn't need one and he was right. Vos was fishing. Jansen didn't take the bait. Michiel Lindeman didn't get any criminal work until Klaas Mulder took over the anti-gang unit in Marnixstraat.

Now, as then, Jansen sat next to his stocky, unsmiling daughter Rosie. When he was in post Vos had tried to understand everything he could about the man who, for a while, was the most powerful home-grown crook in Amsterdam. He'd learned about Jansen's modest childhood and his genuine love for his only child. His ruthless treatment of those who betrayed him and how this was matched by the utmost loyalty for any who stayed on his side.

What Vos found served to paint a portrait of an ordinary Amsterdammer who turned criminal through accident and opportunity not design. Theo

Jansen saw himself as a necessary evil. Someone would run the drug business, control the red-light cabins and the brothels, keeping the dark side in order, maintaining a comfortable status quo in which criminal activity was ring-fenced from ordinary life as much as possible. In Jansen's eyes it made more sense for a Dutchman to take that role. Better that than one of the many foreigners who'd been jostling for underworld power for the last three decades.

Earlier that day the judge had listened to Lindeman and decided Jansen could be released on bail pending a legal review. All he had to do was give an undertaking to stay away from his former associates and report regularly to the police, two conditions to which he readily agreed. The case would be considered in the summer. Until then – and after probably – he'd be a free man.

The hearing seemed so straightforward that Jaap Zeeger, the man whose evidence first sent Jansen to jail then freed him, hadn't needed to come to court.

'I didn't do any of this,' Jansen said as they sat down in an interview room in the basement of the courthouse. To Vos's eyes he looked more like a genial Santa Claus than ever. 'You know that.' He glanced at the woman by Vos's side. 'Who's your friend?'

'A police officer,' Vos told him before Bakker could speak.

Jansen laughed. A gruff, friendly sound. Then ran two fat fingers through his full white beard.

'They really do get younger, don't they? I'm sorry about your girl. Genuinely. If I'd known anything I'd have passed it on. That kind of thing's unforgivable.'

Vos thought for a moment then said, 'I still don't understand why you heard nothing. Those big ears . . .'

Jansen tweaked them beneath the white hair, a sad smile on his broad face.

'It wasn't someone from our side of the street. Not Dutch. Not even those foreigners.'

'Jaap Zeeger . . .'

'It wasn't him either. Jaap's a little fool. Someone fitted him up, Vos. You know that as well as I do. What we do is business. And that wasn't. Sorry.'

Two days after Anneliese went missing they'd searched Zeeger's apartment following an anonymous phone call. Found a girl's skirt, a blouse. The same clothes she'd been wearing when she disappeared. And a doll much like the one sent to Marnixstraat with her hair and blood. Vos dragged the trembling little crook into the station, screamed at him, which was out of character. Got screamed at by the terrified Zeeger in return.

Something didn't fit from the start. Jaap Zeeger was a deadbeat street criminal, a runner for Jansen's dope and prostitution rackets. He didn't have the intellect or the organization to play such games.

Then forensic came back with the news that the

clothes were new, unworn. There was nothing on the doll to connect it to Anneliese. Someone had sent them to Zeeger hours before they'd got the anonymous tip-off. One more twist in a savage game that seemed designed to taunt and torture.

'Where is he now?' Vos asked.

Jansen looked puzzled.

'I don't know. Lindeman said he might have to come to court. The judge decided he didn't need him. Talk to Michiel. Maybe he can help. You don't have an address?'

'If we did we wouldn't be asking, would we?' Laura Bakker said.

'Oh dear.' Jansen laughed. 'She's got a country mouth on her, hasn't she? What do you want Jaap for? He's just a sad little junkie. That clown Mulder leaned on him hard. I don't bear grudges. I hope they're grateful.'

'We're going home,' Rosie Jansen said. 'My father's put up with enough from you people. I won't . . .'

The big man waved at her to be quiet.

'Don't talk to Vos like that. He doesn't deserve it. A city needs good policemen. We won't hear from him again.' He leaned forward and looked at both of them. 'I won't give you reason. You've got my word . . .'

Bakker threw her notebook on the table, tapped the page with her pen. Jansen raised an eyebrow, went quiet. Looked at her. Looked at Vos.

'Zeeger's been staying in a drug house off Warmoesstraat,' Bakker said. 'With Katja Prins. Know anything about that?'

'I've spent the last two years in jail. How would I?'

Rosie Jansen got to her feet, leaned over, took Bakker's pen and scribbled something on the pad.

'Talk to Lindeman. There's his number. He fixed the affidavit. He dealt with Jaap. Not us. We're leaving now. Dad?'

Jansen rose from his seat, hugged her, smiled, patted her back.

The release order meant he had to go straight to his house and stay there, reporting into Marnixstraat every evening. Jansen looked happy enough with that idea.

'Have we fixed a car for you, Theo?' Vos asked.

'You can keep your car,' Rosie Jansen said. 'He wants to walk.'

'Maybe get a beer along the way,' Theo Jansen added dreamily.

Vos frowned.

'You're still covered by a court order. We should take you. Laura?'

Bakker closed her eyes, rolled back her head.

'I'm running a cab firm service for crooks now?'

Jansen laughed.

'I like this one, Vos!' He beamed at Bakker. 'I don't need a cab, kid. But your boss can join us for a beer if he wants. You too if you'll fetch and carry . . .'

He didn't wait for an answer before striding upstairs, past guards and lawyers, past anxious faces and a couple of relieved ones.

Vos liked this place mostly. He'd won here more than he'd lost. That wasn't luck. It was preparation, work and good judgement. Had Klaas Mulder shown the same when he prosecuted Theo Jansen the genial old gang lord would never have set foot out of jail.

Two huge wooden doors, manned by security guards, blocked the entrance. Glass windows above them. The feeble spring sun rose beyond out of a dull, rainy sky. Jansen beamed at the light and said, 'See? That's what freedom looks like.'

Santa Claus, Vos thought again. The beard had got bigger, whiter in jail.

He couldn't understand why there wasn't a specific police team in place. If he'd been the one setting Jansen free the old hood would have gone home in a squad car with a couple of uniformed men by his side.

Bakker called the lawyer on the stairs up. Grimaced and said he was on voicemail. She'd left a message.

'We don't leave messages,' Vos told her.

'Why not?'

'Because Pieter Vos likes to see your face when he talks to you,' Jansen broke in. 'Listen to this man, young lady. You might learn something.'

Vos took no notice. The courthouse was different. They'd redecorated. The place had lost its old patina of dust and age. It was now functional, modern, as boring as any other office in the city.

In the corner one of the uniformed officials was struggling to get into the shadows to make a phone call.

Vos always noticed the furtive, found it interesting. So he watched the man. The way he had his hand over the phone. The shifty, restless cast in his eyes. As if he wanted to be invisible.

This kind of conversation happened in courts all the time, between lawyers and clients. They were rarely conducted by men in uniform.

'Bye,' Theo Jansen called and Vos heard the familiar creak of those old wooden doors. They hadn't been oiled of late anyway.

Laura Bakker came off a short call to the station, livid.

'This was a total waste of time. Prins has left Marnixstraat now. De Groot's furious with us. What are we supposed to—?'

'Shush,' Vos said and put a finger close to her mouth.

She looked at him speechless.

Vos turned to the doors. Theo Jansen stood on the threshold, breathing in the fresh air, beaming at the pale and lifeless sky, his daughter by his side trying to persuade him to walk down the steps.

'This is wrong,' Pieter Vos said to no one.

'What is?' Bakker asked.

'Everything.'

A metallic rattle from outside near the canal,

101

like the chatter of a mechanical beast. Jansen's head turned towards the source. But by then Pieter Vos was running, arms flying, shouting, to the big man silhouetted in the doorway, to the guards, to anyone.

CHAPTER 16

When they climbed the rusty iron ladder, began walking down the road, semi-automatic in one hand, pistol in the other, red kid was trembling, pumped-up, scared. A few steps down the street he found a stray pigeon flying straight at him, grey wings flapping into his face.

Flung his arm in the air, caught the trigger.

A rattle of fire up into the gloomy sky, a shower of feathers and blood raining around them.

'A bird,' blue kid said. 'Shit.'

They were close enough to make out the man from the picture, standing at the top of the steps, smiling stupidly at the wan day.

Stocky. White beard, Father Christmas but not the kind you'd pick a fight with. A big woman was with him, screaming, struggling to get in front of him like a shield.

Too far away. They were idiots in too-bright clothes, walking by the side of the canal carrying Jimmy Menzo's heavy weapons like bad extras from a lousy movie.

'Shit,' blue kid said again, stopped and thought, 'All this down to a bird.'

There were things you could plan for. And things that just happened.

He walked to the edge of the canal, threw the guns in the dull, grey water, turned and ran away.

CHAPTER 17

Vos got outside, yelled at Jansen who stood transfixed by his first sight of the outside world in two years, almost oblivious to the figure in bright shiny red running, weapon in each hand, towards him.

A second burst of fire. Glass flew from the windows of a couple of cars parked near the stone steps to the court, ripped dust from the walls.

Then Theo Jansen moved. Turned slowly, threw off Vos's hands, those of his daughter, pushed her back towards the courthouse, pushed Vos too, strode in behind them.

'Doors!' Vos yelled once they were inside.

Four men, five, in court uniforms raced to close them.

A heavy iron bar fell across the double slabs of wood, locked into place. Vos made them stand back, retreating into the dark of the atrium.

The windows were too high to represent any danger. But there was shooting outside. Two weapons. A semi-automatic. A handgun. Vos watched the glass shatter, the shards rip into the air and fall onto the patterned tiled floor.

A high-pitched, foreign voice screeched something.

Two uniformed cops had appeared from somewhere. Handguns out, ready. Trapped like the rest of them.

Another rip of shells through the broken windows, glass flying everywhere. The people inside stayed quiet, eyes on one another. A second burst. More glass. No one spoke.

After a little while the world beyond the door fell silent. Then came the wail of sirens from somewhere, and the sound of voices. The shape in red was surely gone.

Theo Jansen was on a bench seat, daughter next to him, face like thunder.

Vos walked over, sat next to him, shrugged.

'You can't go home, Theo. Not like this. I'm worried about your safety.' He paused then added, 'I'm worried about what you might do.'

'I'm a free man . . .' Jansen began.

'Tomorrow maybe. Not now. Laura?'

She looked paler than ever. No one heard gunfire much in Amsterdam. It was probably her first time.

'Are you OK?' Vos asked.

She nodded.

He called De Groot, told him they had to go back to the courthouse cells.

'You're not a cop any more, Vos,' Jansen snarled when he came off the phone. 'You're a burned-out wreck living like some hippie bum in a dump of a boat. I hear things. You don't tell me what to do.'

'True,' Pieter Vos agreed. 'But Frank de Groot's still commissaris and he agrees with me. You'll stay in custody one more night until we know—'

An explosion of curses. Jansen was up and towering over him. The two uniformed men came over.

Then his daughter was there, hand on his burly arm.

Vos had never got on with her. The father was so much easier.

But she kissed his bearded cheek and said, 'Dad. We can wait one more day.'

Vos thanked her for that then went to look for the court attendant he'd seen on the phone.

The man had fled the place by the back entrance. He got Bakker to check the staff records. A temp, brought in by an agency that very day.

'His name . . .' she began.

'Doesn't matter,' Vos said.

'I've got his name!'

Doubt, he thought. That was what had eluded him of late. The ability to look at something and keep questioning it until some kind of answer came.

'No,' Vos said. 'You haven't.'

CHAPTER 18

Margriet Willemsen lived in a small, tidy flat in a discreet block not far from the waterfront near the Maritime Museum. Prins had first visited with Alex Hendriks two months before to discuss business. She liked to hold private meetings at home, away from the prying eyes of the council offices. He wondered how many other men had been on the list.

Now they were locked together, naked, sweating in her low double bed, writhing shapes outlined by the pale light struggling through the closed curtains. She rode over him, dark hair moving gently with the steady relentless rhythm of her hips. Telling him what to do, when to move. Like this, entwined, a sighing, panting single creature, nothing else mattered. He could have thrown open the windows and let the world see. Wanted to. The risk was part of the excitement. But mainly it was her.

Bea, his first wife, had turned crazy beyond belief. Liesbeth was proving almost as difficult. He liked their damage, the way he could marshal it, control them. Found the power he had enticing.

But Margriet was different. Unlike any woman he'd ever been with. Fierce, dominating, determined. And so savage when she dragged him to bed he wondered if Liesbeth would see the marks of her teeth on his skin. Not that she looked any more. Or made love much and even then it was in the dark, a short, practical act of duty, not this savage, mindless display of force.

Prins tried to put a gentle hand to her face as she rode him. She thrust it aside, gripped his fingers, pushed him hard into the damp sheets, tore at his hair. Her head came down, her hot breath fell on his cheek. A stream of filthy words in his ear. Then her tongue, damp and warm. And he was bellowing, lost in noise.

A pause between them. She laughed, licked his cheek. Pulled back, hand on him, keeping the condom in place. Without a word she unpeeled the slick piece of thin plastic, climbed from the bed, walked to the bathroom. He heard a flushing sound. Then a radio. The news. The shower.

Prins lay back on the bed, listening as his breathing regained a slow and natural rhythm.

When she came back she wore a white dressing gown and a towel round her head. There was a book in her hand. He never saw her get it. There were so many in this place. Three sides of the bedroom were covered in bookcases. Fiction and biographies. Politics and poetry. She was good with words.

Good with him.

'You need to read this,' she ordered.

He looked. A paperback. An author he'd never heard of.

'Why?' Prins asked, and got off the bed.

She came up, touched him, smiled.

'Because I told you to.'

'Don't push it.'

Her fingers squeezed, tweaked him.

'Ow.'

'A little pain helps sometimes.'

He took her hand away.

'You never stop, do you?' he said.

She bent down, sniffed his hand, put his right index finger in her mouth, sucked on it, burst out laughing, threw back her head.

'One life, Wim. That's all we get.' She was watching him. 'You still screw her, don't you?'

Prins looked around for his clothes. He'd need a shower. There was another meeting, a liaison group, before he could go home.

'You didn't answer . . .'

'Liesbeth was hurt. I thought maybe I could save her. I couldn't do that for Bea. Or Katja.'

There'd been no call from Marnixstraat. Or home.

'If you still love her why do you keep begging to come round here?'

He didn't like being questioned. Pushed into a corner.

Prins put his hand to her neck, kissed her quickly on the lips.

'Six months. When we've got De Nachtwacht

running. If we come out with this now they'll call us hypocrites.'

She glanced at the bed.

'Wait . . .' Finger to her lips, thinking. 'I get it. Bea and the girl failed you. So you ditch them and find yourself a new wife. A new work in progress. And when she's gone?'

'Six months,' he repeated. 'We need to be careful. I'm going to have to deal with this Katja thing too.'

'Sometimes I wonder about you. I mean . . . I know I can be a bitch. But . . . You really don't give a shit about that kid, do you?'

He shook his head.

'If you'd been through what I have . . . Forget it. I'm taking a shower.'

He tried to close the bathroom door. She forced her way through, sat on the toilet watching him. Prins scowled, turned on the water and pointed to the door.

'Can I have some privacy now?' he asked.

'God you're a prude. The worst sort. The filthy kind.'

Margriet Willemsen went back into the bedroom, listened to the shower coming to life.

Looked round. Shelf upon shelf of books. Some going back to college, in Holland, at Harvard when she was working on her MBA.

An organized woman. A touch obsessive. Everything was supposed to be in its place. History books one shelf. Economics next. Then politics. Then art.

A photo collection of Man Ray had worked its way into the travel section. This was wrong. Then she looked again. Someone had been messing with the books in this room. And it wasn't Wim Prins, a man she'd never seen read a thing except council papers.

Slowly, methodically, she worked her way down every row, tidying up, wondering how this happened.

Two shelves down on the wall at the foot of the bed she found something that didn't belong at all. A thick paperback. The name on the spine was that of a writer she didn't know. The title was just as foreign too.

She removed the book from the business titles around it, felt the weight in her hand. Looked at the small circle of glass at the top of the spine. Opened the pages and saw the tiny video camera inside, taped to a mobile phone hooked up to what looked like a series of batteries that filled the rest of the space.

Big enough to have been working for a week. Maybe longer.

She thought about the men who'd visited recently.

Prins came out of the bathroom, towel round his waist, dripping water onto the carpet, looked at her.

'What is it?'

'Nothing,' Margriet Willemsen said, pushing the fake book back onto the shelf, spine to the wall. 'You can go now. I'll see you in the morning.'

CHAPTER 19

A business card. A drawing of a miniature mansion.

Poppenhuis aan de Prinsengracht.

The Doll's House on the Prinsengracht. Except this was nothing like the place he'd expected.

Another of Jimmy Menzo's lies. Blue kid hid behind a couple of cars and watched the door. The house looked derelict, abandoned, a dump. Nothing in the windows except tape holding together broken glass.

He didn't know why he'd bothered. Except . . . where else?

Thirty-five euros in his pocket. A fake ID. Nothing more. The money in the briefcase wasn't coming their way. Maybe never was.

Back home in Surinamese there were hideaways for times like this. Family and acquaintances. Gang members who'd help for a price. But Amsterdam was a world away and full of strangers.

Except for one.

As he looked up the narrow street he saw the kid coming. Red shiny suit, thin face veering between fear and aggression. Sweaty. Scared.

He should have asked his name.

Red kid was fast too. Before he could move the idiot had got to the derelict house, tried the door.

No, blue kid thought. *Don't . . .*

By then he was watching him walk in.

He didn't know why he followed, running, yelling.

A name would have helped.

The door opened into a front room full of old-fashioned furniture covered in dust and cobwebs. A vast curved sofa. Paintings on the walls.

Couples in old-fashioned dress, men and women out for walks. And the colour of the place. Pink like a nursery. Pink wallpaper, pink carpet, pink furniture.

Red kid was walking towards the back, calling out for Miriam Smith.

Blue kid followed, a part of him fascinated. He was looking at the dusty remains of a world he'd only heard about. Rich once. Warm and sensuous. The kind of place he'd end up one day.

There were small rooms on both sides, each with a double bed and everything pink, down to the silly lampshades.

Paintings on all the walls. Young women in costumes. Like dolls. So maybe the name wasn't a lie after all.

Ahead of him red kid was flicking dead light switches and yelling, 'Hey! Anyone at home?'

Blue kid strode through the darkness, took hold of the red jacket, got a fierce look back.

'They're not here,' he said. 'We screwed up. It's not safe. And . . .'

They were never coming, he thought. Whatever had happened outside the courthouse.

The place stank of gas. He could hear it hissing from somewhere close by.

'Need to get out of here, man,' he whispered.

'I want my money! I want my stinking money!'

'We didn't kill him. We didn't do anything they asked.'

The gas was so bad it made him want to gag. How many reasons could there be?

Only one he could think of and it made his blood run cold.

'Outside,' he said, dragging red kid back towards the open door by the collar of his cheap jacket.

'Where we going?'

Straight to hell, blue kid thought. One way or another. And without a name.

The explosion hit just as he got close enough to the door to feel a squally burst of Amsterdam rain on his teenage face. By then red kid had fought free and tried to get back into the place that once called itself Poppenhuis aan de Prinsengracht.

The idiot was yelling for Miriam Smith, screaming idle threats and curses from distant Paramaribo she'd never understand.

Fire and debris and dust consumed them both. When he came to they were on the front patio along with the remains of an ancient sofa and stacks of rubbish and shattered glass. There was blood on the red jacket and the kid's right arm was hanging loose from the socket, shattered at the elbow.

Blue kid choked and gagged on the cloud of grime falling around them then felt himself: nothing broken.

There was a gun by the other one's feet. The Walther that Menzo had given him that morning. Must have kept it tucked into his jacket after he dumped the semi-automatic.

'We're going,' blue kid said and yanked him by the good arm into the street.

Sirens getting nearer. People staring at them, more bemused than scared. Things like this weren't supposed to happen in this nice and civilized city. Two kids from Surinamese had brought it here. With a little help on the side.

'To Africa?' red kid asked, clutching at his bleeding arm.

He dragged him down to the next street. Stopped the first cab, a silver Mercedes. Poked the gun into the driver's face just like a carjack back home. Made the fat old man get out and put red kid in the passenger seat before he climbed behind the wheel.

'Yeah,' he said as he spun the cab round, trying to work out what direction might take them out of the city. 'Africa. Where else?'

CHAPTER 20

They put Theo Jansen back in a holding cell. Twenty minutes after De Groot turned up news came in of an explosion a kilometre away in an abandoned house. His mood was deteriorating by the second.

'Jimmy Menzo flew his plane down to Ostend at ten this morning,' the commissaris said. 'With his girlfriend.'

'The Belgians can pick them up for us,' Bakker suggested.

Vos shook his head.

'For what? We don't have anything to hold them. Jimmy will be back. To gloat. There won't be any obvious connections. There never is. The kid I saw outside—'

'Two of them,' De Groot cut in. 'Came in a boat. One of them turned tail when he saw it was going wrong.'

'We need to get hold of them, Frank. Jimmy will have plans—'

'Yes! I know!'

It wasn't like De Groot to get flustered.

'Is the explosion connected?' Vos asked.

De Groot didn't think so. The fire people said the place was derelict. They thought it was down to a gas leak.

It seemed a miracle the kid who'd been loosing off with a semi-automatic outside the Prinsengracht courthouse hadn't hurt anyone. A few broken windows and some damage to the masonry was all they had.

'Have you heard any more about Katja Prins?' Vos asked.

'Nothing,' De Groot said. 'Her father still thinks this is all a game. Maybe he's right. He knows her better than we do. I've got to go back to Marnixstraat. You deal with things here.'

They walked downstairs, went to the holding cell. Bakker followed. Theo Jansen sat on a bench seat. Vos asked him again where Zeeger might be.

The big hood threw up his hands and shrieked.

'I told you! I don't know. Ask Lindeman—'

'I did,' Bakker cut in. 'He says he hasn't a clue. The last address he had . . . . Zeeger's vanished.'

'Jaap doesn't belong to me,' Jansen answered. 'End of story. I want to go home.'

'Katja Prins lived at that same address, Theo,' Vos said. 'She introduced Zeeger to the place. Now she's missing. Looks like my daughter's case. Same kind of routine.'

Jansen shuffled on the seat then screwed up his eyes and said, 'What?'

'We've got a doll with her blood, her hair. Just like I had.'

'This is nothing to do with me,' Jansen insisted. 'How could it be? I've been in jail for the last two years. I want to go home. The judge said I could.'

'It's a conditional release,' Vos told him. 'We can revoke it any time we like without a reason. I talked to the judge. It's done.'

'To hell with this shit . . .'

'No,' Vos insisted, rising to his feet. 'You're not going anywhere. There'll be a van to take you back to prison in an hour. It's going to have to be solitary I'm afraid. Maximum security. For your own safety . . .'

Jansen got to his feet roaring, fists flailing. Bakker retreated. Pieter Vos stood still and stared into Jansen's furious face. Waiting for the storm to abate.

'Tomorrow you can talk to Michiel Lindeman about your legal options,' he added. 'Not today. Whoever wants you dead placed someone in the courthouse. We don't know who. It was a fake ID. If they can do that maybe they can reach you in jail. I'd rather keep you out of the way.'

With that he turned and went back upstairs. Bakker followed, clucking complaints. At the top he waited for her.

'Vos! You didn't talk to any judge. You haven't booked a van to take him back to jail. You haven't—'

'Have a word with Frank. He can fix it.'

He looked at his watch.

'I need a beer. I need to see Sam's eating properly. He's picky about his food.'

'There's work . . .'

He smiled and that shut her up.

'Not for me there isn't. I said I'd look at some papers. That's all. I'm not part of Marnixstraat any more. This is down to you.'

Then he walked out of the Prinsengracht courthouse, took a good look at the broken windows and the bullet marks on the facade, picked up his old bike and set off home.

CHAPTER 21

Red kid hung on to his shattered arm screaming. Blue kid hugged the wheel as the city turned round and round.

Sirens. Dead-end streets. People on foot leaping out of the way. People on bikes shaking their fists.

This was a strange bad place to be and he'd no idea how they could escape, where they could go.

He turned the Mercedes down a narrow alley, praying for some time to think.

There was always the police. Though he knew what the price for that would be. Someone would pay, even if it wasn't him.

'Shit,' he said and slammed his hand on the wheel as he brought the car to a screaming halt.

A dead end. Nothing but pavement, the inevitable cycle track, and beyond it still, slow water.

'We didn't kill no one,' red kid said, squeezing his bloodied, shattered arm.

'I noticed. So will Menzo.'

The building on the right looked like a warehouse. On the left an abandoned apartment block. He'd no idea what part of the city he'd taken them to.

'We didn't kill no one,' red kid said again and then the old Nokia rang.

He knew who it would be.

'Are you the one with the sister?' Jimmy Menzo asked.

'Yeah,' he said without thinking.

'She wants to talk to you.'

Clicking sounds as if they were patching her through from somewhere different. He held the phone away from his ear knowing what was coming next.

One year younger. Pretty as sin. She'd probably be whoring anyway, not running a coffee shop or bar. He understood that. Appreciated where they stood in the world.

'Stop,' he said when he couldn't take her screams any more.

It went on for another minute or more. Red kid was quiet. Didn't even moan about his arm.

'I said cut it out!'

Menzo came back on the line and said, 'It's up to you, kid. You know what to do.'

He sounded so calm he might have been ordering pizza.

'Say you won't hurt her.'

Stupid words. Pointless.

'I won't hurt her. There.'

Blue kid opened the window and threw the phone out onto the grubby pavement.

Red kid watched him then asked, 'Where are we going if we don't go to Africa?'

'What's your name?'

A moment's pause then, 'Etienne.'

Blue kid wiped his nose with his sleeve and said, 'Forgive me Etienne.'

Then picked up the gun that lay between them, shot him once through the head the way he'd learned on the hard streets back home.

The canal was watching him. Listening. Waiting.

The Mercedes couldn't have been more than six months old. Clean and shiny. Nice black leather. Still had that new smell. He'd have ripped off something like this back home. Jacked it in a flash. Maybe in Cape Town he could have bought one for himself.

Manual though. What an American hood he knew called a stick shift. Not automatic like this.

Blue kid wound his arms around the steering wheel as if he was hugging it. Then he slammed his right foot onto the accelerator and clung on as the silver Mercedes burst across the blocked end of the road, over the cycle track, through the low brick wall at the end, and roared down towards the leaden, opaque water below.

CHAPTER 22

Wim Prins didn't get home till just after eight. Liesbeth was in the living room clutching a glass of Scotch. The TV was on. Too loud.

He sat down and watched the evening news. An extended edition. Talk of gangster wars, violence on the streets of Amsterdam.

'Mulder called from Marnixstraat,' she said without looking at him. 'He wanted to know if anyone tried to contact you about Katja.'

'Of course they haven't. I'd have told him. She'll probably call me tomorrow and say it was all a bad joke. Then ask for something.'

She got up and poured herself another drink.

'Go easy on that,' he said.

'Why?'

'You need me to say?' He watched her top up the glass at that, glaring at him. 'Very smart.'

'Smarter than coke and smack, isn't it? Did Bea get lectures too?'

'Yes. And Katja. They didn't work either. But . . .' He got up and poured himself a modest glass. 'I tried.' He raised the whisky. 'Sorry.'

'What are we going to do?'

'I told you. We wait. She always comes round in the end.'

The TV was so loud. The journalist was saying the gang war might be a response to the council's planned crackdown. That De Nachtwacht brought on this battle between the mobs. He even named Jansen and Menzo as the primary culprits.

Prins came close to his wife, took the drink away, held her hands, tried to look into her damp and troubled eyes. She could have been Bea at that moment and this thought terrified him.

'When I've got everything set with the council we'll take a break. Go to Aruba. Stay there for a little while if you like. Get some work done on the place. I'm sorry. I'm a bit . . . distracted right now.'

She reached up, kissed him briefly on the cheek and said, 'You need a shower. You stink from being in that suit all day.'

He took off his jacket, put it round the back of the nearest chair.

'Why would Katja do this?' she asked. 'To you? To me? What did we do to deserve it?'

'You think she needs a reason?'

In the bedroom his phone bleeped. An email from an address he didn't recognize. A massive attachment, too big for the mobile connection.

Prins sighed, went to the study next door, started the mail program, left it to work.

Then went under the shower. The second in three hours. Lots of water. He wondered if it was enough.

CHAPTER 23

It was a lie about the dog. Sam wasn't picky about his food at all. And Sofia Albers had fed him often enough in the Drie Vaten. Sometimes, when Vos lost it and couldn't function much for days on end, she kept Sam in the bar. He seemed to love it.

Three stops along the way. Familiar brown bars in the Jordaan. Places he could sit and think. Or not think. Just sip at a beer, watch the faces, listen to the music. The singing sometimes. Old songs. Stupid songs. Refrains about the city and the neighbourhood. Community and family. Figures from the past.

Dead people.

Vos had seen too many already. As a cop he was supposed to prevent these tragedies. All too often he'd been nothing more than a prurient Peeping Tom. Even when he uncovered the truth the hurt didn't go away. Vos could give them nothing. Could offer Liesbeth nothing, and so she went off the rails, fell into the waiting arms of Wim Prins. Left him to grieve and scream and rail in the shabby little boat beneath the lime trees where no one could hear, spending evening after evening in a haze of booze or dope.

There were no answers inside that fog. But no questions either.

By the time he got to the Drie Vaten it was gone eight. Laura Bakker was seated in the bar on her own, half a glass of Coke on the table, glaring at him as he went to the counter and asked for a beer. Grease from her bike chain had smeared the legs of her trousers. The grey suit seemed to hang on her even more clumsily.

'Where the hell do you get those clothes?' he asked.

'Auntie Maartje makes them.' She looked him up and down. 'Where do you get those? A charity shop for ageing teenagers?'

'Auntie Maartje's in Dokkum?'

'She's got a sewing machine. Buys patterns. They're cheap.' She picked up a napkin, wiped at the bike grease, made everything worse. 'Practical.'

'Like the shoes,' he said, staring at her heavy black boots. 'I can hear you two streets away.'

'You didn't hear me when I came on your boat. Talking to De Groot.'

Vos's head felt a little fuzzy. He was wearing what he usually wore. Ribbed blue wool sweater. Navy donkey jacket. Jeans. Everything old. A little tatty maybe. But clean. Sofia Albers, who was watching them now, saw to that.

'You're one to talk, Vos. Those are odd socks. One's grey. The other's green. Didn't you notice?'

'They're just socks, for God's sake,' he whined, reaching for the beer.

'Sam's eaten. I asked.'

Behind the counter Sofia gave her a comradely salute at that.

Vos joined her, raised his glass, shut up. The little terrier scampered out from behind the counter and settled beneath his feet. Bakker pointed to a poster on the wall: *Casablanca*. Bogart and a beautiful, sad Ingrid Bergman, a pianist smiling in the background.

'You named him from a poster in a bar?'

She folded her long arms.

'So what if I did? He doesn't mind.'

'De Groot's furious. You can't just walk out like that.'

'Why not?'

'Menzo's still in Ostend. They found the kids. One of them anyway. They stole a car.'

This was new. His head cleared a little, entirely of its own accord.

'What happened?'

'It looks like one of them shot the other. Then drove into the canal.' She shook her head. Her long red hair was down around her shoulders. 'They've got one body. Still dredging for the second.'

Vos nodded.

'It's terrible,' she added. 'They were children.'

'Why don't you say a prayer for them then go back to Dokkum?' he asked.

A sudden flare of anger.

'Is that the best you've got?'

He sipped his beer and wished he'd kept his mouth shut.

'Say a prayer?' Laura Bakker repeated. 'Why? Because I'm the village idiot? Is that it?'

'I didn't say that.' Vos pushed the glass away. He didn't want it in the first place. 'This is the city, Laura. When it turns bad it turns . . . unforgiving. Doesn't choose. Between children and adults. Between good and bad. Guilty and innocent . . .'

'I'm here because I want to be. De Groot can fire me. You can't. Why should those boys die like that?'

'Culture,' he said. 'Jimmy Menzo. The Surinamese hoods take it on themselves. It's a question of pride. Probably family too. And I doubt they had a choice. If they didn't fall on their swords there'd be repercussions.'

His answer seemed to make her angrier.

'See. This is why De Groot needs you.'

'What about Katja Prins?' he asked, trying to shift the conversation. 'Have they found Jaap Zeeger? This rehab place her father sent her. It needs checking—'

'Why ask? You're not a police officer. None of this touches you. I'm just an aspirant about to get fired. Why throw this at me?'

Her voice was flat and furious. The dog was moving beneath the table.

'This is not my doing,' Vos broke in. 'Not my responsibility.'

'No. I can see that now.'

She got her bag. The keys to her bike lock. Looked outside at the black night, the shape of Vos's boat beyond the pavement.

'Do you feel safe here?' Bakker shot at him as she gathered her things. 'Do you feel immune?'

'I'm no damned good!' Pieter Vos roared, half stumbling to his feet. 'Don't you get it? I couldn't save my own daughter. Why the hell does Frank think I can help anyone else?'

The dog was a hunched bundle of white fur beneath the table. That made Vos feel bad. Laura Bakker too from the way she knelt down, stroked his trembling back.

'I can see why,' she said. 'Pity you can't. Here . . . If you need it.'

She scribbled a phone number on a beer mat, threw it at him, walked out of the bar, got her bike, pushed off into the darkness and the rain.

Vos finished the beer, went to the counter and asked for an old jenever.

'Don't be stupid,' Sofia Albers said, arms folded, looking cross. 'Shouting in my bar? Scaring your little dog? Home with you, Pieter Vos. You should be ashamed.'

'It's not been a good day. Another beer then.'

He stood there until she relented. Then spent the best part of a miserable hour nursing it, sip by sip.

What he told Sofia had been the truth. This wasn't a good day. The outside world had seeped back into his life, nudged there by Laura Bakker's sharp, insistent elbows.

Seeing Liesbeth. Realizing she was as miserable, as depressed and introverted as when she left him. Dealing with the case, even briefly. That had brought back memories of the job. And the realization that in some ways he liked and missed it.

Vos picked up the beermat with Laura Bakker's phone number, put it in his pocket, hooked the little leather lead to the dog and walked to the door.

Something he hadn't noticed before. There was a light on in the houseboat. A dim one near the kitchen table.

Bakker, he thought. She probably walked in before she came to the bar. It was easy enough to get inside.

The rain was gentle and cold.

Closer he heard music. 'My Funny Valentine' sung in the sad, broken voice of Chet Baker.

More corpses.

The frail American jazzman had died in the red-light street of Zeedijk in 1988, falling from a window of the Prins Hendrik Hotel. Vos had catholic musical tastes. Venerable hard rock, obscure modern jazz. Even a few more recent artists. But he adored the studied, resigned melancholy of Chet Baker too. The singing and the trumpet playing. He had that CD. Been playing it recently. Top of the pile.

In front of the boat the little dog started to bark. No movement inside that Vos could see. Not that the windows showed everything.

He walked across the gangplank, pulled at the door. The lock lay on the ground, the broken clasp next to it.

Vos pulled out his phone and the scrap of paper Laura Bakker had given him then called her.

Swore when she was on voicemail.

'You pay for any damage,' he said after the message beep. 'Don't ever go into my boat without asking. Just don't . . .'

He pulled open the door, pocketed the phone and went down the steps into the cabin. Sam was yapping wildly. A high-pitched yowl. The sort of sound he made at the vet's when a needle was brought out.

The sort he made when he was scared.

CHAPTER 24

Liesbeth wriggled over to Prins in bed, worked her hand beneath his pyjama top, stroked his chest.

'Busy day,' he said. 'Tired.'

Her fingers weren't listening. Then they gave up.

'Is it me?' she asked.

Eyes closed, head back in the pillow.

'No. It's just work. And all this . . . worry about Katja.'

'You didn't seem that worried.'

'You want me to shout and scream? Do you think I do that? I've lived with Katja and her demons ever since Bea died. They wear you down in the end.'

She retreated from him beneath the sheets.

'Mulder's coming round in the morning,' Prins said. 'We've got to meet anyway. About De Nachtwacht . . .'

'I'm sick of hearing about that crap.' She propped herself up on one arm, looked at him. 'It won't work, you know. People aren't like that. You can't just flip a switch and make things different.'

He stretched, felt bad.

'We've got to do something. If we'd flipped the switch a bit earlier maybe we could have saved your daughter—'

'That's not what Pieter said. Or De Groot. They said it was . . .' She blinked, took on that mask of tragedy she'd worn all the time when she was splitting up with Vos. 'They said it was someone crazy.'

'They haven't a clue who it was.'

'Do you? Even the boss of Amsterdam doesn't know everything, does he?'

'No,' he said with a grim laugh. 'I know a lot less than most people. And every day what I do know gets smaller.'

'Don't leave me,' she whispered, close to him again, hands in his greying hair. 'Don't let go.'

'What?'

'Sometimes I think . . .'

The pain always worked on him. Prins kissed her. Then, before he thought about it much, she was taking off his pyjamas, all over him, desperate.

It was short. Sad. Strange. They didn't say a word after. He could feel her face against his chest, the tears running down onto his skin.

'I need to check my email,' Prins said and climbed out of the bed, walked into the study.

It was an excuse. A poor one. But there'd been the odd message earlier, the attachment that wouldn't download.

In front of the PC he looked at it. The message came from someone calling himself Pop Meester.

A nickname maybe. 'Doll Master'. Same for the subject. No body, just an attachment, an eighty-meg video file.

Prins walked to the door, closed it then returned to the computer.

Somehow he knew what he'd see. There was even a time and a date to help him. This was three hours earlier. Grainy picture, no sound. Naked bodies in the half darkness. Margriet Willemsen arching over him in the bedroom of her little flat. Prins rolling back his head. A silent roar.

He closed the video, shift-deleted the file. As if that would make it gone forever.

Went back to bed and tried to sleep.

CHAPTER 25

The houseboat was deserted. Vos walked over to the CD player, killed the music.

The dog kept barking, sniffing, whining.

He looked round once. Then again. Looked everywhere.

It wasn't that he was drunk. Not quite. In a way his head was clearer than it had been in months. He could see none of this was working. The boat would never get fixed. Nor would his life. Not this way.

And there was Frank de Groot dangling a way back into the old nightmare. The familiar hell.

He went to the window at the stern, opened it. Took out the ID card De Groot had given him. Was ready to throw it out into the water.

'Sam . . .' he pleaded. 'For God's sake.'

The volume of the little dog's barks had gone up a good few decibels the moment cold night air entered the room. Now it turned into a howl.

Animals saw things before people. Could smell things too.

The tarpaulin was half-off the sinking dinghy along the way.

Vos felt his breath catch, his gorge rise. All the old familiar feelings. No way of avoiding them.

He put the lead back on Sam, marched him over to the Drie Vaten, told Sofia Albers she'd have to look after him for the night. Something in his face stopped an argument.

A good woman. One who was soft on him maybe.

'Did you hear anything?' he asked. 'See someone near my boat?'

She looked at the dark night.

'Not a thing, Pieter. What's the . . .?'

He grabbed a couple of paper napkins from the counter, walked outside, went down the steps to the dinghy, looked. Took a napkin for each hand, moved the tarpaulin gingerly away.

Then called Frank de Groot. Found he could talk much the way he used to when he was in the force. Logically, calmly, clearly, even if his head was spinning.

De Groot listened and finally said, 'Jesus, Pieter. Not the Prins girl?'

Vos steeled himself to look again.

A woman's body side on against the dinghy's planking. Gunshot wound to the head. A dark stain leaking down towards one breast. Cradled in the crook of her right arm a porcelain doll in an old-fashioned dress now soaked in blood. The kind Petronella Oortman might have owned.

'Just get here, will you?' Vos said then sat on the chilly stone bank and waited.

PART II

TUESDAY 18 APRIL

CHAPTER 1

Morning. The road along the Prinsengracht was still closed. The bridge, the junction by the statues of Johnny Jordaan's band too. Vos had watched a murder investigation slowly come together, the past rise from the cold dank waters of the canal.

Officers in white forensic suits. Cameras and swabs in their hands. Low voices murmuring into phones, dialogue served in digital fractures by way of answer. Vehicles everywhere. The long black saloon of the commissaris. The cheaper marked squad cars of the uniformed officers there to keep back the sightseers and the press. A forest of bicycles. This was still Amsterdam.

And a gurney. Lifted up beneath searing floodlights, raised from the half-sunk dinghy six hours after he found her there. A morgue shroud round the corpse now. Black plastic covering her dead eyes and bloody skin.

A precise, painstaking ritual was coming to life and Vos couldn't fail to be a part of it. Around five, when he could barely keep his eyes open, he'd spent a fitful hour in a spare room above the bar.

Drank more coffee, ate a pastry when he woke around six thirty. Walked a downcast, puzzled Sam briefly along the canal then left him with Sofia Albers without so much as a word.

It was seven now. De Groot was there with a team of forensic officers and detectives. Laura Bakker hung around at the edge of the crowd, not quite a part of them, shivering by the canal. Red hair tied back, eyes bright and alert. A new suit. Navy this time, almost the same colour as his own shabby jacket, trousers and sweater. She looked like a lanky schoolgirl who'd been up all night.

De Groot caught Vos's eye, clicked his fingers and pointed to a control van. Vos smiled at the young aspirant, lost and ignored. Told her to come too though that got a long sigh from De Groot. The three of them went inside and sat on the cold seats. De Groot got Bakker flipping through reports on the laptop, making calls, checking queries.

Vos felt clear-headed. Sharp almost. It had been two years since he'd found himself inside an investigation, trying to find light in the darkness. Something in him welcomed the challenge. An inner voice he couldn't silence.

'Have you told Theo Jansen yet?' he asked when they'd gone through a summary of the overnight intelligence.

Frank de Groot stared at the laptop and said, quietly, 'No. We need to think that through. He's supposed to get out today. What do I say? His daughter's dead and we've no idea how? Jimmy

Menzo never set foot outside Ostend. We can't trace whoever he had outside the courthouse. Theo's going to go crazy.'

'Why does it have to be Menzo?' Bakker asked, looking up from the computer.

The commissaris gazed at her.

'Who else could it be?'

Vos wasn't so sure.

'Would he really go for the daughter just because the hit on her old man had failed? Those kids outside the courthouse were organized. It wasn't spur of the moment. They were told what to do. It was crude, violent and public. He was trying to make a statement. Killing Rosie Jansen . . .'

He looked at Bakker and asked, 'What would that say?'

'Nothing,' she replied. 'Kill her and it just makes things worse, doesn't it?'

Vos smiled, glanced at De Groot and nodded.

'Quite,' he said. 'More war. A worse war. Not just bloodletting. A vendetta. Maybe it was Menzo. But I thought he was smarter than that.'

'You're starting to sound like one of us again,' De Groot noted with a smile.

Vos picked up the printouts from the computer, got Bakker to run things through the laptop again.

Went over what they had.

Two teenage Surinamese hoodlums had attempted to murder Theo Jansen. They'd failed and died, one shot, one seemingly committing suicide, not that the dive team had yet recovered the second body. Both had arrived legally through Schiphol the week before and stayed in a cheap city centre hostel. Nothing linked them to Menzo or any other known Amsterdam hood.

Jaap Zeeger was still missing. There was no news about Katja Prins. The papers and the TV were full of stories about gang war and the attempt on Jansen's life. None had yet picked up the identity of the murder victim in the Prinsengracht or the fact the Prins girl was missing.

Bakker's phone rang. She mouthed the word 'forensic' and listened to the call, her pale face taut with interest.

'Why are they calling you?' De Groot asked when she was done.

'Because I asked them to,' she said as if the answer was obvious. 'They found something on the doll. The one he left with Rosie Jansen. There was a . . .'

She went to the laptop, scanned her messages.

'A little camera. Taped to the back inside a plastic bag to keep out the water.'

Fingers on the laptop again. Her hand went to her face and stroked back a stray strand of hair.

'It's got pictures. And a video. They're sending it over.'

The three of them waited. A series of images came up. Vos watched very carefully.

'Where is that?' he asked.

'Rosie Jansen's apartment,' De Groot said. 'We knew she was killed there anyway.'

Eight still images in all. Theo Jansen's daughter dead on the floor of what looked like an elegant room. Pale carpet. Modern paintings on the wall. Blood alongside it. Spatter. A single shot.

Scattered furniture. Broken crockery. Glass fragments on the carpet.

'She fought,' Bakker said.

'Like a tiger,' Vos agreed. 'Rosie would.'

'Is there anything new?' De Groot asked with a marked impatience. 'How did he get in? What have forensic got?'

'No sign of forced entry,' she said then tapped the keyboard once more. 'Nothing else. They're still looking. It takes time I guess.'

Vos stared at his feet. Brown suede shoes. Worse for wear. On the way out he'd picked a few clean clothes out of the laundry bag Sofia had waiting for him. Different socks. Still odd, light grey and dark. He'd never noticed. Same navy wool jumper. Beneath it a cheap sweatshirt from C&A. He was dressed for a night listening to a band in the Melkweg. Not a murder investigation.

'You don't have time,' he said. 'Someone's pushing here. Pushing Theo Jansen.' He stared at De Groot. 'Pushing you. Maybe even pushing Jimmy Menzo.'

The commissaris said something about going back to Marnixstraat and talking the case through there.

Vos shook his head.

'Yesterday was a favour. I've paid off your stinking cheese now.'

'Jesus, Pieter!' De Groot cried. 'This bastard

dumped Rosie Jansen on your doorstep. He came inside your home. You're involved whether you like it or not.'

'All the more reason to be out of it,' Vos replied and got up, looked at the pallid day outside.

He could go back to the Drie Vaten. Sleep for a while. They'd release his boat once the forensic people were through. After that he'd tidy up. Change into different old, threadbare clothes. Get back to the work that wasn't really work. The life that didn't add up to much at all.

Maybe sit in the Rijksmuseum again, hour after hour, staring at Petronella Oortman's doll's house, trying to make sense of things.

After that drink a few beers. Maybe smoke something for the first time in weeks.

Wasting time. Because what else was left to do with it?

'Forensic sent over a video,' Bakker added. 'It was on the camera too. Wasn't taken with the other photos. Someone put it in there deliberately.'

'How many pictures do you need?' Vos asked, exasperated. 'Rosie Jansen's dead. Start looking.'

'It's not about her,' Bakker said warily.

Then she pulled up something new on the screen.

CHAPTER 2

Wim Prins sat in the kitchen of their quiet courtyard home. Just after eight. Coffee and toast on the table. Klaas Mulder, the hoofdinspecteur from Marnixstraat, had turned up ten minutes early.

To Prins's annoyance he didn't want to talk about De Nachtwacht. Just Katja.

'If this isn't some kind of game—' he began.

'It's not a game,' Liesbeth spat at him. 'Whatever it is, it's not that.'

Mulder glared at her. She scrubbed at the kitchen table with a dishcloth, not that it needed it.

'If Katja's been taken you've got to expect an approach. Probably today,' Mulder said. 'It's possible this is linked to the attack on Jansen.'

'How's that?' Prins asked.

Mulder shrugged. Picked up his coffee, toyed with a doughnut on the table and said, 'You promised to take them apart. Maybe Menzo thinks this is a good time to throw Jansen and his people out for good. You won't get rid of everything. What's left . . . he gets more.'

'This is about Katja,' Liesbeth whispered. 'Not politics. Not some stupid law . . .'

Silence. Mulder filled up his own coffee cup. Waited.

'It's about my daughter,' Prins agreed. 'She's screwing me around again. I don't doubt it. Not the first time. Won't be the last. But we've got to deal with it.'

The cop shrugged.

'Either way it's serious. De Groot says he's not turning a blind eye any more. If this is all a game she's in court for wasting our time. If someone has her. Menzo say . . .'

Liesbeth Prins put a shaking hand to her forehead.

'Jesus, Wim. Why did you get us into all this shit? What possible point—?'

'Stop it!' Prins yelled. 'You know why.' He nodded at Mulder. 'He does too. The whole damned city. God knows it's been played out in the papers often enough. I had a wife who fell to pieces in front of my eyes. Got a daughter who's gone the same way. It's just—'

'So it's about you, is it?' she asked in a low and bitter tone.

'If you like,' he said more quietly. Then to Mulder, 'Tell me what you want us to do.'

'We need a list of all her friends. Her contacts—'

'Katja left home two years ago,' Prins cut in. 'You know them better than we do.'

Mulder put his notebook back in his jacket, ate

some more doughnut, looked at his watch and said, 'If you're too busy . . .'

'She's still got her room here,' Liesbeth said. 'There are things in it. Some of it goes back to when she was little.' A pause. 'She was happy then.'

'You've looked?' the cop asked.

'Not much. I wondered whether we could throw some of it out. But whenever I asked she flew off the handle.' Liesbeth Prins hugged herself through the thin dressing gown. 'Even after she left. It's not easy.'

'What isn't?'

'Being a stepmother. Or a stepdaughter I guess. Do you want to see?'

He finished eating, shook his head.

'Not really.' Mulder got up, brushed the crumbs from his jacket. 'If someone calls let me know.'

'We didn't talk about De Nachtwacht,' Prins said.

'We didn't. Bit busy right now to be honest. With things that matter.' The grin. 'Missing people. Dead people.'

'This is going to happen, Mulder. Marnixstraat won't stop it.'

'No,' he agreed. 'We won't. But from what I hear we won't need to.'

'What?'

Mulder got up, threw his business card at Liesbeth Prins.

'If you hear anything come straight to me. No one else.'

CHAPTER 3

Laura Bakker ran the video sent by Marnixstraat forensic. Shaky frame rate. Bright summer's day from another time.

It was on the memory card but came from a different camera. The date was a little under three years before. Just days before Anneliese disappeared.

'That's your daughter, isn't it?' she asked.

Frank de Groot had his face in his hands, was cursing.

It took a while for Vos to say yes.

He tried to place the location. Grass. Families with kids. A pale building like a flying saucer in the background.

The Vondelpark. The Blue Teahouse. A quiet place for a drink or a sandwich. They used to wheel Anneliese there in a pushchair when she was tiny and the world seemed whole.

Here she was looking the way she did just before she vanished. Young and beautiful and happy. On the cusp of adulthood, a life beyond home. She was treading barefoot across the grass, laughing and smiling for whoever held the camera. Vos could remember watching her do that. It could have been yesterday. He recalled too the way he used to worry. What if something – a wasp, a piece of broken glass – lurked in the Vondelpark's lush lawn and he failed to see it first?

'That's Anneliese?' Bakker asked again.

Dancing on the green grass as if she'd live forever.

Laura Bakker didn't seem to mind she got no answer. Just went on anyway.

'One of the night team saw this, Vos. They recognized her. I'm sorry. They said it was important.'

'Of course it's important,' Vos said, eyes locked to the small video window. 'Someone wants me in this case. What else did they tell you?'

'Nothing.'

He reached forward and paused the video.

She'd gone missing the third week of July. It was hot that summer. No rain. The city had felt lethargic. Vos had been slaving day and night trying to persuade some low-level hoods in the city gangs to turn informer. No sign of the storm to come.

He leaned forward and looked very closely at the grass, the people around her. She was wearing a pastel blue shirt and jeans cut off below the knee. He could remember being with her when they went shopping for them. A birthday present. He got bored when she took so long to make up her mind.

Liesbeth couldn't come for a reason he couldn't recall.

He shook his head, tried to clear his thoughts. Hit play again.

'Vos . . .' Bakker began.

Anneliese was heading towards the Blue Teahouse. Skipping like the kid she was. Then she sat on the grass, hands around her knees, face full of delight. Of . . .

Happiness. And she wasn't always. He recognized that now.

The picture shook. Whoever held the camera was trying to sit down too, still holding the thing.

Vos moved in so close his nose almost touched the screen. Watched as a figure came into view. Same kind of clothes. A pale shirt, pink this time. Long blue jeans.

Then a face.

Blonde hair. Bright blue eyes. They might have been sisters.

'Jesus Christ,' De Groot murmured. 'What the . . .?'

Bakker reached over, hit pause and scrabbled for some stock shots from the files.

'That's the Prins girl, isn't it?'

Vos kept staring at the screen: two young fair-haired girls in their mid-teens. They might have been cousins. Sisters. He hadn't been at home much but he knew a few of Anneliese's friends. Katja Prins had never been among them.

'Katja doesn't look like that now,' she said.

Three photos. Police mugshots probably. A surly, drawn face, that of a teenager old before her time. Vos turned them over, looked at the dates. They started two years before.

'So the girls knew each other?' De Groot asked.

'Not that I was aware,' Vos said. 'I was working, remember? God knows how many hours a day . . .'

Marnixstraat swallowed him up the moment he walked through those doors. Liesbeth seemed content. Anneliese was growing, busy in the summer holidays. There was nothing for a father to worry about.

De Groot ran a finger over more papers.

'Katja Prins went to pieces after Anneliese vanished. First mention of being taken into police custody three months later. Drunk. High. Prins pulled some strings and got her off with a caution.'

Vos reached forward and hit play. Forty seconds of Anneliese and Katja Prins beaming at the camera like childhood friends, caught in a hot and sunny summer that would never end.

Then the screen went black. He was about to turn it off when Bakker pointed out the video wasn't done. Another twenty seconds to run. They waited.

After a brief gap a light came on. A dark, squalid room. A terrified, bloodless face.

Katja Prins again. Features drawn. Thinner. Made miserable by something Pieter Vos couldn't begin to guess.

Screaming, mouth wide open, spittle flying.

Vader, Vader, Vader. Help me . . .

No one else in the picture. Nothing behind except blackness and plain pale walls.

'Someone's holding that camera,' De Groot said. 'Someone's got that kid.'

The three of them sat for a long minute not saying a word.

Pieter Vos closed his eyes and tried to think. Sometimes you made decisions. Sometimes life made them for you.

He turned and looked at Laura Bakker.

'Where were you last night?'

'What?'

'When I came back and saw someone had been in my boat. I thought it was you. I tried to call. You were on voicemail.'

She didn't blink.

'I was so pissed off with you I didn't answer. I thought you were drunk.'

'If you're going to work with me you pick up the phone.'

She shook her head.

'I'm working with you?'

Then to De Groot.

'I want Koeman, Rijnder and Van der Berg. They can start by getting all the files on Katja Prins. On Menzo and Jansen.' He thought for a moment. 'After which they're mine, along with Bakker here.'

'We're really stretched, Pieter . . .' De Groot said.

'Don't care. Mulder can work on Rosie Jansen. I don't want him sticking his nose in this.'

A nod, the softest of grunts.

Vos got up.

'Where are you going?' De Groot asked.

'I've got a call to make.' Then to Bakker. 'Go

back to Marnixstraat. Arrange for Jansen to be transferred there.'

They looked at him.

'You need an ID for the daughter, don't you?' Vos asked.

'Of course,' De Groot agreed.

Vos pointed a finger at both of them.

'No one tells Theo Jansen a thing. You leave that to me.'

'Then what?' De Groot said.

'Then we put him back in jail. You wouldn't want him on the street, Frank. Not after he's heard.'

CHAPTER 4

Close to the end of another meeting about De Nachtwacht. Hendriks and Margriet Willemsen around the table.

'We had a call from one of the papers,' Hendriks said. 'The reporter didn't want to say why. She says she needs to talk to you. A personal matter.'

Prins slammed his pen on the table and swore.

'I told her that wasn't good enough,' Hendriks added.

Margriet Willemsen's eyes had scarcely risen from the documents for a moment since they began.

'It's about your daughter,' the civil servant added. 'They've heard she's missing again.'

She was looking at him then.

'What's wrong, Wim?' she asked. 'Is there news?'

He'd got used to the idea that everything changed when he entered the council offices. That he shrugged off the world outside, became someone else. But it wasn't true. All the crap followed him, up the stairs, into the office that overlooked the canal and De Wallen.

'I thought it was Katja jerking me around again,' Prins said. 'Maybe I was wrong. It's possible this is something to do with what happened yesterday. The attack on Theo Jansen.'

'How?' she asked.

'I don't know! If the police do they're not saying.'

She said nothing.

'I won't be blackmailed,' Prins said. 'I won't let these bastards win.'

'Best we don't complicate things,' she said.

'What does that mean?'

'We can stall on De Nachtwacht,' Hendriks suggested. 'You should focus on your daughter. It doesn't look good if you carry on as normal. As if it didn't matter.'

Prins slammed his fist on the table.

'We don't back down. I won't—'

'Listen to me.' She reached out and placed her hand on his. 'You're upset. It's understandable. Alex is right. Let's put out a statement. Say we want to make sure everyone's on board—'

'Dammit!' Prins yelled. 'I run this place. I say what happens here. We've got a timetable.' He picked up the project plan, launched it across the table at Hendriks. 'We stick to it.'

They stayed silent.

'Any questions?'

'If that's what you want,' she said quietly. 'We should ask Marnixstraat to put a blackout on any stories about Katja. They'll do that for us, Alex?'

Hendriks was frowning. He never liked raised voices.

'If it's a kidnapping I guess so,' he said.

Then he took his phones and his iPad and fled.

'You shouldn't lose your temper with staff,' Willemsen said when he'd left. 'It can come back to haunt you.'

'Come back to haunt me?' Prins said. Then told her about the email and the video.

She didn't blink, just listened then asked, 'Have you still got it?'

'Do I look like a moron? If Liesbeth saw—'

'What did he say? What did he ask for?'

Prins tried to remember.

'He didn't ask for anything. There was a name. Pop Meester. The file. That was all. For Christ's sake. How the hell did they get something like that?'

She got up, walked to the window. Dark pin-striped business suit. Not a black hair out of place.

'How?' Prins asked again. He couldn't look her in the eye. 'I mean . . . without you knowing?'

'What?'

She came to him, put her palms on the table, looked in his face. Margriet Willemsen never got mad. Just cold and right then she was icier than he'd ever seen.

'Are you asking me whether I filmed us screwing? Then passed it on to some . . . blackmailer?'

'I didn't—'

'Why would I do that? What possible reason . . .?'

'If the press get hold of this. If Liesbeth—'

'Don't be so damned weak.'

'How did this happen?' he asked again. 'They had something in your room.'

Her hand went to his grey hair. Affection. Or control. He wasn't sure.

'I'll deal with that. I'll deal with De Nachtwacht. It can wait for now.'

'No. That's what these bastards want, isn't it?'

The desk phone rang. He hesitated to pick it up. So she did it for him.

Alex Hendriks. Marnixstraat were going to get onto the press. There'd be a blackout agreed on Katja. No mention of her in the papers or the broadcast media. No one to approach the family.

'Someone's really taken her, haven't they?' Prins whispered.

Willemsen sat on the edge of the desk.

'It might be best if you went home.'

'And do what exactly?'

'Be with your wife?' she suggested. 'That would look good.'

CHAPTER 5

Vos was at the Prins house, an awkward meeting punctuated by difficult silences.

'Is there anything I should know?' he asked.

'Like what?'

Liesbeth looked terrible. As if she hadn't slept in days. Almost as bad as she did after their daughter went missing.

'Anneliese and Katja Prins were friends,' he said. 'I'd no idea. Did you?'

They sat at the kitchen table in the comfortable, elegant house hidden away in a select courtyard near Willemstraat. It was nothing like the life they'd lived together. He was working long hours rising through the ranks in Marnixstraat while she brought up Anneliese, taking temporary jobs on the side. They never ran short. Never made much of a fuss about furniture or decorations. All those things seemed irrelevant. They were a family and while Vos wished she'd agree to marry him he understood and accepted why she didn't. What was the point? They had Anneliese, a beautiful child, more precious, more significant than any band of gold could ever be.

'That can't be right,' she said too quickly. 'I'd have known.'

For a while she'd worked in a legal aid organization. Lawyers came and went.

'Did Wim used to come into your office when you were in Damrak? Maybe he brought Katja with him?'

She went to the sink, got a pack of cigarettes, came back and lit one. Her hand shook the way it used to.

'What is this, Pieter?'

He told her about Rosie Jansen's murder, how she was found next to his boat.

'It looks like you're not the only one who wants me involved in this case.' He showed her the police ID. 'I'm back and I never wanted to be. We found a video. Anneliese and Katja in the Vondelpark. They were friends. Not long before she disappeared. No question.'

She thought about it.

'Maybe Wim did bring her. I don't remember. I never really knew Katja until I started seeing him. Liese was dead then. We were history.'

Not dead, he thought. Just missing.

'Teenagers like secrets,' Vos said. 'They cultivate them.'

'You were out day and night when she disappeared. I'd left the law office by then anyway. That summer I had a part-time job. I still took her to school. Brought her home. She never saw Katja as far as I know. Are you really sure?'

'I saw the pictures.'

'Well . . .' A shrug. 'I can't explain it.'

He waited.

'Why are you here anyway? Mulder was round first thing. We told him everything we knew. When someone calls we'll tell you.'

'If,' he said. 'If they call.'

'So you think Katja's playing tricks again? With all this gang shit going on? Mulder said maybe they took her.'

'Maybe they did.'

'Well?'

'I don't know. I'm just asking questions. Waiting for answers. It's all I do.'

He watched her cough on the cigarette, took it from her fingers, stubbed it out in the ashtray.

'You're not my keeper now,' she said.

'I never was, was I? How could I have been? I wasn't there. The job . . .' That was true and he regretted it. 'Sorry.'

Liesbeth always liked apologies. They were a sign she'd won.

'She's still got things here. Her old bedroom. I told Mulder. I thought he might be interested.'

'He wasn't?'

'Him and Wim are at loggerheads over this Nachtwacht nonsense. None of you want that to happen, do you?'

Vos sighed.

'I've been a police officer for all of sixty minutes. Don't ask me to speak on behalf of Marnixstraat. I'd like to see her room if that's OK.'

It was at the front, overlooking the private park in the centre of the courtyard. Small, with a single bed and a studied tidiness that surely came from Liesbeth's fastidious hands, not those of a teenager.

Lurid posters of pop stars on the wall. A wardrobe stuffed full of clothes. A chest of drawers much the same. A desk with the ghostly marks of a missing laptop on the surface.

'The computer . . .'

'Wim said she sold it for dope.'

He rifled through the clothes in the wardrobe. Bags of shoes at the back. Lots.

'She left plenty behind.'

'Fashion, Pieter. There's no value in anything from yesterday.' She looked him up and down, briefly put a hand to his threadbare jumper. 'You never did understand that. You don't look a day older. How do you manage that?'

'Maybe because I haven't done anything of late,' he said with a shrug.

Liesbeth sat down on the bed and looked ready to weep.

He went through the chest. Just underwear, socks, shirts, a few books: vampires and steampunk.

'Do you hate me?' she asked.

The desk had a single drawer. It was full of pens, spent concert tickets, paper clips and crayons. There was a large art pad at the back. He took it out and flicked through some of the drawings there.

'Why would I hate you?'

'Because I ran out when you needed me.'

Vos came and sat down on the bed.

'We were both too broken by what happened. We couldn't talk. There was nothing left.'

They'd never had this conversation and that was a cruel and sad omission.

'You didn't need me,' he added. 'Not that I could see.'

'I . . .'

She closed her eyes, said no more.

'When Wim came along he seemed to take you out of yourself. Out of the misery.' He gestured at the room. 'Took you to a place like this . . .'

Vos laughed and felt no jealousy, no envy. Even the regret seemed to be fading.

'No competition really. Is there?'

She reached out and squeezed his hand. Didn't let go. Looked as if she wanted to say something but didn't dare.

Vos kept looking at the desk.

'Katja and Anneliese knew each other,' he said. 'They were close. Not long before she vanished. Back then . . .'

He couldn't get those images out of his head. The two girls, beautiful and carefree in the park. Was it possible a friendship that seemed so close could be a secret?

'Back then Katja was fine too.' He slipped his hand out of hers. 'When did she start to lose it?'

'I don't know. Ask Wim. He's her father.'

'I will.'

'Marrying me didn't help. I was never good enough. Bea was larger than life. Knew everyone. Did what the hell she liked. And then the dope got to her. And she killed herself. Katja's still a simple child really. She loves a little drama. How the hell could I compete with that?'

When he was an officer in Marnixstraat his head worked well. Had a capacity for dates and linear narratives. Now . . .

'When did Bea die?' he asked. 'I don't remember.'

'That's because you were stinking drunk and doped up too,' she said with a sudden flash of anger. 'It was around the time we split up.'

'How exactly?' he asked.

She glared at him.

'She shot herself. Were you really so out of it you never knew?'

He went and looked at the desk again. Something was stuck underneath one of the corners by the wall. Vos crawled onto the carpet and found it: a USB memory stick.

Smiling, he held it up.

'Mulder's a cretin,' she said.

'You've got a computer? I'd like to take a look.'

She showed him into the study. Prins's desktop was sleeping.

He brought it to life, put the stick into the machine.

'Could you check her bedroom again?' he asked. 'See if there's anything I missed?'

A dark look but she left anyway.

There was a single message in Wim Prins's inbox, sent just a few minutes before. It came from someone calling himself Pop Meester.

An interesting name in the circumstances. Vos thought for a moment, opened the message. There was a zip file with it. Room on the USB stick, just time to get it on there before Liesbeth came back empty-handed. Then he thought for a second and marked the message unread.

'Well?' she asked.

He clicked on the first of Katja's files. Pop music came out of the desktop speakers. Everything on there was an MP3.

'Piracy's bad,' he said, and ejected the USB stick. 'I'd like to keep this anyway.'

'I can make some more coffee,' she said, suddenly hopeful.

'I've got an appointment.'

'You always have. Another time?'

He pocketed the memory stick and said goodbye.

CHAPTER 6

The morgue was on the ground floor at the back of Marnixstraat overlooking the staff car park and the adjoining bike sheds. Lines of marked squad cars ranged outside the window. Diesel fumes mingled with the stink of autopsy, chemical spirits and blood.

One of the assistants leaned against the wall in the yard, smoking a cigarette. A grey curl waved in through the open window.

Theo Jansen stood near the exit looking at nothing through the glass. Tears in his eyes.

'Sorry,' Vos said. 'I wanted to tell you myself.'

'Why?' Jansen shot back at him. 'Do you think this makes us equal?'

Rosie Jansen's body lay on a metal anatomy table in the centre of the small room. Her face was visible above the sheet. The gunshot wound had been cleaned up and covered with a bandage.

De Groot had set a team working on the murder overnight. More than had been allotted to the two Surinamese kids who tried to kill Jansen outside the courthouse. It was early. But still they ought to have more than this.

'Not equal, no,' Vos said.

The white beard was straggly, uncombed. Jansen seemed much older than he had the day before.

'But we do connect. She was left next to my home. The doll in her arms. It's like one I was sent when Anneliese went missing—'

'I had nothing to do with that!'

'I know. You told me and I believe you. But whoever this man is . . . these people . . . They want me in this case, Theo. They left some photos of my daughter with Rosie.'

Angry, baffled, Jansen said, 'You're telling me she had something to do with your kid's murder now?'

'I didn't say that. Someone wants me to get hooked up in all this. I don't know why. I wish none of it had ever happened. But it has.' He shrugged. 'Here we both are.'

Jansen walked to a chair by the door to the yard, sat down heavily. Laura Bakker asked him if he wanted something. A glass of water. Coffee. He shook his head. Vos had arranged secure transport back to prison.

'How did they kill her?' Jansen asked.

Vos took him through as much as they had.

'She opened the door herself. That would be to someone she knew, wouldn't it? Or invited in.'

'Rosie didn't live in fear,' Jansen said. 'She wasn't scared of anyone. Why should she be? No one goes round killing your kids for God's sake.'

He realized what he'd said. Shrugged. His eyes

strayed to the silver table. Bakker called one of the morgue assistants. The man walked over and covered Rosie Jansen's swollen dead face.

'What kind of world is this?' Jansen asked of no one in particular.

'Had she had threats?' Vos asked.

'No.' He leaned forward on his arms, stared at the ground. 'I got a few in jail. Only to be expected. Rosie was just looking after things until I came out.'

'Not a lot to work with,' Vos said quietly.

'Where is he?' Jansen asked. 'That Surinamese bastard. Jesus . . . Coming for me I can take. Expect. But not Rosie. Never . . .'

'He's still in Ostend. Went there yesterday morning. Private plane at the airport.'

Jansen sat upright, leaned against the wall, looked at him.

'He'll be back,' Vos said. 'When he does we'll interview him.'

Silence.

'We both know he'll have an alibi we can't break,' Vos went on. 'We know one of the kids is dead. It's best we assume the second fell on his sword too. So we'll need someone who'll talk. Any ideas?'

'I've spent the last two years in a cell thanks to that bastard Mulder. Why keep asking me these stupid questions?'

Vos nodded and said, 'Because I have to.'

'Going to let me out now?'

'What do you think?'

'Dammit! The judge said—'

'It's conditional,' Laura Bakker interrupted. 'If you read the judgement. Release on bail pending appeal. In the circumstances . . .'

Jansen glowered at her, then at Vos.

'You're on this case now? This is it? The team?'

'We're looking for the Prins girl,' Vos said. 'I wanted to tell you myself. I felt you were owed that. De Groot's assembling a team. Mulder's going to run it . . .'

The big hood jabbed a finger in his direction.

'I want you. Not that clown. If he hadn't put me in jail none of this would have happened.'

Vos frowned.

'You can't think that way, Theo. Keep asking yourself . . . what if ? You'll go crazy. I'm talking from experience. I've found you a single cell in Het Schouw. As close to deluxe as I can get.'

There were six tower blocks in the prison complex of Bijlmerbajes near the Amstel river. Jansen had spent two years in Demersluis, a unit reserved for dangerous prisoners.

'Het Schouw's a holiday camp next to your old place. It still has to be solitary,' Vos added.

Jansen was back staring at the table.

'And Rosie? When do I get to bury her?'

'We'll let you know. Are there relatives we can contact? Her mother . . .'

'She left me years ago. I don't even know where she went.' Tears threatened his vision once more. 'Why are you asking me this? You've got files. You know what I eat for breakfast. When I take a shit. Rosie was all I had.'

Vos checked his watch then asked, 'Is there anything else?'

'Can I make a couple of calls? Private? Friends. I need to talk to Michiel Lindeman too.'

'The lawyer won't get you out,' Bakker chipped in.

'Of course,' Vos said. 'There's a pay phone in the corridor.'

'And the toilet,' Jansen added.

The phone and the washroom were a good walk away. Vos nodded at a young officer to deal with it. When Jansen was gone he spoke quietly to the lab technician working in the morgue and asked him to check some records.

Bakker stayed reading the files.

'What do we do now?' she asked.

He gave her a business card in a plastic evidence sleeve.

'Those two boys of Menzo's had this. The Poppenhuis aan de Prinsengracht. Derelict building. Whatever it was, it wasn't a doll's house.'

'This is that gas explosion?' she asked looking at the card.

'Koeman's out there taking a look. I want to see for myself.'

She didn't move.

'This is a picture of the Oortman house, isn't it? Like the one you got on the first box with the doll in it?'

'Seems to be,' he agreed.

171

'You can get that picture anywhere, Vos.' She handed the sleeve back. 'It's just clip art. You pick it up off the web.'

'Maybe.'

'Chasing a missing kid? On the back of a business card? This . . .' She nodded towards the silver doors of the morgue. '. . . is a murder. Jansen wants you to handle it. De Groot will agree if you ask him.'

'I'm aware of that.'

She folded her arms. The home-made suit seemed to hang on her more badly than the previous day's.

'Laura, there's nothing either of us can do for Theo Jansen's daughter. Katja Prins could be alive. With a little luck maybe we could find her. If you'd rather stay here and play with a computer . . .'

'I'll get us transport then.'

Vos looked out of the window.

'It's not raining, is it?'

CHAPTER 7

Ten minutes after Vos and Bakker left the station Frank de Groot wandered down to the ground floor. The morgue was almost deserted. Rosie Jansen's body was back in refrigeration. The forensic assistant was head down in a computer.

No pathologist.

No officers.

No Theo Jansen.

He walked over to the assistant, a smart young woman, Dutch Muslim, a pink scarf around her head, music fizzing out of the tiny phones in her ears.

'Where is everyone?'

She took out the phones and looked up from the screen. He had to repeat the question.

'They all left.'

'I can see that.'

She looked upstairs.

'Management meeting about the two Surinamese kids who went for Theo Jansen. Seems there's a link with that place on Prinsen where the bomb went off. They were there first.'

'What link?'

'I think,' she said slowly, 'that's what they're trying to work out. That nice new man went off somewhere.'

The commissaris swore under his breath. She looked shocked. He apologized.

'Pieter Vos isn't new.'

'He's new to me.'

'And the crook we had in custody?'

She brightened.

'The big guy? A couple of prison officers came to pick him up.' She shook her head. 'God I hate that part. When they come and see. You've got to watch and you hate yourself for it.' She glanced at the bank of refrigerated storage units. 'Still can't imagine what it feels like. One of your own family . . .'

'Theo Jansen put plenty of business our way,' De Groot grumbled.

'Doesn't mean he doesn't have feelings, does it?'

Everyone answered back these days.

He tried to call Vos and got voicemail. Then Laura Bakker. She was in the street somewhere. On a bike he guessed. Just managed to tell him they were on their way to the bombed-out house on the Prinsengracht when the signal died.

'Christ,' De Groot muttered and got another black look from the young woman in the pink headscarf.

The washroom was an isolated block at the end of a long corridor, close to the car park. He wandered down there, went to the wall, listened to the buses from the station outside as usual, started to take a leak. Said a silent prayer of thanks that Vos was back on duty and starting to look a little like his old bright, sharp self.

A gang war. Katja Prins missing. De Groot had enough to deal with working out how they were going to handle the fallout from Prins's crazed scheme to clean up the city. He'd left most of that in Klaas Mulder's hands and wasn't sure that was such a wise decision.

Zipping himself up he heard a muffled sound. A man, in pain.

He looked along the line of stalls. The last door was half open. A leg, a single black shoe akimbo, poked out from inside.

'Christ,' he said again and walked over.

One of the younger uniformed men, not much older than Laura Bakker, face bloodied, eyes scared. Bundled into the corner next to the toilet, hands bound behind his back, mouth stuffed with paper towels held in place by a torn cloth.

De Groot strode over, removed the rag from his mouth, waited as he spat out the towels, gagging along the way.

It took a while. Then he turned his head to the bowl and threw up, sobbing, choking.

There was no weapon in his holster.

The control room had answered by then. When De Groot started talking the young officer in front of him lost his balance again, tumbled back to the

175

floor. The commissaris gave up on the call, got him to his feet, put the seat down on the toilet, held his arm, made him stay there.

'Theo Jansen's in a prison van on the way to Bijlmerbajes,' he said to control.

'Got that on the list,' the woman said. 'Picked up already. He's going in the Het Schouw block.'

'Put me through to the driver.'

He looked at his watch. Thirty seconds. That was as long as he was going to wait.

But he didn't have to. The woman came back to him and said, 'Something's wrong here. I'm putting out a call.'

CHAPTER 8

Sitting in the security van as it took off for the prison towers of Bijlmerbajes Theo Jansen could picture every street in his head. Turn into Marnixstraat, keep straight on until they hit the busy square of Leidseplein. After that he was theirs. They'd be on busy, open public roads. Little chance of escape. He had to be as quick as he was as a young Amsterdam thug, looking to survive and prosper in dangerous times.

Easy so far. He'd beaten up the skinny cop in Marnixstraat, taken his gun. Wandered out and found the prison van waiting in the yard. The two guards had looked a touch surprised when he turned up, coughing and wheezing a little. Said he didn't feel too good and wanted to go.

They checked the register. Theo Jansen was in theory a free man. It didn't seem too odd he'd made his own way to the yard. So they watched him sit down on a bench, ask for a minute to get his breath back, cough a lot, ask in vain for a cigarette.

Then finally, with a helping hand from both of them, climb inside.

Seconds after they pulled out of the station he held his breath until he began to sweat. A minute later he started hammering hard on the metal wall that separated his secure compartment from the driver and the guard with him.

Three bangs. Three more. Finally the small window came open.

Jansen thrust his red face into the gap, said, 'Sick.'

'You can see the doctor when we get there.'

Theo Jansen gagged some more then keeled over onto his side.

The van rose. The bridge over Leidsegracht he guessed. They were now in the narrowest street along the way. Tram lines, cycle paths, red-brick terraced shops and apartments either side. Brown bars with Heineken signs. The low tan shape of the American Hotel emerging on the right.

Thirty years before, when he did his own dirty work, Jansen had taken down an English gangster in the lobby there, shot three times, didn't die quickly.

He remembered that as he lay groaning on the floor, feeling the van come to a halt.

They wouldn't leave him there. Not without looking. The police had rules. Orders to follow.

When the doors opened he saw them. One big, one small. Truncheons and radios on their belts. No weapons. They were just drivers really, looking bored and miserable.

They climbed in. The little one bent over him and asked, 'What's up?'

Jansen fetched the big guy a kick to the groin, pulling out the handgun, pushing it into the face of the other one.

Big man went down howling. The other froze, terrified.

'Keys,' Jansen said, scrambling to his feet, shifting the weapon from side to side.

Nothing.

He walked over to the door, slammed it shut. Just the low interior light now. No one outside to see.

'Keys or I shoot you,' he said in a quiet, confident untroubled voice. 'Don't make me do that. It's always a waste.'

Jansen looked down at himself. Fawn cotton chinos. A white shirt. Fawn jacket.

'And I hate blood on my clothes.'

It was the big one who took out his keys first.

'And those,' Jansen added, nodding at the handsets on their belts. 'And your wallets.'

When they were done he kicked the radios, wallets and keys to the door. Checked with the little man how to close the van. Opened the handle, said thanks, slid their stuff outside.

Tucked the handgun into his waistband, got out and locked the door behind him.

They were booting the walls in seconds but he didn't mind.

The street was almost empty. He picked up the wallets, pulled out all the cash, then threw them beneath the van with the radios and keys.

Fine grey day. Too cold for clothes like this. Theo

Jansen walked off towards the back lanes of Leidseplein.

The barber's was tiny, a single door, a tiny window, a sign: Maarten's. He strode in, nodded at the man working on a single customer at the mirror, walked into the back room, waited.

A few minutes later the barber walked in.

'You don't look a day older,' Jansen said. 'Got a beer?'

The barber went to the fridge, took out two bottles.

'Jesus, Theo. I just heard on the news. About Rosie. What the hell's going on?'

'I don't know,' Jansen said.

The barber nodded at outside.

'Are you supposed to be loose? The radio said . . .'

'This is my city. Where else should I be?'

Jansen felt the thick white beard, then his long white hair. The change in colour happened in his thirties. He felt he'd looked this way forever. But these were different times.

'Can you take this off me?' he asked. 'All of it. Gimme a crewcut like the kids have. Never had one of them.'

Maarten walked out to the front, turned the sign to closed, drew down the blinds. When he came back Theo Jansen had finished the beer so the barber got another out of the fridge, handed it over.

'You can sit in the chair now,' he said.

CHAPTER 9

The Poppenhuis was a long ride from Marnixstraat, on a quiet stretch of the Prinsengracht opposite the Amstelveld square. Don't-cross tape ran the length of the building. A construction team was attaching plastic sheets to scaffolding on the front. Close to the front door a workman was sweeping up shattered glass.

A lean man of medium height, narrow face dominated by the droopy brown moustache, Koeman was sitting on the bonnet of a squad car by the water smoking a cigarette. The ash dropped on his taupe short winter coat and he never noticed. He waved a hand by way of welcome, watched the way Bakker walked, didn't say a word.

Vos and Bakker followed him to the door. They picked up three hard hats then made their way past the construction men.

'Whorehouse,' Koeman said as they began to walk round the wrecked ground-floor rooms. 'Want to meet the madame?'

Vos had stopped in what must have been the reception area. The smoke and the firemen's hoses had changed the colour of everything but he guessed it had once been pink. Koeman walked up and opened what looked like a tall cupboard behind the desk. Behind the doors was a long painting: the Oortman house, an almost exact copy. But in each open room something different. A display of sex acts, all kinds. Men, faces turned away from the painter. The women, none naked, but dressed as dolls. On their backs. On their knees. In one room splayed out on a wooden contraption, legs akimbo.

'I'd guess you'd call that the menu. At least you had to ask to see it.' Koeman looked reluctant to say something but came out with it anyway. 'This is the thing that drove you crazy when your girl vanished, isn't it? The one from the museum?'

Vos nodded.

Koeman frowned.

'If you were going to call a brothel the doll's house it's pretty obvious they'd use that picture, Pieter. It's famous. Doesn't mean there's a connection.'

'I know that,' Vos said. 'Was this on the books?'

'I ran the address through vice. It's registered as a private residence. We've no records of complaints. Of any visits.' He shrugged. 'Anything.'

'There has to be some kind of paperwork,' Bakker said.

'You haven't worked this beat, have you?' Koeman retorted. 'It's called a *privehuis*.'

Bakker looked at him, bemused.

'Private house. It's like a genteel little party.' He gestured round the room. 'You sit around with

182

the girls. Talk a while. Have a drink. Smile at one. Then . . .'

'You seem knowledgeable,' she said.

Koeman smiled, not pleasantly.

'I've worked this city since I was an eighteen-year-old cadet. You'd be amazed what I've seen. But this place . . .' He shook his head. Looked at Vos. 'It doesn't add up. We ought to have known about it. From what I've seen upstairs it was a bustling little business. Then a little under three years ago . . .' He clicked his fingers. 'Gone. All closed down.'

They walked out back to a small, grubby courtyard. An Asian woman in garish clothes sat on a rusty garden chair smoking a cigarette. She didn't look at any of them when they arrived.

Her name was Amm. Vos found another rusty chair, pulled it up and sat in front of her.

'You're in big trouble, Amm,' he said.

She looked at him and scowled.

'No I'm not.'

'Why did you shut up shop?' he asked.

'Went on holiday for a while. When I came back all the girls had gone.'

'All of them?' Koeman asked.

'I told him,' she said, jabbing a finger his way. 'Every one. Bitches. I brought in some of those kids myself. Got them papers. That's how they repay me.'

Bakker glanced back at the house.

'How old were they?' she said.

'Old enough,' came the straight answer.

'How old?' Bakker asked again, leaning down to get in her face.

'Every one of them nineteen.'

Koeman threw back his head and laughed.

'Oh, I love it. Why not eighteen? That's still legal. For now.' He winked at her. 'But when this new guy in the council gets his way it's twenty-one. And brothel keepers like you are in real shit, aren't you?'

'It was a privehuis,' she insisted. 'We had nice girls and nice customers.' She glared at him. 'Maybe you'd know some of 'em.'

'Meaning?' Bakker asked.

Koeman looked at her and winked.

'A good hostess never talks about business,' the Thai woman said almost primly. 'What's the world coming to?'

Vos stood up.

'Why didn't you open up again, Amm? You could have got new girls. This place . . .' He looked back at the fire-blackened corridor, the paintings on the walls. 'It must have cost a lot of money.'

She wriggled at that.

'Didn't want to. Didn't need to. I got enough money . . .'

'That shithole in De Wallen where I found you doesn't look so hot,' Koeman broke in. 'You work waitressing in a crappy restaurant. And this place is worth . . . what? Three or four million. Maybe more.'

No answer.

'Where does the insurance go?' he added. 'Jimmy Menzo?'

She didn't answer.

Vos pulled a photograph from his pocket. Katja Prins. Showed it to her. Nothing. Then he hesitated for a while, took out another shot. Anneliese. Showed her that too.

The Thai woman looked at him, astonished.

'I don't deal in white girls. Why would I? Those bitches from Russia and those places . . . they'll slit your throats for five euros.' Her hand swept the cold air. 'I never seen these kids.' She looked at the photos again. 'Too young for me.'

'They're Dutch,' he said.

She laughed at him then. One prominent gold canine in her mouth.

'You're crazy. What would a Dutch kid be doing here? We just get your men.'

Vos nodded at Koeman.

'You need to go to the police station with my colleague. We're going to have to check your papers. The legal documents to do with this building.' She was swearing under her breath. 'It's going to take some time.'

CHAPTER 10

Vos started at the top floor and began working his way through, room by room.

Bakker followed and watched.

'What do you want me to do?' she asked.

'What do you think you should do?'

'Go back to Warmoesstraat and see if we can find Jaap Zeeger. That kid there . . . whatever she was called . . .'

'Til Stamm.'

'She had more to say.'

Vos frowned.

'Let's look around first.'

'It's an empty house. Shouldn't we be talking to people?'

Nothing much had been left on the top storeys. Just empty rooms with lurid pink furnishings, a basin and a shower in the corner. A bed. A couple of chairs.

Eventually they got to the first floor. A large room that felt different. Only a tiny window, high up. Thick carpet, fading pink wallpaper, a king-size double bed with a dusty velvet cover stained with smoke. Two chairs. The usual shower in the corner.

A dusty chandelier as if this room was special somehow.

Vos tried to see out of the window. It was too far up for anyone to peer in, even from across the canal.

He started going through the nearest cupboard. Towels mainly. Every one had an image of the Oortman doll's house embroidered in the corner. When he pulled out some sheets they had the same.

'This is a brothel?' Bakker asked. 'With fancy laundry?'

'There's money here. What else do we know?'

She folded her arms.

'Why did you show her those photos?'

He shrugged.

'Why not? It's called the Doll's House. That suggests the girls here were young. Not nineteen. Not eighteen either. If this was just an ordinary privehuis we'd have known about it, like Koeman said. Maybe they were grooming kids. Maybe . . . I don't know.'

She'd got the hint, had started going through a second set of drawers beneath the window. Bakker was tall enough that, when she stood on tiptoe and climbed on the chair, she could see out through the broken, smoke-smeared glass. The canal, the square opposite with a church turned into a restaurant and bar. Two boats, one commercial, the other full of tourists, were making their way along the canal.

'What are we looking for?' she asked as she went

through yet more towels and sheets, all with the doll's house logo on them. 'And why didn't they take this stuff away?'

'She was scared, wasn't she?' he answered. 'The Thai woman. She didn't even want to come inside this place.'

He scratched his head.

Bakker kept on hunting through the drawers.

'I don't know what we're looking for,' Vos said, and sounded downcast. 'I didn't three years ago. I don't now. Frank's going to have to take charge here. I can't . . .'

He stopped. She'd opened the final drawer, at the bottom, and from her face he could see she'd found something.

Vos strode over, almost crowded her out of the way. Ran his gloved fingers through the drawer. Four porcelain dolls. Blonde hair. Dead faces, mouths frozen in a pout. They looked expensive.

The drawer below was full of cardboard gift boxes made for the dolls. A line drawing of the Oortman house on every lid. If Vos had possessed a felt-tip pen he would have drawn the corners of a coffin on one. Not that it was necessary.

'This is what he sent you?' Bakker asked.

He walked over, sat on the bed, said nothing.

'A drawer full of them, Vos. It's like . . . they sold them as souvenirs or something?'

He called the station, got through to De Groot.

'I need a full team,' he said before the commissaris could speak. 'We've found something.'

'What?' De Groot asked and listened. When Vos was done he said, 'That's it?'

'That's it,' Vos agreed.

'You can get some forensic. I can't spare any men. Those I gave you are being reassigned.'

'No, no. Listen to me, Frank. This is important—'

'Theo Jansen just busted out,' De Groot said. 'I don't have time for dead cases. Got too many live ones on my hands.'

'Just give me a chance—'

'Is there anything there that connects with the Prins girl?'

'That's what I'm trying to find out.'

'I'll take that as a no,' De Groot responded. 'You can have some people from forensic. They wanted to see you anyway.'

'About what?'

'About something you asked for.'

'I need officers,' Vos insisted.

'You can have Van der Berg. Keep him sober if you can,' De Groot said then hung up.

CHAPTER 11

Wim Prins was at his desk going through some papers on De Nachtwacht when the PA came through and said a crime reporter from one of the dailies was outside demanding to speak to him.

'Tell him I'm busy. He can make an appointment next time.'

'It's a woman and I don't think she'll go away.' The PA was a middle-aged dragon he'd inherited. Didn't like him much. 'She says it's about your daughter.'

Prins closed his eyes.

'What about her?'

'She won't say. Just that she has something you need to see.'

'Like what?'

The PA sighed.

'Wouldn't it be easier if you asked her yourself?'

The journalist was called Anna de Vries. Somewhere short of thirty, smart, incisive face, self-satisfied smile. Not the least bit daunted in his presence.

'We're really busy here,' Prins said. 'Make this

quick.' She pulled out a voice recorder. 'And put that away.'

She shrugged, smiled, did as he asked. The PA came back with coffee and closed the door behind her. Anna de Vries wriggled on the chair in front of him. Short skirt. Pretty woman. Knew how to use it.

'I decided to come to you first,' she said. 'Before the police. I want this to be your decision. Not mine.' She stared at him frankly. 'I haven't even told my news editor about this. So . . .' She put her hands on the desk. 'Whatever you want to do that's fine by me.'

Then she got her briefcase and pulled out a plain brown envelope and an iPad.

'Funny really. You go for weeks without anyone giving you a break. Then two turn up in one day.'

She placed the envelope in front of him.

'You should take a look at this first. I did. I printed them out for you. They turned up as an attachment in an email this morning. Your name at the top.'

Seven sheets of paper. Laser printouts. A message that read, 'Get a thousand five hundred euro notes. Put them in a small carry-on suitcase. Black leather Tumi. You've got a day. Then we'll be in touch.'

And some photos. Katja, no doubt about it. In the first scared in a plain grubby T-shirt, druggy eyes glaring at the camera. Eye shadow blurring around her cheek or maybe a bruise. In the second exhausted, dead-eyed, hair greasy. In the third . . .

Prins rubbed his temple. Wanted to scream.

Katja in her underwear, strapped to a chair, screaming as something – a whip maybe, even an iron bar – came down on her so quickly the movement was blurred.

'Half a million euros,' the reporter said quietly. 'Wow.'

'This has to go to the police.'

Prins reached for the phone. Her hand came out and stopped him.

'I haven't finished.'

She pulled out the iPad.

'You know,' Anna de Vries added, 'I'm rarely embarrassed in this job. You kind of grow out of it. But right now . . .'

She shielded her eyes theatrically then hit play. Sighed and turned down the volume when the grunts got too loud.

Wim Prins reached over and shut the thing off.

'Coalition politics.' She wore a brazen grin. 'It really does bring people together, doesn't it? Heartwarming, in a sense. Though what your wife—'

'What do you want?'

She blinked.

'Is that a serious question? I'm a reporter. I want a story. My story. No one else's.' She tapped her jacket. 'Mine.'

He waited.

'If I could write this now I would,' she added. 'Your daughter. You screwing your deputy. Christmas come early.'

The grin disappeared.

'You got a media blackout out of Marnixstraat, didn't you? I could fill the first six pages. Except I can't write a damned word. Thank you.'

'What . . . do . . . you . . . want?' he asked again.

She did a rat-tat-tat with her fingers on the brown envelope.

'I want you to get your daughter back. Safe and well. Really. What you do about this . . .' She nodded at the iPad. 'That's up to you. I haven't shown it to a soul. Like I said, not even my boss. It's just you and me, Wim. Take the photos and the note to the police by all means. This . . .' Her finger stroked the little screen. 'I think it can stay between us for now.' A pause, the grin. 'If you're cool with that.'

'Go on.'

Her eyes narrowed.

'Are you being deliberately dense here? Do what you need to do with Katja. Fix it. Then, when it's over . . . when the blackout lifts . . . you talk to me. To me and no one else. The big story.' Her hand swept the room. 'How you won back your junkie daughter. How your family's going to survive. Get stronger.'

Prins waited.

'How you went off the rails for a while. Lost it. Margriet Willemsen's a man-eater. Are you the only mug in this city who doesn't know that? It's her career that's on the line. Not yours. Not if you come clean. Not if we handle this properly.'

She picked up the iPad, put it back in her case.

'I know we're all meant to be good Protestants. But there's a Catholic streak in all of us. We can forgive anything pretty much. So long as someone confesses. It's good for the soul. Don't you think?'

Wim Prins felt sick.

She got to her feet, took out a business card, scribbled something on the back, threw it on the desk.

'That's my private number. My address too. Not far away. If you'd rather talk there . . .' He checked the card. An apartment block near Spui. 'Your decision. Call—'

'No one else has seen this? Any of it?'

'Didn't I just say that? I want this story. I'm not showing it round the office. Not until it's time.'

When she was gone he called Marnixstraat. De Groot sounded agitated.

'How are they going to get in touch?' the commissaris asked.

'Search me.'

De Groot didn't speak for a moment. Then, 'I'll send someone round to get what you have. We'll run it through forensic to see if we can work out if it's genuine or not.'

'There are pictures. I know my daughter.'

'I meant a genuine kidnapping. Not extortion. Either way they'll get back to you. Fixing a meeting. I need to know—'

'Is that it?'

A pause on the line.

'No that's not it. We do have other things right now. Or haven't you heard?'

Prins listened to the news of Jansen's escape and felt guiltily grateful for a moment. At least the police wouldn't be throwing hard questions at him.

Next he called Margriet Willemsen and said, 'We need to talk.'

CHAPTER 12

The Begijnhof was a courtyard of tall houses behind busy Spui. An odd anachronism in the busy modern city: a Catholic community for women going back centuries. Silent, peaceful, remote except for the stream of tourists who found their way in through the little arched doors on the street. Not quite a nunnery but not far off.

Neatly clipped grass, trees, pigeons feeding in the centre. A few tourists wandering past the tidy lawn. Theo Jansen sat in a top-floor apartment close to the window, feeling his rough chin and cheeks.

The beard had disappeared thanks to Maarten's careful work. So had the long white hair. His skin was red and sore. His mind made up.

The woman in the room was two years younger than him. Dyed brown hair too long for her and a pleasant, lined face. She wore a fawn dress, old-fashioned, a plain brown sweater over it. Only a faded tattoo on her right wrist spoke of another life.

'Did she see you much lately?' Jansen asked.

'I was the enemy, wasn't I? The woman to be forgotten. The one who abandoned you.'

'You had your reasons. It wasn't a life for everyone. I never . . .' Jansen fought hard to remember how they came to part. The world was so fast and anxious then. His hold on the drug and nightclub lines was far from secure. He could have been dead in the gutter just as easily as any of those he'd killed. 'I never thought you'd go. And when you did . . .'

This next was true. He had to believe it.

'I never wanted Rosie to be parted from you. I hoped . . .'

'What, Theo? That we could stay friends?'

They met when she was a student, working in one of his bars, desperate for money. A bright girl. Always ready to answer back. Never scared of him, unlike everyone else in those days.

'Suzi. That was what I did. What I do. I didn't know anything else.' He looked at her, saw the combative, beautiful young woman he'd fallen in love with. 'I couldn't run away. Reinvent myself. Or . . .' He waved outside. 'Turn religious or something.'

He scratched his bare head and found it hurt.

'And I never knew you were a Catholic either.' Jansen wagged a finger at her. 'If you'd told me then maybe none of this would ever . . .'

She was crying. He got up, put his arms round her. Kissed her dyed hair and found it didn't smell the way it used to, of flowers and dope smoke.

'I'm sorry,' Suzi whispered. 'I keep thinking it's just a bad dream. I keep hoping . . .'

Her arms fell round his waist and didn't meet the way they once did. He was fat and old. All the same they stayed there for a long while. Then she wiped her eyes with her sleeve and he went back to his chair, sipped at the lukewarm coffee. She'd heard about Rosie's murder on the radio. There was nothing he had to tell her that wasn't public knowledge already. Their daughter was a headline. Thirty seconds on the news alongside the tale of the attack outside the Prinsengracht court. A coming gang war was the real story. People feared for themselves, not a bunch of criminals.

'Thanks for taking me in,' he said. 'I don't know where else I'd go.'

'What if they know about me? This is the Begijnhof. It's for women. I can have you here for a little while as my guest. I'll tell them you're my . . . cousin. That's it.'

Another wipe of her face with her sleeve. This place was a sanctuary of a kind. A prison almost, but a gentle one. Suzi lived in the Houten Huys, the wooden one, split into apartments like the others. A sign on the door said it dated back to the beginning of the sixteenth century. Jansen saw it on the way in and wondered what Amsterdam was like in those days. How different really.

'When will they bury her?' she asked. 'May I go?'

'I don't know. It depends on the case. If Pieter

Vos was in charge like I asked then maybe . . . not long. He's a decent man.' Jansen remembered the look on Vos's face when they argued. 'He knows this kind of pain. But that bastard Mulder . . .'

'Why? Why Rosie?' she asked and that he found the hardest question of all.

After a while Jansen hung his head, rubbed his own eyes, said, 'I can't imagine. Me? Fair game. Why not?' He pushed the coffee aside and wished she kept a bottle of jenever. 'Rosie was never a part of the business.'

She stared at him.

'Not much anyway,' he added.

It was impossible to explain. To apologize. To do anything except quietly set about an act that would appal this woman, someone he'd once loved. The idea of vengeance would have been beyond her even when they were together. Now, in the quiet sanctity of the Begijnhof where she prayed twice a day . . .

'I won't stay long,' he promised.

'Where will you go?'

'Maarten. Remember him?' Jansen rubbed his cropped skull. 'He's a barber now. I set him up in the shop when he wanted out of the business. Pretty good. He can talk to some people. They'll scoot me out of the city. If I get a passport from somewhere we can drive down to Spain. I've got a villa there.'

He tried to smile at her.

'You could come and see me if you like. It's near Malaga.'

Her face was stony and full of doubt.

Jansen said, 'I was going to do that with Rosie when they set me free. We'd agreed. It was what I told the judge. I gave up everything.' He saluted, like a Boy Scout. 'I became a good boy, finally.'

'Then why did you escape, Theo?'

She always was this sharp, while time and prison had blunted his own innate cunning.

'Because if they put me back in Bijlmerbajes Jimmy Menzo's going to kill me there instead.'

That cold, judgemental stare. The one that said: *liar.* Now he remembered why they'd fallen apart, not noisily, not with ill-feeling. It was over a simple and mutual lack of trust.

'What do you want of me?' she asked.

'A bed for a couple of nights. A beer or three . . .'

She laughed at that and the sight cheered him.

'Some fresh herring and sausage. And cheese. And . . .' He got up and kissed her hair again. '. . . your company.'

The sudden tears formed two shining rivulets down her pale cheeks. He wished they weren't there, that there was something he could do.

'God knows I've missed that and I wish Rosie were here to enjoy it too.'

'Beer and herring,' she said getting up. 'I've got the cheese.'

She looked stiff. Old. Not ugly old like him. Good old. A different kind of beauty, more impressive by far than the eye-catching, flirtatious allure that first trapped him.

'I'll do what I can,' she said, and reached out and touched his bristly chin. 'You look nice without that stupid beard and hippie hair. Like a new man.'

'I'm glad to hear it.'

'But you're not, are you, Theo? New?'

He glanced out of the window, trying to avoid her eye.

'I've got to see Maarten later. About money and that passport.'

She nodded, expecting this.

'I won't involve you,' he promised. 'I won't do anything to bring trouble to your door.' He thought about this and knew he meant it. 'Lord knows I've done that enough already and I don't deserve your forgiveness. Do I?'

'No,' she agreed as she went for her coat, picked up her purse, looked through the money in it. 'But then if you only forgive the worthy . . . what's the point?'

CHAPTER 13

Van der Berg turned up with the forensic team. A heavyset man of forty-five with a pock-marked face and fading salt and pepper hair. He smelled of aftershave strong enough to cover the fragrance of beer to come. An old and unsuccessful trick.

'Crazy out there,' the detective said after they put on white bunny suits. 'Theo Jansen back on the streets.' They were in the first-floor room with the double bed, the chandelier, the sheets and towels. Everything pink and smoke-stained. 'All this . . . What the hell's going on?'

Vos asked how Jansen got out.

'Theo was on his own,' the detective said. 'Hit some uniformed kid in the toilet. Got his gun.'

The forensic team were taking photographs. Vos turned to the team leader, pointed at the bare floorboards and said, 'Forget about pictures for now. I want luminol.'

Then he went to the high window and started to draw the heavy curtain.

'It's a little early for that,' the forensic man replied.

'Katja Prins could still be alive. I don't have time.'

The officer in the white suit looked ready to argue then thought better of it.

'Let's do this properly then,' he said.

He opened up the curtain. Talked to his team. Told the three cops to wait outside while they went about their work.

On the landing Van der Berg handed over the report Vos had asked for earlier.

'Did you look at it?' Vos asked.

'Why would I do that?'

Vos shrugged, went into a corner, began to read.

They watched him. Watched as he walked downstairs out into the cold, dull day. Lost in something they couldn't begin to guess.

'What was it?' Bakker asked.

'Something he asked for about his kid's case. Technical report. I don't know.' Van der Berg scowled. 'I don't care what Frank de Groot says. Pieter shouldn't be doing this. It nearly killed him before.'

'Do you expect him to sit at home on that stupid boat twiddling his thumbs? Or in the Rijksmuseum staring at a doll's house?'

He glowered at her.

'I went there a couple of times. Tried to get him out of that place. For a beer or something. Do you think that's what he was doing? Looking at a piece of wood?'

'What else?'

The old detective gave her a kindly glance, just short of condescending.

'It wasn't the house he kept staring at. It was the dolls. I don't know if he thought there was some kind of answer there. Or if his girl was like that or something . . .' He leaned against the smoke-stained wall. 'He wouldn't talk to me about it. Look . . . this is fine if it all works out. But what if it doesn't? What if we lose the Prins girl too? And we still don't find out what the hell's going on?'

He had a lugubrious face, one that smiled easily, but not for long. Van der Berg looked at the wall, drew a long line in the smoke dust. Pink wallpaper underneath.

'Something here doesn't feel right.'

'You worked on Anneliese's case?'

'Damned right I did. Every last one of us tried to help there. But this . . .' He moved out of the way as a couple of forensic people walked into the room carrying aerosols and fluorescent tubes. 'The guy before just taunted Pieter. Never asked for anything. Just wanted to make his life hell. She was probably dead all along. We knew that. So did he.'

'He thinks Katja Prins is alive,' Bakker said.

'Yeah. And usually Pieter Vos is right. In the end.' He nodded down the stairs. 'If a dumbo like me gets an inkling this isn't the same he knows it. Knows a lot more than he's saying too. He always used to drive us nuts with that.'

Bakker went downstairs and found him outside seated on the wall, a cigarette in hand.

'I didn't know you smoked,' she said. 'Ordinary stuff anyway.'

His eyes were glassy. She wondered about him.

'I don't,' Vos said and threw the thing into the gutter.

'Are you all right?'

He was staring at a report, a single sheet on his lap. Vos put it back into the envelope when she started trying to see.

'Anything I should know?' she asked.

'Til Stamm told us Katja was going to a rehab place. Her father paid. It's called the Yellow House. It's a charity. Regressive therapy. Facing up to things from your past.'

Bakker leaned against the plastic sheeting and the scaffolding on the burned-out front.

'Why would forensic send you a report on a charity?'

'They didn't.' He got out a twenty-euro note. 'There's a really good *friteshuis* round the corner. Get us some chips, will you?' He pulled a puzzled face. 'Which sauce? Which sauce . . .?'

She folded her arms.

'Curry if they have it. Get one for Van der Berg too but he'll want mayonnaise. Something for you. Drinks. I'll have water. Still. Not fizzy. I hate—'

'You hate fizzy.'

'How do you know?'

Laura Bakker looked at the money.

'Just guessing. I don't get it. One minute you treat me almost as an equal. The next I'm like your servant. What is this?'

'Saté,' he said, waving the note. 'Changed my mind. If they do saté I'll have that instead.'

CHAPTER 14

In the office, the two of them at his desk, Prins told Margriet Willemsen about the reporter. She looked unhurried, self-possessed. Almost as if none of it were a surprise at all. Then she took Anna de Vries's business card, glanced at it.

He leaned back in his leather executive chair by the window, trying to feel composed.

'You know her?' she asked.

'The woman's a crime reporter. Why would I know her? What else have you done?'

A young woman police officer had picked up the photos and the ransom note. Prins had kept copies. He'd told her the documents were pushed through the council office letter box some time that morning.

'That's really smart, Wim. The police will want CCTV from the building. When they realize there's no one on it . . . what are you going to say then?'

'Jansen busted out this morning. De Groot's got bigger things to chase.'

She picked up the copies, flicked through the photos, stopped at the one of Katja in her underwear, cowering at someone out of view.

'This could still be her playing a game. What are you going to do?'

'I can just about get the money. If I have to. I want . . .' He put a hand to his temple, felt the pressure there. 'I want Katja back. Maybe this time we can make something work . . .'

'How often have you said that? This de Vries woman . . . has she shown anyone else the video?'

'She said not,' he answered, and wondered how Margriet Willemsen had managed to put him on the defensive so easily.

'Do you believe her?'

He'd already asked himself that question.

'She's ambitious. She wants to cut a deal. They can't write the story anyway, not with De Groot's blackout. If I play along and give her an exclusive at the end then she'll be . . . understanding.'

Willemsen nodded, thinking about this.

'Which means you admit to an affair with me, go back to Liesbeth, hand-in-hand with your daughter, and ask the city's forgiveness?'

'For now . . .'

'While I get labelled the scarlet woman. Marriage breaker. Harlot. Do you think I'll survive that?'

He shook his head.

'I think we can negotiate something . . .'

'She's got a video of us in bed, Wim. Do you honestly think she won't use it?'

He didn't have an answer.

Margriet Willemsen took out her phone, made a call to Alex Hendriks. When she finished she looked at Prins and said, 'Listen to me. We can both survive this. Come out stronger maybe. But you've got to trust me. You've got to do what I say. Go along with everything that happens now. I wasn't going to raise this today. But I guess this bitch from the paper's forced our hand.'

He wanted to laugh. But he couldn't. Something was slipping away from him here.

She looked at her watch. Didn't speak until Hendriks turned up. With him was Danny Smit, deputy leader of Prins's Progressive group, a nervous, skinny young accountant from the suburbs. Too shy and too stupid to do anything unless he was told.

'Danny,' Prins said as they sat down. 'Alex. What is this?'

Willemsen stared at him.

'I took Danny into our confidence. About Katja and the police investigation.'

'Thank you,' he said.

'You've been under a lot of pressure over De Nachtwacht. That's been obvious to all of us,' she went on. 'Hasn't it?'

Smit nodded obediently.

'Now . . . with the police investigation . . .'

Prins was getting the message.

'Wait a minute. You can't have these discussions without me—'

'We can,' Hendriks broke in. 'And we must. You have responsibilities to your family. We all understand that. But we have duties to the council too. It's important to bring down the shutter on this before it goes too far, Wim. We've all come to realize that over the last twenty-four hours.'

A red flame flickered at the back of Prins's head. He pointed at Willemsen.

'She was trying to get me to fire you only yesterday. What the—?'

'I don't remember that conversation,' Willemsen interrupted. 'Where did it happen? When?'

Prins closed his eyes and laughed.

'Oh for God's sake. Is this a palace coup or something?'

Hendriks had a document folder with him. He pulled out a sheet of paper, placed it on the desk.

'It's for the best,' Willemsen insisted. 'You stand down from the vice-mayor's office for personal reasons. You keep your seat. You can focus on your family. When things are settled there, come back. We'll find you a good place . . .'

'And De Nachtwacht?'

Danny Smit finally found his voice.

'The consensus in the group is that perhaps we went a little too far. The ideas you were pursuing were more ambitious than we originally agreed.'

'Who got to you, Danny?' Prins snarled. 'Menzo? Jansen? Some other cheating crook who's flooding De Wallen with whores and dope pedlars?'

Smit bridled at that.

'This is for your benefit too. We all think it's best you stand aside for a while. Margriet will take the presidency.'

Prins laughed out loud.

'I'll be the new deputy,' Smit added. 'Then, after six months, when I've got the experience, I'll take the presidency in turn. Unless you're well enough to come back.'

'You think?' Prins demanded.

Smit looked offended.

'You should consider your family. We are.'

Hendriks pushed the sheet of paper closer.

'It's a formality,' he said. 'The decision's already made. We don't need your signature. It's in everyone's interest there's no fuss. De Groot's expecting you in Marnixstraat. That's where you should be. We'll all be thinking of you. Praying—'

'Fuck you,' Prins snarled. 'Fuck every last one of you.'

'We can give you a little while to collect your things,' Hendriks added.

'No we can't,' Margriet Willemsen said instantly. 'You need to go, Wim. No fuss, please. We'll handle the media from now on.'

They sat there, staring at him.

'I'd rather not call security,' she added after a while. 'Don't make a difficult situation worse.'

He laughed. Got up. Looked at the three of them. Hammered his fist on the chair.

'I want this back.'

She nodded and said, 'There's plenty of time to talk about that later. When things calm down.'

Danny Smit looked as if he was stifling a laugh. Prins didn't say another word, just walked quickly from the room.

A long silence.

'Do I get your office now?' Smit asked. 'Today?'

She walked over and took the big leather chair by the window. Revolved in it once.

'No. Tomorrow. You can leave too.' Smit thought about arguing then got up. So did Hendriks. 'Not you, Alex.'

Margriet Willemsen waited till the young politician had left the room.

'I didn't realize we were going to spring this on him so soon,' Hendriks said. 'I thought he might have fought a bit more.'

'Did you?'

She was rummaging around her briefcase.

'What do you want to do about his diary events?' he asked. 'The meetings on De Nachtwacht. The traders. The unions. You want me to cancel?'

'I'll deal with them. It's business as usual. Make sure everyone knows. Wim's taking temporary leave on compassionate, family grounds. That's the story.'

He'd got his iPad out, was checking his messages as she spoke.

'You do love your toys, don't you?' she said with a smile.

Hendriks laughed.

'Yeah. I guess.'

She pulled out the little video camera she'd found in the bedroom.

'What about this? How do you rate that one?'

He picked up the little black gadget, turned it round in his hands.

Alex Hendriks hesitated for a moment. Looked at her. Grinned.

'Pretty good actually,' he said. 'What do you think?'

CHAPTER 15

Outside the Poppenhuis in white forensic bunny suits. Eating frites and sauce out of paper cones.

Van der Berg kept eyeing the bar across the canal. He glanced at Vos who said, 'Not a chance.'

So when they finished the detective took their cones and napkins, deposited them in a bin, then lit a cigarette. He didn't take much notice of Bakker as she waved away the smoke.

'Good frites, Vos,' she said.

He shrugged.

'There are better. Now Vleminckx Sausmeesters if you can be bothered to queue . . .'

'I don't really want to talk about chips. What are we waiting for?'

'Waiting,' Van der Berg said. 'What would life be without it?'

'More interesting?' she asked.

He laughed.

'Anticipation, kid. Learn to appreciate it.'

'I'm waiting for the crack about cows,' she added.

'Cows?' Van der Berg asked, puzzled.

'Never mind . . .'

A forensic officer came outside and told them it was time.

'Stay back,' Vos ordered. 'Watch. Do as they say.'

They returned to the first-floor room. A couple of officers held heavy plastic sheeting close to the curtain to keep out all the light. Three more held fluorescent tubes, turned off. The head man had a camera in each hand, one still, one video. He nodded. The sheeting went up. The tubes came on.

'Thirty seconds,' Van der Berg said. 'A minute. That's all if there's something here.'

The tubes turned to the floorboards at the back. Nothing.

Then the centre. Nothing.

By the front, beneath the small window a small patch of blue became visible. The cameras pounced on it.

'Boss,' someone said.

'Working,' the camera man answered.

'You need to see this.'

Vos walked towards them. On the wall was a bigger splash of blue.

'Good,' the one with the cameras said as he got there, firing with both lenses.

Bright blue. Livid blue. Almost alive underneath the fluorescent tubes.

Vos stood by them as they worked.

'Not much,' the head forensic officer said. 'Could just be a fight. Someone getting beaten up. An accident even.'

Kept filming, snapping. The men with the fluorescents in their hands padded round it, held out the tubes like weapons.

No more blue stains and the ones they had were fading.

The head forensic man turned to Vos and said, 'I told you we should have done this my way. It's all out of order.'

He handed the cameras over to one of his minions then asked for the plastic sheeting to be taken down from the window.

A long silence. Then he added, 'This is old. It can't be the Prins girl. Can't be anyone recent. I don't think this room's been used in a few years.'

'A few months short of three,' Vos said. 'The Thai woman told us that. She was on holiday. When she came back the place was closed and she didn't even think about reopening it.' A pause. 'That was August. When . . .'

He didn't need to say it.

'We can get DNA,' the man insisted. 'I'll make it a priority. As soon as I can run it through the lab you'll know.'

'DNA,' Vos murmured. 'Fine.'

He went downstairs, walked outside, looked at his phone, checked for messages. Found none.

Van der Berg followed. A couple of pigeons eyed them from the pavement as Bakker turned up, scribbling in her notepad.

'You should pull out of this, Pieter,' Van der Berg said. 'It's getting too close. There. I said it.'

216

'Katja Prins is missing.'

'Is that all you're looking for?'

Bakker watched him, waiting for an answer.

'She's out there somewhere,' Vos said.

'Can't see anything that ties her to this place,' Van der Berg pointed out. 'Can you?'

'No,' Vos agreed. He looked at Bakker. 'So what do we do?'

'We go back to Warmoesstraat,' she suggested. 'That's the last place anyone saw her. And that kid. Til Stamm.'

'Why?' Vos asked.

'There was something wrong there,' she said. 'I told you. She was lying to us.'

Vos's phone rang. They went quiet as he listened to De Groot's voice booming out of the earpiece.

'Warmoesstraat can wait,' he said when he was finished.

CHAPTER 16

Margriet Willemsen laughed and realized Hendriks was enjoying this. So maybe she should too.

'I think you should put your toys away now, Alex. We've better things to do.'

Hendriks shrugged, scooped up his phones and tablet, put them in his case.

'How long was it there?'

'Does that matter?' he asked.

'Yes.'

'Long enough. Look . . .'

He got up, went to the window. She came and joined him.

'What Prins wanted was crazy,' he said. 'People were going to get hurt. For no good reason. You can't wind back the clock. I just wanted some ammunition. I don't intend to use it.'

'What the hell are you talking about?'

'What matters is . . .' He nodded at the grey city beyond the glass. 'What's out there. People. Our people. Clean up a little. I'll help you. But we're not the Taliban. Let's not get too judgemental.' A weak smile. 'That wouldn't fit either of us.'

She raised a finger to his calm, bloodless face.

'There's a video out there already,' she said. 'That reporter's got a copy of him and me from yesterday.'

Hendriks screwed up his eyes and said, 'That's not possible.'

'She's got it. Wim saw it.'

He went white.

'I never sent anything to anyone. If Wim kept on with this nonsense . . . if he tried to fire me . . . I was going to let him know then. I didn't—'

'No, no,' she cut in. 'Don't screw around. I want the truth. The reporter . . .'

'What reporter?' he asked.

She was getting cross.

'Anna de Vries. The woman was in here earlier. She had the video. Wim saw it on her iPad.'

Hendriks seemed astonished.

'It didn't come from me. I don't want that out there.'

Willemsen went back to the big leather chair, sat down, told him to take the seat opposite. Picked up the little spy camera, threw it in his lap.

'I want you to delete everything you've got.'

'Sure, sure. But . . .' Hendriks looked scared. 'Truthfully, Margriet. I don't understand this. How can it have got out? Are they going to run something?'

'There's a blackout, isn't there? Because of the daughter. Once that's over . . .' She scribbled something on the notepad in front of her. 'I'll deal with it. Just do what I ask.'

Hendriks was getting nervy.

'I can testify he came onto you if you like. Make you look a victim.'

Willemsen's eyes narrowed.

'Does a victim deserve to run this city?'

No answer.

'I told you,' she said. 'I'll deal with it. Just . . .' Her hand cut the air. '. . . get rid of everything you have.'

CHAPTER 17

Hendriks went down the hall to his office, checked with his PA, got the reporter's name, returned to his desk, looked her up on the Web.

Anna de Vries. Twenty-eight. Crime hack with one of the Amsterdam dailies. No contacts with city hall that he could see. No interest in local politics at all.

He kept all his private material in a cloud account, accessible from anywhere. Music, documents, photos. There were just two worthwhile video files he'd got from Margriet Willemsen's bedroom. One clearly Prins from the day before. The other, the previous week . . . he didn't know. That time it was later and they came in with the lights off. No easy way to tell in the dark. It didn't look like Prins but he wasn't sure.

Hendriks could work computers. The cloud account kept an access log. A text file in the root folder. He looked round the office. Just the PA. There'd been a temp, a scruffy young girl sent along by the work placement people. But she wasn't around.

He found the log, opened it.

There should have been just three IP addresses, his work PC, his home iMac and the mobile account used for his iPad and phone. Hendriks was looking at a fourth. He copied the number, pasted it into an IP look-up site. One of the big telecoms outfits. A company millions of households used for phone and Internet access.

But not him.

He'd been hacked.

With shaking fingers Hendriks deleted everything in the account then went into the trash and removed it all permanently.

Tried to get this straight in his head.

No one had been inside his apartment recently. He hadn't lost a phone in years. Logic dictated that the only insecure place anyone could steal his password was here, in the office. From the desk of the head of the council's general office, a place he regarded – perhaps stupidly – as secure, private, safe.

Sometimes he didn't log off the city hall system at all. Even though it offered, for someone who knew it, a way into that private store of information.

The PA had been there for years. A dull, loyal, obedient servant of the council.

Then there was the scruffy temp. She'd come into the office two weeks before, sent by a charity looking to give her work experience. Turned up sporadically. He'd have sent her packing if it wouldn't have looked bad.

Hendriks got up and walked over to the PA.

'What happened to that girl we had in as a favour?'

She laughed.

'Oh, you mean Til?'

'That was her name?'

'Til Stamm. She came from Limburg. Couldn't you tell?'

Hendriks shook his head.

'I didn't talk to her much. Where is she?'

The woman smiled, shrugged.

'Who knows? She never came back from lunch.'

'Do we have an address for her?'

She tapped the keyboard, found something, printed it out.

'I'm going out for a while,' Hendriks told her. 'Probably the rest of the day.'

'The press office say they're putting out that release about Prins,' she said.

He got his coat and his case.

'The statement's all they get,' he said. 'No interviews. Not another word.'

CHAPTER 18

The barber lived in a tiny ground-floor apartment behind his shop. There was a door out into the alley at the back. Jansen was able to leave Suzi's tall timber house in the Begijnhof, walk out of one of the side gates and scuttle to Maarten's mostly in shadow.

Not that he was worried too much about his appearance. Without the white beard and the long hair no one would recognize him easily. He'd gained weight in prison. A bigger paunch, the muscles softened because he didn't feel confident enough to use the exercise facilities. Jail had been a solitary, deadening experience. He didn't want to go back.

And anyway there was work to do. You're not a new man. Suzi had said that, and as usual she was right.

It was closing on six when he knocked on the back door of Maarten's block. The barber turned up smoking a cigarette. He'd put a notice on the front window: *Closed Due to Illness*. Had spent the rest of the afternoon making quiet calls, assembling the things Jansen had asked for: phones, money, a weapon. And a passport. Belgian with a blank space for the photograph.

The first thing he did when Jansen arrived was offer him a beer. The second was take his picture with a small digital camera.

'I'll get that back tonight,' he said, taking out the memory card, putting it in an envelope with the passport. 'You just have to say when you want to go.'

Jansen slapped him on the arm.

'I'll see you right on all this.'

The barber shook his head.

'You don't need to do a damned thing. What happened to Rosie . . . Jesus. I still can't believe it. You're sure it was Menzo?'

'Who else? Who'd dare?' He looked at the stubby handgun on the table, two boxes of shells next to it. 'What's this? A kid's toy?'

Maarten chuckled.

'Yeah. I wondered about that too. First thing that came to hand. Beretta nine thousand.' He took out the magazine, loaded it with bullets. 'Twelve shots.' Retrieved two spare magazines from his pocket. 'The guy said to watch for the sight catching on your pocket when you take it out. Apart from that it's a good weapon.'

Jansen picked up the handgun, felt the weight.

'It's a really long time since you did street stuff, Theo. Why not leave it to someone else?'

'Not for this,' Jansen said. 'What do we know?'

Maarten had been under strict instructions. Talk

only to people he could trust. That applied to every-one. Especially those they paid within the police.

'Menzo flew down to Ostend yesterday. Setting up an alibi.'

'Who with?'

'That black woman of his. The girlfriend. Miriam Smith. One among many. But he seems sweet on her. She runs things when he's out of town.'

'And?'

'The cops are chasing Wim Prins's kid. They're not sure whether she's jerking Prins around or not. Word is he's got a ransom note. Half a million euros. Vos is handling it. Mulder's still on Rosie's case.' A pause. 'And yours now.'

'Mulder,' Jansen grunted. He could picture the tall cop, grinning slyly in court as all the lies he'd fed Jaap Zeeger got rolled out as truth.

'They're waiting on Menzo getting back. They don't have enough to arrest him in Ostend.'

'Lindeman . . .'

'He says . . .'

The barber licked his lips. Nervous.

'He says what?' Jansen asked.

'He says you screwed up. They were going to let you out anyway if you'd just waited a day or two. This De Nachtwacht crap Prins was trying to bring in won't happen. It's on the news. Prins has stood down from the council. Personal reasons. He thinks he's coming back. He's wrong. Lindeman seemed to know a lot about that. Not that he was going to tell me.'

The barber went to the fridge for more beer. Jansen shook his head and got up to make himself a coffee instead.

'See if you can get me a number for Vos,' Jansen said. 'We may need to talk.'

The barber scribbled that down.

'He's been at that place on the Prinsen. The one we used as a privehuis.'

'Jesus, Maarten. Am I expected to remember every last piece of property I own in this city?'

The barber shrugged.

'I guess not. We kept that one off-limits. Gave the money to some Thai hooker, put it through her.'

'I didn't even know we had a privehuis there. What's this got to do with anything?' Jansen asked.

'Maybe nothing I guess. It's not ours any more. Seems Menzo muscled in there. Got her on his side. It had been closed for a while. With you getting arrested I don't think anyone was watching too closely. If you like I could . . .'

Jansen waved him down.

'What's that to me? A stinking privehuis. I've got enough money to buy a million of them.'

'Yeah well. Vos is interested in it for some reason. The Doll's House. That's what we used to call it. Ring a bell?'

The big man sat down, looked at the barber across the table.

'Dolls?'

'You never went there?'

227

'I told you. I didn't know I had the damned place.'
Maarten the barber wriggled on his seat.

'You?' Jansen asked.

'Just the once.' He grimaced. 'They were kids. It wasn't our kind of thing.'

'Who was running the Thai woman?'

'Not me,' Maarten said quickly. 'I didn't like to ask.' He hesitated. 'It got really rough when you went inside, Theo. It was a war and we were losing.'

Before Jansen could say anything the barber's mobile rang. He glanced at the number, nodded towards Jansen, said, 'Yeah?'

Short conversation.

'Menzo's plane's due in Lelystad at seven,' Maarten said when it was over. 'Probably back here an hour after. He mainly uses a place of his near the station.'

Jansen gripped the gun again, turned it in his hand.

'How many people know I'm here?' he asked.

'Nobody. I told everyone you were hiding out somewhere I didn't know. Just calling me when you needed something.' He laughed. 'It's true, isn't it?'

The magazine went in easily, came out the same way. He could see the sight was prominent. Jansen put the Beretta in his trouser pocket, pulled it out, practised getting the stocky weapon free in one clean movement.

'You want help?' the barber asked without much enthusiasm.

'I want transport,' Theo Jansen said.

CHAPTER 19

Vos sent Van der Berg to question the Thai woman. Then he and Bakker went to De Groot's office. Prins was there with Liesbeth. The politician's welcome, coffee and biscuits on the desk. No one touched them.

Frank de Groot stood over a clear plastic envelope next to the cups.

Vos went and read it, Bakker not far behind. Then flicked through the photographs in their transparent sleeves.

'Are they real?' De Groot asked.

'It's Katja,' Prins said. 'What do we do?'

'You get the money!' Liesbeth barked at him.

They all waited.

'I'll get the money,' Prins agreed. 'I've stepped down from the council . . .' He put a nervous hand to his head. 'Just until this is over.'

Puzzled, Vos asked, 'Why did you do that?'

'It seemed best,' Prins muttered. He pointed at the note and the pictures. 'Is she making this up or not?'

'What do you think?' Vos asked.

All eyes were on Prins at that moment.

'I think she hates me. I don't know why.'

Nothing more.

'They've asked for money,' Vos said. 'They'll come to you with a time and a place. We need to know.'

'Of course,' Prins agreed.

'So what else are you doing?' Liesbeth demanded. 'Apart from letting criminals go.'

'Theo Jansen was going to be free anyway,' Vos replied. 'At least when we get hold of him this time he'll stay in jail. For something he actually did.'

Back to Prins.

'Is there anything else you can think of that might help us?' he asked. 'Anything you've noticed?'

'Such as?'

'I don't know. Somebody acting strangely. Someone in the office.' He looked at the note on the desk, moved the clear plastic across the wooden surface. 'An odd email maybe.'

The politician stiffened.

'No. Is that it? Can we go now?'

'If you like,' Vos replied.

'What are you doing, Pieter?' Liesbeth asked again.

'I told you. We're working.' He looked at Prins again and said, 'Have you picked up any personal email today?'

'I've been in the office. Too busy. Why?'

Vos went round the desk, sat in De Groot's chair, brought the computer to life. Took the USB stick out of his pocket.

'Thing is . . . I've got a confession. I came round

to see Liesbeth this morning. When she was out of the room I took a look at your computer. There was a message there.' An amused frown. 'I wouldn't normally have looked. But it came from someone called Pop Meester. Which made me curious. You know the name?'

Prins blinked.

'You read my email? That's illegal.'

Vos waved a hand and said, 'Lots of things are. Your daughter's missing. The case seems to be connected with dolls. Someone called Pop Meester sends you a message.' He smiled at Liesbeth. 'You want me to do something. Does it matter?'

'What did it say?' De Groot asked.

'Nothing,' Vos said. 'Nothing at all. There was just this.'

He slotted the stick into the computer, found the file. Hit the keyboard.

A video came up. They all crowded round to see.

A dark room, two shapes moving, one over the other. Sounds. Bed springs, creak of wood, sighs.

'That's not me,' Prins cried. 'That's not me!'

Margriet Willemsen naked over a barely seen figure beneath her. Breasts rocking with the slow rhythm. Soft, almost inaudible sighs. Then a final low grunt and she fell on him, laughing. The picture froze. End of clip.

'Pop Meester,' Vos said. 'The Doll Master. I asked you if you knew the name. You didn't answer.'

'I don't know the damned name!' Prins yelled. 'That's not me.'

231

'I never said it was, did I?' Vos pointed to the screen. 'According to the file date this was five days ago. Eight in the evening. You were at a convention in Rotterdam then. I checked. Though you can fake these dates.' He took the stick out of the computer, gave it to Bakker, told her to pass it on to forensic and see if they could bring up more detail. 'It's Margriet Willemsen obviously. Who the man is . . . I couldn't see. Maybe they can work on it. Why they'd send it to you . . .'

Prins was sweating. Looking round the room.

'This is to do with De Nachtwacht, isn't it?' he said. 'Ever since I said I'd go for those bastards they've been gunning for me. You!' He stabbed a finger at De Groot. 'You're supposed to protect us from this.'

Bakker took the note and the USB stick and walked out of the door.

'You're going to get the money?' Vos asked.

'I said I would.'

'Keep it in the bank until I say. Any more questions?'

Even Liesbeth was out of them at that point. The two of them left. Frank de Groot delivered a short lecture about what was and wasn't allowed.

'Dammit, Pieter. I could fire you for that. You could wind up in court.'

Vos pulled out his ID, placed it on the desk.

'All yours,' he said.

De Groot pushed the card back to him.

'Don't be so stupid next time.'

'Why am I doing this?' Vos asked. 'What's the point?'

'The point is I need you,' the commissaris said. 'Isn't that enough?'

'Not really. You've got Mulder.'

'Mulder's busy chasing Jansen and whoever killed his daughter! I don't have the people . . .'

There was something De Groot didn't want to say.

'Come on,' Vos pleaded. 'Out with it, Frank. You don't do shifty well.'

'I got a call from the privehuis just before you got here. Forensic thought I needed to be told first.'

Vos waited. When De Groot didn't go on he said, 'There's nothing there that connects Katja Prins to the place. Theo Jansen put up the money to start it. My guess is Menzo seized it some time after you put Jansen in jail. There's someone's blood there. I don't know but I think it was Anneliese. The DNA . . .'

'They found her bus pass under the floorboards. Her picture. Her signature.'

Vos sat down, closed his eyes.

'It's definitely her,' De Groot added. 'They got a sample back and ran it through the lab straight away. Seems they had Anneliese's DNA records out already for some reason.' De Groot reached out and put his hand on Vos's shoulder. 'I'm sorry, Pieter.'

Vos nodded.

'There wasn't a lot of blood,' he said. 'It doesn't mean . . .' This sounded stupid, but real too. 'It doesn't mean she's dead.'

De Groot sighed.

'When do you want to tell Liesbeth?'

'Not now. What the hell was she doing in a place like that?'

'Sixteen,' De Groot said. 'You don't own them. You don't follow them round every minute of the day, do you?'

'I guess not,' Vos agreed.

Bakker was waiting for him in the corridor.

'There's something you need to know—'

'If it's about the bus pass . . .'

'What bus pass? Jimmy Menzo. His plane just landed at Lelystad.'

Forty-five minutes, an hour back into the city. Menzo lived in a block almost opposite Centraal station. A conspicuous crook these days.

'Van der Berg can check out the privehuis,' he said. 'Let's look at Warmoesstraat on the way.'

CHAPTER 20

Jimmy Menzo parked his Beechcraft in the general aviation airfield hangar at Lelystad. Walked out through the minimal security with Miriam Smith carrying their overnight case.

No one there. Not a single cop. He hadn't been expecting that. They had to be waiting for him in the city.

Light rain falling from a flat sky. They went to the silver Mercedes saloon, didn't speak. There was a rule, one they always obeyed on breaks like these. Business and pleasure didn't mix. No unnecessary phone calls. Only good food, good wine. And whatever else he felt like. They didn't talk about Amsterdam or Theo Jansen, didn't watch the TV. Didn't do anything much except drink and smoke and screw once he'd dealt with the Surinamese kids, patching the call through to the sister in De Wallen.

She'd been dealt with now too. He liked to think himself a patient man, never rushed into things. He wanted time to think.

The Mercedes was in heavy evening traffic, fifteen minutes from home, when Miriam Smith finally flicked through the news headlines on her phone.

'What is it?' Menzo asked when she whispered a low curse.

'Jansen's on the loose,' she said. 'They wouldn't let him free so he broke out. You shouldn't have told everyone to leave us alone.'

'I get a life too sometimes,' he snapped.

He turned the radio from the rock station straight away. Caught the news midway through. Theo Jansen, one-time Amsterdam gang lord, missing after escaping from a van taking him back to prison. Then a brief account of his daughter's murder, how her body was found in a dinghy on the Prinsengracht near the houseboat of a former police officer, not long after the attempt on Jansen's life.

Menzo listened, turned off the radio when the item was finished. He was shaking his head, half-laughing to himself.

'It helps if I know about things, Jimmy,' she said in a tense West Indian drawl. 'Being kept in the dark pisses me off. Especially when there's a war coming.'

The line of cars had slowed to a crawl. The air conditioning made the interior of the Mercedes so cold he could feel his shirt clinging to his skin. Menzo liked that. As a kid in Paramaribo he'd spent too many long and sleepless nights sweating in the tropical heat.

'He's going to be mad,' she said.

'No,' Menzo told her. 'He's going to run. Theo's not stupid. He understands when he's lost. They own some property in Spain. Florida too. He'll go. And you know what?'

He put a finger to his mouth. She knew the gesture, lit him a cigarette, passed it over. Menzo took a long draw then moved it to his right hand.

'I won't chase him,' he said. 'Retired's as good as dead.'

She folded her strong arms, leaned back in the seat, took a long breath. This was as close to mad as she got.

'What's it now?' he asked.

'All this time you've spent fighting that old bastard. And you still don't understand him.'

An ice-blue Beetle cut in front. Menzo hammered on the horn, shook his fist. Got a look back and an apologetic wave.

'Tell me,' he said.

'You killed his kid!' she cried.

They were getting close to the city edge. If the traffic stayed this way they'd be outside the apartment block soon. He could call out for something to eat. Open a bottle of wine. Stay quiet, stay close for a couple of days.

The law would be waiting for them. They surely knew he was back. But there was nothing they could do except ask questions and listen to the silence that followed.

'You killed his daughter,' she said again and stamped her fancy shiny shoes in the footwell.

'That's not in the book. This shit with the Vos guy. Dumping her near his place—'

'For the love of God shut up. I'm trying to think.' She stared at him.

'I'm supposed to know things, Jimmy. If I don't how the hell am I going to deal with all this crap when it goes wrong?'

Nothing more.

'Well?' she asked.

'I was going to ask you about Rosie.' He took the road for the waterfront. Thirty minutes now. No more. 'I thought . . .'

'Thought what?'

'We had a deal,' Menzo told her. 'Me and Rosie. We got on fine. I'd done some business with her before. We met up last week. All agreed. If she could get Jansen out of jail, make him go away, take that place in Spain. That was the end of it.'

She slammed her palms on the dashboard.

'You never told me.'

'What was the point?' Menzo asked, getting loud, getting angry. 'She was game. But then . . .' He'd thought it through carefully at the time. Wished it might have worked. But Jansen wasn't the kind to give up. 'Theo was never going to play. I couldn't risk it.'

'You never told me!'

A white Ford van had appeared behind, came so close to his back bumper he couldn't even see who was behind the wheel.

'Who the fuck are you, Miriam? A jumped-up

hooker who does what she's told. Cut the mouth or I'll stick you back running a privehuis in Utrecht. If you're lucky.'

She stretched out in the seat, shook her head.

He didn't find it easy driving and thinking at the same time.

'You mean you didn't fix Rosie?' Menzo asked. 'A little present on the side or something?'

'I don't go around killing women. Not without a reason.'

Menzo wound down the window, threw the cigarette out into the busy street. Popped open the glove compartment on his side. Walther PPS in there, brand new, plenty of shells.

'Then who the hell did?' he wondered.

And another thought.

'And why are they trying to bring Vos back into this shit? I don't want him around. Not again.'

Miriam Smith didn't answer. She looked scared and it had been a long time since he'd seen that.

Menzo thought for a moment. Hit the right indicator.

'Where are you going?' she asked.

'Back to Lelystad,' he said. 'Time for a holiday. Croatia maybe. Cyprus.'

The road had opened up. Four lanes, two in each direction. They weren't supposed to turn. But there were no traffic cops nearby.

Menzo edged the Mercedes out ready to swing round.

That was when the white van hit, hard and loud,

sending them bouncing out of their seats, the safety belts seizing with the impact.

Another sound. One he knew too well. The glass shattered around them. Something hurtled past his ear.

Jimmy Menzo punched through the broken windscreen until he could see clearly, floored the pedal, brought the Mercedes screaming round a hundred and eighty degrees, fighting to get clear of the van behind.

Far enough away he could see the front. Two men there, one driving, one, bald, with a ruddy face, angry and determined, hanging out of the window, gun in hand.

The saloon spun on the greasy road, back end wheeling round, smashing hard into a motorbike coming the other way. Menzo dampened the sideways roll, got back some control. Saw the road back out to Lelystad, middling night traffic, few gaps.

The white van was making a U-turn too, trying to follow them.

It was Theo Jansen in the passenger seat. Different looking. Madder than he'd ever seen.

Menzo pulled into the outside lane and floored the pedal again.

CHAPTER 21

Six streets from the office to her little apartment near Spui square. Anna de Vries walked through the busy city, distracted. The meeting with Prins hadn't gone well. Now he was standing down from office. That was a political tale. She didn't stand a chance of getting near it.

Waiting wasn't supposed to be part of the job. A story landed. A story got written. Then you moved on to the next. But what she'd told Prins that afternoon was true: her options were limited. Every newspaper, radio and TV station, every news website in Holland had been contacted by Marnixstraat and offered a simple choice: agree to a news blackout on the Prins girl's kidnapping or face the consequences. With a gang war breaking out in the city no one wanted to catch the blame for an innocent death. Not that Katja Prins wore the label 'innocent' easily. De Vries had gone through enough of the cuttings in the digital library to understand she'd had plenty of contact with the police over the last two years, and never wound up in court.

Influence. Wim Prins possessed it when he was

a leading criminal lawyer. As vice-mayor of the council . . .

The time would come. It was a question of being patient. However she worked the Prins story when it broke – whether Katja was found alive or not – Wim Prins was going to be destroyed. He could play the repentant father and husband as much as he liked. The video of him in bed with Margriet Willemsen told its own story, one that needed no script.

De Vries stopped in a quiet bar, ordered a sandwich. She lived alone. There was no food in the place. No time to shop. It didn't matter, not with the story she had on her hands, the biggest in years.

As for Margriet Willemsen . . .

The ice queen of the right-wing EU-haters. Aloof, unsmiling, judgemental. Taking her down would be a pleasure. De Vries could hear the applause ringing in her ears already. Maybe there'd be a prize. Even without it . . .

She ordered a small beer and laughed to herself. The man next to her, tall, middle-aged, serious-looking, smiled and offered to buy it.

'I can pay for my own drinks,' she said and looked at him so hard he shrugged and wandered off.

No time for distractions. She'd fought hard to get a job on the paper. Fought even harder to work the crime beat. And the battles were only just beginning.

Halfway through the beer the phone rattled in the pocket of her coat.

De Vries took it out and looked at the screen. One message. Name: *Wim Prins*. It said, *We need to meet. Cafe Singel. 30 minutes.*

A tiny brown bar, just a couple of minutes away, not far from her studio apartment.

It seemed odd that Prins wanted to see her there. Somewhere so public.

This had better be worth it, she texted back.

No answer. Anna de Vries checked in her bag. The iPad was there. She patted it, smiled then set off into the night.

CHAPTER 22

The Mercedes was careering down the main road out to Lelystad, dodging between traffic. Jimmy Menzo kept glancing in the mirror. He'd punched through most of the windscreen in front of him. Cold April air surged through the vehicle, icy rain stabbing at their eyes.

Miriam Smith looked back. The white van was dogging them, swerving through the cars behind, mimicking their movements two, three, four seconds later.

It didn't look as if it was going to give up.

'Gimme the gun,' she said.

Menzo threw the wheel round, slid past a single-decker bus.

On the left a field came up splashed with colour as if a gigantic painter had swept at it from the sky.

Tulips. Red, yellow and purple, growing in bands a quarter of a kilometre wide. They were out of the city, on the way to the airfield. She tried to picture what might happen at Lelystad. There'd be security again. A flight plan for any international journey.

This couldn't go on.

'Gimme the damned gun, Jimmy!' she screamed again.

He scrabbled down, reached into the glove compartment, found the weapon, threw it over, then a box of shells.

She checked the magazine: full. Unhooked her seatbelt. The warning beep went off. She swore, released the catch on her seat, rolled it as near horizontal as she could manage, scrambled towards the back, heels catching on the leather and the belt, legs flying. After a few seconds her knees found purchase, she got into a crouch behind the rear window, looked up.

Found herself clutching for the door handles to stay upright. The gun fell. Shells scattered everywhere, across the leather, into the footwell. The Mercedes was slewing sideways again. Tyres shrieking. Jimmy Menzo swearing and shouting at the wheel.

Her head slammed against the left door. Then Menzo flung the car from side to side again and she banged up against the right.

A brief moment of dizziness. The feeling that none of this could be real. Her skirt had hitched up around her thighs. Her mouth was sore, salt taste of blood leaking behind her lips.

Head down, hands flailing furiously on the floor. Finally her fingers gripped the gun.

She worked her way up, looked through the back window.

The white van seemed stuck to them, the length

of two cars behind. A couple of men behind the windscreen. The one with the gun was Theo Jansen transformed, without the beard and the long white hair. Santa Claus look gone for good. And he wouldn't take his eyes off her.

'Fuck it,' Miriam Smith said then shot straight through the back window.

Shook off her jacket, wrapped her fist in the fabric, tried to punch a gap in the crazed glass.

After a couple of seconds of hard, screaming motion she could just see through.

The white van was still there. Unmarked. Relentless. Charging down at them, past the fields of red and yellow and purple.

'We didn't do it!' she shrieked and knew they couldn't hear.

Another wild shot through the fractured glass. Still they came on.

'We didn't do it,' she whispered and tried to calm herself. Leaned onto the leather of the bench seat very carefully. Took aim. Not Jansen. That wasn't enough.

The driver, she thought, then slowly started to squeeze the trigger, aware from the motion beneath her feet that something was starting to change.

CHAPTER 23

There was no one in the house off Warmoesstraat except the dull and drowsy dope-heads crowded round the bubble pipe in the front room.

Laura Bakker glowered at them and said, 'They call that high?'

Til Stamm was out, Jaap Zeeger still missing.

They poked around anyway, went upstairs, took a closer look at the rooms. De Groot called from Marnixstraat. Every avenue they'd tried with Theo Jansen had failed. Not one of their current informants had a clue where he might be.

'Maybe he's left the city,' the commissaris suggested.

'Do you believe that?' Vos asked, looking round a grimy bathroom, checking the products on the shelves. What looked like enough for one woman only. This was a place run and occupied by men.

'I can hope,' De Groot answered. 'Are you going to see our friend from Surinamese?'

For what it's worth, Vos agreed. They'd got nothing concrete to connect Menzo to Rosie

Jansen's death. Nothing to link him to the attempt on her father's life. Or Katja Prins.

'So why do you want to talk to him?' De Groot asked.

'I want to see his face,' Vos answered and that was the end of the conversation.

They were on the first floor when they heard a voice at the door. A man. Asking for Til Stamm.

Bakker was there first, grabbed hold of him as he turned to leave. Stood in front to block any hope of escape.

Vos came out into the weak sunlight. These April evenings seemed to fade slowly, as if the city didn't want to give up on the day.

'I know you,' he said.

Middle-aged, slight, smart, intellectual. The last person to be sniffing round a drug house in De Wallen.

'Do you?' the man said.

Bakker showed him some ID then asked for his. The card came out slowly.

Alex Hendriks.

'You work for Wim Prins,' Vos said. 'You run the council.'

'I'm an employee. That's all. Prins runs it. Or he did. And will, when he comes back.' Hendriks didn't look in the least worried by their presence. 'What's this about?'

'We're looking for some people. Til Stamm for one. Like you,' Bakker said.

Hendriks came out with the story. The Stamm

girl was a temp in city hall, working for his office as part of a rehab scheme. She hadn't come back from lunch that day.

They waited. That was it.

'Does a big wheel from the city council usually chase people who take a day off?' Bakker asked.

He shook his head at the question.

'This is part of a social programme. We care about these kids. We want them off drugs and into work.' He looked at her, then Vos. 'Don't you?'

Alex Hendriks waited for an answer. Vos's phone rang.

It was De Groot again. Something was happening east of the city. Jimmy Menzo's Mercedes had been reported driving erratically along with a stolen white van. The two vehicles were headed back towards Lelystad.

'Send me a car,' Vos said.

The city hall man was still waiting when he came off the phone.

'If you hear from Til Stamm,' Vos said, 'you'll tell us, won't you?'

'Why do you want to know?' he asked.

Vos thought for a moment then nodded back at the grimy tenement.

'This is the last place anybody saw Katja Prins. Til Stamm knew her.'

It wasn't easy to read the expression on Alex Hendriks's face.

'But you knew that, didn't you?' Vos asked.

'Of course I didn't,' Hendriks said. 'Is that all?'

Two minutes later a white BMW, orange and blue stripes and *Politie* on the side, turned up lights flashing around the corner. Vos and Bakker climbed in the back.

CHAPTER 24

Jimmy Menzo didn't know why he picked this one narrow lane off the highway. Had no idea where it went. It was a farmers' track he realized once he'd careered half a kilometre down and could see the way the tarmac gave way to gravel and then to slippery mud. Nothing more than a passage into the fields and fields of tulips all around them, blooms for the flower market and export, colours that, this close, were just visible in the slow-fading evening light.

It was an idiotic idea. Like going to Ostend when he should have been home taking care of the fallout from what was supposed to be the killer blow, the last death that gave him an iron grip on the criminal heart of Amsterdam.

Everything came to a close. Careers and kingdoms. Lives and little country lanes.

Looming up was a gate that marked the end of the track. A lone tractor in front of it. Too narrow to turn easily, even if there was time. They were heading down a narrow, remote cul-de-sac with no way back.

'Shoot him,' he ordered and didn't look behind.

'Shoot him!' Menzo screamed.

'I'm trying . . .'

Miriam Smith loosed a round through the broken rear window. Metal buckled on the grille of the white van. Steam emerged from somewhere. And still it came on.

'Just . . .' Menzo said to nothing but the remains of the windscreen.

Just what?

Take me out of here, he thought.

Another shot from behind. Another curse. He didn't even remember her using a gun much. Taking aim through a fast-moving window, trying to target the bouncing cab of a van, however close . . .

Not going to happen, Menzo thought, and slung the wheel round hard, slammed his foot on the brake, felt the ABS pump back in protest.

There was a slip lane down into the nearest tulip field. He aimed for it. Aimed well but the Mercedes was travelling so quickly it couldn't stop before the metal gate. The battered saloon burst through, leapt into the air, came belly down amid the sea of blooms then pegged into the bank of an irrigation channel.

A bright scream, a black shape flying past him, bursting through where the windscreen had been. An explosion. The airbags triggered, in front and right of him, the one from the wheel rising into his chest with a blow like a gentle giant's punch.

He could just see Miriam Smith's broken frame bounce on the battered silver bonnet then fly off into the mass of flowers, taking down stems, taking down their pretty heads, rolling somewhere out of view.

Fragrances.

Sweat and blood and diesel. The sweet asthmatic smell of flowers.

Sounds. The airbag wheezing. The car creaking.

Menzo glanced at the mirror, barely able to move. She had the only weapon the car carried. He was trapped, defenceless.

And the white van was there, a smoky wisp of something coming out of the front grille. Two shapes climbing from the cab.

He fought against the airbag and the seatbelt. Gave up.

A face at the window, gun in hand.

'Theo?' Menzo asked, screwing up his eyes.

The man looked so different. Everything that seemed to define him before, the genial beard, the flowing hair, the smile, was gone.

No answer.

'I didn't touch her,' Menzo pleaded. 'Rosie. I wouldn't do that.'

The other one had walked forward into the field of felled tulips. He came back dragging a bloody, mangled body. Opened the back door, threw Miriam Smith's shattered frame onto the bench seat. Menzo looked. Her mouth was open. Her eyes too, but dead and blank.

'Shit,' he muttered, still fighting against the seatbelt.

Theo Jansen popped a bullet through the airbag. The thing burst. The slug disappeared some-where near the pedals. Menzo took a deep, scared breath.

The second guy had gone to the van and returned with something. A plastic carboy. He came back and took off the top.

A familiar smell. Petrol swamping the scent of the field.

'I didn't touch Rosie. I swear—'

Jansen bent down and put a shell through Menzo's right knee. The Surinamese hood screamed in agony. Then the man outside the shattered window crashed a shot into Menzo's left.

Blood and shrieks. A pain so keen it numbed his frightened mind.

The petrol smell was getting worse. Menzo managed to turn his head, saw the second guy shaking the carboy's contents around the cabin of the Mercedes, on Miriam's bent body. On the seats. The carpet.

Finally on him.

'I didn't . . .' Menzo muttered. The world was closing in on him. It stank of fuel and tulips, had the colour of blood and flowers.

Theo Jansen moved away from the door. He stood among the tall blooms lighting a cigarette. The other one threw the carboy onto the passenger seat and moved out of sight.

Jimmy Menzo watched the lighter move up to Theo Jansen's mouth, raise a small red flame there.

Watched him flick the unsmoked cigarette through the air, turning, turning all the way.

CHAPTER 25

Anna de Vries stood in the bar for thirty minutes. Wim Prins didn't show. She texted a return to Prins's summons.

Three words: *Where ARE you?*

Watched the screen. Nothing. This was pathetic. Like waiting on an unfaithful boyfriend. She knew what that felt like too.

De Vries enjoyed being a reporter. It was a job that kept her on her toes. Something new every day, especially since she came on the crime beat. That meant hanging round with curious people. Lawyers. Detectives. Criminals from time to time.

The most interesting thing: if you took away their professions they mostly looked the same. Men seeking something to make them whole. Give a little meaning to their small lives.

And yes, she thought. Always men. Even in the police the women usually stayed away from the harder, bleaker side of the city. Which was where the stories lay and always would.

Another fifteen minutes. Nothing on the phone. Anna de Vries got bored, found a quiet dark corner, took out her iPad. Slyly watched the video that had turned up unannounced in her inbox that morning.

Prins and the Willemsen woman in bed. It looked as if she was in charge there anyway. Finally a woman got to run things, even if it was handing out a little pleasure to the boss.

She turned it off. De Vries had carefully copied the files she'd been sent into her private account then shift-deleted them from the office address. Every local copy was gone. This was hers alone, sent from a fake ID to the newspaper email address printed at the foot of all her stories.

And when the girl was found, one way or another, she'd give Wim Prins a few moments of peace then hit him with the ultimatum: an exclusive revealing everything, the affair, his future, the state of his marriage. Either that or Anna De Vries would take the crueller option, and put the whole thing, video and all, online.

A moment of amusement.

That would happen anyway. Just not from her. Directly.

They got what they asked for in the end.

A look at her watch. Another five minutes gone. The bastard wasn't going to show.

Then her phone squawked and vibrated.

'About time,' Anna de Vries said and looked at the picture message on the screen.

Blinked, trying to understand what she saw.

She knew the young woman staring blankly out from the little screen, pale, drawn, scared.

Had checked her picture in the files. It was Katja Prins.

Underneath a short message.

Can you hear me howling, Pieter? Don't you care?

Fumbling, uncertain fingers. Drink getting in the way. Anna de Vries tapped out a quick reply:

Katja. This is Pieter's friend. I can help. Where are you?

And waited.

CHAPTER 26

Back in the apartment in the tall wooden house in the Begijnhof Theo Jansen headed straight for the shower. He stank of sweat and blood, smoke and flowers. The white van was a burned-out wreck a couple of kilometres from the field where they'd left Menzo. Maarten had fixed fresh transport. That was now in an underground car park in the city, waiting to be found.

She'd looked at him when she first opened the door, said nothing.

Got some towels when he'd asked. Clothes, newly bought that afternoon.

Afterwards Jansen put on the cheap blue chinos, shirt and sweater, bagged the old clothes, slunk into the night, walked out from the quiet courtyard, dodged through the shadows of the street. Found a restaurant waste skip, left them there.

When he got back she asked, 'Do you want something to eat?'

He shook his head, didn't look at her, sat down, turned on the TV.

Nothing on the news except mention of an

incident on the outskirts of the city. A car crash in a remote field. Fatalities.

Jansen turned off the set. It would take a while. The police would be there now. Wondering how to scrape Jimmy Menzo and his girlfriend from what was left of their saloon. In an hour the news would be out.

She brought a beer anyway, sat down on the stool beside him.

After a while she asked, 'Do you feel better now?'

No answer.

'Did this finish something, Theo?'

'You don't know where I've been. What I've been doing,' he said, recalling the way she threw this shit at him back when they were together. 'You never did and never wanted to.'

He stared at her and knew there was no affection in either of them at that moment.

'But you always wanted a piece of what I got, didn't you?'

She didn't blink. Didn't smile or frown. Just scratched the old tattoo on her wrist. Maybe prayer did this to you, he thought. Removed the fury, the passion, the hunger. Put a kind of living death in its place. A sense of acceptance. A quiet and pious admission of defeat.

'Back then I did,' she said finally. 'Not now. I don't want anything. Except . . .' She toyed with her long brown hair. The dye was good. It almost looked natural, the same colour he'd loved when they were both in their twenties. 'I want you to forgive yourself. Even if you can't forgive me. Or anyone else for that matter.'

He told himself he didn't understand a word she said. That they were the ramblings of a Catholic lured back into the fold, swallowed by comforting false promises and fairy-tale illusions.

That locked behind the doors of this small apartment in an old and tall wooden sanctuary called the Houten Huys it would be easy to live on dreams.

'Do you have Skype?' he asked.

Maarten the barber had found the number he'd asked for.

'I call friends in Italy sometimes,' she said and went to a drawer, pulled out a cheap USB phone.

Jansen got up, smiled, put a big hand to her skinny arm.

'I won't be here long. No more than I need.'

'That's what worries me,' she said.

He took the phone and plugged it into the computer. Some tricks he'd learned of late. He would only speak in person to Maarten and leave it to the barber to deal with anyone else. And even Maarten had no idea where he was staying, could communicate only through a single mobile with a ripped-off SIM inside it.

But phones gave you away. The first thing the police did these days, before setting foot outside fearful of the rain, was check the masts and the location of suspicious calls. Not Pieter Vos. That man was different. The others . . .

Jansen wondered if the rest of Marnixstraat had any idea what had happened the day before. How hard they'd tried. Rosie was dead. He was alive and a fugitive. In a way he made a better, an easier target.

Skype wasn't a real phone at all. They could track down which Internet provider was used to place it. Maybe even a city. But nothing more than that, not unless they got hold of the computer itself, and there were ways round that too.

He'd learned those in prison, taught by one of his foot soldiers serving time for a credit card scam.

It was a cheap laptop, recent. Jansen created a new account, logged on, got Skype running, typed in the bogus account details he'd used from time to time back when he was free. Still nine euros in credit. Enough.

Checked the list of numbers Maarten had got him.

The one he wanted was top of the list. Jansen dialled, listened.

A quiet, thoughtful voice, almost young, answered, talking to someone before turning to the phone and saying, 'Yes?'

'This is Theo Jansen, Vos. We need to talk.'

CHAPTER 27

He took the call standing next to Laura Bakker in a floodlit field. Stink of smoke, charred flesh and the faintest scent of flowers. Vos snapped his fingers at her when he heard Jansen's voice, pointed at the phone, mouthed the word, 'Trace.'

Waited a moment then asked, 'Did you get your beer? Too early for the new herring, Theo. Sorry.'

A forensic team was working in the mangled shell of Menzo's Mercedes. In their white plastic suits they looked like busy ghosts flitting through a nightmare made real.

'Don't waste your time,' Jansen said. 'You won't trace me. I'm not that stupid.'

'You broke out yesterday. Chances are we'd have set you free before the end of the week. You tell me.'

A roar down the line. He could see Bakker on the phone to control, talking rapidly.

'If you're going to shout,' Vos said when the volume died down, 'we can end this now. I'm busy. I guess you know that.'

'Busy finding who murdered Rosie?' Jansen asked.

Vos walked away from the car. They were starting to move the bodies. It was messy. There were things he didn't want or need to see.

'No,' he said. 'That's Mulder's job. I thought I made that clear. These are hectic times. They seem to get more—'

'That clown put me in jail! You think he's going to find the bastard who killed my daughter?'

'Mulder's not the only one . . .'

'This morning. All you wanted to talk about was your girl. And the Prins kid. Not me. Not my girl.'

Vos tried to think back, realized that was true.

'I'm sorry. I was preoccupied. I've been out of this for a while. It's not easy.'

Vos put a hand to his hair. It felt too long now. The job was returning with each passing minute. He couldn't try that trick of throwing his ID card at De Groot again. No one would believe him. Any more than he'd believe it himself.

'I'm struggling,' he said and stepped back to let through a team of forensic people lugging two gurneys. Bakker was off the phone, shaking her head. No wonder Jansen was happy to talk. He wasn't going to be tracked through a simple call. 'Aren't you?'

Silence. Maybe Jansen was gone. Bakker came and whispered in his ear.

'Theo?' Vos asked. 'Seems we found a white van burned out a few kilometres away. There's a crew on it now. We've put up alerts at the airports. The border people. Everywhere. You're not getting out of the city . . .'

'Who says I want to leave?'

'We should meet,' Vos continued. 'Just the two of us. I'll buy you a beer. As many as you want. Then we'll call a car. You can bring Michiel Lindeman along if you like. I'll make sure you get somewhere decent in Bijlmerbajes.'

Nothing.

'No one's going to mourn Jimmy Menzo,' Vos added. 'Plenty of people will say you did the city a favour. Maybe Wim Prins.'

'Jimmy took the Prins girl too?'

Vos struggled for an answer.

'I don't think so. I hope not. If he did we're really screwed, aren't we?'

Jansen grunted something then said, 'He told me he never laid a finger on Rosie. It was nothing to do with him.'

'Did he tell you anything else?'

'He didn't have time.'

'That's a shame. Isn't it?'

A long pause then Theo Jansen said, 'You don't think he killed her, do you?'

Vos moved back to the narrow lane. The bodies were coming out now. By the line of cars and police vans tulips nodded their heads slowly in the flood-lights and the breeze like baffled witnesses to an inexplicable tragedy in their midst.

'Come in, Theo. Let me buy you that beer.'

'Why?' Jansen snapped and Vos knew he was losing

265

him. 'Because we've lots to talk about? We're the same now. That's what you said. So maybe I will call again. Maybe not.'

Then hung up.

CHAPTER 28

Anna de Vries waited close to the bar in Singel. She'd put the video and Wim Prins to the back of her mind. This was a better story all round. The disgraced politician's fugitive daughter, pleading for help.

Why?

She knew the stories. How Katja was a dumb Amsterdam schoolgirl who went off the rails after her mother committed suicide.

There were plenty of places to get lost in the city if you were looking. Anna de Vries could see the spread already. Page after page. All she needed was to find Katja, talk to her, get her somewhere safe, bring in the newspaper lawyers, let them negotiate something with the police.

Once the piece was written. Once the exclusive was put to bed.

De Vries stood in the cold street near the canal, getting frantic waiting for an answer.

She'd need pictures. A solid, reliable photographer. There was a freelance on the paper's books. A quiet, discreet man who took paparazzi shots on the side. She made a quick call, found he was at a loose end, put him on the alert.

'Where?' the photographer asked. 'When?'

'I'll get back to you in a few minutes,' De Vries promised. 'I need to talk to someone first. When she's happy. Then I'll call.'

He didn't like that much. But he wanted the job so she could live with it.

Twenty minutes after that first message the brief exchange began.

Katja writes, *Who are you?*

Anna writes, *Pieter's friend. He's worried about you. He wants to help. Can we meet?*

Katja writes, *Too scared.*

Anna writes, *We can take you somewhere safe.*

Katja writes, *They'll kill me.*

The woman in the skimpy raincoat shivered, wondered what she was getting into.

Anna writes, *No one's going to hurt you, Katja. That's a promise.*

She leaned back against the damp grimy wall. Felt excited. A little scared too. The crime beat was a good one. Produced plenty of front page stories. Brought her into contact with people on all sides of the law. But mostly it was pursued in the bright light of day. Not in the shadows of the rainy city at night.

Katja writes, *Slaperssteeg. After the Oude Kerk. Go to the end.*

Anna writes, *How do I find you?*

Katja writes, *I'll find you.*

She put away the phone, started to walk. Thought about texting again and asking the obvious question . . . *How?*

But her mind was made up by then. That run-down part of De Wallen was less than ten minutes away. It wasn't somewhere she'd usually go at that time of night. But this was her story and it was there for the taking. Like Katja Prins.

CHAPTER 29

They got back to Marnixstraat at nine thirty. Vos was insistent she go home, get some rest. Bakker wasn't in the mood.

Standing in reception he asked, 'Are you hungry?'

'After what we've just seen . . .'

'Where do you live anyway?'

'You asked! Finally, you asked!'

He nodded, waited.

'Near Westermarkt.'

'Sounds swanky.'

'You haven't seen it . . .'

'I've a dog who needs a walk.' He tugged at his hair. 'Sofia's going to have to keep him for a while.'

Mulder's team had drawn a blank on Theo Jansen. There was no new development in Rosie's murder, nothing on Katja Prins since the apparent ransom demand.

'If you buy me a beer and sandwich,' she said, 'I'll walk Sam with you.'

'I like that idea,' Vos agreed.

They cycled down Elandsgracht side by side through fine drizzle. He talked quite brightly to begin with, of the Jordaan, the years he'd spent living in the neighbourhood. But as they drew closer to his houseboat, just ten minutes from her home, Pieter Vos's answers became shorter, until he barely responded to her questions at all.

Instead of going into the bar he went to the canal and chained his bike. The wrecked dinghy had gone into the hands of forensic who were slowly tearing it apart with little success. The team was finished with his boat, which had proved equally unyielding. Two uniformed men stood at the head of the steps. Vos talked to them, told them to go back to Marnixstraat.

For ten minutes they walked Sam in silence along the Prinsengracht. Then they came back and sat beneath the poster of Casablanca: two beers, a couple of cold boiled eggs with salt on the side, two toasted cheese sandwiches, some ham and crisps. She looked at the plain, cheap food and shook her head.

'What's wrong?' Vos asked.

'Do you ever eat in a restaurant?'

'Why would I do that?'

'For something . . . nice?'

He picked up an egg, sprinkled some salt on it, took a big bite then said, 'I suppose you got spoilt in Dokkum.'

'Nah . . . Mostly we just scavenge and live off road kill.'

Sam sat at his feet, staring up all the while, looking a bit baffled. Vos told her off for feeding him crisps.

'Not good for a dog.'

But the ham was OK so she gave him that. Then asked, 'What do we know? Really?'

The bar was empty but he looked round to make sure their conversation was private all the same.

'We know Theo Jansen killed Menzo and his girlfriend. He thought they were responsible for Rosie's death. To begin with anyway.'

'Does he still believe that?'

'Not after we talked.'

'And that's it? One word from Pieter Vos. That's all it takes?'

There was a brief, bright sparkle in his eyes.

'Not really. I suspect Theo knew already. He's an impetuous type. Angry. Violent. But an admirable man in some way . . .'

'Admirable? He's a murderer and a crook.'

Vos nodded.

'And lots more besides. But he has a kind of moral code. He's an Amsterdammer. A practical man. He knows we'll always have criminals. He just thinks they're better home-grown.'

He rolled up a piece of meat and passed it to the dog.

'Menzo would never have murdered Rosie anyway.'

'Why not?' she asked.

'You said it yourself this morning. Nothing to gain and lots to lose. It brings a different kind of blood into the equation. One that spills on everyone in the end. Menzo was no fool.'

'You make it sound so logical.'

The comment surprised him.

'It is. We're dealing with intelligent men here. Businessmen. It's just that their business . . .' He shook his head. 'It's the mirror image of ours. They liberate, in their own terms. While we try to tell people what they mustn't do.'

'We're not in the wrong, Vos.'

He shook his head.

'Sometimes we are. Sometimes we overstep ourselves, like Wim Prins and his stupid scheme. Which is about nothing but power by the way—'

'His daughter's missing!' she cried, too loud.

Sofia Albers gave them a hard look from the bar.

'His daughter's missing,' she said quietly, almost a whisper.

'I'm aware of that,' Vos said with a mournful shrug. 'Do you think Menzo was responsible? Any more than he murdered Rosie Jansen? Or maybe someone employed by Theo, a man who was about to be released from a prison sentence he didn't deserve?'

She finished the beer.

'Search me. Do you have no idea?'

'None,' he said immediately. 'But we know what we don't know. Which is a start.'

There was something he wanted to say but didn't.

'What is it?' she asked.

'We need to look past the obvious,' Vos said, and drained his own glass. 'What if this apparent vendetta . . . it's just manufactured?'

His eyes grew unfocused, tired.

'I honestly don't know. Any reputation I've got is exaggerated and largely undeserved.'

'Don't tell Frank de Groot. He's counting on you.' She hesitated. 'And so am I.'

'For what?'

'An education,' she said straight away.

Something in that made him think. Vos got up and nodded then went to the bar, asked Sofia Albers to keep Sam for one more night and paid.

He looked her in the eye, alert again.

'If I took you off this case and sent you back to shuffle parking tickets in Marnixstraat tomorrow . . .'

She screeched. The dog stared at the pair of them. So did the woman behind the bar.

'If I did that . . .' Vos repeated.

'You can't! They might as well fire me now.'

'You could go home to Dokkum.'

'I don't want to! I want to be here.' She stamped her boots on the wooden floor, one after the other. 'Here.'

'Fine. Then there's something you need to see. In my boat,' he said and without a word she followed him out into the night.

CHAPTER 30

A narrow dead-end alley. Spikes on the windows. A sign in English above the entrance: NO SEX.

At the canal end a single street lamp flickered erratically. A few foreign drunks lurking outside a bar in the main street. A couple smoking weed, arm in arm, as if they were on honeymoon. The big bulk of the old church lay round the corner. But this part of De Wallen was firmly in the grip of the red-light business. Cabins alive with fluorescent tubes, bodies writhing at the window. Dope cafes. Bars and cheap restaurants.

And in Slaperssteeg . . . nothing.

Anna de Vries walked the length of the grubby passageway, from the canal towards the dead end behind Warmoesstraat. Her head was spinning from the beer. She was hungry for some proper food. And tired. It was hard to think straight after a long and eventful day like this.

She slung her bag more tightly over her shoulder, thought of the precious iPad in there. Muggings weren't common in this part of De Wallen. But they weren't unknown.

Phone out, one more message.

Anna writes, *Katja? Where are you? I'm here. Where you said.*

She looked at the screen. Waited. Nothing. Then the letters faded, as if out of boredom.

'Screw this,' De Vries muttered. 'I'm going home.'

Someone had been jerking her around. That was for sure.

Then it rang and the sound made her jump so much she nearly dropped the thing on the filthy cobbles.

One short curse. She looked at the name there and answered.

'It didn't work out,' she told the photographer. 'Sorry.' The inevitable question. 'No. You don't get paid. Nice try.'

When she finished the call she heard footsteps. The street light flickered. She pulled back a step. A man was there, scaring the life out of her for a moment.

Then De Vries saw his face, laughed with relief and said, 'Jesus Christ. What are you doing here? I could have wet myself . . .'

Thought about it.

'Ah.' Finger in the air. 'So Katja called you too. Of course she would. I'm sorry. It makes sense . . .'

She looked at him again. There were plastic bags on his hands. Plastic bags on his shoes.

In the dark and narrow passageway of Slaperssteeg Anna de Vries shook her head. He held something in front of him and it glittered in the waxy yellow light.

CHAPTER 31

The houseboat was neater than she remembered. And touching too, like a teenager's room, plastered with posters, pairs of jeans and socks neatly folded in random piles. Forensic must have done some tidying up after they went through his things, finding nothing at all to suggest who broke in and played an old jazz CD on his stereo. And dumped a body next door, in a way that seemed designed to draw him back into Marnixstraat and a murder investigation.

Bakker felt done in but she wasn't looking to going home. The tiny studio apartment near Westermarkt was a dump, all she could afford. Some of the neighbours stayed up late, playing music. Looked down on her because of the job, her Friesland accent. Because she wasn't like one of them and never would be.

But she wanted to know how this city worked. Wanted to learn. Pieter Vos seemed a good place to start.

He was rummaging around in the bows where two large doors blocked off what looked like a storage area. Bakker went and joined him, helped clear a few pieces of old furniture out of the way as he tried to find something at the back.

'I don't remember it being like this,' Vos said.

'Like what? A mess?'

He turned and looked at her.

'I don't remember it being this tidy.' Then he shifted an old record player to one side and said, 'Ah . . .'

Bakker found she had to retreat a step or two, find a chair, sit down hard.

The thing Pieter Vos had brought her to see was a doll's house. A metre high, perhaps more. An exact copy of Petronella Oortman's, down to the open rooms with their tiny furniture and miniature figures.

'What's this?' she whispered, feeling a sudden chill in the hot, stuffy cabin.

'Can you give me a hand? It's quite heavy.'

She squashed next to him in the bows, both jostling for grip on the dusty wooden walls of the miniature wooden house. Finally Vos managed to half-roll, half-bounce it sideways out of the storage area. She got her fingers under the roof and the two of them lifted it over the edge of the compartment out into the open cabin.

'What is this?' she asked again.

'It's Anneliese's,' he said, as if she should have guessed. 'I had it made for her tenth birthday.' He grinned. 'She loved it for all of three weeks. Then it was kid's stuff and she never looked at it again.'

Vos brushed the dust from the roof with his elbow, peered inside.

'I kept it when we broke up for some reason. I don't know why.' He shrugged. 'You do that with dolls, don't you?'

Laura Bakker reached out and touched his sleeve for a moment.

'Pieter. You should let it go.'

'Why?' he asked, puzzled.

Bakker had no answer.

'You see,' he went on, 'life's like this. A series of rooms. You open one. You walk through.' He poked around the ground floor with his fingers. Picked up the tiny doll from the floor, placed it on the minuscule wicker chair. 'You always think you know what to expect. But sometimes you go through the next door and . . .'

He rolled back his head and sighed.

'I'm sorry.'

Vos got up and walked to his briefcase.

'You need to see this.' He pulled an envelope out of the case. It had the stamp of forensic on it. 'Don't share it around. I want to try to understand . . .'

There were two reports, each about DNA samples. One for Katja Prins. The second for Anneliese.

Bakker read them. Then read them again. Put them down. Looked at him and said, 'So that's why the result came back so early this afternoon? From forensic in the Doll's House? You'd already been asking.'

He'd gone back to playing with the things in the doll's house again, setting the table straight, the tiny figures back in their places.

'Does it mean what I think?' she asked.

'Anneliese and Katja shared the same father,' Vos said. 'Wim Prins. Liesbeth worked for him when I first met her. She did lots of temp jobs over the years. For a while she was a volunteer in a legal advice centre he used to visit. I never . . .'

He stopped for a moment, looking as if he didn't want to continue.

'We were so . . . happy. So normal. So . . . dull and boring and predictable I guess. At least I was.'

'You asked for those records this afternoon. You must have thought—'

'I never thought we were anything out of the ordinary. Just another family trying to do what was right. You lose everything in the end, don't you? Everything . . . everyone you love. They're taken from you, one way or another.'

This was important. She understood that. Understood too that it puzzled Vos in ways he couldn't quite fathom.

'You must have wondered, Pieter,' she repeated. 'Otherwise why check?'

Vos finished fixing the tiny rooms on the first floor.

'I told you. One day you open a door knowing what's behind it. *Knowing.* But really it's just an illusion. A pack of lies. Everything is. Every last thing.'

He set one more tiny shape upright on a chair.

'And the worst part is . . . when you lie to yourself.'

She waited, said nothing.

'I worked and worked at Marnixstraat because I told myself that was what they paid me for.' A shrug, the smile. 'It wasn't true. Not really. I was staying away from her. I guess I must have known something was wrong. I didn't want to see it. Face it. I didn't notice I was staying away from Anneliese as well.'

He nodded, tried to make sure the words were right.

'I lied to myself because it was easier that way. Maybe when Anneliese was older we'd have dealt with it. Maybe not.' The quietest of laughs. 'I'm not very grown up, am I? You wouldn't play these games in Dokkum.'

'People play those games everywhere. Don't fool yourself. What are you going to do?'

'I'll talk to Liesbeth tomorrow. About the blood. About . . . Anneliese.' He looked her in the eye. 'This is between the two of us for now.'

'You can't keep that to yourself.'

'I know. That's why I told you.'

She got up, shuffled her coat around her. Wanted some fresh air.

'Van der Berg thinks you should stay clear of this,' she said. 'Maybe he's right.'

'Would Liesbeth thank me for that? I want to find Katja Prins. I want that more than anything.'

'So you can ask her why your daughter . . . why Anneliese died in an Amsterdam brothel?'

'She was my daughter,' Vos insisted. 'DNA's got nothing to do with it. We brought her up. I'm her father. And I don't know she's dead. Not yet.'

'Not if . . . Not if you say so.'

Laura Bakker stopped. It was as if she wasn't even there. Engrossed, obsessed, Vos had turned to the second floor, the main bedroom. He asked her to reach into his case and bring out a pair of forensic gloves. Then, with the stealth and care of a surgeon, he reached inside, lifted the tiny sheets, pulled something out from beneath the covers.

Another photo. Two young girls, happy, healthy, smiling for the camera. Not in the Vondelpark this time. They were in front of a tall terraced house with tulle curtains in the windows.

Anneliese and Katja Prins posing outside the privehuis called the Doll's House. Before the bomb hit.

'Forensic did a great job, didn't they?'

'Looks like it,' Vos agreed.

'Someone's trying to tell you something, Pieter.'

He nodded, looked at her, surprised perhaps.

'True,' Vos said. 'But what?'

CHAPTER 32

Anna de Vries looked. Couldn't move.

The thing in his hands was a knife. He must have been holding it low down as he stood there, grinning.

It was a knife and it felt cold and cruel as the sharp point took her breath away.

The phone slipped from her fingers and he didn't seem to notice. He was too occupied with keeping the blade tight inside her, the force so hard and insistent she couldn't even scream.

De Wallen. The red-light district. Not a place to wander at night. She'd known that all along.

And this was a mugging of a kind. Just by the last man in Amsterdam she'd have expected.

PART III

WEDNESDAY 19 APRIL

CHAPTER 1

Jaap Zeeger walked into Marnixstraat just after eight in the morning, asked for 'Mr Vos', waited patiently in reception, hands on knees.

They came down and took him into an interview room where Bakker turned on the recorder.

'First time we've met and you haven't cautioned me, Mr Vos,' Zeeger said with a grin.

Bakker had brought along the file. Zeeger was thirty-four. A string of minor convictions, mainly drug-related. Time in jail. Time in state drug treatment.

Vos could scarcely believe it was the same man. Lean, with clean dark hair, a face that was pockmarked but more healthy than before. He looked ordinary. Not the sad, sick foot soldier he'd been when he was one of Jansen's minions. Zeeger had a black leather jacket, black jeans, clean shiny shoes. He said he was working part-time for a courier service and was hoping for a full-time job there soon. He'd been away on holiday at a caravan camp in Texel. Got back the night before. Heard from Til Stamm the police had been looking for him.

Now she'd gone to Texel, to the same caravan he used. One owned by the Yellow House, the rehab charity she'd mentioned and said she had nothing to do with.

Bakker queried that. Zeeger bristled.

'Til's a nice girl. She wasn't lying. They had the caravan going free so I asked. They said she could have it.'

He took some gum out of the pocket of his jacket, popped it into his mouth.

'Don't smoke any more?' Vos asked.

'Gave it up. Gave up all that crap I got fed. And you know where I learned to use that shit? In jail. Where you lot put me.'

'We're terrible people sometimes,' Vos agreed. 'Where's Katja?'

'Dunno. I went off to Texel a week ago. She was still here. Seemed happy enough.'

'What do you know about the privehuis on the Prinsen?' Bakker asked. 'The Doll's House? Nice place for young girls.'

He waved a skinny hand at her.

'I never went there. All I did for Mr Jansen was run round his pot and pills and fetch a bit of money from time to time. He'd tell you that too if you lot hadn't let him go. That brothel stuff wasn't my thing. Besides . . .'

For the first time he looked shifty.

'Besides what?' Vos demanded.

'I heard the whispers. Bad things. Young girls. I don't think Mr Jansen knew, mind. He was dead regular about what went on. Then it closed down and the Thai lady running it got bought out by Jimmy Menzo. I wasn't going anywhere near him. Not even when I was dead sick.'

He balled his fist and thumped the desk. So hard the recorder jumped.

'And I was sick. Not bad. Not evil like you lot said. I was sick and I got myself cured. What I'm telling you's the truth. Don't care what Mr Mulder says any more. How much he beats me round the head and threatens me with all them things I never did. Doesn't—'

'Where's Katja?' Vos asked again.

The lean man in black pushed his seat back from the table. Said he'd like a coffee. Bakker went and fetched three plastic cups. Vos waited, thinking. Silent.

Shushed Laura Bakker when she started to throw questions at Zeeger again.

He wanted to be heard. That much was clear. Wanted to say something in his own time, his own way.

'I wasn't nothing to do with your daughter, Mr Vos,' Zeeger said when he'd taken a swig of coffee. 'You believe that, don't you?'

Vos nodded.

'I don't know who put that stuff in my place. I got home and found someone had left me a package. A doll. Them clothes. I was too out of it to notice things back then. Maybe it was someone else in Jansen's lot. Menzo's. Maybe . . .' His eyes shot briefly to the door. 'Maybe someone here. You think of that?'

'We're not interested in what happened back then. We need to find Katja,' Bakker said.

'Can't help,' he said, shaking his head, starting to look nervous. 'Honestly. She was there when I left. She was good too. We went to the Yellow House that afternoon. Me and Kat had sorted ourselves. No more dope. No more booze.' He raised a finger, as if trying to remember something he'd been taught. 'We're clear and clean. Clear and clean. That's it.'

Bakker swore mildly. This morning she wore a different kind of suit. Green trousers, a too-bright tartan jacket, green sweater with the crucifix on. The colours didn't so much clash as argue vociferously. Nothing fitted terribly well. Auntie Maartje again, Vos guessed. Not that his own clothes – fresh pair of jeans, another dark sweater, a polo shirt underneath it – were much to write home about.

'Where . . .?' she asked.

'I . . . don't . . . know.' He took out the gum, wrapped it inside a tissue, pocketed it. Bit into another piece. 'I'll tell you this though. Thinking back about it now I reckon she was scared.'

Vos looked up.

'Of what?' he asked.

'Of who you mean.'

Nothing more.

'We'll sit here until you say something,' Vos told him. 'If it takes all day.'

'There you go! Just like Mr Mulder, aren't you?' His voice was high and full of a sudden pain. 'Don't matter I fixed myself, does it? As far as you're concerned I'm just another bit of street scum you can lean on any time. Blame the likes of me . . .'

Laura Bakker put her head in her hands and groaned.

Zeeger went quiet.

Then she placed her elbows on the table, looked him in the eye.

'This is really simple, Jaap. Katja's missing. It looks as if she's been kidnapped. The way Vos's girl was three years ago. They knew each other . . .'

His pale, foxy face crumpled.

'They did?'

'They knew each other,' she went on. 'And we don't want Katja to disappear off the face of the earth like Anneliese. Do you?'

Nothing for a while. Then he said, 'Why ask me? I don't count. Not against you lot. Not against all them big people . . .' He nodded at the opaque window, bright sun beyond the glass. 'Out there.'

Vos folded his arms. Checked his watch.

'She didn't talk about it,' Zeeger went on, looking as if he was giving away a secret. 'Only the once and then we're not supposed to say. What happens in session stays in session.'

'Says who?'

'Miss Jewell. At the Yellow House. You can't become clear and clean unless you tell the truth,

291

can you? And you can't tell the truth if you know someone's going to blab it out loud the moment you've left the room.'

Bakker sighed, long and slow.

'It's all right for you!' Zeeger yelled, and at that moment sounded like his old self. 'They won't be banging on your door, will they?'

'Menzo's dead,' she said slowly. 'Jansen's on the run. If we find him he's back in jail for years. If we don't—'

'It's not *them* I'm worried about! Jesus. Kat didn't mess with Mr Jansen or that Surinamese bastard. You lot . . .' He shook his head. Ran his thin fingers through the black combed hair. 'You don't see much, do you? You think the only bad in the world's us. Can't see beyond the end of your stuck-up noses.'

Vos looked interested. Bakker very.

'Go on, Jaap,' she said.

'And end up dead too?'

'I thought Kat was your friend,' Bakker told him. 'Didn't she help you get . . . clear and clean? Don't you owe—?'

'Shut up,' he barked at her. 'Shut up both of you.' He gulped at the coffee again. Cold. Zeeger screwed up his face at the taste. 'She was frightened. I told you. Just blurted it out once when we were in session.'

'With Miss Jewell?' Bakker asked.

Nothing.

'Jaap,' she said, trying to look patient. 'I keep

292

saying this and you keep ignoring it. No one's seen Katja for a week. There's a ransom note. Photos of her. A video . . .'

He didn't react.

'Do you want to see them?' Vos asked.

No answer.

'Fine,' Bakker said, then pulled out her smartphone, put it on the table, pulled up the video that came with the doll on Rosie Jansen's body.

Dark room. Katja in a chair. Screaming. Looking as if she was being hit.

Zeeger couldn't take his eyes off the tiny screen.

'Stop!' he screeched after a few seconds. 'For God's sake turn that off.'

Bakker hit pause. Katja's face stayed on the screen, mouth downturned, frozen in a long, pained scream.

'You know nothing, you lot,' Jaap Zeeger whined.

'That's true,' Vos agreed. 'Enlighten us.'

Zeeger's head went from side to side.

'We'll look after you, Jaap,' Bakker added. 'Nothing's going to happen.'

He laughed at that. But after a while he started to talk. Bakker blinked, checked the recorder, made sure it was capturing every word.

Twenty minutes later when he'd finished Vos stood up, shook his hand.

'I need you to make a statement now, Jaap. Just repeat what you said, on the record. Then sign it.'

'I just told you . . .'

Vos smiled.

'It's how it works. You know that. You're on the right side for once.'

They left him in the interview room, called for two statement officers. Stood in silence for a moment.

'What next?' Bakker asked.

He waited.

'We bring in Wim Prins?' she suggested.

'No. First we look at the files on his wife. I was . . .'

All that happened when he was on sick leave from the force, about to resign. He'd no idea who'd handled the death of Bea Prins. A supposed suicide.

'I wasn't here then.'

He stood back and let two uniformed officers through, pads in hand, witness statement forms.

'I've got to tell Frank. Until yesterday Wim Prins ran this city. If we're going to accuse him of murder . . .'

Vos gestured to the lift. De Groot's office was on the fourth floor, next to the management suite and the technical area that handled computer intelligence and forensic work.

'Point taken,' Bakker agreed.

Still Vos didn't move.

'What now?' she asked.

'You were good in there, Laura,' he said. 'Very.'

Bakker blushed, mumbled something. And they got in the lift.

CHAPTER 2

A silent breakfast. Liesbeth Prins finished her coffee and croissant, lit a cigarette knowing that annoyed him. Unshaven, dishevelled in a creased blue shirt and a pair of jeans he hadn't worn for years, Prins hunched over a bowl of cereal, barely touching it. Her smoke rolled over him. He didn't look at her.

'What time did you get in?' she asked.

'You didn't check?'

'Eleven thirty.'

He pushed the bowl aside, took a deep, pained breath.

'Why ask a question if you know the answer?'

'The papers were phoning here all night. I didn't know what to say.'

'That's unusual,' Prins replied with a sharp, sarcastic smile.

She stabbed the half-smoked cigarette into the remains of the pastry.

'Do you care, Wim? Does it touch you? Do you still think she's screwing us around?'

'Maybe,' he answered with a shrug. 'I don't know anything any more.'

'Where were you last night?'

'I went for a walk. I had a few drinks . . .'

'A few?'

'Not enough.'

He'd scanned the headlines already. Two stories. The murder of a city gangster and his girlfriend. And the shock resignation of the leader of the council. They all reported the official line: this was just temporary. Then went on to rubbish the idea.

Someone had been briefing. He had a good idea who.

'Are you fucking her? The Willemsen woman?'

He laughed.

'What makes you say that?'

'You. The way you've been skulking around. The way you are around her. You're a lousy liar.'

That was amusing.

'We managed to fool Bea and Vos for long enough.'

'You didn't answer the question.'

A shrug.

'For a while. It was stupid. Over now.' This part still puzzled him. 'Thing is . . . when you're in that place it's politics and I was never a politician really. You have to remember it's not real. I didn't—'

The dregs of warm coffee flung in his face. Then she flew at him, nails scratching, cursing, shrieking.

Sharp pain on the cheek, crockery on the floor. Crumbs and cereal spilling onto the geometric black and white kitchen tiles.

He escaped her flailing fingers, held her wrists, waited until the spitting fury subsided a little.

'There was just you and Bea up till then,' Prins said. 'I wasn't cut out for it. That's why I did it I guess. I always thought . . .'

The pressure of her arms against him eased and so did the swearing.

'I guess I missed the secrets. You didn't object when it was the two of us.'

'Bastard . . .'

This was ridiculous and he said so. Theirs was a pact made between illicit sheets, stolen moments. Twice they took holidays in Aruba, Prins telling Bea it was to work on the villa, Liesbeth lying about going with a girlfriend.

She dragged herself away. He picked a napkin off the table, wiped the coffee from his face. Felt his cheek. Pain and scraped skin. Prins ran a finger across it, held it out for her to see.

Blood on his fingertip. He glanced at his reflection in the window, framed by the light-green lime trees in the courtyard. A stripe down the right of his face. One that would take a while to heal.

'Don't ever do that again,' he said in a low, cold voice. 'We're not angels. Neither of us.'

'I never pretended to be, did I?'

The doorbell rang. She went downstairs. Prins watched her go. Hair a mess, clutching her dressing gown around her. It wasn't like this when they were slipping away together in the early days, full of the heat of being young.

'Post,' she said coming back upstairs, ripping open a big brown envelope, special delivery.

'You're reading my letters now?' he asked, looking at the name scrawled on the front in thick black felt tip.

'No more secrets to hide. Are there?'

Prins shook his head, walked to the coffee machine, set it up to make more. The morning routine. That was all life had become. A series of mechanical actions and gestures, leading nowhere, achieving nothing.

Liesbeth had gone quiet. It was a silence he knew. One that demanded something of him.

The coffee machine stopped grinding, started whirring.

'What?' he asked and walked over to the table.

A single sheet of white paper. Thick black ink. The lettering looked juvenile. Like that of a clumsy school kid.

It read: *Zeedijk and Stormsteeg. 11.30 am. Tumi case. Money. Wait there.*

She didn't say a word.

Wim Prins went back to the coffee machine, poured a short black cup, sipped at it. Read the note again.

Glanced at the clock. Almost nine.

'The bank won't be able to deal with this till ten. They don't give me much time, do they?'

'You mean you can't get it?'

Thinking.

'I'm going to have to take a passport or something.

You can't get that kind of money out of a cash machine.'

'Can you do it?'

'Yes,' he insisted. 'But I need time. And I need space.' He stared at her. 'I don't want you passing this on to Vos for an hour. OK?'

A shake of her anxious head.

'Don't start screwing around now, Wim. This is about Katja. Not you . . .'

He lost it then. Was on her. Shaking her slim bony shoulders. Face in hers, furious. Lost in the rage.

Almost landed a blow. Which would have shocked him as much as her.

Prins let go. Still mad. Fighting to control it.

'I have to wash coffee off my face. Try to look half human. Try to work out how I can get more money than I've ever seen in my life, stick it in a stupid suitcase and stand out in Chinatown like a horny tourist hunting a hooker. Don't make it harder. Don't you dare.'

He went after that. Into the bathroom. Then the bedroom. Came out with a plaster on his cheek, bright sweater, casual trousers, brown shoes. Like a man on holiday, or heading for one.

Then into the study to pick up some things.

She stayed in the kitchen, miserable at the table, smoking. Looking at the note.

At ten past nine he got his jacket and coat, made her swear to keep quiet till ten, then left.

Liesbeth Prins wondered why she listened to

299

him. What good reason there was not to phone Pieter Vos at that moment. She wanted to see him anyway. She missed his easy, quiet, amiable company. What once was routine and dull now seemed affectionate and caring.

None of that mattered back when she was slinking off to Wim Prins's bed.

One more glance at the note. She wouldn't call. Not until the time he'd demanded.

He'd been right about one thing. They weren't angels. No use pretending.

CHAPTER 3

Frank de Groot looked as if he hadn't slept. He stood by the window of his office on the top floor of Marnixstraat, gazing out of the window. There was work being done on the bridge over the Lijnbaansgracht. Men with pneumatic drills hammering at the pavement, pedestrians struggling through the chaos. The noise leaked into De Groot's office. It didn't help the mood.

He listened as Vos outlined what Jaap Zeeger had told them and said, straight away, 'Forget it.'

'Forget it?' Bakker cried. 'Zeeger told us—'

'Zeeger's a convicted criminal. A thief. A dope pedlar. You're going to set his word against that of an elected politician? A lawyer for God's sake?'

Vos coughed into his fist and took a seat in front of the commissaris's desk. De Groot got the message, sat down opposite. Bakker folded her arms, leaned against the partition wall, sulky as a teenager in a foul mood.

'We've got to look into it, Frank,' Vos said. 'He's made a statement.'

'Bea Prins shot herself in the Beursplein car park.

She was an addict. Plenty of witnesses for that. I'm not reopening the case on the back of hearsay from a criminal.'

A moment's silence then Vos asked, 'Did you handle it?'

'Yes!' De Groot bellowed. 'Me. And no. I wasn't the right officer for the job. If you'd been halfway sane I'd have let you look at it. But you weren't.' Then more quietly, 'And I understand why. We were all in a mess then. We'd been chasing Anneliese for three months and getting nowhere.' A hard look across the desk. 'I know you suffered. You weren't the only one.'

'I need to see those files.'

'Fine, fine. And if you spot something, tell me. But don't pull Prins in just because Jaap Zeeger's walked through the door looking all fine and dandy and decided to tell a few cock and bull stories. We put Theo Jansen in prison because of that little bastard and look where we are now. Why the hell we should believe him—'

'Prins has been trying to walk away from this ever since it started,' Bakker interrupted. 'He's never looked like a man who's lost his daughter. According to Zeeger Katja went to pieces because she suspected Prins killed Bea – and he knew that. Doesn't it fit with what we saw?'

'You need more than the word of a lowlife crook. One who's a self-confessed liar,' the commissaris repeated. 'Until I see that—'

'Give me some people then,' Vos demanded. 'I've

got Bakker here. Access to forensic. Van der Berg. I can't . . .'

Another angry flurry then De Groot threw a printout across the desk.

'Seen this? Heard the latest?'

Vos picked it up. Crime report. Timed at six thirty-four that morning. Body in the Oudezijds Voorburgwal canal in De Wallen near the Oude Kerk. Local woman aged twenty-eight. Single rising stab wound to the abdomen. Fished out of the water after a street-cleaning crew saw her at daybreak. The duty team thought it was a mugging gone wrong. She was a newspaper reporter from one of the big city titles. They'd got the ID from her phone, found in the alley where she was attacked.

'I met that girl a couple of times,' De Groot added. 'She came on the crime beat after you quit. So I've got Jansen loose and everyone screaming at me for that. Menzo and his woman murdered last night. Now this . . .'

Bakker said, 'Katja Prins is missing. She believed her father killed her mother. Somehow this hooks into Vos's daughter's case too. Maybe—'

'Maybe what?' De Groot demanded. 'Tell me.' He jabbed a fat forefinger at her. 'Give me something solid. Something I can show to the people who run this place and say: here. This is why I stopped officers chasing a murderous thug loose in Amsterdam. You don't know if this kidnapping's for real. Or if Prins is right and it's just that kid screwing around again.'

'True,' Vos admitted.

'Start screaming for resources when I can see there's something to do with them. Not now, Pieter. You know I can't do that.'

Vos shrugged. Bakker stayed silent.

'So what are you waiting for?' De Groot asked.

Vos stopped in the corridor, stared out at the view over the bus station towards the Westerkerk.

'The man's an idiot,' Bakker grumbled. 'Why . . .?' She stopped when she saw the look in his eye.

'He's not an idiot. He's right. It's just hearsay. Barely that.' A look at his watch. 'Frank never worked homicide. Not if he could help it.'

Footsteps along the corridor. Van der Berg walked up holding a blue folder with the name Beatrix Prins on the cover. He opened the window, let in the cold spring air. Smiled, bleary-eyed, a smell of booze about him even at this hour.

'Did you deal with this when it happened, Dirk?' Vos asked.

'Sadly no, boss. I was on holiday with the wife.' He screwed up his eyes. 'Beer tour of England. It rained a lot.' He grimaced. 'I needed a break after all the shit we'd been through here.'

Vos rapped his fingers on the folder.

'I want you to sit down. Go through every line. Forget what conclusions anyone else reached. See it with a fresh pair of eyes.'

'With a view to what?'

'Telling me if it adds up.'

Van der Berg nodded and walked off to the lift.

'Will it keep him out of the bar?' Bakker asked when he'd gone.

'Best murder man I ever had,' Vos said. 'Don't judge people by appearances.'

She tipped him an ironic salute.

Vos shook his head.

'And where do we go . . . boss?'

He waited.

'The Yellow House,' she said when Vos stayed silent. 'Oh, and let me guess. We take our bikes.'

CHAPTER 4

'There's a chapel downstairs, Theo. Would you like to see it?'

Bright morning. A few tourists in the part of the Begijnhof courtyard open to strangers.

He had a headache. Had sat up drinking all four beers she'd bought until, some time around two, he'd crawled onto the sofa and gone to sleep. Even after another shower, a fresh set of clean clothes, he felt dirty and stupid.

There was nothing on the news to worry him. No messages from Maarten. He'd told the barber to lay low, stay quiet. Not to trouble him unless it was necessary. Still he felt lonely and somehow ashamed. He'd believed Menzo when he'd said he hadn't killed Rosie. Didn't need to hear that from Pieter Vos. And still he'd burned the man alive, with his dead mistress in the back seat.

Once that wouldn't have worried him much. Now something nagged.

'You want me to pray?' he asked, half-joking.

She wore a loose grey dress falling almost to her ankles. A white blouse with round collars. Her face seemed insufficiently lined by age. Suzi was at peace in a way she'd never been with him.

'No,' she said. 'I just thought . . .'

That flat line of a smile. It judged him and he never did like that.

'I just thought you'd want to get out of here for a while. No one's going to see you.' Her eyes were so steady. They never left him. 'No one would know you. Not the way you are now.'

She walked up and touched his bristly cheek.

'I like it. I bought you a razor and some shaving foam. They're in the bathroom. You should use them twice a day. Also . . .' She went to a shopping bag by the window and pulled out a box with a pair of hair clippers inside. 'I got this. You need to use it.' She waved a finger in his face. 'So the old you doesn't come back.'

Jansen drank a cup of coffee. Ate a croissant and a couple of bitterballen with mustard from the fridge. Then he went to the bathroom and did as she asked.

When he came out she had a coat on and was holding out a new jacket, sleeves ready for him.

'If you want money for this . . .' he began.

'I don't want your money. Can we go now?'

More tourists outside, a big party among them led by a Japanese woman bearing a flag. They took pictures even though a sign asked them not to. Made a little noise which seemed out of place in this peaceful sanctuary just off the busy Spui square.

He sat next to Suzi on a bench in the private

grassed area. She glowered at him when he asked about lighting a cigarette. So he put his hands in his pockets like a naughty child. Was both glad and annoyed that she didn't try to make conversation.

When the group left the courtyard she got up and walked him to the chapel. Told a story about a nun from the seventeenth century buried in the gutter outside because she felt the church had been tainted by the presence of Presbyterians.

'So you get gangs in religion too, huh?' Jansen muttered as they went through the low door.

A modest shop with souvenirs on the right. A tiny chapel on the left. Nothing much to interest him.

'There's always a conflict, Theo,' she said, smiling at him. 'I wouldn't argue with that.' Suzi tapped his chest. 'Inside or out. We never lose it.'

'Don't try to change me,' he said. 'I'm a hopeless case.'

She stayed silent.

'And they'll bury me in the gutter too,' Jansen added. 'It's where I came from. I'll just go back where I belong.'

'Your father was an honourable man. He worked all his life—'

'And got paid piss all. Didn't even own the place he lived in. Didn't . . .'

His old man was a proud, taciturn working-class underling on the Heineken production line. Jansen's mother had died when he was seven. His father fell to throat cancer on the day Jansen turned thirty.

He'd never uttered a word about the work his son did. It was as if everything took place in another world.

'Sshhh . . .'

Her soft finger went to his rough lips. Jansen's voice had turned too loud for the dark and quiet interior of the Begijnhof chapel.

'I suppose you pray for me now,' he whispered, desperate to get out of this place.

'No,' she said lightly. 'I pray for everyone. I wouldn't presume . . .'

She stood in front of him, folded her arms. At that moment he could picture the two of them, young and strong, bodies locked together on the bed of his little flat, before the money began to flood through his life.

Nothing was complicated then. Every day was a battle, to be won or lost. He'd craved victory because he knew the alternative was defeat, shame, death. Never imagined for one moment the price of that triumph would be losing her.

'I can't think of anything I have to give you,' she said. 'But take what you like. Stay as long as you need. Ask for whatever you want. You can have it.'

She closed her eyes. He could see tears at the corners, like tiny transparent pearls.

'There's enough pain between us. Let's not make more.'

His cheap phone rang. In the darkness of the small, stuffy Begijnhof chapel all eyes turned on him. This was somewhere he didn't belong.

Jansen walked out into the porch, answered.

Maarten. Wanting to know what to do.

'About what?' Jansen asked, aware that she'd marched past him, out into the spring morning, determined not to hear.

'Everyone wants to know, Theo. Are we back? I've even got some of the Surinamese guys calling me. They don't want a war now. Not with Jimmy gone.'

Jansen felt stupid. He'd never thought about the fallout from killing Menzo. There was no obvious leader to take over. The man had ruled like an old-fashioned despot. Miriam Smith was effectively his number two and she was dead as well. A war would happen. It had to one day. But not now. There were supply lines to maintain. Debts to be collected. Bills to be paid. Lives to be led.

'What are people saying?' he asked.

'They want you back . . .'

'Marnixstraat is going to keep looking until they find me, Maarten. You know that can't happen.'

'Not if we get you out of the city. You can run this from abroad. You . . .'

Jansen wasn't listening. Suzi was staring at him with those knowing sad eyes. She always understood the politics of crime. Better than him sometimes. She probably guessed this was on the way.

'We need to meet,' the barber said. 'You and Jimmy's people. Michiel Lindeman said he'd be there. He can . . . mediate.'

A lawyer willing to talk to a man on the run. That was an interesting idea.

'Fix something,' Jansen said. 'Get back to me.'

He went back with her, out of the public area of the Begijnhof into the private courtyard, then the tall wooden house and her modest apartment.

'I'm going shopping later. What would you like for lunch?' she asked as she closed the door.

'Herring,' he said. 'Good bread. A beer. Just one.'

Fifteen minutes later Maarten called. A meeting had been arranged. Soon.

'Forget the food,' Jansen told her when he was finished. 'I'll be out of here. I'll get my own.'

CHAPTER 5

It was yellow but not a house. Just a low post-war building one street behind the flower stalls and bulb shops of the Bloemenmarkt. Wedged between a restaurant and a bar, ochre paint, giant sunflowers stretching up to the bright clean windows, it seemed oddly clean and out of place amidst the grey buildings spreading round the flower market.

The sign on the door said: *The Yellow House, Director Barbara Jewell.*

Vos and Bakker chained their bikes to the railings at the front, negotiated the bland receptionist in the bland reception area, and found themselves in Jewell's office without an argument or the least hesitation.

Van Gogh paintings everywhere. Quotations from a variety of gurus, everyone from Sufi mystics to Steve Jobs. Jewell sat next to a large iMac, tapping at the keyboard as she listened to them. She was a sturdy American around forty, short dyed orange hair, piercing blue eyes. A matching blue business suit that looked expensive. From the outset she spoke English in a firm, determined tone.

Bakker asked what they did.

'We cure people,' Jewell answered with a frank, interested smile. 'If we can.'

'Did you cure Katja Prins?' Vos asked.

Jewell's hefty shoulders shrugged.

'I believe so. Do you have reason to think otherwise?'

'Didn't Til Stamm tell you?' Bakker asked. 'When she came for the keys to your caravan?'

The American smiled, puzzled.

'Tell me what?'

Vos filled her in. She looked shocked, worried. Then started to tap at her keyboard again.

Bakker was getting mad.

'Can you leave that for a moment?'

'I'm looking for the last time Katja was here,' Jewell replied. 'I thought you'd want to know.'

She found something, hit the keyboard. A printer at the end of the desk started to whir. Barbara Jewell passed over the single page it produced. An appointment for eleven in the morning. A three-hour period called 'session training'.

Bakker asked what that meant.

'It meant we might give Katja a job somewhere along the line. A teacher needs to understand her subject. Katja knows it better than most. Drugs. Drink.' She hesitated. 'Abusive relationships.'

'You mean with her father?' Bakker asked.

The American woman sighed, looked apologetic.

'This is awkward,' she said. 'I want to help as much as I can. But there are confidences here.'

'You're not a priest,' Bakker retorted.

'No. But I'm still someone who hears secrets that people don't want revealed. If you told me something in private would you be happy if I passed it on?'

'If it saved a life I would,' Bakker said. 'You've got a duty—'

'How much did Wim Prins pay you?' Vos cut in.

She took a leaflet off her desk, passed it over.

'We work on donations. If people can afford to contribute they're welcome. If they can't . . . or won't . . . that's fine too.' A brief, ironic smile. 'No one's getting rich here if that's what you mean.'

She waited. The two of them struggled for a question. Then Vos asked, 'Who saw her this last time?'

'That was my session. Katja was a great subject. Attentive and motivated. She'd worked through a lot with us. I had high hopes.'

'Who were her friends?'

Barbara Jewell frowned.

'We're about wellness and healing. Being . . .'

'Clear and clean,' Bakker said. 'Yes. We know. Who were her friends?'

A shrug.

'She got on well with Jaap Zeeger. They were in the same group. Apart from that . . .'

Bakker scribbled something on her pad then asked, 'Did she say where she was going?'

'Home, I assumed. She rented somewhere near Warmoesstraat. I think she'd got Jaap a room there for a while. He needed somewhere cheap.'

314

'You don't seem in the least worried Katja Prins is missing,' Bakker said.

For one brief moment Barbara Jewell's calm face broke. She looked annoyed.

'People here come and go. I wouldn't read anything . . .'

Vos outlined some of the details about Katja's disappearance.

'Either she's been kidnapped. Or pretending to be,' he added.

'What exactly do you want?'

'Your files on Katja and Zeeger.'

She hesitated, shook her head.

'I'm sorry. That's not possible.'

'There's a young woman in trouble somewhere,' Vos told her. 'I don't know the circumstances. But I do know she's in some kind of danger. My daughter disappeared—'

'Ah!' She raised a sturdy finger. 'You're that one. Katja mentioned you.' Fingers on the keyboard again. 'And your daughter. They were friends. You knew that, didn't you?'

Vos shut his eyes for a moment. Bakker was getting furious by his side.

'I could wrap you in lawsuits,' he said. 'I could cripple this place.'

Barbara Jewell didn't like that.

'We're a charity. We work hand in hand with the government, the city council. The voluntary agencies. I don't think I need to listen to this—'

'Jaap Zeeger told us what Katja Prins said anyway,'

Bakker broke in. 'We just want to hear it from you. Otherwise we'll have to . . .' She was thinking. 'We'll have to arrest him for wasting police time.'

'He made a signed statement in Marnixstraat,' Vos added. 'If it's nothing but mischievous fantasy we can have him in front of a judge this afternoon. Wim Prins is a man trying to deal with a kidnap. I wouldn't give Zeeger much chance in those circumstances . . .'

Jewell stared at them and said, 'Jesus. Is it any wonder why these people find it so hard to get their lives back on track?'

She tapped at the wireless keyboard again.

'This doesn't come from me. OK?'

The printer started whirring. A transcript of what the Yellow House called a 'breakthrough group'. Everything on the table, however shameful, however deep the scars.

'Katja's a deeply troubled kid,' Jewell said. 'Borderline autistic and I don't think she ever got any treatment. I could see there was something there but I had to drag this out of her. It was like sucking poison out of a wound. She needed it.'

Just three of them in the room: Jewell, Katja and Jaap Zeeger. Every word he said confirmed. Katja was convinced Prins had murdered her mother. That this was to blame for her breakdown after Bea died.

'And you never thought of calling Marnixstraat?' Bakker asked, astonished.

'Would you have believed her?' Jewell wondered.

'The word of a junkie? Not too bright. Known to the police. Would you have taken her word against that of a man like Wim Prins?'

It was their turn to fall silent.

Outside, hearing the bustle of the tourists on the flower market quayside, Vos was about to call for Prins to be picked up when his phone rang.

De Groot. Liesbeth had been trying to reach him. There'd been a ransom note. Prins was out picking up the money.

'Where is he?' Vos asked.

'She doesn't know. He's not answering his phone,' De Groot said. 'I put Mulder to work on it since you were out. Zeedijk and Stormsteeg. Eleven thirty. We'll be there. Pieter?'

Vos was thinking.

'I'll get back to you,' he said.

Bakker stood in the street, leaning against the giant painted sunflowers on the wall. Puzzled now, not tetchy as she might have been the day before.

'That was easy in the end, wasn't it?' she said.

'Something should be. Thanks for coming up with that idea about Zeeger. I was struggling there.'

That cheered her up.

'I suppose there's a reason you didn't tell De Groot the woman in that nut hutch just confirmed everything he said about the lovely Wim.'

'The lovely Wim's got a ransom demand. We've little more than an hour to put together a surveillance and a snatch team for Chinatown,' Vos told her. 'It can wait.'

CHAPTER 6

Ten minutes on, after a fast bike ride, Vos and Bakker marched into Marnixstraat. De Groot had summoned a briefing on the fourth floor. Koeman managed to intercept them as they walked down the long corridor.

'No time,' Vos said, trying to brush him to one side.

'Make time,' Koeman insisted.

He blocked their way until he got through what he wanted to say. Anna de Vries, the murdered reporter, had visited Wim Prins in his office the previous afternoon.

'Why?' Bakker asked.

'I don't know,' Koeman said. 'Here's something else. Last night no one knows where Wim Prins was. Not the people in the council. Not his wife. He told her he went drinking on his own. Didn't get back till eleven thirty. We think the woman was murdered about an hour before that.' Koeman winced. 'One of the street girls says she heard a scream around then. Not that she did anything, naturally.'

'Later,' Vos said, trying to push past.

'That's not all,' Koeman went on, pulling some photos out of a plastic envelope. 'De Vries's phone fell into the gutter in the alley where she was stabbed. We got it back. There's a message supposed to be from Prins asking for a meeting in the Cafe Singel. He never showed. I checked. Then another supposedly from Katja Prins. She mentioned your name . . .'

Koeman thrust a piece of paper in front of his face, pointed a couple of lines down.

Can you hear me howling, Pieter? Don't you care?

Vos struggled to speak.

'You got one like that. Supposed to be from Anneliese,' Koeman said. 'It's in the files here. Except that one called you father. Not Pieter. How many people know that? Except the bastard who sent you it?'

Too many possibilities. Too many memories.

'These are all fakes,' Koeman went on. 'Rogue SIMs. The calls went through the same mast so it's the same person with two phones. Someone was reeling in that woman like a fish on the line. We need to get Wim Prins in here. Find out where he was last night. Jesus . . .'

He scratched at the brown walrus moustache.

'I met her a couple of times. She was a nice enough kid for a hack.'

Vos tapped the page of messages.

'If this was Prins . . . would he use his own name?'

'I don't know,' Koeman said straight off. 'Would

319

she have turned up if he called himself Donald Duck? Let's ask him.'

'You just hate politicians,' Vos said and did get past that time.

A high, angry voice down the corridor behind him.

'Don't we all?' Koeman cried.

CHAPTER 7

Wim Prins had used the same bank for almost a quarter of a century. A small private institution based in a turreted mansion in the Museum District. His account manager for most of that time had been Kees Alberts, a dour senior official familiar with international tax legislation and investment opportunities. It was through this man that Prins had bought the villa in Aruba, carefully diverting some of his income from the legal practice which then numbered Michiel Lindeman among its partners. There were other investments around the world too. Another villa in Greece. Some retail sites in Florida. Share portfolios based in a variety of Caribbean havens.

Money never bothered Prins much. His net worth, every last asset taken into consideration, was pushing the ten million euro mark. But most of that was tied down in funds and property. He'd needed little in the way of liquid cash for years and in truth had no idea whether he could raise half a million euros easily at all.

Alberts soon put him straight. After Prins called

the day before he'd worked out some swift calculations. Prins had immediate access to two hundred and forty thousand euros. The money sat on the banker's desk, in a black leather Tumi case as he'd demanded. Four hundred euros for that already deducted from the pile.

'There must be more,' Prins insisted.

'Lots more,' Alberts agreed. 'I just can't turn it into cash the moment you click your fingers. Give me till tomorrow and I could probably add a hundred thousand. A week and we could probably liquidate a million. Most of your money's in property, Wim. I can get you loans against that. Expensive loans. But not overnight. And . . .'

The banker gazed at him.

'I have to ask why. There are rules these days. About money-laundering . . .'

'Do I look like a money-launderer?'

'The rules don't ask what you look like. Only what you do. And why.'

Silence.

'And why?' Alberts repeated.

'Because it appears someone's kidnapped my daughter. And unless I give them half a million euros . . .' He glanced at his watch. 'One hour from now she could be dead. Check with Marnixstraat if you like. They know all about it.'

The banker went white.

'You asked,' Prins said.

'This is a bad time, isn't it? What with the stories in the papers—'

'Forget about the papers. How can I get more money?'

Alberts shrugged.

'You can't. Not from here. Maybe the police can come up with a solution. Marked notes. A case with dye in it or something. That's why they're there.'

'No time. And they won't do me any favours.'

'This is the twenty-first century, Wim. We don't keep vast sums of cash lying around. Who wants it? Who needs it?' He tapped the case. 'Most of that I had to get from somewhere else.'

Prins waited. Nothing more.

'If you don't want it . . .' Alberts began, reaching for the case.

'It's mine, isn't it?' Prins snarled then snatched it from him and walked out into the bright cold day.

De Nachtwacht was such a simple plan, one he'd thought of while staring at Rembrandt's colossal painting in the Rijksmuseum just a few minutes away. A group of sturdy Amsterdam worthies, ready to go out into the city. Drums beating. Weapons at the ready. There was a young girl too, bright-eyed, golden-haired, a dead chicken mysteriously attached to her waist. Some kind of symbol, he guessed. He'd never known. Never been interested in the finer detail. This was a canvas about men willing to fight to take control of something they cherished. The city. To make it safe for their families. To bring light out of the darkness.

Was it vanity that made it so appealing to him?

For most of his marriage he'd been unfaithful. Slyly sleeping with Liesbeth on the side. How many of Rembrandt's men in their fine costumes, good churchgoing wealthy burghers, were up to the same tricks? Was it the city he wanted to purify? Or himself ?

Prins watched the traffic move lazily down the long straight road of Weteringschans. A cab meandered towards him. That morning he'd bought a pair of cheap, heavy-rimmed sunglasses from a tourist store near Leidseplein. As the Mercedes drew to a halt he put them on then climbed into the back, sat there, hand on the Tumi case.

Said nothing.

'Is this a date or do you want to go somewhere?' the driver asked.

'I want to go somewhere,' Prins said. 'Doesn't everyone?'

The man shrugged, waited.

Wim Prins looked at himself in the mirror. Just one more middle-aged man, grey hair, heavy sunglasses, big and cheap, hiding most of his face.

'Schiphol,' he said then placed the black case on his lap.

Hand baggage. Good enough to take him halfway across the world.

CHAPTER 8

Margriet Willemsen was at the window when Hendriks walked in. She'd taken a call from a detective, Koeman. Told him as little as possible. Simply confirmed what he already appeared to know.

This didn't make Alex Hendriks happy.

'That dead reporter was here yesterday. She had the video for God's sake. What do we do?'

'We distance ourselves,' she said, coming back to the desk. 'We stay calm. We tell them the truth as far as it goes. We wait and see what happens. This doesn't affect us, Alex. Keep cool.'

'Cool?' He screwed his eyes shut, wondered what was coming next. 'We need to talk to Prins. Work on our story.'

'Wim's out of this place for now,' she insisted. 'You leave him to me. Do you know what happened?'

He had to say it.

'I got hacked. There was a girl in the office. A temp from one of the drug charities. Now she's pissed off somewhere. I'm pretty sure she got into my account. She must have sent it.'

'You know, Alex, if I didn't think you'd run screaming to Marnixstraat I'd send you naked out into the street right now.'

Hendriks scowled.

'But you do,' he said. 'And I need you. I just wanted to rein him in. That's all. Where the hell is he? I tried calling home. His wife sounded . . .' Hendriks liked Liesbeth Prins. There was something fiery and independent about her. He couldn't understand what she saw in her dry, introverted husband. 'She sounded dreadful.'

'I don't know where he's gone,' Willemsen said. 'Who cares? Marnixstraat have got enough on their hands. If they start asking more questions put them on to me.'

'It doesn't work like that! They're the police. They can do whatever they like.'

She nodded.

'And I'm vice-mayor of the city council. Mulder's our link man for De Nachtwacht. If anyone from Marnixstraat comes on tell them they need to talk to him.'

Hendriks nodded. There was another question. It wouldn't go away.

'That reporter . . .'

'They think it was a mugging gone wrong,' she said.

'You don't think . . . Wim . . . Jesus, he was mad as hell when we threw him out of here. Liesbeth said he was out last night. She doesn't know where. If they start—'

326

'For God's sake, Alex, will you shut up?' she yelled. 'You kicked this nightmare off, didn't you?'

'Not really,' Hendriks snapped back. 'I just threw a little fuel on a fire that was already burning.'

She didn't like it when people answered back. Didn't have any good response either.

'Hell of a coincidence if someone mugged that woman just a few hours after she was in here scaring the shit out of him,' he added.

Margriet Willemsen smiled then. The smile from the election posters. Broad and insincere.

'A coincidence,' she said. 'That's all it is. We're in this together, Alex. We'll weather it together too.' She waved at the door. 'You can go now. Just do as I say. Everything will be fine.'

Outside in the corridor his phone buzzed. Hendriks looked at the screen. An incoming text.

Til Stamm writes, *u want me?*

Oh yes, Hendriks thought. There were so many questions.

Alex Hendriks writes, *We need to meet. Where? When?*

A long pause. He thought he'd lost her. Wondered what he'd do if that was the case. Then . . .

Til Stamm writes, *zeedijk & stormsteeg 1130*

Hendriks leaned against the windows looking out to De Wallen. He knew the city so well he could picture that junction in his head. Two old narrow cobbled streets meeting at a crossroads never meant for modern traffic. Chinese restaurants and a couple of shops. A brown bar he visited sometimes, the Cafe Oost-West.

Why the hell would a druggie temp who'd raided his private account want to meet him in Chinatown in the middle of the morning?

Alex Hendriks writes, *Come into the office. Everything's cool.*

Another pause and he really thought he'd lost her. Then . . .

nothings cool alex. didnt u notice? B there.

CHAPTER 9

Nineteen men and one woman in the Marnixstraat briefing room. Mulder at the front issuing orders, Vos and Laura Bakker in the first line of chairs.

De Groot had outlined the arrangement beforehand. Mulder would run the operation on the ground. Vos would deal with any subsequent interviews. The logic seemed unbreakable. Vos was newly returned to the service, dealing with men he hadn't worked with recently. Mulder had been a serving senior officer throughout, knew all the latest codes and buzzwords.

Argument over before it had even begun.

Vos and Bakker listened to the stakeout plan. Men in plain clothes on the street. In offices overlooking the crossroads. A couple in the Cafe Oost-West. Cars ready to block off all the exit routes. A surveillance helicopter swooping high over the city, not fixed since that would only serve to create suspicion. Fast links into all the nearby mobile phone masts, ready to trace calls as they came and went.

All in position from fifteen minutes before Prins was due. Still no word of the man himself. Just his wife downstairs, waiting in reception, waiting on news.

Vos heard that, closed his eyes, made a mental note to leave with Bakker by the back. Then, when Mulder's briefing was done, asked, 'And us? Where do we go?'

The tall officer looked at him and shook his head.

'You wait here,' Mulder said. 'We've got a team in place. I don't have room for novices.'

Bakker started squawking straight off, only to be quietened by a fierce word from Frank de Groot.

'It's a team, Vos,' Mulder repeated. 'You don't know how we work and I don't have time to start giving lessons now.' He pointed to one of the computers on a desk at the edge of the room. 'We've put some temporary CCTV cameras in place. If you can find a spare desk you can watch it all from here. We bring in the contact. If we can get a location for Katja Prins then we deal with that too.' He looked at his watch. 'Thirty minutes to be in position. If you've got any questions . . .'

Laura Bakker put up a hand, like a schoolgirl wanting to ask a question.

'What?' Mulder asked.

'Bring Wim Prins in, will you?' she asked. 'Just so we can tidy up a few things.'

Mulder looked at Vos.

'Yes,' Vos said. 'I'd like that too.'

CHAPTER 10

Schiphol. Prins walked straight to the KLM counter, paid almost five thousand euros for a one-way business class ticket to Oranjestad in Aruba. The plane was due to leave at eleven forty-five. Nine hours fifty minutes to fly from a chilly Amsterdam to the warm Caribbean. After that a cab to San Nicolas, a hired boat to cover the twenty-seven kilometres to Venezuela, an easy haven beyond immediate Dutch jurisdiction.

There he could put the money into the safest haven he could find. Think. Wait. Drink.

Maybe even smoke and find a whore. Everyone else did. Why not? This was a new time, a new world.

Hand baggage only. The counter gave him a boarding pass. Within three minutes he was through immigration with his electronic passport. Didn't even have to look a border guard in the eye.

The airport was always busy, a sprawling complex of gates and shopping arcades that seemed to stretch forever. There was a business lounge. He avoided it. There might have been someone there he knew. Instead Prins wasted time in a free display of paintings from the Rijksmuseum then sat alone

331

in a tucked-away bar, sipping at a beer, picking at a hot dog, clutching the case, the heavy sunglasses on his face all the time.

Just after eleven now. The police would be flooding Chinatown. He looked at his phone. Messages from Liesbeth. She'd gone to Marnixstraat but didn't say any more than that.

Where are you? Why don't you call?

He thought about this, tapped out a reply.

Everything's fine. Be patient. We'll get through this.

She came straight back.

I need to talk to you, Wim.

But you don't, he thought. You haven't. Not for a long time. Since the marriage. That changed everything. Before, when it was an affair, illicit, secret, stolen, they were joined by an unspoken, interior passion. A frantic heat that a wedding ring extinguished almost overnight, rendering the magical mundane.

I'll call when I can.

From Venezuela. Isla Margarita maybe. He'd been there once with Bea. She spent most of the time coked out of her skull.

Liesbeth wasn't like that. Not yet. And he would call her. Sometime. But not soon.

He looked at the phone. They could trace him through that if they wanted. So he turned it off. Took out the battery. Sat on his own, feeling like a criminal, praying for the moment he could step on board.

CHAPTER 11

Vos and Bakker found an office with a PC hooked up to Mulder's CCTV circuit. It was just after eleven. Nothing much happening from the six cameras on the street. That didn't seem wrong. Then he asked her to fetch Liesbeth, a couple of coffees and leave them alone.

Two minutes later she was back with a miserable-looking Liesbeth Prins and two cups of coffee from the best machine, one forensic owned and rarely allowed anyone else to use. Laura Bakker could be persuasive when she felt like it.

She left to find a hot desk somewhere else. Vos turned off the PC screen. Liesbeth sat down by the window, didn't look him in the eye. Didn't answer when he asked if she knew where her husband had been the previous night. Where he was now.

After a series of questions she barely acknowledged she said, 'He's got the money. Or so he said. What else do you expect?'

Gently, he asked again about Anneliese and Katja. How they might have known each other. Whether there was any suggestion they'd gone to a house on the Prinsen in their free time. He was used to awkward questions. But none so close and painful as those he knew he had to broach now.

'She was sixteen years old,' Liesbeth said wearily. 'You were never there. I had a life of my own too. Do you think I knew what she did every minute of the day?'

'The place she went on the Prinsen was a brothel,' Vos said, not taking his eyes off her.

'What?'

'A privehuis. A kind of club. Probably one where the girls were . . . pretty young. Getting groomed.'

Nothing.

'We found her blood there. Her bus pass. She was in that place. Maybe with Katja. God knows who else . . .'

She shut her eyes tightly for a second, mouth a taut grimace of fury and pain.

'Liesbeth,' he repeated. 'We found Anneliese's blood—'

'Are you happy?' she shrieked. 'Can you sign off the death certificate now? Mark the case closed?'

'No. I can't. I don't know what happened. I'm trying to find out.'

'Why are you pushing this shit at me? I did my best. I was there when you weren't. Not every minute. Every fucking second. But I was . . .'

'This isn't about blame,' he said. 'I don't feel that. I don't think you do either.'

She wouldn't look at him. Gulped at the coffee.

'What's it about then?'

'The truth. Honesty,' Vos said with a shrug. 'What else have we got?'

'You sound like Wim. Begging for votes. Talking in easy riddles that mean nothing—'

'There's a procedure,' he broke in.

'What procedure?' she hissed.

He folded his arms, kept his eyes on her.

'Something we go through in every case. DNA. We've got Anneliese's obviously. Now we've got Katja's.'

Alongside the tears welling in her eyes there was anger and fear.

'It doesn't matter what a drop of blood says,' Vos added. 'She's my daughter. *Our* daughter. I guess . . . I was out working a lot. At night. Pretty boring when I was around too. And Wim . . . with all that money . . . a wife who didn't love him . . .'

Half hunched, clutching at the coffee cup, she glared at him.

'I stayed with you because I couldn't marry him,' she said. 'Is that what you want to hear?'

'Not really.'

'And you never suspected, Pieter? Not once. If you'd asked me . . . if you'd just noticed I wasn't around when I should have been . . .'

'Then you'd have left me,' Vos said and had to ask himself: had he realized this all along? Had a part of him silenced that troubled, suspicious voice for fear of the consequences if he listened to it?

'I guess.'

'Did they know they were half-sisters?' he asked.

'Did Anneliese have any idea Wim was her real father? This could be important. I'm trying to understand . . .'

'No.'

He waited and when she said nothing asked, 'Are you sure of that?'

'Yes.' A pause. 'I mean . . . I didn't tell her. You couldn't. Wim . . .'

'He knew?'

The coffee cup went flying. Not at him. Just at the wall, at the world.

'For Christ's sake! Do you think this is easy? I never knew. I didn't want to. She could have been yours. I wish to God she had been. Maybe things would have turned out differently. Maybe . . .'

'Is it possible Bea knew?' he asked. 'Could Anneliese have found out from her?'

She shrugged, looked at him.

'You don't even want to face it now, do you? I don't know what Bea thought. I wondered sometimes if she suspected. She looked at me in the law office and—'

'This is important. If Anneliese knew—'

'Liese,' she said sharply. 'That's what she was called. She wasn't a child any more. *Liese*. A teenager. Getting inquisitive. Getting . . . devious too.'

'Liese.'

He'd no idea why he never shortened her name. It hadn't seemed necessary somehow. And now that simple, easy omission seemed to condemn him. He wasn't a bad parent. Just a neglectful, distracted one.

'I didn't think . . .'

'No,' she said. 'You were too busy saving other people. You're so good at seeing into the lives of strangers, aren't you? But you couldn't see what was happening in front of your own nose. In your own home.'

He didn't answer.

'Or if you could,' she added, 'you didn't have the courage to mention it.'

Her frail hands touched his chest.

'If you'd said something. If I'd seen I'd hurt you . . .'

Silence between them for a long moment. Then she said, 'I hated the way you worked and worked. It made me feel small and unimportant. When you did come home you only paid attention to her. Never me.'

'I'm sorry,' he whispered. 'I guess I don't show things . . .'

'You didn't notice, Pieter. Don't make excuses.'

'Perhaps not. If I can find Katja . . . If that takes us to what happened with Anne . . . with Liese . . .'

'She's dead,' Liesbeth Prins said in a flat, defeated voice. 'Don't you know it? Can't you feel it?'

'No. I can't.'

'Not until you see her corpse? You never left this place, did you? Not in your head. I stopped wishing for that long ago. I didn't want to go mad. Not like you. That was too easy.'

He nodded.

'If there's something else I should know . . .' Vos said.

'I couldn't control her that summer. You were hardly there. She wasn't at school. I was working part-time in forensic here. You got me that, remember? I wanted something to do. I said we needed the money.' She laughed. 'That was a lie. I was just bored. Sick of nannying an ungrateful teenager and watching you come home exhausted every night, too tired to talk.'

Vos remembered now. She was on the payroll in Marnixstraat for just a few months that summer, filing, doing clerical work on the top floor for a while.

'You never saw it,' she said. 'But she was running wild. Getting back late. Wouldn't say where she'd been. Who with.'

'You could have told me.'

Liesbeth Prins laughed, and it was so sudden, so unexpected the sound chilled his blood.

'Why? You'd have given her some money and told her to go and buy some new clothes. Please . . .' She reached out for his fingers. 'You were a soft touch. Always were. For her. For me when I bothered to ask.'

She must have seen something in his face.

'Oh dear,' she said. 'Here I am shattering all your illusions again. How many times do I have to say this before you get it? We weren't the perfect family, Pieter. Wouldn't have been even if I hadn't been screwing around with Wim. Life's not like that. All neat and tidy . . .'

338

'No,' he said and took away his hands.

She bit her lip, thought over what she wanted to say.

'One day I saw her with this girl. They looked so alike. I kind of recognized her. I didn't know where from. Wim and I . . . we were always discreet. It was never that house of his. Of . . . ours now.' She shrugged at that. 'So I followed them. All the way to Vondelpark. Watched them buy ice cream. Sit down. Look . . . beautiful and happy.'

A bitter, sour look.

'Then along came Bea. And she sat there too. Not like me. An outsider. The enemy. It was as if she was one of them. Another kid. Part of the deal. Whatever it was. I never knew . . .' Her finger traced a circle in the spilled coffee on the table. 'I never dared ask. And then a few days later Liese was gone.'

'You could have told me . . .' he repeated.

'Don't be stupid. I didn't want to open that can of worms. Besides . . . You all said it was those gangsters getting their own back. Or some madman. I'd nothing to tell. Still don't.'

'Did Bea see you?'

A quick, grim laugh.

'Oh yes. I went over there and introduced myself. Liese wouldn't even look me in the eye. Bea did though. Crazy bitch.'

'You could have told me.'

She stared at him, puzzled.

'How? Why?'

Almost two decades together. And still a gulf between them. Invisible walls, dark secrets beneath.

'The place we found her blood . . . the privehuis . . . was on the Prinsen. Opposite Amstelveld. You know it?'

She shook her head.

'Her blood?'

'Not much,' he said. 'I don't think she was killed there. But this place . . .'

'I didn't follow her. I didn't spy on her. She was a teenager. What good would that have done? I'm not like you. Always looking for something to put right. The world's broken. You can't put it back together. No one can.'

Vos didn't know what to say. Then Laura Bakker saved him.

Walked in, didn't knock, came straight to the computer, turned on the screen, started fiddling with the keyboard, said, 'You've got to see this. Something's happening. I don't . . .'

'Don't what?' he asked when she didn't go on.

'I don't get it.'

She looked at Liesbeth Prins.

'I think you should leave,' Bakker said.

But by then the feed from the CCTV camera was up. Figures milling round the crossroads between Zeedijk and Stormsteeg. The occasional crackle of a police transmission over the radio channel.

'Where's Wim?' Liesbeth Prins asked. 'I can't see him.'

Vos glanced at his watch. Twenty past eleven.

'Ten minutes to go,' he said.

'He's always early, never late,' she whispered. Looked at him and said, 'I'm sorry. All the things I did . . . just happened. I never asked for them. Never wanted them really.'

'You should leave!' Bakker said more loudly.

But Liesbeth Prins's eyes were locked on the screen.

'There's that little man from the council,' she said, placing a finger on a figure moving slowly across the cobblestones. 'The one who works for Wim.'

Vos wasn't watching. He scribbled a note, passed it to Bakker, told her to check it out with intelligence.

CHAPTER 12

'What the hell's he doing here?' Theo Jansen grumbled as he sat down in the back room of Maarten's shop.

The place was still closed. The barber looked harried and tired. Nervous at the two men who'd joined him in the apartment, sipping at instant coffee, eyeing each other warily.

Michiel Lindeman had come willingly when Maarten went back to him. The reluctance of the previous day was gone. There were reasons. Jimmy Menzo was dead. Control of the entire city was in the balance.

'He's here because I invited him,' Lindeman said without a blink. 'Because he's needed.'

Short, muscular, thirty-five or so, dark-skinned, shifty eyes, Max Robles smiled too much, laughed too much. Had been a go-between when Jansen was dealing with Menzo before. As trustworthy as any Surinamese hood could be.

'I'm not sure I need you,' Jansen told Lindeman. 'The likes of him . . .'

'Jesus, Theo. A touch of gratitude wouldn't go amiss,' the lawyer replied. 'You're a criminal on the run. A murderer. Any of us could go down just for being in this room with you.' Jansen sniffed, didn't have anything to say. 'Do you think you can get choosy now?'

'Gentlemen,' Maarten intervened. 'Let's deal with this calmly. There's business on the table. Some practical problems to solve. We need calm heads.' He glanced at Jansen in a way he would never have done before. 'From everyone. OK?'

'Theo.' Robles was beaming as usual. Big white teeth. Vast hand extended across the table. 'Last night you popped my boss. I'm here like Mr Lindeman asked. Don't that show goodwill?'

'You tell me,' Jansen answered. Then nodded at Maarten. 'Did you shake him down for a gun when he turned up?'

Robles laughed. So did Maarten. Then the barber pulled a small pistol out of his trousers, showed it round the table.

'Why am I here?' Jansen wanted to know. Then listened.

It was Lindeman talking mainly. Of the need for a peace. Of pressing business decisions to do with money and supply lines. And how Theo Jansen could stay the titular king of Amsterdam from afar. In a day or two when the heat died down they could put him in a car south, down to Belgium. Fix a private plane from Ostend. The same place Jimmy Menzo had flown to the previous Monday.

After that . . .

'Anywhere you want,' Maarten said quickly. 'Anywhere.'

Eight per cent of the action for nothing at all. The day-to-day work would be down to the remnants of Menzo's men working under Max Robles, alongside any willing troops from Jansen's former ranks.

'That's a lot of money for sitting in the sun,' Jansen said.

'True,' Robles agreed. 'But what's the alternative?'

No one spoke.

'I'll tell you,' he went on. 'We carry on fighting. You and me. And then the Turks come in. The Serbs. God knows who else. They're sniffing round already. Getting above themselves.' He tapped his index finger three times on the table. 'There's a black hole out there and someone's going to fill it. Either we let them know their place or we're gone.'

'Two days ago you tried to kill me,' Jansen said.

The swarthy man opposite him nodded, said, 'Yeah. That was rude, wasn't it? But think about this. Jimmy and Miriam are dead. So are those two kids who came for you. If we're willing to forgive and forget—'

'Someone murdered my daughter,' Jansen broke in. 'I don't forgive that. I don't forget it either.'

'No,' Robles said. 'I'd feel the same. Honestly.' He held out his hand again. 'It wasn't us. We'd nothing to do with that. Jimmy didn't used to talk to us when he went down to Ostend with Miriam.

That was their private time. I guess even he didn't know till he got back.'

The hand stayed in front of him, steady as a rock.

'Shake on that if you believe me,' Robles said. 'If you don't we're all wasting our time.'

Jansen didn't move, just said, 'Someone killed her.'

'Not us,' Robles replied and the good humour was gone from his voice. 'Why would we? Jimmy wanted you dead.' He looked round the table, nervous for the first time. 'Here's the truth. He and Rosie had a deal. They talked, two weeks before you were due back in court. If you got out, went away, didn't try to get back in the game . . . that was it. No more nonsense.'

'So why'd he try to shoot me?' Jansen snorted.

And still the big dark hand stayed over the table.

'Because he didn't think you'd listen,' Robles answered. 'Jimmy could be stupid sometimes. But on that . . . I think he was dead right.' He waved his hand. 'If I take this away it doesn't come back. We both suffer. Think about it.'

Theo Jansen rose from the table, faced him, furious, going red.

'Who killed my daughter?' he roared.

It was Lindeman who spoke first.

'Whoever's snatched the Prins girl,' he said. 'Isn't it obvious?'

'Not to me it isn't,' Jansen told him. 'Who—?'

'I don't know who!' Lindeman yelled.

So loud it surprised Jansen. The lawyer was one of the most composed, collected men he knew. He'd never heard him raise his voice before.

'Someone screwing with everyone,' Lindeman added. 'With you. With Prins. I don't know . . . with Pieter Vos too. Why else did they dump her in that boat next to his? Someone's trying to get him back and—'

'Rosie had nothing to do with the Vos girl,' Jansen cut in. 'None of us did.' He looked at Robles. 'Did we?'

'I don't think so,' the man from Paramaribo agreed.

Lindeman sighed, folded his arms, waited for Jansen's attention.

'Jimmy sent those kids of his round to that prive-huis,' the lawyer pointed out. 'He must have known something—'

'It was just insurance,' Robles cut in. 'He wanted them dead and some money back from that place. It had been sitting on the books ever since he got it. A privehuis didn't interest Jimmy much. Not enough return in a game like that.'

Jansen didn't look convinced.

'It's the truth,' Robles insisted. 'Believe it or not. Your choice.'

'The truth?' Jansen looked at the three of them. 'What do we know from Marnixstraat? I had men there. Menzo must have some too. The same ones for all I know . . .'

'They're struggling like the rest of us,' Lindeman

said carefully. 'It looks like Prins could be in the frame for something. I don't know what.'

'Wim Prins?' Jansen asked. 'Mr Clean? Your old partner?'

'Sometimes you think you know people,' Lindeman said with a shrug. 'Sometimes you're wrong.'

Jansen grunted something, took the hand in front of him. Shook it.

'Find me who killed Rosie,' he said, 'and you can have anything you want. Take the eight per cent. Split it between you for all I care.'

The three of them looked interested.

'I'll make some calls,' Robles said. 'Talk to people.'

'You do that,' Jansen agreed. He nodded at the barber. 'Maarten can reach me when you've got something.'

Outside again he was desperate for a beer. Jansen looked at his watch. One minute to eleven thirty. There was a bar round the corner, quiet and discreet.

He strode towards the door. There were a couple of uniformed cops down the street. One of them looking his way.

Theo Jansen crossed the road, walked on, back towards the alley that led into the Begijnhof. He felt a stranger in his own city and that was new.

CHAPTER 13

Klaas Mulder sat in the near-empty Cafe Oost-West stirring sugar into a sludgy double espresso. Happy with the disposition of his men. Not so pleased the officer he had closest to him was Koeman, someone who never quite possessed sufficient respect for his superiors.

'So what happens?' Koeman asked. 'If we snatch whoever's turned up for the money? How does that help us get this poor kid free?'

'The poor kid should have been inside long ago,' Mulder retorted. 'We're not dealing with a school-girl here.'

Koeman tugged on his moustache.

'Sorry. I'm struggling for the relevance of that remark.'

Mulder walked to the window, surveyed the cobbled intersection between the streets.

'And where the hell is Prins?' Koeman asked. He looked at his watch. 'He's got five minutes to show. If this was my girl I'd be—'

'It's not,' Mulder said. He peered at a diminutive middle-aged man in a smart brown coat standing outside the Chinese restaurant opposite. 'Who the hell's that? Get a picture of him. Run it through intelligence.'

Koeman came to the window.

'Alex Hendriks. Something big in the city council. Runs the general office or something. I looked him up in the cuttings this morning. Before I called there. He works directly for Prins. Sorry . . . *worked.*'

'How'd you know?'

Koeman came straight out with it. How Anna de Vries's paper had told him she'd visited the offices and talked to Prins the afternoon before she was murdered.

'He's a politician,' Mulder said. 'The press talk to him all the time. It was a mugging. We'll deal with the dead when we've got the living out of the way.'

The detective bristled. He got out his book and read aloud the messages on De Vries's phone.

'Why didn't I know about this?' Mulder demanded.

Koeman waved a finger in the air and said, 'Because you were busy running round organizing a snatch squad?'

'You'll push me too far one day . . .'

'Can't wait.' Koeman checked his watch, looked out into the street. 'Eleven thirty on the dot. I see no sign of Mr Clean. Just that Hendriks character. Maybe we should pull him in. Maybe . . .'

He stopped.

'What the hell's that?' Mulder asked, looking down Zeedijk.

CHAPTER 14

Security at Schiphol was close to the gate. Prins walked up, placed his phone in the tray along with his belt then, to make sure, his black business shoes. The woman by the scanner tapped the Tumi case.

'Laptop?'

'No laptop.'

'No liquids. Nothing sharp. No . . .'

He kept the sunglasses on and smiled at her.

'I'm very boring really,' he said and watched as the case slid into the scanner. Then he strode through the arch, no beep, picked it up, walked on.

The KLM gate just ahead. No queue for the business line.

He looked at the bright blue and white plane beyond. One of their oldest MD11s. Gave the desk his pass, went on board.

Three rows of two seats at the front. He was by the left-hand window. Most of the business cabin was empty from what he could see.

A glass of champagne turned up, half a smile from the flight attendant.

Everything seemed to be a lurid shade of blue. That and the early drink gave him a headache.

Prins sipped at it anyway. Waited, hoping. Finally heard the doors close, felt the pushback.

Then looked out of the window and watched as the aircraft taxied slowly towards the runway.

CHAPTER 15

Five devils on the street, black, red, orange, blue and livid green, twirling their tails, playfully jabbing their pitchforks at passing strangers.

The tallest was blacked up head to toe, with tall goat-like horns, and looked near-naked. He was carrying a big stereo on his shoulder, cavorting like the rest of them to a deafening pop song.

His teeth were dyed red and he smiled a lot. They all did.

Red teeth. Lurid costumes. Cocky attitude.

Koeman was racking his brain. He'd seen this bunch before.

'This is all we need,' Mulder grumbled.

The shortest one, bright in lurid scarlet, chased one of the plain-clothes men, chattering wildly, prodding with his fork, making monkey noises loud enough to reach the cafe.

The song became clear.

Stevie Wonder. A happy number, at odds with the strange, half-sinister spectacle on the street.

It came through loud and unmistakable as the five demons danced to the chorus.

'Happy birthday . . .' sang the refrain across the cobbled junction between Zeedijk and Stormsteeg.

'Happy birthday?' Koeman whispered. 'What the fu . . .?'

Mulder was on the secure phone. Koeman looked at his watch. Twenty-five to twelve. It was hard to imagine a lawyer-turned-politician missing the drop-off for his own daughter's ransom.

Even harder to imagine a kidnapper closing the deal with these clowns outside.

Too many coincidences here.

'He's not coming,' Koeman murmured to himself. 'This was never going to happen.'

Not that Mulder was listening. The hoofdinspecteur was barking down the line trying to raise someone. Vos by the sound of it. And getting nowhere.

Koeman walked over, waited for a break in the heated one-way conversation and said, 'He's not coming, Mulder.'

The bunch of devils was getting closer, looking round the streets. The tall, blacked-up one pulled out a sheet of paper from somewhere.

Koeman recognized the face now. A bunch of buskers from one of the anarchist communes. They liked to parade round the city doing quick street shows then shaking a hat at any tourists stupid enough to stop.

'He's not . . .'

'I know . . .' Mulder began.

Then a voice cried, in a strained, foreign accent,

'Prins! Oh Wim! Happy birthday, Wim!' The music got louder. They began twirling round again, waving their arms, clapping to the song. 'Happy birthday.'

Koeman couldn't work it out. Couldn't believe it.

There was no Wim Prins. Just the man from the council, Alex Hendriks, wandering around like a lost idiot.

'Screw this,' Koeman said. 'He's mine.'

Didn't wait to hear what Mulder thought. Just walked straight out into the busy street.

People stared at the demons screeching falsetto, 'Wim! Wim! Where are you? Oh, Wim . . .'

Mulder was behind him. Had called down officers from the surrounding shops and offices. It was all wrong, had been from the start. There never was a pick-up here. Prins or no Prins. They'd been fooled.

The team gathered round the entertainers. One of them grabbed the stereo and turned off the music. The devils started to realize what was going on. Amsterdam was a tolerant, laid-back city. Ordinarily they might have got away with this and received a quiet word at the most.

Not now.

Koeman had it worked out in his head already. Someone had paid this bunch to come here. Told them a man called Wim Prins had a birthday. That he'd be around the corner just waiting to be surprised.

There'd be no footprints back to whoever placed

the order. Probably paid for in cash. Even if the dancing devils did know who it was they'd never say. They were a tribe, lived apart from the police, from the rest of the city. Different creatures on a different planet.

So all they had was Alex Hendriks, a staid, middle-aged council official, standing at the corner of Zeedijk and Stormsteeg looking confused and lost. And more than a little frightened.

Definitely the latter when Koeman marched up, showed his ID, introduced himself.

Koeman smiled, pointed to the bunch of devils. 'What do you think of the entertainment, Alex?'

'I was just passing . . .'

'Don't say that!' Koeman put a hand close to the man's face. 'Whatever you do, don't say that. *I was just passing.* No. It's downright rude.'

The detective looked back at the cafe and winked.

'We've been in there for the last fifteen minutes. Ten of them I've been watching you stand here looking ready to piss yourself.'

A police van was turning up, lights flashing, siren howling. The demons were going inside, however hard they protested.

'I've got to go back to the office,' Hendriks said, trying to summon up some courage.

'Your old boss was supposed to be here,' Koeman said. 'Eleven thirty on the dot. Meant to hand over half a million euros ransom for his daughter.' A smile. 'He didn't show. You did. Along with a bunch of dancing devils yelling out his name.'

355

Koeman put away his ID card, glanced up and down the narrow streets.

'Do I look like a man who believes in coincidence? Or just a fucking idiot?'

Hendriks was shaking then.

'We're going to Marnixstraat,' Koeman said. 'For a long and interesting chat. The only question is . . .'

He frowned, took out a pair of cuffs, juggled them round on his right index finger.

'Are you coming willingly? Or do I drag you there?'

CHAPTER 16

It would be warm and sunny in Aruba. He could picture the thirty-minute ride to the coast. Haggling with one of the fishermen about hiring a boat to Venezuela. That would take a thousand euros at least. And if he picked the wrong man . . .

Prins found his fingers wandering to the case tucked into the storage compartment by the window. That was all he had now. All that stood between him and oblivion.

'Sir . . .?'

The business class flight attendant was a pretty young woman, curly fair hair tucked beneath her blue hat, bending over him solicitously, wanting to take the glass. Prins looked round. One other passenger in the cabin and he was on the far side. The next nine and a half hours would be peaceful. Perhaps he'd sleep. If he did the case was going beneath his feet.

'I need your glass for take-off.'

Prins drained the champagne in one and handed it over. Looked round the cabin again. Wanted to laugh. Life was like this in the sprawling council offices next to the Opera House. Cocooned. Protected

357

from the world outside. It had been the same in the law too, even when Michiel Lindeman was walking the tightrope between the police and the underworld. Nothing from outside ever touched him there. No one.

He looked out of the window at the flat fields stretching to the low grey horizon. This two-dimensional land had always enclosed him, trapped him, held him close. Was it odd to think he could escape it? That a simple act of flight could detach him from the boundless past like a conjuror's trick?

Drink wasn't one of his vices. But for the next few hours . . .

The plane kept moving. A line of others ahead. Then the last one cleared. He pulled his belt more tightly around his waist. Felt for the case again.

The flight attendant was strapped in opposite. He looked. She smiled. Then the phone rang next to her. She answered, glanced at him briefly, took off her belt, got up and went towards the cockpit.

Prins looked out of the window. Another plane came into view. It went to the piano keys at the end of the runway. Lined up. Ran noisily down the asphalt.

The flight attendant didn't come back. The plane didn't move. He looked at his watch. Almost midday. He wondered what had happened at the cobbled crossroads between Zeedijk and Stormsteeg. Knew that he would never see that grimy street in Chinatown again. Or anything of Amsterdam.

Then the sound changed. The engines winding

down. He looked out of the window. A Volvo estate, white with blue and red police markings, had pulled up on the taxiway ahead. A couple of airport vehicles followed it. Behind them was a set of long steps, the kind they used when there was no jetway available.

The young woman in the blue uniform came out. Looked at him. Embarrassed.

'Mr Prins. There's a problem . . .'

'Don't worry,' he said, undoing the belt, taking out the case. Smiling at her. She was extraordinarily pretty and he didn't like the idea he'd interfered with her day.

The rear doors of the white police Volvo were opening. He knew what he'd see there. Pieter Vos. A man who never ceased looking. Vos got out in his creased blue coat, swept back his too-long brown hair, looked up at the plane, bright, keen, alert. Young too somehow, as if the past had somehow frozen him the moment his daughter went missing. A man who knew what he wanted straight away, Prins thought. Then came a tall, slender young woman with red hair flying loose, sweeping all round her in the choppy wake coming off another jet that had just started to lumber down the runway, ready to rise free from the unforgiving grip of gravity. To escape.

To escape.

That was all he'd wanted. A moment of peace. Some distance from the grasping, grubby world.

He got up. Brushed down his clothes. Clutched

the case beneath his arm. Followed the flight attendant to the door. Waited and watched as she worked the long handle beneath the porthole window.

Finally she got it free, pushed with her slim shoulder, brought sharp Schiphol daylight streaming into the cabin, an icy breeze alongside.

The steps weren't there yet. Beyond her outstretched arm he could see everything now. Fields and asphalt. Planes and tiny people gathering below. To take him back to the city. To Marnixstraat and so many questions that'd never end.

The woman kept her arm out, holding him back. But she wasn't looking. There was no need.

Prins simply pushed her sideways, walked on, stood on the lip of the plane door, gazed down, held his breath.

Grey taxiway, grass growing through the cracks. Fifteen metres or so to the ground. Enough he guessed and leaned forward, opening the case as he went, twisting so he fell head first, silent, eyes closed, wreathed in a cloud of flying banknotes.

An escape. A quick and easy one, no going back.

CHAPTER 17

Jaap Zeeger finished his statement just after eleven thirty. Waited for a while. Realized no one was much interested. Marnixstraat seemed to have better things to do.

Outside he shuffled his cheap windcheater around his shoulders, crossed the street, walked down towards the Prinsengracht. It was cold and looked like rain. A coffee somewhere. Something to eat. Maybe call in on the Yellow House and do some of the painting and decorating he'd promised. Then, at four, clock on with the courier service for the late shift.

Plenty of things to do. He didn't need dope or booze or cigarettes to achieve them any more.

Clear and clean.

That was what Barbara Jewell promised them. That was what they got.

This part of the city was so ordinary. So quiet. So . . . normal. Down Elandsgracht people walked their little dogs, cleaning up after them as they went. Shoppers and the odd tourist. People buying bread and meat from the organic butcher's. De Wallen was nothing like this. One day, Zeeger told himself, he'd move to the Jordaan. Get a full-time job. Settle down. Maybe find himself a girlfriend. A wife even. Fall into the kind of life he once sneered at. Away from uncertainty and the sudden threat of violence.

He walked past a coffee shop, wrinkled his nose at the stench of the joints from a couple of lowlifes hunched on a bench seat outside. The statues of Johnny Jordaan and his band were ahead of him. The bridge. The way back into the centre. Some time to waste. Some time to think.

A voice called.

'Hey, Jaap!'

He walked on.

One of the deadbeats smoking outside the shop looked familiar. No name. Just a reputation.

Picked up speed. The canal. Boats. The cop Vos lived near here somewhere. He knew that too.

'Hey . . .'

A hand on his arm. Firm and strong. A miserable, bearded face, dark with dirt and smoke. Lost eyes. Black and malevolent.

He'd looked like this once. Before the Yellow House saved him.

'Remember me?' the bum asked. His friend was next to him. A big guy too. No cops nearby. Just ordinary people and they knew best to walk on.

Zeeger said, 'I think you've got the wrong man. Sorry . . .'

The other was on the phone.

'There's a call out for you,' the first one said,

moving closer, putting his arm round Zeeger's skinny shoulders. 'People want to talk.'

He tried to struggle free. Mumbled, got scared, confused.

The way things used to be. He didn't feel so clear and clean any more.

So he did the stupid thing, the old thing. He kicked out with his feet, got the guy in the shins, started to run, down towards the bridge and the little bar on the corner.

Didn't get more than four steps before they were on him. Dope didn't make everyone slow. Or peaceful. He got a couple of kicks to the legs to bring him down, a couple more in the gut to keep him quiet.

Someone over the road was shouting. Talking about calling the police. But from what Zeeger'd heard in Marnixstraat the last thing they'd have on their minds would be a reformed druggie getting a shoeing from a couple of deadbeats in the shadow of Johnny Jordaan's statue in Elandsgracht.

He crouched on his knees, tried to roll into a ball, mumbled something pathetic.

'They want to talk to him, moron,' the other guy said. 'Leave the bastard some teeth.'

'Yeah . . .'

The boots stopped. No point in running. No point in doing anything but wait.

Jaap Zeeger had spent most of his life getting told what to do, what to think, how to feel. If it wasn't Jansen's minions shoving dope down his throat it was Barbara Jewell talking patiently, endlessly, trying to unravel the mess that was his life.

That was the way of things. It was never going to change.

A couple of minutes later a black Mercedes drew up. Two tall men in suits and sunglasses got out. Talked to the dope-heads. Gave them some money and told them to scram.

One of them reached down and picked up Zeeger by the collar.

Another face he knew. One of Jansen's, one of Menzo's, he wasn't sure.

'People want to reacquaint themselves, Jaap,' the man said pleasantly. 'Get in the car, will you? It's only polite.'

Zeeger struggled to his feet, wiped some blood from his mouth. Felt himself. No ribs broken. No damage really. He'd had worse.

Then walked to the Mercedes, climbed in.

CHAPTER 18

Blood on the asphalt. Lavender banknotes flying round the stranded jet like leaves caught in an exotic blizzard. Emergency vehicles. Police and ambulance. Prins on a gurney, medics round him working frantically.

Vos followed them inside the nearest ambulance, Bakker behind him.

Four medics working. Lines. Monitors. Syringes.

He wasn't breathing. Head a mess. Shoulder to one side, blood leaking through his shirt.

Vos found a gap between the two men working on his right, leaned, tried to get close to his ear.

'Talk to me, Wim. For God's sake . . .'

The man's eyes were open, unfocused, flickering in fear and bafflement.

'Talk to me,' Vos repeated, the volume of his voice rising. 'Your kid's missing. Mine's gone.' His hands gripped Prins's sleeve. 'Talk . . .'

The ambulance lurched forward. They were leaving the taxiway. Laura Bakker pulled down a tiny seat built into the back door, sat there arms folded, stony-faced.

'Vos . . .' she said.

He wasn't listening. Had the stricken man by the arm and the medics were getting uppity now.

'You need to get back,' the nearest said.

Vos took out his ID.

'I'm a police officer. This man's in the middle of a kidnapping. A murder. I don't know—'

'You don't know?' the medic said, shoving him out of the way. 'That's so interesting. Now . . .'

'Pieter!' Bakker called.

The monitor flatlined. Prins's eyes turned blank. A long continuous beep. One of the medics swore, called for the defib. Bakker reached out, grabbed Vos's flailing arm, pulled him to the back of the ambulance. Kept hold of him while he flapped until finally she said, 'He's gone. Can't you see . . .?'

'No.' Vos tried to get free from her, but not much. 'He can't be . . .'

'He threw himself out of the bloody plane, for God's sake!' she yelled at him. 'You saw it. What the hell do you think . . .?'

The medic walked over, leaned down, said, 'If you two don't shut up I'll stop and throw you out in the road right now.'

One of the others said something about standing back. A sudden jolt, a bang. Prins's bare chest jumped with the shock.

Still the continuous drone. Flat line.

'He's dead,' Bakker said. 'I know what that looks like. So do you.'

The argumentative medic was back at the table, working, no longer saw them at all.

366

'He's dead,' she repeated. 'Not your fault. There's nothing we could do.'

'I should have got his name out to immigration as soon as Zeeger walked into the office.'

'If De Groot wouldn't let you bring him in how could you?'

'Not waited till I heard Liesbeth. Not . . .'

Something in her face silenced his aimless fury.

'You don't look back,' Laura Bakker said in her plain, flat northern voice. 'You don't ever look back. He's dead and that's it. Start thinking, will you? What the hell do we do now?'

He'd never asked about what happened to her parents back in Dokkum. De Groot said she'd seen them after the car crash. Asking questions seemed an embarrassing imposition. And yet he'd so easily thrown all his tortured history in her direction.

'That's all there is to it?' Vos asked.

She wrinkled her nose.

'What else is there?'

Twenty minutes it took to the hospital. The medics never stopped trying. Pumping drugs into the man on the table. Going back with the defibrillator time and time again.

Then they were there. The doors opened. Bright midday sun poured into the ambulance, onto the blood and the discarded ampoules, and the exhausted medics crowded round the body in their midst.

One of them was drawing a sheet over Prins's corpse.

'Sorry,' the nearest one said and started to tidy away the wires and the syringes. He nodded at Bakker. 'She was right. He didn't stand much chance after a fall like that.'

A glance at his stained and gory tunic. A shrug. 'Still. You've got to try.'

CHAPTER 19

They didn't keep Hendriks long in Marnixstraat. Better things to do once the news came in from Schiphol. When he returned to the council building he walked straight into Margriet Willemsen's office. Waited until she slowly raised her head from the papers in front of her.

'Prins is dead,' he said.

Nothing.

'Did you hear me?'

His voice was fractured, high.

'They called,' she said. 'Do you know what happened?'

The briefest of details. Prins had failed to show for the ransom meet, tried to flee the country instead. Flung himself from the plane when it was stopped on the taxiway just before take-off.

'What the hell were you doing there?' she asked.

'I got a text. From Til Stamm. I think she was the kid who got into my account. Took that video. She said to meet her there . . .'

Willemsen thought about this.

'Did you tell the police?'

A shake of the head.

'Of course not. They'll be back though.'

She put down her pen, pushed away the papers in front of her. Went and stood at the window. Much as Prins had done the day before, when everyone was scheming behind his back, plotting to bring him down.

'Let me get this straight?' she asked. 'Some temp here raided your files and got those videos?'

'Looks like it,' Hendriks agreed.

'And she wanted to meet you where?'

'Chinatown,' he said. At the same time Prins had been summoned to hand over his daughter's ransom money.

Willemsen rarely looked lost. But at that moment . . .

'I need to sit down and clear this up with Marnixstraat,' Hendriks said. 'It's out of hand. You can have my resignation. I know I should never have spied on the pair of you. I just wanted to stop this idiotic Nachtwacht nonsense—'

'Don't be so stupid!' she yelled at him.

Hendriks bridled at that.

'Wim's dead,' he said. 'His daughter's still missing. Til Stamm must know something—'

'You've no idea who sent you that message,' Willemsen broke in. 'Jesus, Alex. You really don't think things through, do you?'

'We're out of our depth here. People are dying. Wim. That reporter woman. Marnixstraat are starting to think he killed her too. That he had something to do with his daughter going missing. I don't want any part of this. Have my head . . .'

She sat down again, stared at him so hard Hendriks shut up.

'It's not just your head, is it?'

'We can't bury this, Margriet . . .'

'Of course we can. Wim's dead. It can go in the coffin beside him.'

He laughed and wished he hadn't.

'That's ridiculous. We've got to tell them—'

'Do that and I'll cut you off at the knees,' she snarled. 'You could face criminal charges for putting that camera in my bedroom. You don't just lose your job. You wind up in jail. Ruined.' She glanced round the office, out of the window at the rooftops of De Wallen. 'If I lose all this you lose a whole lot more—'

'Katja Prins is still missing, for Christ's sake! What if we know something that can help?'

'Like what?' she asked. 'Truly? What?'

He was wavering. Til Stamm knew Katja. The police had said that. Til Stamm, or someone using her name, had led him to the crossroads in Chinatown where Prins was supposed to hand over the ransom money. Except he was sitting on a plane at Schiphol at the time, hoping to flee the country.

'You know what I think?' she said with the briefest of smiles. 'I think Marnixstraat's right. This was down to Wim. He was deceiving all of us. He never worried much about that girl of his, did he? You saw that. I think . . .' She made a note.

371

'That's our position. We don't sit in judgement. We were just . . . puzzled.'

'Puzzled?' he repeated.

'Correct. We draw a line under it here and now. Let's—'

'If you say "move on" I think I'll scream.'

She laughed.

'Let's move on,' Margriet Willemsen told him.

CHAPTER 20

Frank de Groot's top-floor office. The day darkening beyond the windows. Spring rain on the way. Vos, Mulder, Bakker and Koeman going through the latest case notes.

The hunt for Theo Jansen was getting nowhere. Mulder had made no progress with the search for Rosie Jansen's killer. A woman officer had taken a statement from Liesbeth Prins. She'd no idea where her husband was the night before. Had seen no corroborating evidence to suggest the kidnap plot was real. Prins had been coy and cool about Katja's disappearance throughout, something noted by his colleagues in the council too.

The street entertainers who'd turned up in Chinatown dressed as devils had been released. Someone had put an envelope through their front door the previous day. It had five hundred euros in it. Promised five hundred more if they turned up at the junction of Zeedijk and Stormsteeg at eleven thirty the following day. Birthday surprise. It was hard getting them out of Marnixstraat; they wanted to know when they'd get the rest of their money.

'If Prins was behind Katja's disappearance,' Bakker said, 'surely he'd play the distraught father. Wouldn't he?'

'The man was a cold fish,' De Groot said. 'He couldn't put on an act like that if he wanted. We have to look at this as the first option.' He stared at Vos. 'You do see that, don't you?'

'Looks that way,' Vos agreed.

De Groot laid out a possible version of events. Katja Prins had come to believe Prins had murdered her mother. Bea had introduced Katja and Vos's daughter to the Doll's House for some reason. Anneliese had been seized there.

'Are we saying Prins was one of the customers?' Koeman asked. 'If so I have several problems . . .'

'I don't know,' De Groot interrupted. 'You find out.'

'So you think the mother *and* the father were using the same teenage brothel?' Koeman asked.

'You tell me!' the commissaris barked. 'Get Jaap Zeeger back in here. Talk to the Thai woman again.'

'That council guy, Hendriks,' Koeman grumbled. 'We shouldn't have just let him walk. He knew something. What the hell was he doing hanging round Chinatown just when Prins was supposed to be handing over the money?'

De Groot muttered a curse. Nodded at Mulder, said, 'You tell them.'

'I got a call from the council offices before we came in here. I was their contact for that Nachtwacht crap. I guess the Willemsen woman didn't know where else to go.'

Koeman glared at Mulder, heaved a long sigh and stretched back in his chair.

'Til Stamm used that cafe on the corner,' Mulder went on. 'The council's been looking for her. They were worried when she disappeared. Hendriks wondered if—'

'He runs the council's general office,' Bakker broke in. 'Why's he wandering the streets looking for a temp?'

'Priorities,' Mulder said. 'Hendriks isn't one of them right now. Here's something else Willemsen told me. Anna de Vries came to see Prins about the kidnapping. She had some kind of information. He was agitated afterwards. They've checked the CCTV, the internal courier. No one delivered anything for Prins that morning. It had to come from her.'

'This was yesterday!' Koeman cried. 'Why are we finding out now?'

'They only just looked,' Mulder said with a shrug. 'Work it out. Prins's daughter thought he was a murderer. She's missing. Something that reporter said shook him up. He invents these photos. The ransom note. He was out when she got killed last night. Then this morning he gets all the money he can from the bank and tries to hightail it to Aruba. Works for me.'

He looked round at each of them in turn.

'Works for me too,' De Groot agreed.

'In that case . . .' Vos said and got up from his chair.

'Where the hell are you going?' Mulder asked.

'Van der Berg's found Bea Prins's car,' Vos said. 'It's in the forensic garage. Got sold on afterwards.' He picked up a folder. 'I'd just like to take a look. Read the original case notes. Unless anyone . . .?'

'So you're going to make me out to be a fool?' De Groot asked.

'You said I could look at the files.'

'You . . .' De Groot jabbed a finger at Mulder. 'Keep looking for Jansen. Let's get more on his daughter too. Work on the assumption these two things are separate now. The Jansen side of things is down to the gangs. Katja Prins . . .' He sighed. 'We'll see.'

Bakker shook her head.

'What is it now?' De Groot asked.

'Someone left Rosie Jansen next to Vos's boat. Left a photo for him inside the boat. How can they not be linked?'

Red-faced, the commissaris ordered everyone out of the room except Vos and Bakker. She got up and stood, arms folded, against the wall.

'Listen to me, girl,' De Groot barked. 'This isn't Dokkum . . .'

'I'm not a girl and I'm aware where I am, thank you.'

'I could take you off this case now. Send you back home. We don't need to wait for the assessments—'

376

'No, Frank,' Vos cut in. 'You can't. Not if you want me in too.'

The commissaris glowered at them.

'This is the new team, is it? One aspirant and someone who's been out of the force sitting in his houseboat, smoking himself stupid for the last two years?'

'You asked me back,' Vos pointed out. 'If you want to change your mind—'

'Here's what I want!' De Groot yelled. 'Something tied up round here. I've got the mayor, the Ministry of Justice and the media breathing down my neck. Four unsolved murders . . .'

'Two,' Bakker said. 'We know Theo Jansen killed Menzo and his girlfriend.' She held up a couple of slender fingers. 'Two. Rosie Jansen. Anna de Vries. Wim Prins didn't kill Rosie. He was at home that night if his wife's to be believed. And why? The reporter . . .'

She looked at Vos. He was checking the messages on his phone.

'Hello?' Bakker said. 'Anyone home?'

Vos put the phone away.

'Rosie Jansen's Mulder's business, Laura. The commissaris has made that clear. Let's do what he asks, please.'

De Groot brightened a little with that.

'If it turns out this was down to one dead politician,' he said eagerly. 'That would make everyone's day. Just a thought.'

'Just a thought,' Vos agreed.

De Groot still looked uncomfortable.

'Somebody's got to talk to Liesbeth,' he said. 'She knows he's dead. But . . .' His big shoulders seemed to dip beneath an invisible weight. 'It's got to be done, Pieter. If you'd rather it wasn't . . .'

'No problem,' Vos said.

CHAPTER 21

Jaap Zeeger wasn't sure where they'd taken him. Somewhere industrial. Near the water. He could hear the sound of traffic. Distant ships. There were three of them with him in what seemed to be a cold empty warehouse, bare dusty floor, a single table. Chairs. One square barred window set in the wall. Bright spring sun shining through.

He was nervous. They watched him pee into a bucket, sent out the third man, a swarthy thug with a foreign accent, to empty it.

That left him with Theo Jansen and the man he knew only as Maarten.

Zeeger sat on the flimsy chair they'd given him trying not to shake.

'I'm sorry about Rosie, Mr Jansen,' he said. 'She was always good to me.'

Jansen sat stroking his stubble, smoking a cigarette, not looking at him.

'And all that nonsense back when that bastard Mulder got hold of me . . .' Zeeger added. 'I didn't want to say that stuff. He beat me up. Said he'd do things.' A shake of his head. The memories. 'Horrible man. I was dead scared of him.'

'You're dead scared of me, aren't you?' Jansen asked, turning his hard, cold eyes on him.

'I am that,' Zeeger agreed. 'More than him. You got reason to be mad at me. I sent you to prison, didn't I?'

Maarten swore. Jansen nodded, said nothing.

'Well I'm sorry,' Zeeger added. 'I really am. I shouldn't have done it. If it had been now . . . I wouldn't have.'

Jansen looked up and asked, 'What's changed?'

'Me. I'm different. Clear and clean. I don't drink no more. Don't do drugs. I got a job. Only part time. But I'll go full before Christmas they said. So long as I keep my nose clean. And I will.'

'You're a hero, Jaap,' Maarten said in a gruff, disbelieving voice.

'No I'm not,' Zeeger spat back. 'I know exactly what I am. Know what I was too. A chump for you lot. Doing the crappy jobs that didn't count much or earn much. And what did I get for that?' He wondered whether to say it. Why he even dared. 'I got someone fitting me up for Mr Vos's girl, didn't I? Putting what looked like her clothes in my flat. And a doll too. They nearly pinned that on me—'

'Wait,' Jansen cut in. 'What are you talking about?'

Zeeger got close to cross.

'I suppose you were too busy to notice. I'm talking about someone trying to blame me for that kid's murder. They sent that stuff . . .'

'Not us,' Maarten told him. 'Why would we do that? Honestly, Jaap—'

'Well someone did it, didn't they? I know who I am. Just a bug on the street to you lot. Who else knew me?'

Silence.

Then Jansen asked, 'So when Mulder came along . . . you were already pissed off with us?'

'Might say that,' Zeeger agreed. 'I don't rightly remember. I was a mess back then. I said I'm sorry, Mr Jansen. Truly I am. Can't change it—'

'Tell us about Katja Prins,' Maarten interrupted.

So he did. Everything he'd said in Marnixstraat that morning.

Theo Jansen listened carefully then, when Zeeger was finished, laughed. Looked a little like his old self, genial and threatening at the same time, when he did that.

'You're saying the stuck-up bastard who thought he was going to clean up Amsterdam murdered his own wife?'

'I'm not saying it. Katja did,' Zeeger answered. 'She seemed pretty sure.'

'He's dead now anyway,' Jansen said. 'Guess she is too.'

Zeeger blinked. They told him what had been on the news.

'Makes sense then, doesn't it?' he said when Jansen had finished. 'If he was running away with all his money.'

Then they asked about the privehuis on the Prinsengracht and Jaap Zeeger started to fidget on the shaky seat.

'You ought to talk to that Thai woman. Not me. She ran the place. All I did was ferry money and stuff from time to time. Never went past the front door.'

'She's flown,' Maarten told him. 'Marnixstraat picked her up yesterday. Moment she got out of the station she took a plane back to Bangkok. So we're asking you. What went on there?'

He wriggled.

'It was your place, Mr Jansen. Why ask me?'

'Because I don't know!' Jansen roared. 'I was running an empire, for Christ's sake. I didn't manage every damned piece of it.'

The swarthy thug had come back in. He smelled of cigarette smoke. Had been biding his time. In his hands he had a hammer and some nails.

Zeeger was shaking again.

'That's how that Thai bitch managed to sell the whole thing to Jimmy Menzo under my nose,' Jansen bellowed. 'And then God knows what went on . . . God knows . . .'

'I didn't have any dealings with that man,' Zeeger said. 'Don't ask me about him . . .'

'Something happened in that place!' Jansen yelled. Big finger pointed across the table. 'I think you know what that was. I think it's why I don't have a daughter any more.'

Zeeger blinked.

'I don't know nothing. It was yours when I was around. Not Menzo's. He only got it later. After . . .'

One word – that was all it took. One word.

Jansen glowered across the table. Just like the old days. The ones Zeeger believed would never come back after all the time and pain and work he'd put in with Barbara Jewell at the Yellow House.

'After what?'

'You knew, didn't you?' Zeeger shrieked. 'You must have done. Maarten . . .' Jansen's sidekick sat unmoved. Seemingly baffled too. 'You tell him. I thought you all knew.'

The thug with the hammer and the nails sat down, put the tools on the table.

'I never heard the details,' Zeeger went on. 'Didn't want to. We weren't supposed to go near or put any business that way. They had kids in there. And then . . .'

Those times were a blur when they were happening. Even more so now.

The man he didn't know picked up the hammer, weighed it in his hands, started to play with the nails.

'It was Rosie who ran the Doll's House. Rosie who used to make me fetch and carry for it.'

Jansen's face was a mask, frozen in anger and disbelief.

'Rosie who sold it to Jimmy Menzo. I thought . . .' Jaap Zeeger pulled at his lank hair, felt the sweat start to run on his face. 'I thought you knew. She was your daughter, Mr Jansen. You had to, didn't you?'

CHAPTER 22

Downstairs interview room. Liesbeth Prins slumped in a corner smoking constantly, an empty coffee cup in front of her. She didn't look up when Vos and Bakker walked in. Didn't even seem to notice when he sat next to her, Bakker on the other side, voice recorder out, notebook and pen.

Vos knew all the phrases for these occasions. The simple meaningless questions: how are you? The useless expressions of sympathy and regret.

Went through them in a distanced, unreal fashion, trying to give as much meaning to each word as he could. He hated seeing her like this. It was just as bad as the time Anneliese went missing. She seemed drained of all life. When they were breaking up she stopped eating, lived off booze and ciga-rettes, spent hours staring out of the window of their small apartment in the Jordaan, looking down an empty street for a young, bright figure who would never come.

Now even that was beyond her.

Halfway through she looked up at him and said, 'You were there? At the airport?'

He nodded.

'You saw?'

'We both did.'

She glared at Bakker and asked, 'Why's she here?'

'Because this is an interview. And those are the rules,' Laura Bakker said quietly, with a sympathy Vos hadn't noticed much before.

Liesbeth Prins glared at her.

'Not much use are they? Rules. Wim thought he lived by them. Thought all he had to do was teach us to do the same and everything would work out.'

Vos glanced at Bakker. Wanted her to keep out of this as much as possible.

Then told Liesbeth what Jaap Zeeger had said this morning. Watched as her face screwed up in disbelief.

'Are you serious? Wim never hurt a fly. He never even raised a hand to me. God knows I gave him reason.'

'The rehab place Katja was going to confirmed she said it,' Vos told her. 'We've got to look into this.'

'Why? They're both dead now.'

'And maybe Katja too . . .' Bakker slipped in before a look from Vos silenced her.

'Katja hates us both. I don't know what did that. I tried with her. Really I did. Wim too.'

'She thinks he murdered Bea,' Vos repeated.

'He didn't. It's impossible. Katja's not all there. She's a junkie living in a world of her own. In some squalid den somewhere . . .'

Vos shook his head.

'I don't think so. We've three witnesses who say she was off drugs. Katja had straightened herself out. No one's seen her for more than a week. Is it possible the kidnapping was something . . .?' He hesitated to say it. The words didn't sound right. 'Could Wim have made this up? The dolls? The calls? The photos?'

'How?' she asked. 'You're the police. You tell me.'

'If he tried he could,' Bakker said. 'Is there another property in the city he uses? A flat? An office?'

'No.'

'Did he mention a reporter called Anna de Vries?'

The laugh again, and sharp, angry eyes.

'The one who was killed? This is ridiculous. He was out last night getting drunk. They'd dumped him from the council. He wasn't going back whatever they said.'

'You don't know what he was doing,' Bakker pointed out.

'He wasn't murdering someone in De Wallen. I know my husband. Is this the idea, Pieter? Blame everything on Wim now he's gone?'

'I've got to find Katja,' he said.

She shot a furious glance at Bakker.

'I want to talk to you. Not her.'

'This is an interview,' Bakker pointed out again. 'It needs two officers otherwise . . .'

'The interview's over,' he said and nodded gently at the door.

One low curse and then she was gone, taking the recorder and the notebook with her. No protests this time.

'She's a stupid northern cow,' Liesbeth moaned when Bakker was gone. 'Is that the best you've got?'

'I like her,' Vos said. 'She's different. A determined young woman. Wants to make her mark. A bit bemused. A bit out of her depth.' He frowned. 'Laura Bakker's not alone in that. Are you going to be all right? Is there something I can do?'

'Such as what?'

'I don't know. That's why I asked.'

'Wim didn't kill anyone,' she said. 'I never saw him violent. He hated confrontations. It used to drive me mad.' A brief moment of amusement. 'He was like you. I could shout and scream and throw things at him. And he'd just sit there and take it.'

'But he ran, didn't he?'

'So did you,' she said with a sudden vehemence. 'Don't you remember? Ran right inside yourself and hid there, frightened to come out.'

'Katja—'

'I can't help you with Katja. I've told you everything I know.' The cold sad eyes fixed on his. 'More than I ever wanted.'

Her fingers reached out for his hand.

Vos got up. Saw Laura Bakker's red hair at the frosted window by the door. Leaning against it like a teenager, scribbling something on her pad.

'What's she doing here?' Liesbeth said. 'She's just a kid.'

'I know. That's what worries me.'

'When can I bury my husband?'

'Soon,' Vos told her. 'I hope.'

CHAPTER 23

Theo Jansen looked at Maarten the barber. Then Max Robles.

'Nothing to do with me,' Robles protested. 'I never knew Jimmy did that deal for the privehuis until it was all over. He kept all that stuff to himself.'

'He didn't do a damned thing with it afterwards,' Jansen threw at him. 'Why?'

Robles shrugged.

'I don't think he really wanted the place. A creepy flophouse for little girls or something. That Thai woman wanted out of there. We didn't know anyone who was into that kind of thing. Jimmy wasn't stupid. He picked it up for the property. Said he got the place so cheap it was stupid to turn it down.'

Maarten wriggled on his seat, uncomfortable, silent. Robles put a plank next to the hammer and the nails on the table.

'Let's see what else he knows? Gimme a little time—'

'He knows nothing!' Jansen bellowed.

Jaap Zeeger sat on the chair, rigid as a schoolboy in trouble.

'Except about Rosie.' Jansen looked at the thin,

frightened man opposite. 'You're sure about that, Jaap?'

'I'm sure she got me running things there, Mr Jansen. That's the truth. I thought it was for you. I thought you'd know . . .'

'Yeah, well. I didn't.' Jansen leaned down, looked Maarten in the eye. 'Did I?'

'Once I went there,' the barber said. 'Once. Rosie asked me to check out the Thai woman. See if she was lifting more than she should from the books.'

Jansen asked, 'And was she?'

'Sure.' He shrugged. 'I gave her some advice. Got out of there dead quick. It was a creep's place, Theo. Like Jaap said. Men in suits and little girls. We thought it was yours. You running it. Your business. Not ours. So we stayed clear . . .'

'And left a teenage brothel in my name?'

'You were the boss, weren't you?' Maarten cried. 'The only person I knew brave enough to stand up to you was Rosie. She had the damned place in the palm of her hand. And then . . .' He looked at Robles. 'Then she sold it on to Jimmy Menzo when you were inside. We were all glad of that.'

Jaap Zeeger nodded.

'Glad,' he agreed.

'Who was Rosie keeping sweet in Marnixstraat?' Jansen demanded.

'I don't know,' Maarten said. 'She never talked about the place. Not to most of us. It was a private

390

thing. We didn't want to intrude.' He hesitated then said it anyway. 'To be honest I don't think anyone dared.'

Jansen held out his hand, palm open. Maarten shook his head and asked, 'What?'

'Money,' Jansen said. 'As much as you've got.' He looked at Robles. 'And you. Take it out of the pot when we get back. With interest.'

The man from Paramaribo reached into his jacket. It looked as if he'd been out collecting debts. With Maarten's wad it came to almost five thousand euros. Jansen checked it, passed it across the table to Zeeger.

The thin man there looked at the cash, more scared than ever.

'I don't want this, Mr Jansen. I've got a job—'

'Forget about the job. I want you out of the country until this blows over. I want . . .'

Jansen tried to get this clear in his head. It was more about an apology than anything.

'We fuck up people's lives, right?' He looked at Maarten, at Robles. 'But not our own. Not our families. I always looked after the men who worked for me. Always will so long as they deserve it. Something I don't understand went wrong here. Until I know what it is I don't want you around, Jaap.'

He held out his big hand to Zeeger.

'It wasn't your fault. Shake on it. You can walk to Centraal station from here. Get a ticket on that new train to Brussels I heard about. Go have a holiday somewhere warm. Call Maarten here in a month. He can fill you in.'

Gingerly, Zeeger took his hand. Then just as tentatively scooped up the money from the table, stuffed it into the pockets of his leather jacket.

Got up, looking at them as if he couldn't believe this. Walked to the door, went outside, free.

Maarten and the man from Surinamese didn't know where to look.

Jansen couldn't get the picture of Jimmy Menzo out of his head. Trapped in the front of his smashed Mercedes. A bullet through each knee. Maarten pouring petrol everywhere. The dead Miriam Smith in the back.

I didn't touch Rosie. I swear . . .

'My own daughter was screwing around behind my back all the time. Even before I went to jail. After . . .' He was racking his brains to make sense of this. 'What didn't I give her? All she had to do was ask.'

Maarten's hand went to his arm.

'You did everything you could, Theo. You were a great father. The best—'

'Bullshit!' Theo Jansen screamed.

His big hands went beneath the table, flung it up, turned it over. Coffee cups on the floor with the hammer and nails.

A sudden act of violence. The old Theo. The one who'd never died.

You look good without that stupid beard and hippie

hair. Like a new man . . . But you're not, are you, Theo? New?

'Get me out of here,' Jansen ordered. 'I want to go home.' A stupid thing to say. 'Wherever the hell that is.'

CHAPTER 24

Almost six o'clock, past the end of the shift, and they were still in the forensic garage looking at Bea Prins's white BMW 3 series soft top. Van der Berg had been kept out of the Chinatown exercise. So he'd spent most of the day wrapped up with the case reports on her death and chasing down the car.

The new owner was a doctor. She wasn't pleased to have her shiny toy taken from her. Even less so when Van der Berg explained the history that meant he needed it.

Vos and Bakker sat at a desk in the garage listening to him run through the files.

Bea Prins was forty-one when she died. Her medical records showed sporadic treatment for drug and alcohol abuse. The effects of both were evident in the autopsy report. There was a statement from Wim Prins in which he spoke of a difficult though loving marriage. Both had determined to stay together for the sake of their daughter. Bea had worked briefly as a legal secretary in her twenties, which was how they met. A nanny looked after Katja most of the time. There'd been no other job.

They went through the contents of the car when it was found with Bea Prins's body in it. A handbag, nothing in it except money and some personal belongings. Three hundred grams of cocaine in a plastic bag in the glove compartment. No note. She'd been shopping, her husband said, which was why she took the car not her bike.

'No woman goes shopping and kills herself,' Bakker said.

'Maybe she couldn't find what she wanted?' Van der Berg suggested.

She glared at him.

'It was a bad joke,' the detective added. 'Sorry. There was no shopping in the car. She hadn't been seen on any of the CCTV cameras in the nearby stores. She was lying.'

The nanny was away for the week. Prins said he'd stayed at home reading and watching TV. Katja was on a school trip. When Bea didn't come home he assumed she was out late with a 'friend' and went to bed. She wasn't there when he woke up so he called the police.

Her body had been found by then, first thing when the car park opened for business. Time of death was thought to be between eight and ten the evening before. One shot to the left temple from an unlicensed .38 Ruger LCP pistol. Powder residue on the left hand. The weapon in the passenger footwell. The bullet lodged in the rear seat.

Vos flicked through the last of the pages.

'Did she kill herself?' Bakker asked.

'Frank knows his job. It's thorough. Professional.'
A pause. 'Routine.'

'Everyone was worn out by that stage,' Van der Berg chipped in. 'We'd spent months chasing Pieter's girl. Got nowhere. It's not Frank's fault he didn't have enough people to go round.'

'No,' Vos agreed. 'It's not.' Van der Berg wasn't nagging for a beer. This was unusual. 'So what's bothering you?'

The detective picked up one sheet from the forensic report and walked them over to the white car on the ramp. The two duty mechanics dealing with it had worked in the garage for years. This hadn't been one of their jobs when the car came in. Both had been on holiday at the time. Temporary staff from an agency had handled the investigation. No one knew who they were, how thorough they'd been.

One line in the forensic report bugged Van der Berg. It showed minute traces of isopropyl alcohol on the upholstery and the dashboard. There was no explanation given.

The first mechanic stared at him when he read this out and said, 'Valet. They use that stuff when they're cleaning the car. It's no big deal.'

Van der Berg wasn't convinced.

'But you'd also use it to wipe something down for evidence, wouldn't you? Get rid of prints?'

The second man rifled through the glovebox, came up with the service records. The car had been in for an annual service the week before.

'BMW,' he said. 'They come back nice and clean. No surprise there.'

Van der Berg asked them to lower the ramp. Both doors were open. He got Laura Bakker to sit in the driver's seat, walked round to the passenger door on the right.

'Imagine this,' Van der Berg told them. 'Bea Prins is behind the wheel. Say she starts fiddling with her bag. Wondering whether she needs a quick snort for the ride home.' His fingers rapped on the door window. 'Someone she knows turns up. Maybe it's arranged. Her dealer. Who knows? He opens the passenger door. Reaches over.' His hand went up to her face. 'Bang. Straight to the temple. Dead.'

They looked at the direction of his arm. The bullet would have been where they found it.

'There was residue on her left hand,' the first mechanic said.

Van der Berg nodded, walked back round to the other side. Took Laura Bakker's hand, pressed a pretend-gun in her fingers, pretend-fired it out of the open passenger door.

'Residue,' he said. 'And yes, she was left-handed. So this was someone who knew her.'

'Evidence?' Vos asked.

'Give me time,' he said. 'The car park was mostly empty at night. I need to go round and see if there's any sign of a second shot. But it's possible.' The mechanics didn't say a word. 'Tell me it's possible.'

One of them had gone back to the long bench

to sort through the tools and forensic instruments there.

'Two shots?' the remaining engineer said. 'Two to three years ago?'

Van der Berg nodded. The second engineer came back with a spray.

'From what I can see,' he said, 'they found gunshot residue round the driver's side. Where you'd look. Logically.'

Not just on her hand. It was in the plastic and fabric of the seat and the door too.

The engineer with the spray said, 'Everyone out of the way please.'

He talked about how long powder residue might last. How a careful killer, one with time, might try to get rid of all the traces using isopropyl alcohol wipes. But that was impossible. The blast of a weapon forced tiny particles into the fibres of the seat, the porous fabric of the sidewalls, the plastic trim. It would stay there for years. If Van der Berg was right . . .

One of the men filmed as the other climbed in and started to puff round the interior with a white bottle spray.

Then they got out, kept the camera running, waited.

A pink cloud emerged close to the top of the column by the passenger door. Small, faint, unmistakable.

'Go buy the man a lollipop,' the first mechanic said. 'Two shots here. Second to get residue on the woman's hand. Higher position. Outside the car. I'd put money on it.' He waved a finger at them. 'This is why you should never employ idiots from agencies.'

'Forget the lollipop. I'd rather have a beer,' Van der Berg answered, suddenly happy. 'Just the one.'

Vos looked at his watch. Well past the end of their shift.

'A beer,' he agreed. 'Just the one.'

'What?' Bakker shrieked. 'You just worked out Bea Prins was murdered and you're going to a bar?'

'She's been waiting a while for someone to find that out, kiddo,' Van der Berg said. 'A little longer won't hurt. Besides . . .' He sighed. 'If it was the husband it's all a bit moot. Doesn't help us find that kid of his.' He scratched his head. 'Just means she was right. She knew and he knew she knew. Christ. She's dead, isn't she?'

No answer. In his crumpled and worn blue suit he looked deeply miserable at that moment.

'Your own daughter. I'd like to say it's unthinkable. Except if you work here long enough you get to learn not much is.'

'Also,' Vos added, 'I need to check on Sam.'

'You're really going?' she asked. 'Now?'

'I don't live here, Laura. Once maybe. Not any more. Are you coming or not?'

She didn't move.

'Your choice,' he said. 'We're gone.'

CHAPTER 25

Back at the little flat in the wooden house in the Begijnhof. Suzi had returned from shopping. She was fussing round with a duster, not looking him in the eye. Jansen had taken a shower. That usually calmed him. Then he sat down to watch the news.

One story. Wim Prins. The man who the day before had ruled Amsterdam. Dead after throwing himself off a plane at Schiphol. Scandals starting to grow round him. Rumours that he might have been behind his own daughter's disappearance. That he was suspected of the murder of a crime reporter who appeared to have been blackmailing him. And now Marnixstraat was reopening the files on his first wife, Bea, found dead from a gunshot wound in a city centre car park more than two years before.

Jansen listened, growing more morose by the minute. Nothing about Rosie. Menzo and his mistress came well down the newscast. Alongside them was the first mention of his own name. Prime suspect. Gang master newly escaped from a prison van. An Amsterdam native through and through. Focus of an intense search by the police that appeared to have thrown up not a single lead.

'You hide well, Theo,' she said, coming to sit next to him. She was back in another plain grey dress. Almost that of a nun. Had a mug in her hand. He caught the fragrance of herb tea and wondered how they'd ever got together in the first place. Stayed a couple long enough to gain a child.

'No I don't. They're just too busy with all this other shit. The police are only human. Just got so many people they can use.'

Not a single line on TV to connect what happened to Prins with him, with Rosie, or Menzo. Did Marnixstraat really believe that? Could it be true?

'They're looking,' he added. 'Sooner or later someone will talk. They'll find me.' He turned to her. 'If I stay long enough. One more day. Two. Then I'll be gone.' A pause. 'Is that OK with you?'

'Does it matter what I say?'

He didn't like that.

'Yes. It matters. Tell me to go now if you like. I can.'

'Then they'll find you. And you'll hate me again.'

'I'll be in jail. So what?'

She didn't say anything. Just gave him that judgemental look he loathed.

'Oh,' Jansen added. 'I get it. What matters is . . .' He gestured at the ceiling. 'What *He* thinks. Did she do right by a sinner? Did he do right by her?'

'Don't mock me. That's beneath you.'

He'd been thinking all the way back from the

talk they had with Jaap Zeeger. An interview he fully expected to end in Max Robles using the hammer and nails he'd brought for the occasion. But it didn't. Zeeger was telling the truth. Not all of it. That wasn't to be expected. But enough to be real. To be honest. In a way that hypocrites like Wim Prins and this woman never knew.

Theo Jansen was happy deceiving others. That was part of the job. But he never lied to himself. Wouldn't have allowed that.

'Is it expensive living here?' he asked.

'No. Of course not.'

'Still costs, doesn't it?'

She didn't answer.

'And you never came to me for help. Not once.'

'I didn't want your money. Even when we were together.'

He laughed. She didn't appreciate that.

'What's so funny?'

'You.' He nodded at the window. 'This.' A finger pointing at the grey dress. 'That. The act. The pretence. The lie.'

'I think you should go.'

'No.'

'You said you would.'

He went to the kitchen, got a beer, raised the bottle.

'I changed my mind.'

Jansen waited. She didn't speak.

He picked up the phone, handed it to her.

'Call Marnixstraat if you like. Tell them I'm here.

402

I can wait.' The bottle rose again. 'You've got more beer. I can hang around all night if they want.'

Suzi didn't move and he knew then he was right.

'All those years. Me feeling guilty because I'd deprived Rosie of her mother. But that wasn't true, was it? That was just me being stupid.'

He could picture the moment too. Maybe ten years before when Rosie started spending less time with him. He thought there might be a boyfriend but one never showed up. It was good that she was getting more interested in the business. Not that he bothered to check much. She was family. The same blood. Family didn't steal or deceive. Not in his world.

'I never gave you a penny. Yet you've got no job. I don't think you've ever had one. And still . . .' He smiled. 'This is a nice place. I went through your room while you were out.'

'You had no right!' she screamed, hands flying towards him.

One look stopped her.

'I had every right.'

He pulled the snapshot out of his pocket, threw it on the table. Rosie and Suzi in front of a temple somewhere. The Far East he guessed. Statues of colourful monsters and dragons behind them. They looked beautiful. Happy. Mother and daughter. The perfect, secret couple.

'The question is . . .' Jansen said. 'The Doll's House. This place on the Prinsen. Were you running Rosie? Or was she running you?'

She didn't look frightened. She was one of the few who never did.

'It was ours,' Suzi said in a low, hard voice. 'That and a few other things you never knew about. Sorry, Theo. I know you think you owned us. Like everything else round here. But you didn't.'

'And now she's dead.'

'And . . . now she's dead.'

He brought his chair closer, put the beer on the table, forgot about everything except this woman and the daughter they'd brought into the world.

'Why?'

She shook her head. Tears again and they stemmed from anger now. This was so clear.

'I wish I knew.'

They talked. Long and low, as the Amsterdam evening fell slowly on the quiet and empty Begijnhof courtyard beyond the windows.

It was almost eight by the time they finished. Jansen told her to get out of the place for a while. He didn't want to see her. And he needed to think.

Then, ten minutes past eight, he reached for the computer and the cheap Skype headset, started to think about what he'd say, what he'd do. Who to call.

CHAPTER 26

Vos had picked up Sam from Sofia Albers at the Drie Vaten and his clean washing too, took the clothes to the houseboat, Van der Berg watching him warily as he unpacked them and folded them into the chest of drawers near the bows.

'No offence,' Van der Berg began as the dog started to scamper happily round the boat retrieving toys from beneath the dining table and the chairs. 'But . . .'

'Don't say it.'

'Say what?'

'New clothes.'

Van der Berg picked up a blue sweater. Held up the elbow. Poked his finger through the hole.

'I'm going to have to darn that now!' Vos protested.

A blue denim cowboy shirt came out of the basket. Collar frayed to the material underneath.

'Only detective I ever met who looked like he was about to audition for bass guitarist in an Iron Maiden tribute band,' Van der Berg declared.

'I *hate* Iron Maiden.'

'Well there you go. Have you bought any new clothes since you walked out on us?'

He thought about it. Shook his head.

'And,' Van der Berg added, 'don't give me that "I'll have to darn it" nonsense.'

Vos snatched the shirt and the sweater, stuffed them roughly into a drawer, slammed it shut. Sam came up to Van der Berg, a rubber bone in mouth, put his paws on the man's knees begging to play. The cop grabbed the end of the toy, hung on as the little dog tugged and growled cheerily.

'Let me get this straight,' he went on. 'Sofia looks after Sam. Does your washing and ironing. Serves you beer and sandwiches. And probably nags you from time to time.' He beamed. 'What's missing from this relationship? Oh, I know! Sex and marriage.'

'Ha, ha.'

'Shame she doesn't do haircuts too.'

A flurry of curses. When Vos had finished, guilty already for the uncharacteristic outburst, Van der Berg was holding his hands over the dog's ears. Sam stared at Vos with big round eyes. Not scared. Just baffled by something new.

'This little chap's too young to hear language of that sort,' Van der Berg announced archly. 'We're going outside for a ride and a refreshment somewhere. The Pieper I think since I can't bear to see that nice woman behind the bar of the Drie Vaten making cow eyes in your direction. Should you find the self-control to manage your temper you may join us.'

Vos bunched his fist, laughed, howled at the houseboat roof. Came over, picked up the little terrier, held him, kissed his head. Dirk Van der Berg watched, smiled and said, 'Oh for the love of God let's go. I'm thirsty.'

They cycled side by side, Sam in the basket of Vos's bike as the two men rode alongside the still canal, its surface mirroring the lights from the tall terraces opposite and the odd tourist boat purring along full of gawping visitors. From the lime trees came a constant flurry of falling leaves. Then the bar, little more than a house with a front room for drinkers, greeted them as they reached the Leidsegracht bridge.

Van der Berg said he liked the place for the beer. Vos was fine with that. Sofia did so much for him and got nothing in return but his thanks and a little money. Not enough of either probably.

The Pieper was one of the more popular old brown bars at the very edge of the Jordaan but on this midweek night it was little more than half full. A couple of well-oiled men at the counter were starting to sing. Van der Berg put his hands over Sam's ears again and then they discussed beer.

English that night, they decided. Some new brews just in.

Vos found an isolated table at the back next to a line of ancient show posters. Sam sat the way he usually did in strange places: half on Vos's right foot, leaning against his trouser leg.

'Proost,' the detective said and chinked his glass

against Vos's then stopped and picked up the bottle. 'Look at the crap on here.' He pointed to a label on the back. 'Please drink responsibly. What in God's name does that mean? Don't spill it or something?'

'Probably,' Vos thought.

Van der Berg sipped the beer, pulled a face, went back to the bar and returned with something Belgian.

'What the hell's this about, Pieter? Do you have a clue? And if you do, will you enlighten the office jester?'

'If I thought you were the jester would I have asked you to chase Bea Prins?'

A shrug.

'If it's honesty you're after let me tell you the truth. You shouldn't be near this case and you know it. Too close.'

'Tell that to De Groot.'

'He's just desperate. Mulder never made the grade. That stitch-up with Jansen's going to work out badly whether we catch the old bastard or not. Frank's short of quality players. He needs you. He likes you.' Another chink of the glass. 'Everyone does. But he'll thrust your hands into the fire, Pieter. If that's what it takes. Management. It's what they do.'

Vos nodded, said nothing.

'And your farm girl . . .'

'She isn't mine,' Vos pointed out. 'I'm not sure she knows or cares much about farms either.'

'They'll still send her packing. She sticks out a mile in that place. And then she'll hang around anyway. Won't be any easier to shake off than your friend in the Drie Vaten. The kid looks like a duck out of water. I mean . . . watching the pair of you.' The dog was relaxing. He wandered beneath the table. Van der Berg stroked his soft head. 'What a sight. You looking like you visited the charity store. That kid as if she'd just inherited her old mum's wardrobe.'

'Her Auntie Maartje makes her clothes,' Vos said, half-seriously. 'From patterns. In Dokkum.'

'Her Auntie Maartje needs a new hobby. It's bad when things get personal. This nightmare's going that way. Time to stop.'

Vos laughed, shook his head.

'Don't get smart with me,' Van der Berg added. 'We're off duty now. I can say what I like.'

'I never realized you needed a private moment for that.'

A moment of tension, almost hostility between them. The dog seemed to notice and came to sit equidistant between their legs. Got a pat from each in return.

'You're a clever man,' Van der Berg added. 'Except you don't know when to stop. And you don't see anything in front of you except whatever it is you're chasing. That Bakker girl's like that too if you ask me. Bad enough having one blinkered obsessive in the office. Two's unhealthy.'

'Is this why we came out for a beer?'

409

'Partly. I'd also like to know if you're going to give Frank what he wants. Wim Prins's dead head on a plate. For the wife and the daughter. And that reporter they found in the canal this morning.'

'Too soon to know,' Vos said.

'Oh come on. You're Pieter Vos. Everyone's waiting to hear . . .'

'What do you think?'

Van der Berg lifted his glass, drained it.

'I think this is a two-beer problem. Not English either.'

He went to the bar, came back with a couple more local brews. Local Brouwerij't IJ with an ostrich on the label.

'Bea Prins was murdered,' he said in a bored monotone. 'I'll go along with that. The daughter . . .'

A candid, forthright man. He didn't look at Vos at that moment.

'Does that mean he took Anneliese?' Van der Berg wondered. 'Then made it look like the same thing happened to his own girl? I don't know. Unless . . .'

He fidgeted, didn't want to say it.

'Unless?' Vos prompted.

'Unless he was a customer at that privehuis. And he met Anneliese there.'

Vos kept quiet.

'If it was him you're never going to find out, are you? About Anneliese? Or his own kid?'

'That would seem to follow,' Vos replied with

care. 'Not that we've the least evidence either of them is dead.'

'Hope's a wonderful thing,' Van der Berg said quietly. 'So long as you don't let it blind you. I still struggle with the idea he'd go from running Amsterdam one minute to stabbing a reporter to death the next. Alongside all the rest.'

Arms on the table, he looked at that moment as if he lived in the Pieper. But Dirk Van der Berg had that happy habit with any bar he visited.

'And so do you,' he added. 'Which means Frank de Groot's going to be disappointed . . .'

Vos's phone rang. He pulled it out, looked at the screen expecting to see Bakker's name there, hearing her call him back to Marnixstraat for some reason.

Instead it said, *Number unknown.*

He answered over the hubbub of the Pieper.

'You're in a bar,' a familiar low, miserable voice said. 'I can smell the beer from here.'

Vos told him exactly where.

'Bastard,' Theo Jansen replied. 'You're lucky I talk to you at all.'

CHAPTER 27

After the brief spat with Vos Laura Bakker walked into the basement canteen, bought a bottle of water and a cheese salad. Sat on her own at a table near the window.

Other officers came and went. No one spoke to her. No one took much notice.

Then, when she was nearly finished, Koeman, the beady-eyed detective back working with Mulder on the Jansen case, came over and took a chair.

He didn't ask. Didn't look like the kind of man who ever did.

About forty, nice casual clothes. A nice face too when she thought about it, though the overlong brown moustache was stupid. The kind of thing a drug squad officer might have affected once. Koeman had greedy, wandering eyes too. He looked at every woman who passed through Marnixstraat that way. Didn't mean anything, she guessed. The others said he was happily married. Just a habit, one he probably never even thought about.

'Tell me about cows,' he said then tucked into a flabby-looking burger.

'Not a lot to say about them.'

'Do they go moo up in Friesland? Or talk funny? Like you.'

She smiled sarcastically. Picked up her tray. His arm came out, stopped her.

'Let's chat,' he said. 'There's time.'

'Why?'

He took his hand away and sighed.

'Because I was trying to be friendly. That's all.' He put down the burger. Swigged at a pack of orange juice. 'Really. I know people have been a bit . . . off with you.'

'I never noticed,' she lied.

Koeman laughed at that.

'You stand out, kid. You look different. You talk different.' He gestured at the floors above them. 'This is a big place. We don't like different.' More quietly. 'Makes us feel awkward. Sorry.'

She tried to remember the last time anyone in Marnixstraat had apologized to her about anything.

'What does it matter anyway?' she asked. 'I've got the assessment next week. They're going to kick me out. Everyone knows.'

Koeman shook his head.

'Next week's next week. A lot can happen between now and then.'

'I don't fit here. You said it. Vos said it. De Groot—'

'No one *fits* here,' he interrupted with a sudden vehemence. 'I didn't when I turned up. Pieter Vos neither. It's a police station. Not a hospital or a monastery or something. We're not here to fix things. Just find them if we can. Then pass the problem on to someone else.' He shrugged. 'The law.' A wry laugh and then a nod at the window. 'People outside. The . . . *general public*. Who mostly despise us if we do our job. And can't wait to take a pop at us if we don't.'

He was trying to tell her something and she wasn't sure what.

'I don't give a damn if they kick me out,' Bakker insisted. 'I can do something else. Something sane. Something . . .'

'You'll mope and scream and cry.'

'You don't know me, Koeman!' A couple of tables away people were starting to stare.

'I know more about you now than I did on Monday. Back then I thought you were this dumb, frightened, talentless kid who'd somehow got on the wrong train. Found herself in the big, bad city. Too scared to go home. Too scared to stay.'

Bakker folded her arms. Watched him tuck into the burger again.

'And?' she asked.

'And I was wrong. There's something about you. Vos can see it. You're like him, a bit anyway. He's scared too. Scared of us. Scared of going back to where he was, because it was all so bleak and grim.' He pushed aside the half-finished burger with a scowl. 'Not just for him.'

'He'll be gone the moment this case closes,' she said. 'If it turns out Prins was behind Katja's disappearance. That there's nothing to connect the girl with his daughter. Or nothing he can find . . .'

'Fine,' Koeman said. 'If that works for him.'

'But it won't, will it?' she said slowly. 'He wants to know.'

'Don't we all?'

'Is there something you want to tell me?'

He groaned.

'God you're hard work.'

'Koeman—'

'No. Listen. This is important. We may be slow and stupid. We may be pigs from time to time. But we notice things. Like what you've done for Pieter since he came back. Maybe that's all we do.' He looked at her. A frank and friendly expression. 'We're good at it though. Noticing. Looking.' A pause. 'Hunting.'

She felt slow and stupid.

'I haven't done anything for Vos! Are you suggesting . . .?'

'No! No!' He climbed to his feet, grabbed his tray. 'I give up. This is impossible.' He glared at her. '*You're* impossible. I'm trying to help, Laura. So's Vos.'

'He's sad,' Bakker said in a quiet, frail voice. 'Can't you see that?'

'I can,' he agreed. 'But when he's around you he's alive. Something makes him think. And when Pieter Vos thinks . . . eventually things happen. If we're lucky. And God knows we could use some luck right now.'

He had to go back to work, he said. Koeman held out his hand. She took it automatically, getting to her feet, tray in hand. It tipped, tilted, was about to fall onto the floor, scattering plate and glass everywhere.

Another clumsy moment. But this time Koeman was there and grabbed it before the disaster happened, caught the thing and held it safe.

'You haven't been kicked out yet, kiddo,' he said. 'Go home. Get a good night's rest. Think about it. Tomorrow's likely to be a big day around here. Make your mark. Or try to. Get noticed for the right reasons for a change. That's all.'

CHAPTER 28

A few spots of rain out by the canal. A sharp wind. Vos stood next to the line of parked cars along the pavement.

'Let's end this now,' he said. 'You can't keep running, Theo. You're too old for this. So am I.'

'What are you talking about? You don't look a day older than when we were locking horns on the street.'

'I feel it. What's left to prove?'

'Who killed Rosie for one thing.'

'I'm not on that case.'

'I wonder why. Do you know who took your girl?'

Vos hesitated then said, 'No. I don't. But I think we're starting to get an idea about what happened to Katja Prins. And maybe that will take us there.'

A cyclist went past. A young woman on a granny bike. Stiff and upright, face in the wind. The way Laura Bakker rode.

'You really think Prins killed his own daughter?'

'I don't know,' Vos answered. 'I just think . . . we're closer. This is my business. Not yours.'

Jansen grunted, asked about the Doll's House. Vos answered carefully. Talked about Menzo and how they'd learned the Surinamese gang had secretly taken control of the place from him.

'Is that it?' the voice on the line asked. 'Is that all you have?'

'Would I tell you everything?'

'You should. You and me are in the same boat. We're the innocents here. Don't you get that?'

Vos thought of the scene out in the tulip field. Two burned corpses in a wrecked Mercedes.

'Not entirely.'

'We've been lied to. Strung along like fools. Those kids Menzo put on me. He sent them to that place out of laziness. He picked it up on a whim. Wanted out of there. Wanted the insurance.'

Van der Berg had come to stand outside the bar. He was smoking a cigarette, leaning against the windows, watching from across the narrow street, holding Sam's lead while the dog sniffed around the pavement.

'You know that, do you?'

'I do,' Jansen said with a pained sigh. 'Whatever happened in that place – don't ask because like I told you I'm an innocent. It was still on my watch. Not Jimmy's. I didn't know about it. I didn't even know I owned the stinking dump. Kids? Little girls? Not my kind of business.'

Van der Berg was trying to get a trace on the line. Had his own phone to his ear. Shook his head as Vos watched.

'You're a good businessman, Theo. I find it hard to believe this was news to you.'

418

There wasn't the expected explosion. Just the long sigh again.

'You know what?' Jansen said. 'So do I.'

'I'm standing out in the freezing rain,' Vos went on. 'Let's discuss this face to face. A beer.' He thought about this. 'Maybe we can go our separate ways afterwards.'

There was laughter then, a long throaty boom.

'What's this? Pieter Vos? The straightest cop in Amsterdam? He's going to talk to a wanted criminal? A murderer? Then let him walk?'

'Not forever. Just until we're both . . .' He couldn't find the right word to begin with. 'Satisfied.'

'We lost our daughters. Nothing makes up for that.' A pause. There was something new and broken in Jansen's voice. 'Does it?'

Vos stayed silent.

'I apologize,' Jansen added. 'Am I boring you?'

'Frankly, yes.'

Silence. Maybe he'd gone.

Then the gruff voice in his ear said, 'Let me give you something to think about then. Rosie was running that place behind my back. With someone else.'

'Who?'

'Patience, Vos. Indulge me and maybe you'll find out. It was Rosie's all along. She knew something bad happened there. Got scared and passed it on to Menzo behind my back. She tried to sell me out to him too. Families, huh? You think you know where you stand . . .'

419

Van der Berg started to cross the street. Vos put up a hand. Didn't want him near.

'Why are you telling me this?' he asked.

'Your head really did get screwed up after you left, didn't it? You're slow now. You know that? Slow and stupid.'

'Doing my best. A little help would be appreciated.'

The laugh again. Short and without feeling.

'This is the state we've come to, huh? You and me.'

'Theo—'

'Two possibilities. Maybe someone on my side killed Rosie because I wasn't the only one she was screwing. Second . . .'

He stopped. Vos had to prompt him.

'The second . . .' Jansen went on. 'Like I said she knew something. Maybe about what happened in that Doll's House place to close it down. Don't ask me. No one I've talked to seems to know either. But I haven't got to them all yet. And I will. So that's why we won't meet up for a beer. Not now.'

Rosie Jansen. One shot to the head. The gun was unlicensed, prints wiped. They found a pack of shells in a drawer of the flat. The forensic report indicated a struggle. It was possible whoever went to her place simply wanted to talk. That the gun was Rosie's. She'd pulled it out, started a fight, lost it.

'I'm not sure whoever it was went there to kill her,' Vos said. 'If that helps.'

'But they did. And then they left her on your doorstep. Why was that?'

Vos had been asking himself that from the start.

'I already told you. I'm supposed to be a part of this for some reason. It's a mystery to me too. Do you have anything else for me?'

'Just a promise,' Jansen said calmly down the line. 'I don't like being cheated even when it's my own lying daughter. I'm going to rip the heart out of whoever did this. Get in my way and I'll tear you to pieces. I'll squeeze the life out of this whole damned lying city if I need to.'

'Would that make you feel better?' Vos asked.

Silence. He was talking to emptiness.

Van der Berg walked over then and asked, 'Anything?'

'I'm not sure.'

Vos felt tired. Confused. Hungry. They went back inside the Pieper and got some sandwiches. Ate them then finished their beers mostly in silence.

'The innocents,' Vos whispered as the dog grew restless at his feet. He wanted his bed.

'What?' said Van der Berg.

'He says we're the innocents. Me. Theo Jansen.' Vos felt Sam tugging on the lead. He needed to be outside. 'Maybe he's right.'

'Jansen's a criminal. You two have got nothing in common.' Van der Berg put a hand on his arm. 'Nothing.'

'You'd think. But I've never heard him like that.

He's as mad as hell. We need to find him. Theo's in a bad way.'

Van der Berg laughed.

'As if we should care.'

'We should,' Vos said. 'We should care a lot.'

CHAPTER 29

Koeman had left her with an invitation. A challenge. She didn't shrink from them. Laura Bakker went back upstairs to forensic, laughed when the one remaining officer joked about her clashing green trousers and tartan jacket. Then charmed him into talking about the work they'd done on the growing collection of photos and videos in the system. They'd fought to extract every piece of information they could from the pictures of Katja and Anneliese. It was fruitless. What they knew now was exactly what they knew when the photos first appeared. The girls in Vondelpark. Katja, apparently in distress, in an unknown location, against a plain background.

The newest pictures had been taken with a common smart-phone. Recent dates, though they could be forged. No secrets inside. No subtle hints. No giveaway clues. It was as if the girl had been placed against a cinema blue screen, snapped, recorded, and every last detail of background information then removed.

'Clever,' Bakker said, going through the images one by one.

'No,' the forensic officer said. 'Competent.' He looked at his watch. Close to nine. 'I'm going now. We'll take a look tomorrow. Play around if you like. But don't change a thing or . . .'

He was wriggling. He knew.

'Or that'll go on my record too?' she asked. 'With the bent car and all the bumpkin stuff.'

'It will,' he agreed.

She watched him leave. Stayed playing with the computer. Flicked through all the various files there. Finally came upon one from another source. The email sent to Wim Prins the previous morning, snatched by Vos without his permission. An unknown man in bed with Margriet Willemsen. The woman now in charge of Amsterdam was arching, thrusting wildly, lost in herself.

No sound. No sign of the man's face. She recalled Prins shrieking it wasn't him. They seemed to accept that but she didn't know why. It was impossible to see. The room was dark. Her pale body hid his face. And . . .

Laura Bakker pushed her chair back from the laptop. Watching this made her feel uncomfortable. Voyeuristic. Wrong.

A sound behind made her jump.

Tall figure there. She looked up. Klaas Mulder. Stony-faced as usual. Not a man to mess with. He wanted to know what she was doing in forensic at that time of night. So she told him: hunting.

Mulder came up to the screen, stared at the frozen image there, smiled.

424

'Hunting?' he asked with a snide grin. 'You ought to get your kicks for real at your age.'

'Thanks for the counselling.'

'We've had professionals going through this material all day long,' Mulder said. 'People who know what they're doing. They found nothing.'

'Maybe they missed it.'

'Go home,' he ordered.

She went back to the screen.

'I said go home.'

'I work for Vos. Not you.'

Two naked bodies moving. Most of the technicians were men. They'd looked at this briefly and she knew what they'd stare at first. It was logical in a way. Bodies. Faces. Identities. But these were people making love in a busy bedroom. Crammed bookshelves on the walls. A duvet thrown on the floor. Clothes. There were other possibilities.

Bakker grabbed the mouse, drew a rectangle over what looked like a suit and a pair of shoes. Zoomed in.

Mulder sat on the desk next to the computer, close enough to make her uncomfortable.

'If I tell you to leave, you leave.'

'When I'm ready,' Bakker said.

'Aspirant—'

'If they're going to fire me next week what the hell does it matter, Mulder?' she asked. 'You'll get rid of me anyway. All you've got to do is wait.'

'You're not fit for this job,' he said in a mild, infuriating tone. 'You're clumsy. You don't understand discipline. Team work. Preparation. Planning. You don't belong here. You don't belong in this city. Go back to—'

'No, no. Don't say it,' she broke in. 'Go back to shovelling cow shit. Come up with something new, please. You're stuck in a loop alongside everyone else round here.'

Shirt. Underpants. Socks. Shiny shoes. Black she guessed. Men's office shoes. Sturdy. Not as tough as her own boots. But serious footwear and she always appreciated that.

He put his hand on her shoulder. Bakker turned and stared at his fingers.

'Remove that now or I swear this gets formal in the morning,' she said very calmly. 'Maybe I'll make up something about harassment too.' She did glance at him then. Koeman ogled women and barely knew he was doing it. Mulder watched them covetously. She recognized that look. 'Why do I think they might just believe that?'

Mulder removed his hand, smiled a bleak smile, shook his head.

She went back to the screen. Saw something in the corner near the discarded trousers. A wallet. A few of the contents had scattered out when it was flung on the carpet. Credit cards. Money.

'I'm not saying this again,' Mulder growled.

'Don't then.'

Another zoom. Up to maximum resolution. There was an icon on the toolbar to enhance the image. She hit it. A credit card upside down. Except it

426

wasn't. She blinked. Long day. Trying to make sense of this. Mulder got closer.

What was on the screen was familiar and she was struggling to understand.

Then one last look and Laura Bakker hit undo, threw the zoom out straight away. Stood up. Smoothed down the crumpled lines of her baggy tartan jacket. Tried to smile at him.

'You're right,' she said. 'Sorry. I got carried away.'

Didn't look in his eyes. Didn't want to see what was there.

Walked to the lift. Forensic was on the fourth floor. Her bike was in the shed at the back, at the end of the narrow brick alley that led to the street.

Mulder came into the lift with her, leaned against the wall. Didn't push a button. Just stared.

'Ground,' Bakker said, pointing. 'Please.'

He pressed it then. Kept looking at her as they went down. Stood in the reception area as her shaking hands struggled to get the bike keys out of her cheap fake-leather shoulder bag.

There was a uniformed officer behind the desk. Bakker checked out with him. Left Mulder in the station, marched out of the side exit, trying not to run. Found her bike in the damp, dark shed. Shook her hair free because that made her feel better somehow. Climbed onto the saddle trying not to fall off.

Rain spitting from the sky. The roar of an unseen bus pulling away from the stop behind the wall.

Phone out, fingers jabbing clumsily at the buttons.

She should have put Vos on speed dial. It was idiotic. Juggling the handset in one hand, the bike handlebars with the other, big feet clattering against the pedals, wobbling to keep her balance as she walked astride the saddle towards the gate.

High brick walls in the lane to the street. Outside another bus roared past and the fetid wash from its wake flew over the wall, sent her loose hair flying into her face.

Bakker tried to sweep it away with her arm as she kept the phone in her right hand and eased along the alley that led to the road. Started punching the buttons before she got there. Reached the last one.

Heard footsteps behind. Didn't look.

One vicious punch took her clean off the bike, down to the hard ground, phone scuttling away, head slamming hard on the paving.

A shape above. Laura Bakker shook her head and hoped to clear her vision.

It was clearer now.

A long sharp line of silver glinting in the distant street lights.

CHAPTER 30

The phone in Vos's pocket rang. He looked at the screen.

'Laura?'

No one on the other end. Just sounds. Muffled. Indistinguishable.

He waited, listened. Nothing more.

Shrugged and put the phone back in his pocket.

Then the two of them cycled back along the canal, slumbering dog in the basket, Van der Berg chatting happily by his side. The talk in the bar had been worthwhile. Some things needed saying.

As they got closer to the Drie Vaten Vos told him some more about the call from Jansen. Van der Berg, a smart and thoughtful man, listened, scratched his chin for a moment, eyed the bar coming up on the corner.

'No more beer for me,' Vos said quickly. 'Early night.'

Van der Berg lived on the other side of the canal. Ten minutes away.

'Good idea. This thing about Jansen . . .' The two of them had interviewed the man many times. They thought they had the measure of him. 'He loved that kid, Pieter. She loved him too. Or so I thought.'

'She did,' Vos agreed. 'But still she betrayed him.'

'Theo wouldn't take that lightly. He's an old Amsterdammer. Big on family. Big on trust.' They came to a halt by the junction with the statues. 'If he knew she was cheating on him he'd be mad as hell. Could he have sent someone round to talk to her?'

'Why tell me then?' Vos asked. 'We're both innocents. Remember?'

Van der Berg shrugged, smiled his sad wan smile.

'Then I don't know. This whole thing's . . . wrong somehow. If . . .'

He was a sharp man. Saw things before Vos sometimes. Now his eyes were on the water ahead of them. Vos followed where he was looking, remembered two nights before and shivered. A pale shape in the sunken dinghy next to his home.

Van der Berg was off his bike, leaning it against a tree, not bothering to lock it and that was unusual.

'You didn't leave the lights on,' he said, walking towards the dark hulk in the water.

But there they were. Bright throughout the long hull of the boat.

Van der Berg patted his pocket. Opened his coat. Gun there in a shoulder holster. Vos didn't have one. He'd need to go back through training first. And Laura Bakker hadn't yet made the grade.

'Put that damned thing away,' Vos ordered as he climbed off the bike. Gently he lifted Sam from the basket, passed Van der Berg the lead, told him to take him to the bar.

CHAPTER 31

A thought as she hit the ground rolling. No cameras here. A bike gate onto the road. They didn't need them. So she kept moving. Took a kick to the back that didn't hurt too much.

Looked up, saw a long tall shape. Wanted to yell, 'But I didn't see you on the video, idiot.'

Just the white and blue ID card with the word 'Politie' and the yellow flame logo.

If it wasn't for the way he'd wriggled and sighed behind her she'd never have guessed.

Which seemed . . . funny. Or should have. Except now Klaas Mulder held a knife above her in the little brick-lined alley that ran from the Marnixstraat bike sheds down to the main road and the canal.

Long legs on both of them. But she had almost twenty years' advantage, scrambled away against the damp brick wall. Mulder came for her again, blade flashing. She lashed out with her big heavy boots, got him hard in the shins. Heard a muffled grunt and a curse. Rolled sideways again. Got upright. Kicked out once more, as hard as she could, saw him go down, another flying blow, hard boots against soft flesh. Left him there, panting.

Three quick steps to the gate and the street. Laura Bakker launched herself towards the metal grille, hearing the man behind her struggle to his feet. Got to the iron railings. Shook them.

Remembered.

Security. The thing was always locked. One way out only and that was to use the intercom by the side and get the duty officer on the desk to hit the remote release catch.

She slammed her fist on the button, began to yell a stream of pleas and imprecations into the plastic housing.

Sometimes the gate opened quickly. Sometimes he was away from the desk. Or talking.

Bakker turned. Mulder was up again. So was the knife.

'I need this open now!' she yelled, yanking hard at the iron grille. Looked up. The top was a good head higher than her. She could reach it. But it wasn't going to be easy to get over. And she'd be exposed, back to him. Easy target. Dead and gone.

Which left one choice only.

Turn and fight.

The moment she turned, long legs bracing for the first opportunity to kick out, Mulder was on her, elbow at her throat, face in hers.

Grinning. He liked this.

Back against the hard iron railings, facing the stronger man, eyes darting between his and the knife close by her cheek, she thought about this, measured the options.

Did something she'd never have tried in Dokkum. Not if someone might see.

Spat full in his face then jerked her right knee up, tried to catch him in the groin. But he was wise to that. Beefy arms pushing her sideways. Laura Bakker tipped off balance, twisted hard into the brick wall.

His big left fist came out and caught her in the side.

Winded, gasping, racked with a sudden sharp pain she stumbled back against the gate. Down on the ground now, one hand keeping her upright.

Klaas Mulder wiped the spittle from his face. One long slow movement of the arm.

Then waved the blade once in front of her.

'This is going to hurt,' he said. 'This . . .'

Another sound. A barked order. One he didn't listen to.

Then a burst of blazing light and a roar so loud, so bright there was nothing to do but close your eyes and wait.

CHAPTER 32

V os walked straight into the boat, looked down the length of it. Saw a slight figure hunched, head down at the table.

A girl. A young woman. Hard to tell. Greasy, dirty hair, fair, streaked. She sat hunched in nothing more than a grubby cream nightdress, shiny and stained, that finished at her thighs. Legs filthy. Bare feet caked in mud.

She was crying. Vos could hear the sobs. Tried to place them. To think. To hope.

Walked to the table. Still she didn't look at him.

Three years. They changed. Got older. Got bigger.

'Anneliese,' he whispered.

Remembered what Liesbeth had said, had scolded him with.

'Liese.'

The grimy fair hair didn't move. Face locked on his battered, bare pine table. Her hands were covered in muck. Black grime beneath her short fingernails.

He sat down opposite her, held his hands tight. Knew he wanted to touch her. Knew too this was the last thing he should do.

'You're safe now,' Vos said in a quiet, shaking voice. 'Your mother. She needs to know . . .'

The face lifted. The lank hair fell back. He looked and realized that Theo Jansen was right. He was an innocent. Naively looking for something that wasn't there.

Bleak dead eyes, pink from tears, wide with dread, young face lined and full of hurt, Katja Prins stared at him across the table. Opened her mouth. Said nothing. Tried. No words.

'Safe,' Vos whispered and still he had to stop himself reaching out and touching her scrawny, filthy fingers. 'I'm sorry we couldn't . . .'

Footsteps on the old boat's planks. He looked up, saw Dirk Van der Berg coming towards them. Phone out. Watched him sit down too, look at the girl.

'Jesus . . .' Van der Berg stared at Vos. 'Pieter—'

'We need an ambulance for Katja,' Vos broke in. 'I want her seen by a doctor before anything else. I want—'

'Pieter!'

Vos felt angry and that was rare.

Fighting to control his temper he turned to the man and said, 'Are you even listening to me?'

Van der Berg nodded.

'I am. I'll fix it. But something's happened. In Marnixstraat . . .'

Katja Prins's head went down on the table, rested on her bare, thin arms.

'I'll call then,' Vos said and took out his phone.

CHAPTER 33

It was Suzi's idea to go to bed. Jansen wondered about the wisdom of it. Sex hadn't bothered him much, not for years. It wasn't what drew him to her in the first place. Or the thing that had divided them in the end. In truth the naked ritual was more a way of saying something neither could phrase in words. An expression of affection or regret. A way of closing an argument that would otherwise have festered.

They wrestled wordlessly on her double bed, locked together the way they used to be, panting, sighing, heads over shoulders, eyes not meeting. No fond kisses. No words. Just a desperate stab at affection, a hunt for release.

And then it was done. He held her, since this was what she wanted. Felt the damp stain of her tears against his shoulder. She kissed his cheek very quickly, whispered a single word. *Sorry.* Rolled half over, looked at the ceiling. Closed her eyes.

From the courtyard of the Begijnhof came the low soft crooning of a pigeon. A few passing voices, footsteps tapping across the cobblestones. The light never left this room. It streamed in yellow as a dying sun from the old lamps beyond the tall wooden house, close to the cobbled gutter where an old woman asked to be buried so that coming generations would step over her bones.

Soon she was asleep. He recognized the rhythm and sound of her breathing. That was the same as ever. Her neck had grown folds and wrinkles, her skin pores and blemishes that were never there before. Still she was beautiful and always would be. Unlike him, an ugly man from the start. Irredeemable. Black inside.

Theo Jansen knew what he was. Knew too that he hated this place. Hated Suzi after a fashion. Even hated, if he tried, their daughter. A man like him had ways of dealing with treachery. Brutal means to bring about brutal ends. That was his business. His life.

And now the woman who'd schemed with Rosie lay next to him, slumbering. In a kind of peace. A brittle, hypocritical pact with an uncaring God. One that allowed her to cheat and steal and lie, but excusing the fact always because of who he was. A criminal. The fallen. A blind and gullible idiot when it came to the most intimate conspiracy of all, the one called 'family'.

Slowly, he rolled over, looked at her in the yellow light falling on the soft down duvet.

His hand stole slowly towards her neck, stopped just short. He found himself entranced, captured by the sight of her. A face that seemed so little changed, still lovely and now, in sleep, without the pain and doubt and guilt that had come to mark her waking hours.

Jansen's huge fingers hovered over the soft pale skin below her chin. Darker than he remembered, marked with wrinkles.

We are old, he thought. The line that joined us from vivid, loving youth to here is broken. And in its place . . .

Until the day before he'd never harmed a woman. But that was principally from purpose not principle. There hadn't been a need. Or any gain.

But now . . .

Twenty minutes later, dressed, wallet replenished with the money he'd asked her to retrieve that afternoon – five thousand euros, all small notes – Theo Jansen let himself out of the house. Walked through the dark, damp streets of De Wallen. Bought a razor, shaving foam, soap and some cheap clothes from an all-night shop along the way.

Then went through the door of a cheap flop-house in Zeedijk and booked a room for the night.

It was the kind of place that asked no questions. Which was just as well.

PART IV

THURSDAY 20 APRIL

CHAPTER 1

A face on the pillow. Eyes closed. Gentle rhythmic breathing. Fair hair cleaner now. Sleep seemed to take away so many lines on a face that might have been sixteen. Not pushing twenty.

Vos stood at the door of the private room in the hospital in Oosterpark, watching her. Watching Liesbeth by the girl's side too. It was seven on a bright spring morning, the sun strong even behind the hospital venetian blinds. The night had been long and busy. Just two hours' sleep, snatched in Marnixstraat. Then here to find . . . silence.

A uniformed woman police officer had stayed with them. She confirmed Katja hadn't spoken a word. Post-traumatic stress. Liesbeth stayed with her throughout, held her hand, tried to talk. But it was useless. She'd been sleeping now, medicated, for five hours. No sign when she'd wake.

The case was edging its way to a resolution of a kind. Katja Prins was alive. Loose threads were being tied. Everyone seemed, if not happy, close to satisfied.

Everyone except him.

'You should take a break,' Vos said in a low, concerned voice and got the stare. Liesbeth motioned to the corridor. They stepped outside. He'd talked to the doctors again. Katja was physically unharmed as far as they could see. But whatever experience she'd been through had taken its toll. They'd bathed her, fed her. Made her comfortable. The block still remained and could stay for days. Weeks even.

Liesbeth dragged him through the doors to an outside patio and lit a cigarette.

'Why don't you trust me?' she asked.

'You mean now? Or generally?'

'Why do you need a policewoman in there with us?'

'Because Katja was abducted. We don't know what happened. Where she was. How she got free. It's possible she could wake and try to leave. Or that . . .'

He didn't go on. She knew what he was thinking anyway. They'd lived together long enough for that.

'Or that I try to stop her telling you something?'

'This is a criminal investigation, Liesbeth. Don't expect favours.'

Nothing.

'Do you still think Wim couldn't be behind her disappearance?' Vos asked.

Eyes tight shut. That look of pain he'd seen so often.

'We lived together for years and still you didn't

know me. I was married to Wim for less than two. Why . . .?'

'You knew him longer than that.'

A brief smile, not bitter.

'True.' She launched the half-spent cigarette into a nearby bin. 'He always seemed gentle to me. Unhappy, disappointed in some ways. I thought I could help him. He thought he could help me.' A shrug. 'I guess we were both wrong.'

Her eyes turned on him and they were sad and serious.

'So perhaps he did. He was at the end of his tether with Bea. I know that. If Katja found out he'd harmed her . . .' She was considering this as a possibility, for the first time it seemed. 'I don't know what she'd do. Something. But why now?'

This had been troubling him too. He'd got Koeman to look into the Yellow House's methods. Regressive therapy involved forcing 'patients' to face up to hidden secrets from the past.

'Because he sent her for counselling,' Vos said. 'Recovered memory or something. Or maybe Katja just finally found someone who'd believe her.'

'What happens next?'

'We wait. An officer stays with her. With you.'

'In case—'

'In case of nothing. We can't press the girl. The doctors wouldn't allow it even if we wanted to. We've got to explore other possibilities.'

'Like what?'

'I can't go into that.'

'Something happened, didn't it? Last night? I heard the policewoman talking to one of the nurses. She said it was terrible.'

Vos glanced at his watch. Time to go.

'It's on the news,' he said. 'Probably more than I can tell you anyway. When Katja's awake . . . I'll come back.' He waited until she was looking into his eyes again. 'You're going to have to look after her. She'll need someone. You're all—'

'She hates me,' Liesbeth Prins said. 'Will you never listen?'

'Then why are you here?'

'Where else would I be? What happened, Pieter?'

'They'll have a TV somewhere,' he repeated.

Then went downstairs, over to the emergency department. This was where they took Laura Bakker the previous night while he and Van der Berg were waiting for a team to deal with Katja Prins. This was where she stayed.

Vos waited until seven thirty. The time he was given.

Then he asked at the desk. Was guided to a public ward a few minutes away. For women only and it was outside visiting hours. So a scowling nurse cast a suspicious look at his police ID card and told him to stay in the waiting room.

Ten minutes later she marched in. Small pink plaster on her cheek. Bruise around her eye. Tartan jacket. Green trousers. Shiny black boots.

'How dare they keep me in here?' Laura Bakker

446

demanded in her loud northern monotone. 'What right do they—?'

'They were worried about concussion. Worried about you. We all were.'

She frowned. Puzzled.

'I wasn't the one Koeman shot.'

'No. But . . .' He pointed at the garish tartan jacket. 'Shall we call at your place on the way? Get you a change of clothes?'

Hands on hips. Pale face livid.

'I'm sick of all these cracks about what I wear.'

'It wasn't a crack exactly.'

He pointed again. Laura Bakker looked at her right sleeve. Held it up. A long knife slash had torn the fabric in two.

She ran her fingers along it and said, 'Auntie Maartje's going to be mad about that.'

A shake of the long red hair then she pulled out an elastic band and started tying it back behind her neck.

'Mulder's dead, isn't he?'

'Let's talk along the way,' Vos said.

CHAPTER 2

The Begijnhof was quiet in the morning. They didn't let the tourists in early. Still she'd rarely slept this well in years. And she'd told him, finally. A burden lifted.

Suzi Mertens still didn't understand why she'd taken him to bed. Why he'd so easily accepted the invitation. She didn't feel the need to apologize. Rosie was adamant: they were owed something. This wasn't a man's world any more. They deserved a part of it too. Their own cut of a business so large everyone else was taking something on the side.

'I earned that, Theo,' she said aloud, naked, cold, alone.

Now he was gone. Just like the old days. Vanished in the morning without a word.

She got up. Showered. Got dressed. Forgot about breakfast for a while, walked down to the tiny chapel, stepped over the gutter and the old hidden bones, went inside, prayed.

For understanding more than forgiveness. What had occurred was a sin. Rosie paid for it in the most brutal of ways. The weight of that would never leave her. No matter how many times she got down on her stiff legs, knelt on the hard chapel floor, put her hands together, tried to talk to God.

But Theo Jansen was just a man. Both ordinary and special. Decent and flawed. A man she'd loved. Perhaps still did even though she hadn't appreciated the fleeting, dull hatred in his eyes the night before when he forced the truth from her. A truth he knew already.

She opened her eyes. Looked around. Alone in the small chapel at that time of the morning. The smell of fresh flowers mingling with wood polish and an undertone of damp. Rosie never came here. Didn't laugh when Suzi asked. She was a good girl. A loving daughter. Had the strength and the temper of her father from time to time. But the two of them never argued much. Not even when something dark and bad happened at that place on the Prinsen.

She climbed to her feet, pulled her coat around her in the bitter chapel.

Theo would go back to jail. That was inevitable. A display of humility and regret might bring some clemency. She would encourage him in that. Support him publicly. It would be the end of her time in the Begijnhof. She couldn't in all conscience stay there any more.

And then . . . when he was released.

He thought himself old now, though he wasn't quite sixty. By the time he came out he'd be a name in the newspaper archives. Forgotten largely.

Perhaps with most of his fortune sequestered by an avaricious state.

She and Rosie had money hidden away in secret accounts. That would be safe surely. After all the years of milking Theo perhaps she could return the favour and provide his pension. He wasn't an arrogant man. The idea might even amuse him.

Suzi Mertens shook her head. Wished she could think straight. The previous night was a way of saying goodbye and both of them knew it. There was no love left to be rekindled. Only respect underlined, in her case, by the smallest amount of fear.

Theo was who he was. A part of him might die. But the rest would never change, however hard she tried.

That was one more reason why there could never be a lasting reconciliation between the two of them. Too much distance, too much rank history. It was all a stupid dream, one that vanished the moment she looked into his cold and disappointed eyes.

She walked outside. Still no tourists. Pigeons flapping, cooing. A solitary man in a black winter coat, too heavy for the morning, sat hunched on the bench in the public area, his back to the tall wooden house where she lived.

A glimpse of face. Old, pale, whiskery. Neat grey hair. Vaguely familiar.

Suzi Mertens sat down next to him and said, 'Will it ever be summer?'

450

Looked at him more closely. She did know him. There was even a name. Maarten. A foot soldier from the past.

He'd always seemed cheerful before. A nice sort, as much as any of them were. One of the lads. Full of bawdy jokes and laughter. Now he was miserable and downcast like her on this chilly April morning.

'Not for everyone,' Maarten said.

He was opening his coat. There was something there, grey and gleaming. A gun.

'I never meant to hurt him,' she said softly. The words sounded pathetic even as she spoke them.

'But you did.'

'Yes. Both of us. Rosie and me. We didn't betray him. Not really. We just wanted something we could say was our own. Something we made ourselves. That wasn't handed down from him.'

She wasn't going to run. Not from a middle-aged crook who'd soiled this precious quiet place already.

A long and steady look into his old and miserable face. He didn't want this. Theo had sent him here.

'And now he wants me dead,' she said.

You weren't supposed to question. You were meant to cower, to shiver, to plead.

Maarten got up, stood over her. Coat just open. Hand on the weapon.

CHAPTER 3

Klaas Mulder's home was on the first floor of a block in De Pijp. Overnight the duty team had begun to penetrate behind the dead hoofdinspecteur's mask revealing a different side to the stiff unyielding man Vos had worked with for more than a decade.

The apartment, a place no serving police officer appeared to have visited, told its own story. Top-floor penthouse, three bedrooms, in an expensive modern building. Original paintings on the walls. Fancy modern furniture. A gigantic TV in the living room. It spoke of money. They'd extracted some of the man's bank statements and were starting to run through them. Mulder had more than a hundred thousand euros stashed in offshore holdings in the Caribbean.

The switchblade he'd used in the attack on Bakker had been identified as the same weapon that murdered Anna de Vries. The reporter's iPad had been found in a drawer in Mulder's flat. No time, it seemed, to erase it. A couple of the team were running through the video of Prins and Margriet Willemsen when Vos and Bakker turned up.

'Busy woman what with running Amsterdam and everything,' Bakker noted, watching the two of them in bed.

She was back in a new clean grey suit with a fresh pair of shiny black boots. Trying not to seem affected by the night before.

Mulder had three different unallocated phone SIMs in his jacket when he died. One of them was used to send De Vries the text messages, supposedly from Wim Prins and Katja, to lure her to a bleak dead-end alley in De Wallen. That case, at least, seemed closed.

Just before nine De Groot turned up with a tired Koeman. Bakker went out of her way to thank him. The man looked embarrassed. Still shocked. Beyond the room white-suited forensic officers continued to tear the place apart. It wasn't a fruitless exercise.

'So now I've a corruption case on my hands?' De Groot asked as they sat down at the table in a lavish kitchen.

'It looks like the money came from Surinamese,' the lead officer on the night team said.

'He was working for Jimmy Menzo?' the commissaris asked.

'Seems so,' the man agreed, handing over some sheets. 'There are these too . . .'

Phone records kept coming in for the SIMs in Mulder's possession. None was more than a month old. It looked as if he changed them regularly.

Vos looked at the names on the printouts.

'He called Rosie Jansen,' De Groot said, peering at them too. 'Six o'clock. On the day she died.'

'He was off duty,' Vos said. 'Theo had been kept in custody. Maybe he was just being friendly.'

De Groot didn't like that.

'We need to nail this down, Pieter. Today if we can.'

Vos wanted to laugh but didn't.

'Meaning what?'

'Meaning I want an end to it,' De Groot replied. 'God knows we're going to get enough shit thrown our way as it is. Menzo having his own man inside the force. A senior one at that. We know Prins staged this nonsense with his daughter—'

'No we don't,' Bakker cut in. 'We haven't heard her story yet.'

De Groot waved her away.

'What other explanation is there? How else . . .?'

'We'll look into it,' Vos said. 'When she can talk.'

The commissaris didn't like the tone of his answer.

'I want this closed,' he repeated. 'Prins was pulling this stunt with the daughter. He murdered his first wife and the girl found out. Mulder was Menzo's man inside Marnixstraat. He killed that reporter. We know he was in contact with Rosie Jansen just before she died.'

'And he was in the area,' the night man added. 'We've got CCTV of him in Dam Square early that evening. She lived just round the corner. No one knows where he went after work.'

'Then he dumps her on your doorstep just to fool us all,' De Groot said. 'Jimmy Menzo wanted Theo Jansen dead. When that failed he sent round Mulder to kill his daughter instead. I want you to take control of everything. Prins. Mulder. Jansen. This is getting political. Be discreet. Be prompt. Any questions?'

Vos could think of lots. Just none he wanted to ask just then.

'I'm sorry this didn't turn up anything about Anneliese,' the commissaris added. 'Sounds like Wim Prins was playing a cruel trick on you and Liesbeth there. Mulder just added to it. Maybe when this is done with we can look again—'

'But it is about her,' Bakker cut in. 'There's got to be a connection . . .'

'The connection's Wim Prins,' De Groot said. 'He knew exactly what happened when Anneliese went missing. Maybe . . .' He couldn't look Vos in the eye. 'Maybe he knew more than that. Talk to that girl of his when she comes round. You'll see.'

A uniformed officer, a woman in the night team from Marnixstraat, came in from the other room. She had her phone in her hand, looked at De Groot.

'We've just been sent a sheet of phone records from the city council,' she said. 'Came through the door first thing this morning. Don't know who sent them.'

'And?'

'It looks like Margriet Willemsen called Mulder before Anna de Vries was murdered. Not long after the reporter walked into the council offices and talked to Prins.' She picked up the iPad in her gloved hands. 'With her home movies.'

'I don't want any more politics in this than we've got already,' De Groot said.

'It's there, for God's sake,' Koeman cried. 'She was screwing Prins and Mulder. Prins knew about that video. What's the betting she called Mulder to tell him and ask for a favour?'

De Groot growled something no one heard.

'Also,' Koeman added, 'we need to bring in that little council guy. Hendriks. I still don't buy the way he kept popping up.'

'You want to arrest the vice-mayor and one of her officials?' De Groot demanded.

'No,' Vos said in a calm voice, trying to keep down the temperature. 'We just need to talk to them. Their place not ours for now. And besides . . .'

'Besides?' De Groot asked.

Vos shrugged and said, 'Katja Prins apart – and she's not talking – what else do we have?'

CHAPTER 4

Theo Jansen found the hair dye he bought the night before. Put it on his stubbly head and beard. Looked at himself in the mirror in the cheap Zeedijk hotel. Saw a fool stare back from the stained, cracked glass.

He had money. A gun and plenty of ammunition. An untraceable phone. A long, empty day of waiting ahead. Any other time, free like this, he'd have gone for a walk, taken a couple of beers. Stopped at a canal stall and downed some herring. The way he used to for Rosie when she was a kid, pretending to be a pelican, dangling the raw cold fish and onion over his gaping mouth.

Any other time . . .

There would be no more days like that. No pleasant hours with his daughter. No reconciliation with Suzi. His life had come to focus on a single act of vengeance. The death of the person who'd stolen the life of a treacherous daughter. Was that for him? Or Rosie? He wasn't sure. Didn't care. Only one thing mattered and that was the deed itself.

Jansen screwed up his face and examined himself in the mirror again. He wouldn't want to go back to prison like this. At least there he had a kind of dignity.

Then the phone rang. Twenty minutes to get to a coffee shop near Rokin. One he owned. Or used to. He wasn't sure any more.

Jansen got his things, all of them, didn't plan to stay more than one night anywhere until this was done. Paid forty euros to the surly Sri Lankan at the desk. Walked outside into the bright city day.

He'd never thought about Amsterdam much growing up. It was the only home he knew. The only place available, not that he disliked that idea at all. A civilized city, genteel in parts, rough and dangerous in a few well-defined quarters of De Wallen. A man who knew those streets, understood where to go and why. These dark alleys made him once he used his strength and cunning to despatch or possess everyone who stood in his way.

He dawdled down the narrow street of Zeedijk, eyes on the cobblestones, glancing in the windows. Realized he'd never walked around the city in this timid, anonymous way before. He was a proud man. Liked to stare people in the face. To judge them. To let them judge him. Just like Pieter Vos, the sad, smart officer from Marnixstraat. A man Jansen could deal with. Never control. He knew that because he'd tried.

More little shops. A couple of tourists, drunk or stoned. It was hard to tell. Down a lane a line of cabins, red lights, big women in underwear. Jansen stopped in front of the nearest. She had shiny ebony skin, huge, pink satin knickers, pink satin bra. Mouthing something filthy, making a gesture with her finger between her lips. Waving him in with a pink nail, grinning, pointing to the intercom.

One press of the button. How much? Fifty euros? A hundred? He'd no idea. These places probably belonged to him. If not then Menzo or his heirs. What happened in them was someone else's business. Theo Jansen had never paid for a woman in his life. Never wanted or needed that. He'd have stayed with Suzi from beginning to end if she'd allowed it. But that love died as the empire grew. More cabins. More coffee shops. Restaurants and supply lines running into the Dutch hinterland.

It was work. Just a job. Like his father's. But better paid and, for those who prospered, richer rewards.

And someone would do it, always. Because that was the nature of life, of Amsterdam. Of every city he'd ever visited. However much the church and prudes might wish it otherwise. Theo Jansen gave the public what they wanted. Treated well those who were loyal to him. Punished those who weren't. The way the government did. And they were there forever too.

The coffee shop was ahead of him. Maarten stood outside the door. Big heavy coat. Long miserable face. They went to the tiny smoking room at the back. Kicked out a couple of dope-heads who took one look and didn't argue.

'Well?' Jansen asked after the black guy from the

counter served them a couple of fierce coffees and left them alone.

'Well I did it.'

Maarten looked different. Not as scared or submissive as he used to be.

'And?'

The barber took a deep breath then a swig of coffee and recounted what had happened with Mulder.

'Christ,' Jansen muttered. Could think of nothing else to say.

'I thought he was still ours. But turns out he was Menzo's,' Maarten added. 'I talked to someone in Marnixstraat. Last time I'll get that privilege. There's going to be an internal investigation. People are shit scared. Mulder killed this reporter woman. They're working on the idea he murdered Rosie too. It was Jimmy thinking . . . if I can't have her old man I'll have her.'

'You believe that?'

'I don't know what to believe any more,' Maarten said quietly.

'Jimmy wanted me dead. Not Rosie. He told me that himself.'

'Jimmy was a lying bastard.'

'He wasn't a fool!' Jansen bellowed.

The more he thought about it the more stupid it seemed.

'Why would Mulder do something like that himself ? Why take the risk?'

'He killed this reporter woman, didn't he?'

'Maybe he had a reason there. Not with Rosie.

460

She'd been talking to Jimmy Menzo anyway. She'd done business with him over that privehuis for God's sake. Why would Menzo want her dead?'

'Then . . . I give up.'

An awkward, pregnant silence between them. Finally Jansen said, 'Suzi. You did it?'

'I said that, didn't I?' the barber snapped.

Different city. Different time. Maarten had never spoken to him this way before.

'I sat down with her. Showed her the gun. Said either she walked into Marnixstraat and told Pieter Vos everything she knew. Or someone was going to deal with her because that's what you wanted. I think . . .' He screwed up his eyes as if this recollection shamed him. 'I think she actually thought I'd do it myself. Certainly felt that way.'

'Good . . .'

'No, Theo! It's not good.'

Voice too loud in the little room with the cloying, acrid stink of dope. The barber glared at him across the beaten-up brown wood table.

'God knows I've done things I don't want to remember,' he said in a low, angry voice. 'But I never went around picking on women. We didn't do that kind of thing, did we?'

Not often, Jansen thought. Only on the rare occasion it was needed. Like now.

'She's going in there when?'

'I left that to her.'

Jansen pushed back his chair. Wondered where

he'd go next. Not to Maarten's shop. He didn't like that idea at all.

He held out his hand. The barber just stared at it.

'I've been thinking,' Maarten said. 'I owe you. If it comes to getting you out of town. Getting money. Passports. Putting you somewhere safe so we can make that deal with Robles work . . . I'm fine with that.'

'Very generous,' Jansen noted.

'It's what you're due. But this other shit.' He opened his coat, took out the weapon he'd shown Suzi Mertens, pushed it across the table. 'Forget it.'

The barber looked Jansen straight in the face.

'I mean that. I'm old. We both are. I'm old, I'm tired and I want an easy life. Don't want to spend it in jail for no good reason.'

'Rosie's good enough reason for me.'

'And you think this is just for her? Not about the fact you lost? *We* lost. Or that she and Suzi screwed around behind your back?'

'We didn't lose,' Jansen repeated. 'Not yet.'

'Everything falls apart in the end, Theo. Nothing you can do to stop it. Me and Robles and that Lindeman creep tried to put together a deal to get you out of this. But you won't take it, will you?'

'When I'm ready. When I know . . . about Rosie.'

The barber groaned, got up, looked at him and said, 'Where are you going to go now?'

Jansen laughed.

'I own half of De Wallen. You need to ask?'

'You don't own as much as you think. If you walk into the wrong place they'll give you up. The word's out. You're an embarrassment. Dangerous. Crazy.'

'People don't talk to me like that,' Jansen said. 'It's not wise.'

'Once upon a time maybe.' The barber handed over a new phone. 'I suggest you use this from now on. I don't know if the one I gave you's safe any more.'

'Suzi . . .'

'Suzi's got that number. I've got it. No one else.'

Jansen picked up the gun from the table, stuffed it into the spare pocket of his coat. Two weapons now. He felt like small-time muscle waiting on an opportunity.

'If you change your mind and want to get out of town we can do that today,' Maarten added. 'Gladly. Right now. I'll drive you all the way down to Spain myself . . .'

'Don't let me keep you,' Jansen replied.

A sour, judgemental scowl. He'd never have got that before. Then the barber was gone.

CHAPTER 5

Vos and Bakker started to cycle to Waterlooplein. Halfway down Elandsgracht he stopped suddenly, excited by something he'd seen.

'Croissants!' he declared and dashed in to the cheese shop, came out with a couple, pushed his bike to the benches near the statues of Johnny Jordaan and his musicians. She sighed, joined him.

'Aren't we supposed to be working?' Bakker asked.

He pulled out the phone log someone had shoved in the postbox of Marnixstraat that morning. Together they went through it.

'Best cheese croissants you can get round here,' Vos added. 'I like to have one every morning around eleven.'

'It's always good to have a schedule,' she observed.

Bakker looked at the croissant he'd given her. Still warm. Cheese crispy round the base. Perfect soft pastry. She picked at the thing, then finished it in a couple of bites. Purred for a moment.

A couple of pigeons started to hang around, looking for crumbs. Then an old woman with a dog meandered past, said she hoped Sam was well and learning to be less excitable, got a smile and a salute from Vos in return.

Cars and bikes. A sign in the little island between the narrow traffic lanes declared 'The Pearl of Jordaan!'. On the next bench a couple of dodgy-looking men were smoking weed. A mother went past pushing a pram, snapping at a kid who was trying to pluck the strings on the double bass on one of the statues.

'Who needs restaurants?' he asked. 'When you've got . . .'

'Yes, yes! Best cheese croissant ever. OK?' She tapped the phone log. 'What about this?'

It was for the office landline in Willemsen's office. One call to Mulder. Ninety seconds. Nothing else.

'Not much there, really. We'll need to scare a bit more out of them than that.' A grin. 'Are you up for it?'

She balled up her napkin, took his and the bag from the cheese shop, disposed of them carefully.

'I believe so,' she said and they cycled on to Waterlooplein.

He let Bakker lead the way, big boots clumping into the council offices. Before Vos could say a word she'd asked for Margriet Willemsen. The day was getting brighter. Summer waving in the distance. The flea market outside was busy with tourists and locals. Everything seemed so very normal. Whatever normal was.

The receptionist came back and said Willemsen

was busy in a meeting. She could fit them in around one in the afternoon.

Vos nodded and leapt over the security gate, waved his police ID at the flapping, worried guard. Checked the department list by the lift doors. He'd been here before. The executives worked on the top floor. Where else?

Bakker was right behind him. No one argued.

Willemsen had occupied Prins's old office. She was in the seat by the window with the view out to De Wallen, rooftops and church spires, red and brown, black brick and golden in the sunlight. Alex Hendriks opposite her when they marched in ignoring the squawks of the secretary who'd followed from reception.

'This is a meeting?' Laura Bakker asked and pulled up two chairs next to Hendriks.

Vos smiled and said, 'It is now.'

Bakker took out her voice recorder and notebook. Hendriks got up to flee for the door.

'You can stay,' Vos ordered. The council man groaned, sat down.

Willemsen looked furious.

'This is outrageous.' She picked up the phone. 'I'm calling De Groot. You can't just walk in here—'

'If you like,' Bakker cut in, 'we can discuss this with De Groot in the room. At Marnixstraat. He sent us.'

Vos looked at her. Nodded in agreement.

'Sent us straight here,' he added. 'No stopping. Or you go to jail.'

Then he held up the call log. Official city council stamp at the top. No arguing.

'Where did you get this?' she demanded.

'A good fairy pushed it through the door this morning,' Bakker said.

Willemsen lost it then. Stormed about confidential documents. Breach of trust.

When she calmed down a little Vos asked about the call to Mulder.

A pained sigh then Willemsen said, 'He was our link man at Marnixstraat for De Nachtwacht. Don't you know that?'

'That's why you called him?' Vos asked.

'Yes. We had a meeting coming up. Why else?'

He hesitated for a moment then said, 'This is a little delicate.' Looked at Hendriks. 'But anyway . . . You were sleeping with Klaas Mulder. You were sleeping with Wim Prins.'

A furious silence.

'Probably around the same time if the dates on the videos are to be believed,' Bakker added. 'I don't mean *simultaneously*. As far as we know. Just kind of . . . a little while apart.'

Margriet Willemsen blinked and asked, 'What videos?'

Vos smiled, waited for a moment then said, 'You don't know? One on the iPad Mulder took from the reporter he killed two nights ago. That was you and Prins. Another got sent to Prins at home. That was you and Mulder.' He scratched his cheek. 'Bit of a mix-up there perhaps . . .'

She didn't look flustered. Simply puzzled.

'I haven't a clue what you're talking about.'

Bakker scowled.

'Anna de Vries was in here on Tuesday. She had that on her iPad. She told him. And he never—?'

'Wim said nothing about it to me,' Willemsen insisted. 'I never talked to the woman. Neither did Mulder as far as I know.'

'You slept with both of them!' Bakker cried.

A shake of the head. Every last black hair in place. Willemsen looked confident.

'What's my private life to you? Or anyone?'

'I shouldn't be here,' Alex Hendriks announced and got to his feet. Vos let him leave. Willemsen watched him go. Eyes boring into his back.

'Two men you were involved with are dead,' Vos said when Hendriks had left the room. 'We need to understand why.'

'I'm a single woman. What I do outside of here is my business. Not yours.'

'That reporter could have destroyed you,' Bakker said. 'One story from her . . .'

Margriet Willemsen laughed.

'This is Amsterdam. Not whatever cow patch you grew up in. People don't give a shit who I sleep with.'

'You know something about this,' Bakker insisted, a little of the confidence knocked out of her voice.

Willemsen thought for a while then looked at Vos.

'Maybe I do. They're saying Wim killed his wife. Kidnapped his daughter. I had a fling with Mulder.

That's all it was. But I can tell you. Those too were close. They went out together. Drinks. Parties.'

'There was a privehuis on the Prinsen,' Vos asked. 'Three years ago . . .'

She shook her head.

'I don't hang around brothels. Mulder and Wim were close on De Nachtwacht. Much more involved than I ever was. To be honest Wim was obsessed with all that for some reason. I never did understand why.'

A thought, seemingly stray, then she added, 'Wim would be really mad if he thought someone had a video of us. He had a terrible temper. I can tell you that.' The steady, confident smile. 'I don't. Ask anyone.'

She glanced at the clock on the wall.

'I really do have meetings. If I could help I would. But . . .'

CHAPTER 6

It took ten minutes for her to calm down enough to summon him. Then she called Hendriks back into the office. Watched him take a seat. A small man. Scared and lost. And still there was something she didn't get.

'What do I do with you, Alex?' she asked.

He blinked at the bright sun beyond the window, kept quiet.

'Really? You cause so much trouble. So much unnecessary pain.'

Hendriks bowed his head, looked briefly mutinous.

'I've apologized for the videos. I didn't expect them to get out of here. Someone stole them. They were just . . . insurance.'

'You mean blackmail?'

'If that's what you want to call it. Not that I used—'

'You sent Marnixstraat that call log, didn't you?'

Hendriks shrank into the seat, stayed silent.

'You sent them a call log because you think I'm responsible.'

'I didn't say—'

470

'You think I called Mulder and got him to deal with that woman.'

'Deal with? She was murdered.'

She laughed.

'If you believe I'm capable of that . . . aren't you being just a bit, well, slow?'

'This city doesn't belong to you, Margriet! Any more than it belonged to Wim. To any of you.' A finger stabbed at his chest. 'It's ours.' A wave at the window. 'Everyone's. You can't come in here and tell us how to live. What to think. What to feel.'

She wanted to scream at him. Instead, calmly, she said, 'You don't think Wim would have got anywhere with De Nachtwacht, do you? It was his pet project. An obsession for some reason. We went along with it to get a seat at the table. That's all. For Christ's sake, Alex. You didn't need to spy on us. It was never going to happen. Not with me around.'

'So I gather,' Hendriks replied without thinking. Then realized. Twitched, nervous on the seat.

A long silence between them. At the end Margriet Willemsen said in a tense, taut tone, 'You've been under a lot of pressure. I don't think you cope well. The best thing for all of us would be for you to resign. Right now. Just clear your desk and go.'

'You think so?'

'I do. I'll sort out the severance. Don't worry. It'll be generous.' A glance at the window, then at him. 'Go home. Wait there. I'll send round someone from human resources. Straight away. We can do this subtly.' A frank look. 'Nothing need go on your record. You get the pay-off. I'll find you something elsewhere. Just be supportive. No more cameras. No more leaks. No more screw-ups . . .'

'I won't be th-threatened,' Hendriks stuttered. 'Not by the likes of you.'

'And what exactly am I, Alex? Please. Do tell.'

He didn't answer. Got up. Unsteady. Walked out the same way.

CHAPTER 7

Suzi Mertens was waiting when Vos and Bakker got back to Marnixstraat. A serious, pretty woman with a sad, drawn face. Drab brown coat and dress, like an off-duty nun. She'd asked for Vos by name at reception. Said nothing else except that she'd wait.

They listened to her in an interview room. After five minutes Vos stopped the conversation, called for a third officer. Issued the warning and turned on the voice recorder for the rest of her story.

It made a kind of sense. The privehuis was hers and Rosie's. Theo Jansen knew nothing about it, even when they closed it and sold on the property through the Thai woman, passing it to Jimmy Menzo.

'Why did you do that?' Laura Bakker asked.

'Because Rosie wanted to.'

'Why?'

No answer.

Vos turned off the recorder, nodded to the third officer, asked her to go. When it was just the three of them he asked, 'What made you break up with Theo?'

'I hated watching him change and never notice.'

She kept wringing her hands. Looking at the frosted-glass window bright with the sun.

'I just wanted a normal life. A family. Someone . . . you could talk to round the table. Take your kid to the beach. Pick them up from school.' The fingers moved more frantically. 'Wasn't much, was it? But Theo . . . Every day was a battle. A war. Anything we wanted he'd buy. Whatever we asked for. But we didn't get him. Not after Rosie was born. We weren't family. Just something else he owned.'

'You could have taken her with you,' Bakker said.

A short, cold laugh.

'You think so?'

She put her hands on the table, aware she was fidgeting. Recovered something of herself.

'What happened in the privehuis?' Vos asked.

A shake of her head.

'I honestly don't know. Rosie dealt with everything. She said it was best I wasn't involved. One day she closed the place down. Said we could sell it on to someone else and let them deal with it. You didn't argue with Rosie. She was like her father that way. It was pointless.'

'They were young girls,' Bakker said with a sudden vehemence. 'Little more than children. Older men grooming them.'

'I never knew,' Suzi Mertens answered very easily.

'But Rosie did,' Vos said.

She didn't answer.

'You live in the Begijnhof,' Bakker said. 'Do you pray in the church there? Ask for forgiveness—?'

'I did my best!'

Her sharp voice echoed round the room. They waited.

'I did my best,' she said again more gently. 'Something went wrong. Rosie was proud of that place. She said they got interesting customers. Businessmen. Politicians. Movie stars sometimes. People with money. And class.'

'They were paedophiles,' Bakker told her. 'Abusing young girls who couldn't protect themselves. While you made money out of it—'

'I didn't set the rules,' the Mertens woman interrupted. 'I didn't go there.'

'You knew though, didn't you?' Bakker said grimly. 'You had an idea something funny was going on.'

Suzi Mertens stared at Vos.

'Rosie said she had people from the police among her regulars. So I assumed I wasn't the only one who turned a blind eye.'

'Anyone with a name?' Vos asked.

'He killed her, didn't he?'

'Mulder . . .' Laura Bakker whispered.

'Is that why he did it?' Suzi Mertens asked. 'To keep her quiet? I've got the right to know. So has Theo. Why do you think he sent me here?'

'Where is Theo?' Vos said.

'I'd tell you if I knew.' She waited. 'Is that why Mulder killed my girl?'

Vos got up. Warned her she'd be cautioned for

475

hiding Theo Jansen on the run. Charged when the station got round to it.

'You didn't answer my question,' she said.

'I didn't,' he agreed.

CHAPTER 8

Alex Hendriks didn't wait to get his coat. After he left Margriet Willemsen's office he took the lift downstairs, walked straight out into the cold Amsterdam morning, stood for a long while among the office workers and tourists, watching the boats on the canal, the hawkers in the market.

A ten-minute stroll back to his bachelor flat. Along the Amstel, across the Skinny Bridge into Kerkstraat.

There he'd wait for the embarrassed drone from human resources. The council rarely fired officers, and never senior ones in his experience. But there was a process to be followed. He'd written it himself.

This was a walk he'd taken every day for nineteen years, working his way up the council hierarchy. Doing what he was told. Being a good civil servant. Along the canal then to the pretty pedestrian bridge where the artists sat and painted, trying to sell their canvases to any passing tourist. A quiet, solitary stroll. If there was time he'd stop by the painters, admire their work. Tell them he wished he could draw too, which was true though in truth he'd never much tried. There was always work.

Papers to be dealt with. Decisions to be made. Councillors to be obeyed. Levers and switches that needed pulling in order to keep the city running.

Sometimes he'd think about those choices as he sat by the Amstel, glad to leave the council building and De Wallen behind. Tourists would ask him to take photos of them beneath the white wooden arms that rose from their supporting arches to make way for boats moving up and down the broad, busy river. He always agreed. For all its faults he loved Amsterdam, was proud of his native city.

His small, modestly decorated flat was just on the other side, close to the point at which Kerkstraat met the tree-lined street that bore the river's name.

On this strange day he walked straight past the artists, didn't even look at them. Then stopped. The white arms were rising. A large commercial barge edged slowly down the river towards the Skinny Bridge. Tourists had their cameras out. Cries of delight.

A bridge. A boat. A hiatus in the day his old life ended.

Hendriks stared at the rising arms. Could see his building on the corner of Amstel and Kerkstraat beyond.

A silver-grey Mercedes parked outside. Four swarthy men in business suits were getting out. They looked busy, anxious. One went to the door, pressed the bell. The other three were looking around.

Transfixed, Alex Hendriks watched them. He'd entered a different world since Wim Prins and Margriet Willemsen seized the helm of the council. Perhaps that explained his actions. Or so he liked to think.

The bridge kept slowly rising. Across it his eyes caught those of one of the men in suits.

Recognition. He felt it. Felt the way his blood ran cold.

A shout. The other two turned. The fourth at the door gave up and looked too.

The twin levers of the Skinny Bridge moved slowly towards the bright spring sky. One of the men was dashing towards the crossing. Hendriks kept gazing at them, unable to move. It felt like a dream. A slow nightmare seeping up from the cold waters of the Amstel, freezing his limbs as it crept around him.

The lights on the bridge started flashing. A low klaxon. The nearest suit got to the rising edge, tried to cling to it.

One hand out. In it something so unexpected it made Hendriks turn his head sideways, like a curious bird.

A gun. It had to be.

Two of them now and at that point Alex Hendriks found his legs. He turned and ran, kept on going along the opposite bank of the Amstel, fleeing for his life.

There was a Volvo estate near the main road. White, red and blue. *Politie* on the side.

He glanced back. The white arms were all the way up. The figures in suits swarmed angrily on the other side. Too far to chase him down the opposing bank.

Hendriks opened the back door of the police car and fell in. Saw two uniformed officers turn and stare at him.

'Marnixstraat,' he said.

'We're not a taxi . . .' the cop at the wheel began to say.

'You want to know what happened with Klaas Mulder, don't you?'

They were quiet then.

'Take me to Vos,' Hendriks ordered, and slunk down into the back seat.

CHAPTER 9

Fourth floor of Marnixstraat. A forensic officer was working archived CCTV material on one of the big-screen workstations. Vos, Bakker and Koeman watched. A map of the area around Rosie Jansen's apartment near Dam Square was in the corner of the screen. Van der Berg sat busy at another desk, poring over more phone logs.

Vos had checked repeatedly on Katja Prins's condition in hospital. She was awake now. Liesbeth was still there. Katja still hadn't spoken a word to anyone.

'Here.' Laura Bakker pointed to a tall figure in the corner of the CCTV coverage. 'That's him.'

'Mulder,' Koeman agreed. 'Rosie Jansen's apartment's round the corner. Narrow pedestrian street. No camera coverage there. This puts him in the vicinity. There's nothing to say he was in her place. Nothing we've picked up in his apartment either.'

The detective looked tired and out of sorts. There'd be an internal inquiry into Mulder's death, beyond the usual inquest. All firearms incidents generated them.

'He's nailed for the De Vries woman,' Koeman

481

added. 'No question there. Rosie . . .' He frowned. 'I don't see it. Are we bringing in that woman from the council and her little imp or what?'

De Groot had listened to Vos's report of that meeting with an expression on his face that said, 'I told you so.'

'The commissaris thinks we don't have enough,' Bakker told him.

'We need the Prins girl to start talking,' Koeman grumbled. 'This doesn't look right.'

Vos went over the street map around Rosie Jansen's apartment. It would have been easy to approach the place without crossing the busy Dam Square. Mulder could have gone to see her. He could have gone anywhere.

The CCTV rolled on.

'We're screwed here,' Koeman grumbled.

Bakker placed a long forefinger on the screen. Her nails were short and clipped, like those of a schoolgirl.

'There,' she said.

Vos looked. Wondered. Ignored Koeman's bleats. Asked someone to fetch Suzi Mertens, still downstairs, waiting to be charged.

When the woman came up he pointed to the figure on the screen and asked, 'Do you know who this is?'

She took out a pair of glasses and peered closely at the monitor.

'I don't think so. Should I?'

On the adjoining computer Bakker typed a name into the ID database.

'This woman was with Rosie?' Mertens asked.

'She was in the vicinity,' Vos said. 'Maybe it's nothing. You're sure you don't recognize her?'

Suzi Mertens took off her glasses, glanced at the screen again, leaned forward.

'I already told you. Who is she?'

'You can go back downstairs,' Vos said. 'You might want to find yourself a lawyer.'

'Who . . .?'

Vos nodded at the door. The desk phone rang as she walked out. Koeman answered it.

'Don't pull up records when we've got witnesses around,' Vos told Bakker.

'It was an ID card! She couldn't see—'

'If I can interrupt the argument,' Koeman said, hand over the phone.

He was smiling. Beaming. Happy again.

'You know I said we should have pulled in that dork from the council,' he said gleefully. A chuckle. 'No need. He's here. And he wants to talk.'

CHAPTER 10

Leidseplein didn't look much different. Forty years before Theo Jansen did grunt work here. There was money to be made from drink and drugs and sex down the dark lanes that spread out behind the busy square.

He'd decided to heed the barber's warnings. Steered clear of De Wallen. Hung around cafes drinking endless coffee. Waiting for someone to call.

Behind the ugly sprawl of the casino, wandering aimlessly, he came across a blind alley. A dark cobbled cul-de-sac leading off the street. Found himself staring at it, mind wandering, struggling to focus.

A memory. Somewhere down this dank lane he'd done door duty for an early privehuis. A cheap and nasty dive. One of the first to mix dope and women, not long before the gang wars began. Jansen had been given responsibility for keeping it hidden. Paid off some police officers and a few people in the council. Kept the business running and tried not to look too closely at the clientele.

One night a big Hollywood star, a man everyone

recognized, turned up waving a fist full of guilder notes. He didn't mind being seen in an illicit Amsterdam whorehouse. That was what the city was for. So Jansen took his wad, made sure no one snatched any photos or asked for autographs. Then left him with three teenage Thai hookers and a bag of weed.

The idiot seemed happy enough.

Jansen took a couple of steps down the alley, remembering how he saw the same actor in a family film not long after. Playing the perfect father, a role the papers said he performed in real life. Rosie was five or six at the time and loved that movie. Jansen had watched it with her, feeling sick most of the time.

The black brickwork didn't look any different in this dark cul-de-sac. Same smell of drains.

Did he own this place now? Or was it part of the Menzo estate that Robles and his thugs controlled?

He didn't know, wasn't interested in finding out. Just found himself transfixed by the memories. Maarten was right. People got old, got weak and stupid. And the city rolled slowly on forever. Where he was stood was a short walk from the Museum Quarter with its Rembrandts and Van Goghs, the Concertgebouw where he and Rosie sometimes liked to go when the music was light enough for a working-class Amsterdammer's taste. But they were different places. Bright and elegant and refined. The two of them were interlopers there and knew it. This was home, hemmed in by dank bricks and the daily grasping round of seedy business. Life had been like this here long before he was born and would stay that way when he was dust. It was a place people needed to visit from time to time. The dark side. Somewhere they could throw off the crippling mantle of respectability and let the hidden animal inside loose for a while.

Then go home, to little wives and little lives and dream of the next time they might be free.

Not him. He was their servant. Their slave. A well-paid one but that was all.

Alone, lost for where to go, what to do, Jansen found himself gripped by a sudden urge to see the place that started him on this path. Walked down the narrow alley. A purple door. A name: Lazy Elephant. It was all coming back.

Found himself in the darkness at the end. The door was shiny black now, freshly painted. A set of bell pushes for the floors above. He stared at them. An accountant. A public relations firm. A Chinese import and export business.

He was wrong. This place had changed. Maybe for the worse. He was never a thief. The men who found their way through the door of the Lazy Elephant got their money's worth. He wondered if these people could say the same.

Someone had plastered a stick-on sign on the wall close by. A warning about pickpockets and muggings.

They happened, Jansen thought.

It was a grim, desolate alley. He was alone. An

old and now anonymous man. Stupid place to wander.

They were there when he turned. Three young hoods, one Asian, the others he wasn't sure. Ugly and skinny, with crowing looks on mean faces. The smallest was at the front, the other two behind. The way cowards worked.

He had a thin knife out. Said, 'Give me your wallet, Granpa.'

Waved the blade.

Theo Jansen wondered how long it had been since he'd dealt with scum like this. Not far from here either.

Bent down, put a hand to his ear, said in a croaky voice, 'What's that, sonny? I don't hear so well.'

A flurry of curses. The knife flashed in front of him. The little idiot put his hand to the front of Jansen's coat.

'Gimme the fucking money, man.' Another swipe. 'Or it's this.'

Jansen nodded, said, 'Ah.'

Slowly opened his coat, put a hand in, wriggled it round, listening to the kid's language get louder and worse as they glanced around wondering if someone could see.

He had long black greasy hair. This was so easy. Jansen closed his right hand round the gun, brought it out. While the kid stared at it, eyes wide, mouth open, Jansen's left hand wound itself into his scalp, pulled his head hard, banged it against the wall.

The knife clattered on the cobblestones. The other two scampered off in an instant. Just the two of them now, close against a set of bell pushes. A man approaching sixty. A youth maybe twenty at the most.

Theo Jansen jabbed the barrel of the pistol hard into his sallow cheek. Listened to the stream of whimpered pleas, jabbed harder. Told him to shut up.

'What's the lesson today?' he asked calmly.

'Didn't mean it, mister,' the kid whined. 'Didn't—'

'What's the lesson today?'

He'd roared that in his best angry voice and it felt good.

Silence.

'Sometimes you pick the wrong guy,' Jansen said after a while. 'That's the lesson. Learn it.'

The gun barrel didn't move. The kid's eyes stayed wide.

'Repeat after me . . .' Jansen began.

'Sometimes you pick the wrong guy,' the kid said quickly.

Street-smart, Jansen thought. Just the way he was. But no muscle. Probably no decent parent either. In a way this kid had an excuse he'd never possessed.

'Get yourself a job, sonny. You're not cut out for this stuff. Listen to me. I know.'

The kid laughed, a flash of anger in his eyes.

Spat back, 'A job. Where've you been?'

'Jail. And I'm going back there or somewhere else very soon.'

He took the gun away from the skinny youth. The kid glanced at the cobbles, the knife there.

'You can forget that,' Jansen said.

The door opened. A middle-aged woman in a smart business suit stared out at them, asked warily, 'Is there something wrong?'

'We were looking for the Lazy Elephant club,' Jansen said. 'But I think we're too late.'

Then he half-shoved, half-kicked the kid back out into the street. Jansen watched him lope off. Cursed himself for the crack about a job. That was an old man's response. He'd have been insulted by it too.

Back in the square he found a herring stall. Looked at the fish. Old, not new. Got a grunt from the man behind the counter. Ordered a *broodje*, watched as the man put the thin white fillet, some onions, some pickles in the bread roll.

Walked round Leidseplein eating. He should have had a beer first. Or a jenever. That way he might not have noticed the thing barely had any taste. This was his city and it seemed to be recoiling from him. No one looked at him. No one did anything but get out of his way.

A crazy old man eating *broodje haring*. Thinking of a dying crook, consumed by flames in a field of flowers. And his daughter, murdered, left next to the houseboat of the only cop a man like Theo Jansen would ever trust.

Maybe Mulder did kill her. And then what? Hard to take revenge against a dead man. He'd heard nothing from Maarten. Nothing from Robles or

Suzi. Three, four hours, that was all he'd give it. After that he'd sit in a bar somewhere in the Jordaan, drink himself stupid, make the call and wait for Vos to turn up.

A few minutes later the phone rang. It was Suzi outside Marnixstraat.

'You didn't need to send that man,' she said. 'Or threaten me. You could have just asked.'

'Confession comes naturally I guess.'

'You're a bitter, crazy old fool. You know that?'

'Yeah. But we've all got our faults. I never lied to you though. Did I?'

Silence. He thought he'd pushed her too far.

'They say they're going to charge me with hiding you. When they've time. I could go to jail.'

'It's not so bad. They've got priests and things.'

'Theo!' she shrieked. 'Don't blame me for everything! It was Rosie's idea. Not mine. She was pissed off you didn't want to know me. I didn't have two pennies to rub together—'

'You could have asked!' Jansen bellowed.

'Begged you mean. Gone on my knees.'

Maybe that was true, he thought. He'd built walls around himself over the years. No one came close. Not even Rosie it seemed.

'If it was Mulder I may as well come in,' he said more quietly. 'What's the point?'

She didn't answer.

'Am I talking to myself here?'

'Vos doesn't think it was Mulder,' she said. 'He didn't say so but I could tell.'

490

Even after thirty years he could still hear the edge in her voice.

'So who's he chasing?' he asked.

'A woman. I wasn't supposed to see but they had her name on the screen.'

'Someone I might know?'

'She's American. Barbara Jewell. Runs something called the Yellow House. I looked up the address. It's behind the flower market. They've got her on CCTV near Rosie's place.'

'The Yellow House? What the hell's that?'

'I don't know! He couldn't wait to get me out of there. They've got hold of the Prins girl. Vos wants to talk to her about that place on the Prinsen. But she's sick or something. Can't speak. They kept asking me what happened there—'

'What did?'

'I don't know,' she cried. 'That's the truth. But that kid does. They seem sure of it.'

'Thanks,' he said.

Ten minutes to the flower market on foot. He could ask about the place there.

'That's it? Thanks?'

'I'm sorry I sent Maarten. I didn't want to see you myself. I couldn't face that.'

'Do I frighten you, Theo? Is that it?'

'Maybe,' he agreed. 'Most things do if I think about them.'

CHAPTER 11

Vos sent a couple of uniformed officers to fetch Margriet Willemsen to Marnixstraat, met her in reception. They got three cups of coffee from the worst machine, headed down the corridor. He'd picked the route carefully. Along the way Alex Hendriks sat inside another room with Koeman and a young detective. Vos stopped at the door and looked through the glass. The little civil servant's head rose from the table. Terrified when he saw her.

'I'm here because of that cretin?' Willemsen demanded. 'You know I just fired him? Did he tell you that?'

'He told us you sent him home and there was a bunch of thugs waiting for him,' Bakker said.

Willemsen laughed. Shook her head.

'What is this? Alex Hendriks has lost his mind. He planted a camera in my bedroom. Tried to blackmail Prins. Then some temp raided his secret home-made porn store and started this nonsense. He's the criminal. Not me.'

Bakker was ready to rise to the bait. Vos kept her quiet. Then they went to the adjoining room.

Hendriks was shaking, terrified when the uniformed men delivered him to Marnixstraat. He had his own iPad with him. The phone log they'd seen already. The two videos. Some unrevealing email exchanges between Willemsen and Mulder the previous week.

And one thing of substance: four months of statements for a private bank account in the name of Willemsen's political group. Vos had got the numbers printed out. Passed them across the table after they sat. Then placed another set of statements, pulled by the night team from one of Mulder's offshore accounts the previous night.

'You need to look at this,' he said, tapping the first printout.

Willemsen didn't even blink.

'Once a month Mulder was getting eight thousand euros paid into an offshore account,' Bakker said. 'We've traced the source. Menzo.'

'A crooked cop's your business. Not mine.'

'Here.' Vos placed a finger on the second statement. 'Once a month he transfers four thousand euros over to you.'

Willemsen calmly picked up the sheet and examined it.

'Not me. That's a party account. I don't run it. I don't even know what's in there.' She frowned, thinking. 'From what I remember this is used for operating expenses. We get lots of individual donations. Every political party does. You should talk to our financial officer. He can explain—'

'For God's sake!' Bakker yelled. 'You've got the biggest crook in Amsterdam paying you a monthly stipend. Like you're . . . the phone company or something. What did he get for it?'

'Mulder's finances are nothing to do with me,' Willemsen replied, head to one side as if puzzled, not flustered at all. 'I slept with him from time to time. It was sex. Not friendship. We didn't do a lot of talking.'

'Three days after Menzo paid him you got your kickback,' Vos said.

'Lots of people make a monthly donation. I do it myself out of my own salary.' She smiled and asked, 'Is that it?'

'Not even the start,' Vos said. 'Hendriks told us you went for the deal with Prins so you could kill De Nachtwacht from inside. You were placed there for that.'

'He's a fantasist. Totally delusional.'

Bakker cut in, 'He thinks these thugs you sent round were going to kill him.'

She laughed at both of them.

'You mean I'm a murderer too? Have you found these imaginary people I supposedly sent there? Do you have anything to corroborate what he says?'

Vos had despatched a team down to the Amstel but they'd drawn a blank.

'Listen to me,' Willemsen said. 'I will speak very slowly in the hope you might understand. Alex Hendriks is insane. Delusional. Pissed off I fired him. I'm offended you even give him the time of day. And this will go further. I promise.'

She leaned back in her chair and stared at them.

'You dragged me from my office because of the ramblings of a disgruntled employee? The fact one of your own officers was making a contribution to a political party? Which was his right by the way.'

She picked up her briefcase, checked her watch, got up from the table.

'Are you charging Hendriks over those videos he made? I hope so. I'm going to be talking to a lawyer too. About libel. About wrongful arrest . . .'

'We didn't arrest you,' Vos said. He looked at the three untasted plastic cups in front of them. 'We just invited you here for coffee.'

She did smile at that.

'You're a funny man. I hope you're still laughing tomorrow.'

'You can't walk away from this, Margriet,' Vos told her.

'There's nothing to walk away from. And we're not on first-name terms.'

'Dirty money's going into your campaign funds. Even if we can't prove it went to you. We can show it went to your party. And those videos . . .'

She sat down again.

'Forget about the money, Vos. You've nothing there.'

'The videos,' Bakker repeated. 'The trouble is . . . they're so *available* these days.'

'They haven't leaked,' Vos added. 'Which is a

small miracle, given at least one of them was in the hands of a reporter.' He sighed. 'The trouble is . . . I don't know if I can guarantee they won't get out there in the future. From here. From wherever else they happen to be.'

Laura Bakker nodded in agreement.

'Even if the money doesn't get you,' she said. 'I don't think Amsterdam's going to warm to seeing its council leader humping two dead men on YouTube.'

'You're threatening me,' Willemsen said, to Vos not her. 'I thought you were smarter than that.'

'I need to know about Mulder and the prive-huis on the Prinsen. I think you went there. I think—'

'Once,' she snapped. 'Once only and it was with Wim. Not Mulder. Your man was there already when we turned up. This was a couple of years ago when I was just coming into politics. It was supposed to be some kind of . . . I don't know. An initiation. A meeting place for like minds. OK?'

'With Prins?' Bakker repeated.

'That's what I said. I think he was new to it too. Mulder fixed it.' She shrugged, looked briefly regretful. 'Middle-aged men in suits. Young girls in party dresses. Sitting on their laps mostly. And God knows what else went on upstairs. I didn't stay to find out, and neither did Wim. If you . . .'

Margriet Willemsen was lost for the right words and that seemed rare.

'If you people had been doing your jobs . . . if you hadn't been taking kickbacks . . . none of that would have gone on.'

'Didn't stop you taking Jimmy Menzo's money,' Laura Bakker said with a smile.

'You start from where you are!' Willemsen yelled. 'Not where you'd like to be.' Then more quietly. 'Wim didn't get that. He thought he could tear up everything and begin again. Life's not like that. Everything's a compromise. A negotiation. Anyone can make peace with their friends. It's cutting a deal with your enemies that counts. That changes things. With Mulder around we could have reached an accommodation. No more visible brothels. No drugs near schools. Turn down the red lights a little.'

She stopped. Had said too much and knew it.

'I was trying to make things better in a way that was going to work. Believe it or not. Now we're back to square one. With Menzo dead and Jansen God knows where . . . I don't know who'll be calling the shots. I will talk to your superiors about this, Vos. They're not naive. They live in the real world. Not the fairy-tale one you people seem to inhabit.'

He didn't object when she went to the door. Bakker was starting to tick, demanding to know why.

Vos sat in silence, running his fingers through his long, straggly hair. Then excused himself, went down the corridor, walked into the washroom,

497

went into the first empty stall, made a long phone call, thought about the answers he got. Issued an instruction.

Bakker was outside waiting for him.

'Hello?' she said. 'Anyone there?'

'I went to the toilet.'

'You're up to something. Where's your mate Van der Berg?'

'Til Stamm. Why would a casual housemate of Katja Prins, someone who said she wasn't even a friend, try to steal information on Katja's father?'

'She didn't kill anyone,' Bakker said. 'Why are you bothering about her when that bloody woman—'

'I don't have time for this,' he said and marched through to the next room, pulled Koeman out of the interview. He'd got nothing fresh from Alex Hendriks. The records he'd brought proved Willemsen had communicated with Mulder. That Mulder had contributed to the party funds. That was it.

Vos leaned on the wall by the window, staring at the street outside, listening to the rattle of the pneumatic drills.

'He wants protection?' Koeman asked. 'Does he get it?'

A puzzled frown.

'Of course not. I'd really like a decent coffee. Not from the machine. Forensic have got a new one . . .' He looked at Bakker. 'And some biscuits. What kind do they do these days? Can you fetch a list?'

She was taking a deep and angry breath.

'That was good,' he added quickly. 'The thing about the videos. She'll be on the phone to the people above Frank right now. But what the hell . . .?' A tug of the long hair again. 'I really need to know why Til Stamm would do a thing like that. Good coffee might help—'

'I am *not* your waitress, Pieter Vos,' Bakker declared.

Koeman threw his hands in the air.

'Oh for God's sake I'll fetch the coffee. You don't get a biscuit list. Any news from the hospital?'

Vos looked at his phone. A message from the officer there saying Katja Prins was ready to be discharged soon. She still hadn't said a word. When they let her go she'd be staying with Liesbeth under medical supervision.

'Two biscuits,' he said. 'No chocolate. I hate chocolate on biscuits.'

Koeman stomped off. Bakker started to squawk again.

'Quiet,' Vos said. 'I'm trying to think.'

'It would be nice to be included.'

'Depends what I'm thinking.'

'I won't give a damn when they kick me out of this place next week. I'll go willingly and find a job working with normal people . . .'

'Normal people will bore you, Laura. They do that.'

A door along the corridor opened. Frank de Groot, red-faced, furious.

'In!' he shouted. 'Both of you.'

'I'm waiting for my coffee and biscuits, Frank,' Vos objected.

'In!' the commissaris roared.

CHAPTER 12

It wasn't hard to find the place. Yellow sunflowers on the wall. One street behind the fragrant busy market where tourists paid through the nose for bulbs they'd never grow. Jansen stood outside in the cold, wondering what to do.

A name. That was all he had. Nothing to link the American to Rosie. He didn't even understand what the Yellow House was.

Then a white Volvo estate parked clumsily along the road, a familiar figure got out and lumbered towards the building.

Didn't look at the big man with the dyed stubble darting into the shadows.

Jansen fought for the name. He used to be good with these. Never forgot a face. Now it took a while.

Van der Berg. A big, boozy friendly detective. Someone Jansen once thought might turn out to be flexible. But that was part of the act. In truth he was as stubbornly honest as his boss Pieter Vos. Who surely sent him here for a reason.

CHAPTER 13

De Groot closed the door and told them to sit. Read a kind of riot act. About all the things they'd done wrong. How Margriet Willemsen was bringing down the wrath of distant gods.

Vos listened patiently. Laura Bakker squirmed and twisted in her chair.

'This,' De Groot declared, 'is where it finishes. I know there are holes. I want to hear what the Prins girl's got to say just as much as you do. But it's not going to change anything. We've got two names to put on the sheets. Mulder and Wim Prins. Both dead. I want that done. As far as the Willemsen woman's concerned—'

'She's lying through her teeth,' Vos intervened. 'You know that.'

'Maybe I do! But she didn't kidnap Katja Prins. She didn't murder that reporter or Rosie Jansen. Most of all we can't prove a damn thing. You can't . . .'

Hendriks's car with the suits near the Skinny Bridge had been spotted on CCTV. False plates, no IDs for the men inside. It looked suspicious but there wasn't a single footprint back to city hall.

'If we've got photos of them—' Bakker started.

'We can do what?' De Groot asked. 'Spend days finding them and then? They didn't do anything. You don't have a scrap of evidence to put her in the frame alongside Mulder. Or for corruption either.'

He turned to Vos and asked, 'Am I wrong?'

'Probably not. You might want to pass the file to the anticorruption people.'

'That's my call,' the commissaris answered. 'Not yours. I want to see the paperwork drawn up on Prins and Mulder. I want to be able to put out a statement. Case closed.'

The two of them sat silent at that.

'It's not too much to ask,' De Groot added. 'I don't see the point in chasing dead men. Leave Margriet Willemsen to me. And find Theo Jansen. If we can put him inside I'll be able to sleep at night.'

'Lucky you,' Bakker said. 'We still don't know what happened to Anneliese. Why Mulder would have dumped Rosie on Vos's doorstep—'

'He was screwing with us!' De Groot yelled. 'He hated the idea Vos was back here. Maybe . . . I don't know . . . thought it would be fun to give him some more pain. Do you think we're going to find an answer to everything? Life's not like that here. This isn't . . .'

'Dokkum?' she asked. 'Got that, thanks.'

De Groot folded his arms. Kept quiet.

'Can I see Katja Prins home first?' Vos said. 'She's not talking but they say she can leave hospital. Liesbeth's going to look after her. They both need some support.'

'Wouldn't you be better off looking for Jansen?' De Groot demanded.

'We don't have a clue where he is,' Vos said. 'No one does. Even his own men I suspect. Maybe . . .' A thought. 'Maybe Theo will find us when he wants to. He's out there for Rosie. If we put out a statement saying Mulder shot her—'

'Don't be long,' De Groot ordered. 'I want that on the evening news.'

Back in the corridor Laura Bakker said, 'De Groot doesn't like me.'

'What makes you think that?'

'Because he doesn't.'

'Frank's in a corner,' Vos told her. 'The Willemsen woman's causing him pain.' He dragged on his old blue jacket. 'Do you know what Barbara Jewell and the Yellow House do?'

'Cure people? That's what she claimed.'

'Regression therapy,' he said. 'Heard of it?'

She nodded.

'That's where you say hello to your monsters. And then you end up . . . clear and clean.'

'Does it work?'

'I don't have any monsters,' Bakker said straight off. 'It's just you complicated city folk . . .'

Vos laughed.

'What's funny?' she asked.

'You.'

'I can't believe that Willemsen woman's going to get away with this. You saw her. We both—'

'Politics, Laura. Sane people stay clear. Frank's right too. We don't have anything to throw at her except a couple of bedroom videos and a few suspicious bank records. Let's try to fix the world bit by bit, shall we? The easiest parts first.'

She nodded, a brief smile at that.

'So are we going to the hospital now? I'll get a car.'

He glanced outside the window.

'Too nice for that. I want some fresh air.'

An exasperated sigh.

'We can't cycle all the way to Oosterpark. If we're picking up Katja . . .'

He waggled his bike keys and smiled. She glanced back at De Groot's office. The door was closed.

'So where are we really going?'

'Mystery tour,' Vos said.

CHAPTER 14

Just before noon Van der Berg came out of the Yellow House, phone in hand, having a conversation he didn't seem to like. The sun was close to warm. The street had a few tourists clutching flowers and stupid souvenirs: clogs and pointed white hats.

There was a woman with the cop. Maybe forty, stockily built with dyed hair. She wore a mannish long black jacket and an expression of bafflement. Didn't want to be with Van der Berg. Didn't have a choice. That was obvious.

While the two of them stood outside the house with the sunflowers, Van der Berg gently arguing, eyeing the Volvo, Jansen quickly ducked out into the sunlight, looked at the street. A cab was trundling along looking for business. He clicked his fingers, summoned it. By the time the driver got there Van der Berg was back at the Volvo opening the door for the woman Jansen assumed was Barbara Jewell.

Jansen pointed at the white police car, said, 'Wherever they're going.'

The driver hesitated.

'Friends of mine,' Jansen lied as he climbed in.

'Then why don't they give you a lift?' the driver asked.

Jansen threw a couple of fifties on the front seat. 'That's why.'

The Volvo edged out towards the end of the street, looking for an opening in the busy traffic. The cab driver frowned, picked up the notes.

Two cars distant they followed Van der Berg through the cars and trams.

Then they got to the Prinsengracht and the police car bore left.

One way down the southern bank, away from Marnixstraat. A long, leisurely drive. After a while the squat white barn-like shape of the Amstelkerk came into view with the green open space of the park beyond it. Children playing on the swings. Rosie had come here when she was little and Jansen a single father, trying to be the best parent he knew.

Another white patrol car came and parked outside the burned-out building opposite. Jansen stared across the canal. He knew where he was going now. A place he should have visited long ago.

CHAPTER 15

Two uniformed women officers took Katja and Liesbeth Prins from the hospital to the blackened shell of a building that was once the Doll's House. They were waiting in the street with their wards in the car as Vos had instructed. Watched as he and Bakker leaned their bikes against the smoke-blasted railings, took out the set of keys he'd brought from Marnixstraat, removed the padlock and the chain and pushed open the new metal security door.

Bakker followed him in, looked around and said, 'De Groot's going to kill you.'

'I'm not doing this for Frank. Didn't you notice?'

'And I get fired too.'

'If you want to go back to Marnixstraat . . .'

A wry smile. Nothing more.

Another marked police car drew up. Van der Berg with the Jewell woman.

'Send everyone back to the station,' Vos said. 'I just want Katja and the two women in here. And you.'

Inside the place was cold and stank of bitter smoke. Charred wallpaper, barely pink, hanging down like peeling bark. Floorboards brittle and creaking under foot. Vos took the stairs slowly. He went into the first-floor room at the front, couldn't force from his head the picture of the blue fluorescent tubes and the stains that emerged like magic.

Lost in his own thoughts for a while. Someone coughed. When he turned they were there: Bakker to one side leaning against the wall, watching everything the way she liked. Liesbeth wild-eyed and baffled. The Jewell woman puzzled, suspicious. And the girl . . .

Katja cut a skinny tense figure in a plain blue coat and jeans. Her hair was clean and tidy now. She seemed more sixteen than nineteen. Had that troublesome adolescent glint in her eye, the hard-set look of a surly teenager waiting for the inevitable reprimand.

Liesbeth didn't meet her darting eyes. Barbara Jewell did and looked distraught and concerned.

Vos introduced the American to Liesbeth then walked over to the wall, brushed his fingers against the rings of forensic marks. Looked at the same thing on the floor. Pointed them out and said, 'Here.' Then, 'Here.'

'What is this, Pieter?' Liesbeth asked. 'We're all exhausted. We want to go home.'

He came back to them. Bakker kept quiet for once.

'Anneliese was in this room,' he said. 'That was her blood. Someone attacked her. I think she fought back. She didn't look her years. To me anyway. But she wouldn't give in easily. I know that.'

Another glance at the wall. The stains weren't standard blood splatter. It couldn't have been much of a fight.

'That was three years ago and we never knew. Never would have done if a gangster hadn't inherited this place because Theo Jansen's daughter was too embarrassed to keep hold of it. Then sent his hoodlums here because he wanted them dead and his sorry little privehuis off the books.'

He'd thought this through. There could be no other answer. Menzo and Jansen inhabited a small world. It was no great surprise the way the different parts hooked up.

Vos tried to catch Liesbeth's eye and it wasn't easy.

'Did you hear what I said? Anneliese was here. A brothel. Don't you want to know—?'

'Of course I do!' she shrieked. 'But not now. Katja's sick. Give her some peace for God's sake. You never took much interest in your own daughter. Do you have to put someone else's through hell to make up for it?'

Katja slammed her hands over her ears, walked over to the bed, sat down on the stained mattress, stared at the thick grubby carpet.

This was the look she'd had the night before. Lost in herself. Mute and unresponsive to everything outside. Simple almost and he was sure it was an act.

Vos sat next to her, peered into her face, stayed that way until she returned his gaze.

'Why won't you talk?' he asked gently.

'Stop this,' Liesbeth snapped. 'Do you want me to get the doctors here? She's sick. Leave her alone.'

'She was sick before,' he said then glanced at Barbara Jewell. 'But you cured her. You unlocked something and made her . . .'

The words eluded him.

'Clear and clean,' Bakker butted in.

'Clear and clean,' Vos repeated. 'Because something hidden, something stuck in the past came to the surface. And then—'

'You can't do this,' the American woman said. 'I won't allow it.'

'You tell me then,' he said. 'What was it you found?'

'You know already!' Jewell replied. 'We've been there. Her father. What she believed. This isn't the place to start repeating myself . . .'

Vos pointed to the ghostly stains.

'But it's the only place. It began here.' He looked at Katja again. 'Didn't it?'

Nothing.

Laura Bakker came and sat the other side of her on the bed.

'This is dead simple,' she said. 'We don't need to know what happened.' A long, determined look. 'Where . . . have . . . you . . . been?'

Katja Prins folded her arms tightly around her skinny waist, kept looking at the floor.

'I'm calling De Groot,' Liesbeth said, taking out her phone. 'I don't believe for one minute he knows you're torturing this poor kid . . .'

Bakker was up in a moment, snatching the phone from her fingers.

'Where were you . . .?' Vos asked more forcefully.

The girl muttered something. He bent closer to her, said, 'Can't hear, Katja. I can't hear.'

Whatever words she said were lost.

'We're going,' Liesbeth told him. 'I'm going to crucify you for this, Pieter. How dare—?'

'Anneliese was here,' Vos said again, getting to his feet. 'Something happened three years ago. It started everything. From the death of Bea Prins all the way to Rosie Jansen. Katja knows what that trigger was . . .'

Back to her again, he said, 'You're not simple, Katja. Not an idiot. I don't think that. You know—'

'Don't,' the girl whispered in a low, hard voice.

One word and it didn't feel much like a breakthrough.

'Where've you been, Katja?' Bakker asked again. 'At least tell us that. People have died because of this. Liese . . .'

Slowly, with all the resentment of a trapped teenager, she spat out, 'Don't . . . know . . .'

Face creased with pain and anger. Voice young and broken.

Vos shrugged. Pulled something out of his pocket. Set it in front of her.

A single sock. Black. Small.

'I found that on the floor of my boat last night. After you turned up in a grubby nightdress.'

The expression on her face changed. Went from anger to fear.

'That's not mine . . .' the girl whispered.

'Except you didn't,' Vos went on. 'You arrived in a taxi. Someone in the bar saw you. Normal clothes. I guess you must have thrown them in the canal. Dirtied yourself up from the deck or something.'

He picked up the sock.

'And forgot this. The game's over. Where were you?'

Shaking, eyes straight ahead, expression blank. Back where she was the night before.

'You can tell me here,' he added. 'Or Marnixstraat. You choose—'

'She was with me!' Barbara Jewell cried.

The American came and sat next to her. Put an arm round her tense, hunched shoulders.

'She was with me,' she repeated. 'I thought it was the safest place to be.'

CHAPTER 16

Theo Jansen watched Van der Berg and the two uniformed women leave in their cars. Looked at the upstairs window. Saw Vos there. The young woman from the courthouse cell. They weren't alone.

He felt weighed down by two guns. Weighed down by something else he couldn't name. Walked over to the nearest rubbish bin, dumped Maarten's weapon and the shells in there. Just the one pistol. That was all he needed. The Beretta nine thousand. He still had a full magazine left over from the two the barber gave him.

The way into the privehuis he once owned but never visited was half open. Jansen took out the Beretta, looked at it, stuffed the weapon into the right-hand pocket of his jacket, walked in, quietly went up the stairs.

Heard voices. Listened. Looked around at the grimy, tasteless wallpaper, the lurid pictures on the walls. Hated this place. Hated himself.

Took out the little gun, didn't snag the sight on his pocket along the way.

CHAPTER 17

'What haunts us breaks us,' Barbara Jewell said in a practised, hypnotic drawl.

Next to her on the bed, young head bowed as if in prayer, Katja Prins listened, eyes half-closed. The woman's low and mesmerizing voice might have been a drug itself.

'We're not really interested in your lectures, thank you,' Laura Bakker interrupted. 'Just tell us what happened.'

'Lectures?' the American asked. 'We fix people. We don't judge them. Good or bad. Or throw them in prison. We help—'

'You let this genie out of the bottle,' Vos said as gently as he could. 'With the best of intentions I'm sure. But it didn't quite work out, did it?'

She looked at Katja. Downcast, lost on the bed. Started to speak. Vos listened, knowing somehow what he would hear.

That session she'd talked about in the Yellow House. A pivotal, cathartic breakthrough. Katja's admission that she believed her father killed Bea. And one more secret, spelled out slowly in Barbara Jewell's steady, mesmeric words.

She kept it short. When she was done he said, 'So this was all a pretence? A game? You try to fool us Katja's been kidnapped. You copy the way Anneliese vanished. And you think that's going to tell us where she went?'

'I know where she went! He took her!' Katja Prins screeched, eyes on him now. 'My dad. Don't you get it?'

By the wall Liesbeth Prins closed her eyes, swore under her breath.

'Took her where?' Vos asked.

'I don't know!' A bitter, self-recriminating tone. 'I don't . . .' Eyes closed. Remembering something again. 'Mum brought us here. I don't know why. She said Dad came too sometimes. They all did. The politicians. It was . . . their secret.'

She looked at him, at Barbara Jewell.

'Mum . . . did things sometimes. Stupid things. Bad things. But Liese . . .' Her eyes were on Liesbeth. 'She wanted to get back at you. You wouldn't let her come to the beach with us. You wouldn't let her stay out. Do anything she wanted—'

'Not true,' Liesbeth said. 'Not—'

'That's what she said,' the girl insisted. Her face was immobile, her voice a dull, sad drone. 'Mum asked her first. She knew I wouldn't want to come. But I wasn't letting Liese here on her own. One time. That was all. Nothing happened. We laughed about it afterwards.'

Face up, staring at Vos then.

516

'She wasn't supposed to come back. Not without me. But you couldn't tell Liese anything . . .'

Her finger pointed to the thick carpet.

'The time I came we stayed down there. Tea and cake and dirty old men who wanted you to sit on their laps and let them tell you you're beautiful. I knew I wanted none of that and I was the stupid one. Why she . . .'

She unwrapped herself from Barbara Jewell's arm.

'When Liese went missing Mum wouldn't talk about it. But she knew. I could tell. Then I met the Thai woman who ran the place. She was scared. She said someone had asked for her. Big and important. A lawyer. Someone nobody dared touch.'

'It wasn't Wim,' Liesbeth murmured. 'It couldn't be—'

'I'm telling you!' Eyes wide, voice shrill. 'After Mum died I could see it in his face. Don't blame me. I never knew. I never wanted this—'

'You didn't,' Barbara Jewell said. 'It's not your fault.'

'Easy for you . . .'

Then a guilty silence. Angry tears.

The Jewell woman got up, stood next to Vos.

'This was my idea from the start,' she said. 'Not Katja's. She didn't want to do it. I forced her.'

'Don't lie to them, Barbara,' Katja mumbled. 'Don't—'

'She needs to bury Bea. Your daughter too.' A

brief and apologetic shrug. 'The details were all out there. In the newspapers. The dolls. What happened afterwards. You were public property, Vos. We wanted to make it seem the same. So you'd look again. Just harder this time. Make you people take notice and ask some questions he'd never faced. Without that . . .' A glance at the girl on the bed. 'You'd never have believed her. A junkie. Against the likes of him. She deserved better. She's innocent. God knows the kid's suffered enough . . .'

A hand to Katja's head. The girl stared at the grubby carpet, grim-faced, silent.

'I made her stay with me. We sent those dolls, those messages. We got a friend to work in the council and see what trouble she could stir up there. I wanted to make that bastard's life hell. Any way we could. Until he broke. Or someone talked. Until you people finally did something. We never . . .'

The calm, the self-control seemed to desert her for a moment.

'We never meant to harm anyone. We just wanted justice. For Bea. For your girl. For Katja too. But I guess . . .' Her voice had fallen to a whisper. 'I wanted to help. I didn't want any of this . . .'

Something stopped her.

'And Rosie Jansen?' Vos asked.

'We just wanted to talk. Truly we never meant . . .'

Barbara Jewell was looking right past him.

'Pieter . . .' Laura Bakker said quietly, starting to move.

Too late. The gun slammed hard against Vos's head. Sent him sprawling down to the floor, aware of nothing but Katja's terrified screams.

CHAPTER 18

Seconds, minutes. He wasn't sure which. When he came to Jansen stood above him, his elbow pinning Barbara Jewell to the wall, the gun jabbed up against her neck.

'Theo . . .' Vos said, climbing back to his feet.

Katja was screaming like a furious, scolded child.

'You want to talk?' Jansen yelled at the American woman. 'Talk now. I lost a daughter. I've got a coffin waiting to be buried too.'

Jewell, head back against the charred wallpaper, glared at him, unafraid.

'You owned this place, didn't you? You let this filth go on.'

'I didn't know . . .'

'You owned this place!' she yelled. 'You flood this city with drugs and hookers and all the shit this kid's been trying to drown herself in. Then plead innocent—'

The gun went up. A blast into the ceiling. Pink plaster raining down and flakes of paint.

'I didn't know!' Jansen shouted. 'Rosie was my daughter.'

520

Silence for a moment. Then Barbara Jewell's calm, slow voice.

'She ran the Doll's House. She knew what went on here. That's why we went to see her. To beg. To ask for her help. She knew—'

'It's business! Giving people what they want.'

'They were children,' she said quite calmly. 'Innocent kids getting groomed by middle-aged men in suits. Who did what they wanted then went back to their offices and their wives . . .'

Jansen brandished the weapon in her face.

'That's how it is here. How it's always been. If you don't like it . . .'

Vos came closer. Bakker too. She had her phone in her hand. Fingers moving over the keys.

'But you don't like it either, Theo,' Vos said. 'We both know that.'

The old hood glared at him.

'My daughter's dead and you did nothing. Just like your own kid—'

'Backup on the way,' Laura Bakker interrupted, thrusting the phone into Jansen's line of vision. 'Two minutes and they're here.'

The American scarcely heard her, just stared Jansen in the face.

'We wanted to talk,' she told him. 'That's all. To ask for her help. We didn't know there'd been that shooting outside the courthouse. We just went round to see her. She went crazy. Started screaming. Pulled out a gun. I was scared she was going to use it—'

'And then you shot her?' Jansen said.

A long moment. Barbara Jewell hesitated, started to say something. The frail slight figure on the bed flew at them, gripped Jansen's arm, struggled to grip the gun in his hand.

Got her fingers round the weapon. Took Jansen by surprise so much her desperate clawing nails almost snatched it from him.

Hands free, arms flailing, Jewell got loose.

Just the big hood now in the centre of the room with the skinny, slight girl, hands round his, black pistol waving.

'I shot her, mister . . .' Katja hissed. 'Me. Not Barbara. I did it—'

'Katja,' the American woman said.

Sirens outside. The sound of tyres screeching.

Tears and fury in a young hard face.

'I shot her,' Katja repeated. 'She was yelling at us. Waving a gun. If you want to kill someone, kill me.'

Jansen stood back, lifted the weapon, aimed it straight at her.

Finger on the trigger. Eyes on a young and damaged face.

Didn't fire.

Footsteps on the stairs. Van der Berg and Koeman leading the way, weapons out, ready.

'What would you have said, Theo?' Vos asked, still holding out his hand. 'If you'd known about this place?'

'If it wasn't me, someone else . . .' Jansen said with a sigh.

'But it wasn't you. It was Rosie. She knew you'd have hated this. That's why she closed it down. She wasn't worried about us. Mulder kept it off our books. We'd given up on Liese's case. Rosie was terrified of you, no one else. What would happen if you found out.'

'You sound desperate, Vos,' Jansen muttered.

'So you've got limits. Just like us. Just the same . . .'

His hand, extended out for the weapon, didn't shake. He caught Jansen's eye, nodded.

'I'm sorry we never had that beer. One day. We've got lots to talk about. Lots to share.'

Jansen stared at him and the broken, frightened girl.

'Just give me the damned gun, Theo,' Vos said. 'We're done here.'

'You talk too much,' Theo Jansen grumbled then handed him the Beretta.

'True,' Vos agreed, then ordered the others to put their weapons away. Told them to take everyone to Marnixstraat, wait for him there.

He stood with Bakker and watched them leave.

'Only one lawyer I can think of,' she said when everyone was gone.

She held up her phone again: the address was there already. Not far away.

'You might have told me about that sock.'

He frowned.

'What sock?'

She folded her arms.

'Katja's sock?'

'Oh that? I made it up. It's one of mine.'

A pause then she said, 'And you've still got Jansen's gun.'

'I know.' He stuffed the weapon into the inside pocket of his jacket. 'We'll take the bikes.'

CHAPTER 19

Almost two and the sun spoke of summer. Locals cycling in a determined fashion along the track between footpath and road. Vos and Bakker were headed for a quiet back street in the Canal Rings. Closing on Leidseplein. He pedalled quickly, steadily. She kept up all the way.

As they rounded the corner to the square she said, 'I don't suppose this is a slip of the memory, Vos. But shouldn't we call for help?'

'You'd think that.'

He was sure she tut-tutted then.

'Yes, actually. I would. I mean . . .'

Vos heaved on the brakes, both feet on the floor, just managing to avoid a couple of tourists dawdling in front of them. Bakker came up beside him, stomped her big black boots on the ground. Waited for an answer.

'Did you have a doll? When you were little?'

She winced. Almost blushed.

'Just the one. I wasn't really into dolls.'

'You don't say?'

'To be honest I hated the bloody thing. But my

uncle bought it. Which shows how well he knew me. I really didn't want to hurt—'

'Have you still got it?' he interrupted.

Bakker laughed out loud. So much a couple of tourists stopped and gawped.

'If I didn't want a doll in Dokkum I'd hardly need one here, would I?'

She got ready to pedal off. He wasn't done.

'But did you throw it away?'

She thought for a moment.

'Well . . . no. I don't think so. It's at . . .'

'Auntie Maartje's?'

'Aren't you the clever one? I wouldn't chuck out something like that, would I? You don't do that with dolls. You . . .'

Her hand went to her mouth. Her eyes were wide open.

'You said this once before and I wasn't really listening. You keep them.'

'You keep them,' Vos agreed.

Then pedalled on.

CHAPTER 20

A lawyer's house in a quiet street overlooking a peaceful stretch of still canal. Pale brick, tall windows, four storeys tall, a swinging hook on the gable roof. Red geraniums by the shiny black front door.

On a low bridge nearby a herring stall was open for business. One customer alone, chatting to the man in a white coat behind the counter. A quiet, lazy, affluent corner of the Canal Rings. A mansion probably three hundred years old, the walls thick and impenetrable.

By the front steps a few sacks of cement, a mixing board, scraped grey mortar.

Vos got there first, threw his bike onto the pavement, strode up the steps, put his finger on the bell. Kept it there.

Bakker close behind him. She looked around. Thought about the house. Big place for one man.

There was a smell too. Fresh paint and plaster.

Still Vos kept his finger on the bell. An angry voice from behind the black painted wood. Middle class, middle-aged.

The door came slowly open, just ajar.

Michiel Lindeman didn't look the way he did when he was working. No grey suit. No slicked-back hair. He was in grubby stained overalls, flecks of white and grey on his shoulders. The building smell about him.

'What's this?' the lawyer asked.

Vos just stood there, looked at him. Bakker leaned against the shiny frame. Smiled.

One moment and that was all it took. The man's face fell, went from angry and resentful to terrified. He was trying to slam the door but Vos's elbow was there already. Lindeman began yelling something about warrants when Vos put his shoulder to the wood, Bakker joining him, the two of them forcing the lawyer back inside.

A light entrance hall, a chandelier, paintings, thick carpet. Sacks of sand and cement against the right-hand wall. Lindeman had stumbled under the force of their sudden entrance. Crouched on the floor, making threats, starting to wheedle and whine.

'Close the door,' Vos ordered and so she did.

Then he took out Theo Jansen's gun.

CHAPTER 21

In the dark she sits, hands on lap, fingers playing with the fabric of tiny pink and white squares.

That's all she can move now. All he's left her.

My little doll . . .

How many times had he said that? How many times had she fought?

Pink gingham pinafore frock. Soft cotton puffy sleeves. A halter neck.

The black patent shoes are gone. The dress is frayed, too small for her.

No longer the expectant, innocent schoolgirl. Now she knows. Now she sees, even with the blindfold over her eyes, the thick black tape across her mouth.

The room is full of dust and darkness.

My little doll, goodbye.

No light, only cold. The vile plastic blocks her nostrils, covers her mouth. Coarse fabric scratches at her eyes.

Kindness, he said.

This was the best he could do.

Love of a precious sort.

And then she was alone. For the first time, it felt, since she walked alone into the place on the Prinsengracht one sunny day a lifetime ago. Thinking this was nothing more than a stupid experiment born of boredom and resentment. That soon she'd persuade her mother to let her go to Bloemendaal aan Zee, the party and the beach. Be with someone of her own age. Not sad and desperate old men in shiny suits.

Memories.

Tea laced with something else. Meagre meals served on a simple plastic tray while she listened to his stories, his pleas, his apologies. Trying to black out the sudden furious rush, the need, the violent, desperate lunge, hands tearing at her, at his own clothes too.

Afterwards he'd weep. Talk of love. But that wasn't for her. It was for the costume. The pretty pink fabric. The billowing dress. The memories of something lost before he could claim it. She didn't exist. Only the doll did. And that wasn't human at all.

Trapped inside the basement cell he'd made she'd daydream. Recall the easy, comforting tedium of home. A TV programme, some music. A lost toy. The stupid doll's house her father bought then put away for storage when she laughed at it. At him.

These memories, both sweet and painful, fill her tired and troubled head. He'd fed her something that morning. It was different. Not funny tasting tea. An orange juice, sweetly metallic. She'd taken a sip, looked at him. Saw the guilt and sorrow on the only face she'd known of late.

Pink bed. Pink sheets. Pink pillows.

How long had she been here?

She didn't know. Her head was aching, roaming.

Dreams.

One came now with such sly and vivid detail it felt real.

She was floating somewhere near the ceiling, like a small creature hiding in a high, safe corner. Beneath she could see a young girl strapped to a chair, drugged and blindfolded, mouth taped, locked in a sealed and airless room decked out in a single colour. Not frightened as the poison started to rush and roar through her feeble veins. Not worried any more. Just grateful that this endless night was coming to a close.

Aware too that a storm was gathering somewhere, above her, not near, not distant.

Sounds she'd never heard before in this new, small life. Other voices, angry desperate ones.

Shouts. Cries.

Then the short and cataclysmic roar of something like thunder.

CHAPTER 22

Michiel Lindeman cowered on the floor in his grubby overalls, looking up at them, scared and furious.

'Where's your warrant?' he yelled. 'You can't do this—'

'This is the warrant,' Vos said, took one step forward, pointed the barrel of the black pistol straight into the lawyer's face, raised it, loosed a bullet at nothing. 'Where is she?'

Bakker was beside him, looking round, doing what he was supposed to: thinking, reasoning, imagining.

Lindeman, no fool, got himself into a crouch, put his hands round his knees, screwed up his weasel face and said, 'What?'

'My daughter. You took her from that privehuis. Where is she?'

'You've lost your mind again, Vos,' the lawyer muttered and shook his head. 'This time you'll pay for it.'

The gun was back on him, closer now.

'Pieter,' Laura Bakker said quietly. Reached out with her hand, guided it away. 'I think maybe—'

'Where is she?' Vos bellowed. 'It was you at the Poppenhuis. Rosie Jansen said so—'

'Rosie Jansen's dead,' Lindeman yelled. 'Are you crazy enough to talk to corpses now?'

Vos nearly lost it then. Would have done if Bakker hadn't dragged Lindeman to his feet. Said in a cold, determined voice, 'We're looking round this place, mate. Everywhere.'

Then kicked and shoved him down the hall.

Sitting room, living room. Kitchen. Bathroom.

On the floor above an office, a small home cinema. Bedrooms, spare rooms. Empty spaces full of junk.

Three more storeys. Twenty minutes.

Not a sign of anything out of place. No woman's clothes. Not a picture of a doll. Nothing young at all. Just room upon lavish room in a solitary middle-aged lawyer's Canal Rings mansion.

Lindeman kept getting more confident with every fruitless step.

At the end they were back in the hall. The lawyer was throwing around heavier threats, demanding they leave, promising to call De Groot. The gun hung loose in Vos's hand. Options lost. Ideas absent. Nothing to imagine except the worst: she was gone, disappeared, dead somewhere he'd never know.

Laura Bakker walked behind the two of them and started to examine the bare fresh plaster there. Put a finger to it.

'This is still damp,' she said. 'Amateur-hour stuff. My uncle's a builder. You're rubbish at it, Lindeman.'

'If I want your opinion—' the lawyer started.

'You're getting it anyway. Why's a man like you doing this?'

'Money,' he said with little conviction.

Vos came and looked. He knew nothing about buildings. Couldn't even work on his own boat.

'The rest of this wall's fine,' Bakker said, walking along, rapping on the plasterwork. 'Why do just this bit?' She looked at the tools and empty bags on the floor. 'And all this stuff you've got? It's for more than that.'

'I want you gone,' Lindeman said. 'When I talk to De Groot—'

'Ooh, not big, bad Frank. That's scary,' Bakker said then pulled a pickaxe from behind the cement-stained wheelbarrow along the wall.

'What the hell do you think you're doing?' the lawyer asked.

She smiled and swung it long and hard, fetched the sharp end into the fresh plaster. Once. Twice.

Looked at Vos and said, 'There's a door behind this. He's got a basement down there I reckon, and he's blocking it up.'

Lindeman made for the front of the house. Vos tripped him, caught him by the collar, took the pickaxe, gave her the gun, told her to watch him.

The plaster was wet and soft. After a few blows he could tear it off with his hands, ripping long lines and curls until they littered the floor.

The door behind was black, painted recently. Bronze handle. Locked.

He looked at Lindeman, asked for the keys.

'I'll see you in jail,' the lawyer said. 'Assault. Illegal entry. This is my home . . .'

Bakker pocketed the gun, found a sledgehammer amidst the tools, took three long powerful swings, shattered the fitting, kicked it open.

A light switch behind. Vos grabbed Lindeman. Took him with him, hit the button.

A fluorescent tube below flickered into life. Long stairs. Bare stone. Laura Bakker ran down the steep steps.

'It was a wine cellar,' Lindeman said wearily. 'I didn't need it any more. The damp—'

'Vos!' Bakker shouted from below. 'There's another wall he's blocked up here. Probably did it this morning by the looks of things.' She nosed around. 'And there's wine too.'

She returned to the bottom of the bannister, letting the hammer hang loose by her side.

'You must have been in a big hurry. Shutting off this place before you could even take out your booze.'

Vos grabbed the pickaxe with one hand, the lawyer with the other. Down the steps, pushing Lindeman in front of him. A long flat facing wall. Plaster in the middle, a tall rectangle still fresh enough to show damp stains in places. He put his ear to it, heard nothing.

'This is a big mistake,' Lindeman said. 'You don't know—'

'Shut up,' Bakker said and took a swing at the wall.

The sledgehammer bounced off easily. Vos let go

of the man, heaved with the pickaxe. Kept swinging, blow after blow. Was aware she'd dropped the hammer now and was dashing in between, ripping at the thick brown shreds. Aware that Lindeman was slinking away too.

'Get him,' Vos ordered and went back to work.

There was a rhythm to it. A steady pulse that took away his thoughts.

A noise from above. A shout. A scream. Vos glanced back, saw Bakker and Lindeman on the stairs. She fetched him a kick with her big right boot straight into the shin, sent the lawyer flying down the steps, turning, rolling, shrieking to the cold hard floor.

'Oops,' Bakker said when she got to the bottom. There was a length of wire cable in her hands. She wrapped it round the lawyer's wrists, tied the end to the bannister rail. Came back, started heaving the sledgehammer alongside him.

Mindless work. Repetitive. The only thing he wanted right then.

She was the first through, almost fell on her face as the hammer broke another wooden door hidden behind new plaster. One more lock to be shattered. A final obstacle to be removed.

Then they stood there breathless, Lindeman whimpering somewhere, apologies, excuses. Nonsense about love and devotion and how no one really understood.

Laura Bakker put down the hammer.

'Trouble is, mate . . . they do.'

Vos kicked through the black wood, reached in, found a light switch on the left, flipped it.

Pink, he saw. Pink walls. Pink carpet. Pink chair. Pink bed. And something else.

A shape on a chair, bound to it with rope. Head slumped forward. Blonde hair. Slight figure. Childish pink and white gingham dress.

'Anneliese,' he whispered and walked inside.

PART V

NINE DAYS LATER

CHAPTER 1

Summer arrived early. The morning cyclists along the Prinsengracht were in shirts and shorts and skirts, sunglasses on their heads as they went about their daily rounds, pedalling beneath the green lime trees.

Vos's boat was still a mess. There'd been other cares. Dealing with the aftermath of his invasion of Michiel Lindeman's mansion and the ensuing arrest. Seeing both the lawyer and Jansen into court and jail where they'd remain. The same process for Katja Prins and Barbara Jewell. They were out on bail on manslaughter and blackmail charges, headed for a suspended sentence from a judicial system that was already showing signs of sympathy. And probably the same for Suzi Mertens who was with Jansen when Vos went to interview him in prison. Arguing his case. Closer perhaps than the man himself wanted. But Vos was glad to see her there.

The fallout had provided a field day for the papers. A bent cop. Warring gangsters. A dead politician and his partner, a crooked city lawyer who'd groomed and made captive the daughter of the detective in charge of tackling organized crime. And most of all the discovery that Anneliese wasn't dead at all. A miracle of a kind. It was made for the headlines.

Margriet Willemsen remained vice-mayor of the city council, unchallenged, untainted largely. Alex Hendriks had fled, taking a large pay-off to London to look for another job, a different life.

Then the media moved on to other stories. There was only so much scandal Amsterdam could take. What remained best suited criminals, be they lawyers or dead police officers, not a hard-bitten woman politician who seemed to have an answer for everything.

De Groot had dropped the investigation into Mulder's – and Menzo's – illicit payments. That was the price of turning a blind eye to the illegal entry into Lindeman's house.

Vos wasn't minded to argue. Anneliese was free, slowly emerging from her imprisonment and the sedative Lindeman had given her. Beneath the pain and passing bewilderment she was still the daughter he knew: bright, inquisitive, determined. But different too in ways Vos struggled to appreciate. There was a gap between father and daughter, even without this extraordinary hiatus. Her relationship with Liesbeth was closer, more intense, complex and difficult at times.

There would be thoughts they'd share he'd never hear about. He didn't worry or mind. His daughter would, the doctors assured them, recover one day.

542

The scars of Lindeman's doting incarceration might take years to heal. Even with help and counselling a few might never disappear entirely, not that he wanted to think about that right now. But she was alive, and the legal side of the case could proceed without her. Lindeman would plead guilty on grounds of insanity, arguing that he was himself the victim of an obsessive, selfless form of love. There would be no need for witnesses, cross-examinations in court. She would at least be spared that.

He sat on a rickety old stool on the boat deck, between the dying roses and a few pots of herbs, Sam at his feet. The little dog was excited by the presence of someone young, listening to the footsteps echo through the cabin below. She was with Liesbeth, the two of them talking in low voices. Rootling around the boat she'd found the old doll's house and to his relief had been able to laugh at it. Thrown at him the old accusation: *How could you? Don't you know me at all?*

And at that he'd left her there with her mother. Stayed outside watching the traffic on the canal, people ambling to the rickety pavement tables of the Drie Vaten.

'Dad?' she said, climbing up onto the deck, putting on the pair of sunglasses she always wore outside. Her eyes had grown weak trapped in Lindeman's basement. She was making her first hesitant steps back into the world. It would all take time.

Her voice had altered too. A couple of tones lower than he remembered. Adult and knowing.

Two cases were by the gangplank. This was a goodbye, a temporary one though painful still.

'Why do you live here?' she asked, pulling up another flimsy chair to sit beside him. 'What's wrong with a flat?'

'I like my boat. I'm fixing her up. By the time you come back she'll be finished. You'll love her. When you go to sleep you hear the water. When you wake up you hear the ducks. It's beautiful. I've never slept so well in my life.' A shrug. 'Not for the last few nights anyway.'

Liesbeth had followed her up the stairs. She didn't look any different. Still hurt. Still grieving for Prins he guessed.

'You'll never fix this thing,' she said, eyeing the long street both sides of the bridge. 'You won't have time. De Groot's going to make sure of that.'

'You could be right,' Vos agreed.

Two seats booked onto the same flight Wim Prins tried to take, direct to Aruba. They'd stay in his villa there, the one Liesbeth had secretly visited while she was living with Vos. Anneliese knew nothing about that, any more than she realized Prins was her real father. Vos had demanded Liesbeth's silence on those matters from the outset. She hadn't argued.

'Will you find the time to come and see us?' Anneliese asked. 'Mum says . . .' She looked uncertain. 'We're going to stay there for six months or so. I need to get my head in shape. Being some- where else . . .'

'If the doctors say it's a good idea . . . if you think so too . . .' He touched her arm. 'Come back when you're ready. No pressure. I'm not going anywhere.'

'It would be good to see you,' she said in that steady, determined way she'd had since she was little. 'You look as if you need some sun.'

'Don't worry about me. If there's time . . .'

It was a lie. They both knew it. He looked at his watch. The taxi would turn up at any moment. Vos got to his feet, smiled as she joined him.

He put his arms round his daughter, kissed her soft cheek. She was tall and beautiful, summer shirt and new jeans. Hair cut short now, not the childish locks Lindeman had demanded.

'You can always find me here,' Vos said. 'I will always love you. If you need me, just ask.'

She took off the sunglasses. Blinked back tears. Perhaps the child in her thought he and Liesbeth would toy with a reconciliation. While the adult knew differently and always took the bleaker view.

'I need a minute with your mother,' he said. 'Go and have a coffee over the road. It's better than the stuff I make.'

'I never said thank you, did I?'

'You didn't need to. I'm sorry it took me so long. I gave up. I thought I'd lost you. That there was nothing I could do.'

'What changed things?'

'Not what but who. Katja Prins I guess. And a very stubborn young woman from Dokkum.'

'What . . .?'

'Another time,' he said. 'Not now.'

Arms round his shoulders she reached up and kissed him again. Both cheeks. Love between them. The quiet yet fierce devotion of family. Something Pieter Vos thought he'd lost forever.

Then she strode over to the Drie Vaten, sat at a table among the tourists, ordered a coffee. A couple of young men were eyeing her. She wasn't just beautiful in his eyes. There was a charming, affecting, perhaps illusory innocence about her. It turned heads. Had done for the obsessive and lonely Michiel Lindeman, looking for his own private marionette to own, to shape, to adore, three years before. Sooner or later another man would come along. A good one this time he hoped. And not too soon.

'You're welcome to come and see us, Pieter,' Liesbeth said. Arms folded. Face emotionless, impenetrable. 'Make a change from this dump.'

The dog sat upright, stared at her. Vos was sure he heard a low growl.

'I like this dump. The Jordaan's my home.'

She didn't appreciate that.

'And now Aruba's going to be yours,' he added.

'I want to be somewhere warm and sunny. Somewhere we can be happy. Liese needs that as much as I do.'

'It's best you stay there.'

She cocked her head to one side, puzzled.

'If that's what I want. Wim's estate here needs sorting out . . .'

'The bank can do that. You should leave it to them.'

'What happens about Bea?' Liesbeth asked. 'Does that go down on Wim's file too?'

'What's it to you?'

'I was married to him. Remember?'

She'd asked so few questions. A part of him wished it could stay that way.

'I'll leave that open for now.'

The dog got up and walked to the bows, sat there, back to them, posing for the snapping cameras of a pleasure boat cruising down the canal.

'Why?'

'Because he didn't kill Bea. You did.'

The same frozen expression. Not a flicker in her eyes.

'And there I was,' she said blithely. 'Thinking you were getting better.'

'I'm fine, thanks. Someone had wiped down the seats of her car.' Vos's attention strayed to his daughter. Sofia had come to sit with her, probably to make sure none of the men did. The two of them were sipping coffee. Chatting. 'Forensic thought it happened when it went in for a service a few weeks before. I got Van der Berg to check. The garage didn't use wipes on that model. The seats were leather. They needed polish.'

'You expect me to believe—?'

'The wipes were very specific. Bigger than the kind you buy in a shop. Exactly the same size as the ones we have in forensic. Where you were working at the time.'

'That's it?' she asked. 'The best detective in Amsterdam. That's all you have?'

'It's a start. Or it will be if you come back from Aruba. I don't want Anneliese staying more than six months either. Not unless she comes here and tells me to my face that's what she wants.'

'You arrogant bastard . . .'

'Wim knew all along, didn't he?' Vos had thought this through. Kept it to himself. 'De Nachtwacht was a part of that guilt, I guess. Thinking he could clean up the city and atone for something on your conscience. I guess it wasn't so hard for him to jump from the plane—'

'He was a coward. Weak. Just a man. That bitch stole my daughter. While you were pissing about going crazy in Marnixstraat, getting nowhere. She took Liese to that privehuis. It was her fault—'

'No. Lindeman seized her. No one else.'

'Bea started this! Are you listening? Are you still asleep?'

Her voice had got too loud. A young, concerned face watched them from a table outside the Drie Vaten.

'I just wanted to know,' Liesbeth said more quietly. 'Wim was at his wits' end with the woman. I didn't set out to kill her. She laughed in my face.

548

Said she'd known about me and Wim all along. What she did to Liese was her revenge. Not on me. On my daughter.'

That hadn't occurred to him. It should have, Vos realized.

'And you just happened to have a gun. Some wipes from Marnixstraat forensic to clean up afterwards.'

'I'd worked it out, Pieter.' She prodded him in the chest. 'While you were getting nowhere. I knew.'

A white taxi was edging along the Prinsengracht, the driver looking out for someone.

'Come back and I reopen the whole thing,' Vos promised. 'I'll use every officer I've got until I see you in court. Believe that if you believe nothing else.'

She smiled, waved to Anneliese outside the cafe. Shouted in a calm and friendly voice, 'Ready?'

Looked at him, still beaming then asked, 'And break your daughter's heart twice over? I don't think so. If you were going to do it, you'd do it now. Don't fuck with me. You're not up to it. You never were.'

She held out her arms. The promise of a final embrace.

'Make a pretence. For her sake. Not mine. Bea's dead and buried. So is Wim. Liese's alive and I won't let anything in the world hurt her. You can count on that.'

The briefest of hugs, a cold peck on the cheek.

Then he lugged their bags to the road. Held his daughter in his arms one last time, whispered fond words in her ear, kissed her and watched them go.

He was still standing there, lost in his thoughts, his doubts, when a cycle bell rang.

CHAPTER 2

S am came running down the gangplank, yapping wildly, dashed to the bike, put his feet up against her legs.

'You forgot, Vos. I don't believe it.'

He felt slow and stupid. A tall young woman on a modern bike with a basket on the front. Her red hair was long and down around her shoulders, carefully combed. She wore an old-fashioned print dress, white and green, cut just above the knee. Pale brown leather sandals, not heavy black boots. And a pair of modern sunglasses which she pushed back from her nose as he watched, then planted on her head.

'Laura?'

'I should have known, shouldn't I? We agreed. Remember?'

'You look... different. The clothes. Auntie Maartje?'

'She doesn't make everything I wear. I'm off duty.' Slowly she repeated the last two words. 'Do you even know what that means?'

He recalled a promise: she could take Sam for a ride and a walk somewhere. At the time he'd been trying to turn down an offer of a beer from Van der Berg. Hadn't given it much thought.

'Vondelpark,' she said, stroking the dog's head after she leaned her bike against the rail. 'If that's all right . . .'

The little terrier's tale was wagging like an over-worked metronome. She picked him up, kissed his head, got licked in return, placed him in the basket on the front.

'That's new,' he said, pointing to the handlebars.

'De Groot's confirmed me in post. I got the letter yesterday. A present to myself.'

'Good news,' he said, nodding sagely.

'As if you didn't know. Not that he had much choice. I'd have caused such a stink if they booted me out. After all that nonsense with Katja and Mulder. Ooh . . . you can't begin to imagine . . .'

'I can actually.'

She stroked the dog.

'Are you all right? You look distracted.'

'Never better,' he said, aware she was staring at his threadbare blue shirt, the worn jeans, old trainers. A thought. He pulled up his jeans and pointed. Two matching socks. Bright red.

'Congratulations,' she said. 'It'll be evening dress next.'

'It's a start.'

'Do you want to come to the park too?' she asked, hovering over each word like an adult talking to a child.

Vos pointed to the boat.

'Work to do here. Lots of it.'

'Will it ever be finished?'

'Probably not.'

'Will you?'

He hesitated then said, 'Is anyone?'

A nod towards the Drie Vaten.

'Besides . . . there's some washing waiting for me over there.'

'That is truly shameful.'

A sheepish grin.

'I know. Don't let him eat crisps.' He pulled an old supermarket carrier from his pocket. 'Make sure you clean up . . .'

She reached beyond the dog into the basket and showed him a brand-new pack of something called poop scoop bags.

'Last chance ever, Pieter Vos,' Laura Bakker said, pulling down the sunglasses. 'I won't ask again.'

He shrugged, smiled a wan smile. Watched as she muttered something under her breath then set off along the canal.

Sam did something he'd never seen before. Instead of facing forwards, enjoying the wind in his fur, he turned and looked at the woman pedalling him to the park. She was chattering to him as she cycled slowly along the Prinsengracht, red hair flying over her shoulders, lost to everything but the dog.

Vos glanced at the run-down, battered boat.

Then the Drie Vaten serving up the first cold beers of the day.

Tugged at his too-long hair.

Scratched his cheek. Felt briefly torn.